HALLOWEEN PARTY 2019

HALLOWEEN PARTY

2019

DEVIL'S
PARTY
PRESS

MILTON, DE
19968

HALLOWEEN PARTY 2019

HALLOWEEN PARTY 2019 (and all contents within except memoir) is a work of fiction. Any similarities between actual persons, places, organizations, corporations, products, events, ghosts, ghouls, goblins, spirits, demons, and the undead are entirely coincidental.

ISBN: 978-1-7340918-0-9

devilspartypress.com

CONTENTS

HALLOWEEN PARTY 2019

"The oldest and strongest emotion of mankind is fear,
and the oldest and strongest kind of fear is fear of the unknown."

H O W A R D   P H I L L I P S   L O V E C R A F T

INTRODUCTION

DAVID YURKOVICH

IN OCTOBER 2017, Devil's Party Press emerged with its first short-story collection, *Halloween Party 2017*. The 132-page anthology featured the work of nine contributors. Our plan at that time was to publish a new horror collection biennially. Time passes, and so here we are, two years later, with a new collection of scares.

We now present to you *Halloween Party 2019*, a significantly larger and more diverse collection than its fledgling predecessor.

Included in this edition are stories of the macabre, ghosts and spirits, psychological terrors, urban legends, weird fiction, monster horror, witch tales, cannibal escapades, and zombies gone amok.

I suppose it's easy enough *not* to care about the horror genre. And yet, there exists in each of us a need to delve into the darkness, into worlds only imagined, into our fears, and all our "what-ifs."

It is this desire to dance with death and survive (or maybe not) that keeps alive a genre that began over 250 years ago with the publication of Walpole's *The Castle of Otranto*.

As Di and I edited this tome, we remarked to each other time and again how our dreams had been corrupted, our sleep ruined, our quiet time terrorized by the stories herein.

We suffered.

It is time to gift that terror … to you.

Dim the lights and prepare to embrace the fear.

DY

FALLEN HERO

LISA FOX

THE MAN WALKED.

His scuffed work boots pushed pebbles with each step down the gravel path toward town. Ashen dust clung to his faded dungarees and the faint aroma of smoke lingered in the crisp fall air. Hands tucked in the pockets of his tattered black leather jacket, he strode beside the rusting tracks peeking through tufts of brittle overgrowth, the rails warmed but once per week with the slow rumbling of the CSX train as it passed through Mineville, brimming with coal. In the distance, endless rows of dilapidated houses settled beneath the shadow of shale mountains.

After 20 years away, the man returned to the only home he had ever known. Nothing changed here—*nothing ever changed here*. But, had he? His rounded and hunched shoulders belied his former stature; it was easier for him, *better for everyone*, to slink by in a world where he was no longer welcome than to rise to his true height, walk with purpose and show them that he was different now; he'd done his time, made peace with the past. The man welcomed the camouflage of age, his graying hair and beard painting him in a sad, non-threatening invisibility that he hoped would allow him to blend in with the landscape and help others forget.

His hazel eyes, magnified by the thick lenses of his oversized and bent wire-framed glasses, fixated on the dust that swirled in eddies beneath his feet. He studied the impression his soles made in the terrain and the way the gravel reset itself as he marched forward, his presence as fleeting as his footsteps.

The boy emerged from the shadow of a burnt-out home in the distance. Its porch drooped in a macabre frown; the charred wood frame shedding history with each cinder that fell and drifted. *Some relics aren't worth preserving*, the man thought, wondering why the structure remained. *It's like propping up the dead among the dying.* The boy moved toward him with a bounce and a hop, a gait reserved for the very young. His cherry-red cheeks and curly, flaxen hair glowed in technicolor contrast to the decaying landscape beyond. Small fingers flipped at the lid of a tarnished, silver Zippo lighter. It clicked and snapped with each flick of the boy's thumb.

Click, click. Click, click.

Metal on metal.

"Hey, mister!"

The man stopped.

"You got a lighter like this?"

The boy flipped the lighter open, producing a small blue flame, which he cupped to shield from the autumn breeze. The child's hands were rough and cracked, as if gloved in old-man skin. *Boys' hands should be plump and dimpled,* the man thought, *cradling fireflies, not fire.*

The man shook his head. "No," he said, the train whistle in the distance drowning out his reply.

Sparks danced in the boy's eyes. "A lighter like this is dangerous, ain't it, mister?"

A slow gap-toothed smile spread across his face as he thrust the lighter upward, just beneath the man's beard.

The man flinched.

"Shame, shame, I know your name!" the boy taunted.

"I think it's time for you to go," the man said, jaw tightening. "You don't want your mama worrying about you."

The boy licked his fingertips, extending them over the flame as if willing it to dance. He shook his head, mesmerized by the light in his hands.

"Mama's not worried," the boy said, a reddish glow reflecting in his eyes. "She's sleeping. She's always sleeping."

The train whistle blared a warning. The man and boy looked up, their eyes locked as the ground rumbled, the vibration shaking the man to his core. The boy smiled and skipped toward the approaching train.

"Stop!" the man yelled, reaching for the boy, who leapt over the tracks just before the locomotive barreled through.

The man watched as a carousel of boxcars sped by, the clacking of the wheels a drumbeat against the whooshing and whistling that had devoured the silence. Amid the cacophony, the man lost sight of the boy; when the train passed, the boy was gone. The open lighter lay at the man's feet, its flame charring the dead leaves that blanketed the gravel road.

—

Head down, the man shrunk from the stares of the townsfolk shopping at the Five and Dime. He tucked his parcel under his arm—a carton of Marlboros, canned tuna, crackers, and three cans of wood varnish—and was met with the hard eyes of the shopkeeper. The meaning of his glare was clear: *Get Out of My Store.* This town's memory was as deep and unyielding as a barren mine. *Perhaps it's better to be invisible to the world than to be remembered by it,* he thought. The man pushed through the store's exit, the jangle of the bell a welcome respite from the cold silence inside.

Across the cobblestone road, three young firemen polished Mineville's newest engine, their arms coated in a sweaty sheen, their pride reflected in the gleaming red metal. The man smiled, wistful. His great grandfather founded Mineville Engine Company Number One in the late 1800s, in the days when horses pulled the rig. His grandfather, father, uncles, cousins, and brothers all heeded the call, just as he did in his eighteenth year. The brotherhood bound them with a force far stronger than blood—generations connected by the same yearning. *Seize power over fire.* But that bond was broken the day the man had left Mineville. Cousins and brothers drifted to unknown towns, faceless and nameless with the hope of starting anew. The uncles retired, retreating to their cottages on the outskirts of town, spending their final days rocking on creaky porches, swilling beer from sweating cans and talking about the old times. And his father—some say he died of a broken heart.

The man stepped off the curb, drawn to the fire station like a spark to kindling. He recalled the adrenaline rush that came with each call; the quick catch awakening his gut as he rushed to don his gear, his heart pounding like a caged eagle as he jumped on the rig. And the sweet euphoria of storming a burning building; he was a soaring bird whose talons reached through walls of flame, bold and unscathed. Beneath his wings the flames cowered, upon his back the helpless were whisked from harm. He breathed fire, taming chaos at will; a god whose actions determined who might live, and who might die.

Tires screeched as an oncoming sedan swerved around the man and slammed on its brakes. "Get out of here, before you get somebody else killed!" the driver yelled, wild-eyed and waving a fist through the open window. The firefighters paused from their work, shaking their heads and staring at the man, their lips pulled tight, eyes narrowed.

The man had dropped his parcel; the canned tuna rolled in the gutter. As he retrieved his package from the asphalt, he noticed the boy sitting on the hood of the fire engine, an oversized helmet falling over his eyes. The boy waved furiously, a red handkerchief balled up in his palm.

"Hey, mister," he yelled, releasing the fabric. Caught in a light breeze, it floated toward the pavement like an ember. "This belong to you?"

The man removed his glasses, his eyes following the cloth in its descent. As it touched the ground, the wailing of the fire signal mobilized the men. They pushed their buckets aside, the cleaning rags dropped and forgotten as they scrambled to gather their gear. The boy laughed as red lights flashed atop the firehouse and he clambered into the back of the truck; the firemen leapt into the cab and sped toward danger.

The wheels had rolled over the fallen handkerchief, leaving a filthy imprint in its center. The man crossed the empty street and crouched down to retrieve it. He spread the cloth over his thigh, dirtying his fingers as he ran them across the rough cotton.

———

The man trudged up the rickety wooden staircase to the apartment above his great aunt's barn, a one-bedroom unit initially built as a boarding house for coal miners who drifted in and out of town. With few exceptions, those who were born in Mineville usually died there; newcomers were as transient as the seasons.

He had been homeless after 20 years in the state penitentiary. Great Aunt Martha was the only one who paid him any mind after he was released; she gave him a place to stay, though he doubted she'd visit. Like his life, the man's dwelling space was on loan. The furniture was mismatched and tired: a red velvet couch with cigarette burns and sagging cushions, a tan leather easy chair that began its life as ivory, a wobbly kitchen table. Wallpaper in the pattern of pink peonies curled down from the corners of the room. It wasn't much, but it was home, a comfortable solitary confinement after years of bunking with criminals.

When he unpacked his groceries, the man removed a crisp Marlboro from its carton. He reached in his pocket for the lighter that the boy left behind. It had belonged to the man, a gift from a long-forgotten fiancée. He hadn't seen it, or her, since the night of the Walnut Street fire. That was his last night as a fireman, the last night of his life. The night he went to prison.

Where had the boy found it?

He ran his fingertips across the engraving. "J.D." His initials—the initials of the man he used to be. He flicked his thumb across the igniter, lighting a low blue flame. A plume of sweet smoke encircled his cigarette, and he took a long drag. He plopped down on the couch, sinking into the velvet. The lighter lay nestled in his rough palm, the luster of silver dulled by time.

Sighing, the man extinguished his cigarette in the ashtray, another loan from his great aunt. "Hero" was painted on the ceramic, along with a picture of a helmet and axe. That ashtray had survived through years of fire and ash, of guilty pleasures lit and snuffed out. The man recalled playing with that ashtray as a child, stacking burnt-out cigar and cigarette butts as he sat under his aunt's dining room table—the smell of stale nicotine absorbed into his skin. He leaned up against the legs of his father and his uncles that surrounded him like a fortress—*a prison cell*—entranced by their stories of rushing and rescue.

Heroes. All of them.

The man stood and stretched; there was important work to do. As part of his community service, he was tasked with refurbishing town relics damaged by a recent flood—starting with a collection of wooden plaques commemorating the history of the Mineville Fire Department. He lifted the first plaque from the pile on his kitchen table. "Fallen Heroes" was etched by hand at the top with his father's name, the name they shared, immortalized in the wood.

The plaque lay like a tombstone in the man's hands. With reverence, he laid it gently on the table. He reached for the can of varnish and dug his nails under the lid, pulling. The metal indented his fingertips, but the lid wouldn't give. He scratched his beard, intent on remembering where he left his screwdriver to jimmy it, when he heard a familiar sound.

Click, click. Click, click.

Metal on metal.

The man spun on his heels, knocking the sealed varnish can off the kitchen table.

"Hey, mister!" The boy sat on the arm of the couch, his ruddy face rivaling the scarlet fabric. He held the lighter between his thumb

and forefinger, opening and closing the lid of the Zippo in a maddening staccato.

"How did you get in here?" the man asked, his pale cheeks
flushing. He looked toward the closed door, the deadbolt still secure.

The boy closed the lighter and tapped it against his forehead.
"I've always been here." He grinned. "J.D."

The man shook his head, running fingers through his hair.

"I don't know why you're following me, but you need to stop."
Fists clenched, the man stomped toward the door. He screamed as he
touched the doorknob, his skin singed by a surge of heat. Pulling his
hand away, he saw the knob glowing red. Blisters sprouted from his
smarting palm.

The boy giggled as the man raced toward the kitchen sink and
plunged his hand into a cool faucet stream. The man grunted with relief, and in pain.

"Get out of my house," he said, through clenched teeth.

"Your house?" the boy said, materializing next to the man as
he tended to his injury. "This is not your house. Nothing belongs to
you any more, does it, J.D.? Except this." He ignited the lighter, dangling the flame in front of him.

"Scram." The man waved a shaking hand toward the door.
"Get the hell out of here, kid."

"Kid? Why are you calling me *Kid*?" The boy closed the lighter
and let out a belly laugh, clutching his stomach as it jiggled. "My name
isn't Kid. It's Billy. Why are you making believe you don't know me?"

The man pushed past the boy, heading toward the wall phone.
"I'll call the cops."

"9-1-1!" the boy said in a singsong. He skipped around the
man.

The man reached for the phone, his uninjured hand resting on
the receiver.

"That's who my mama said I should call if there's an emergency," the boy said. "9-1-1." He stopped moving and stood very still.
His shoulders dropped, and he sighed. "And I did. I called them. But
they were no help."

The boy clicked the igniter and ramped the lighter fluid to full
strength. The man watched, wide-eyed, as the fire morphed from an
innocent sliver of candlelight into to a brutal blowtorch. The boy dangled his pinky finger over the flame, then plunged it into the amber
core.

The man retched at the acrid stench of burning flesh. He stepped backward, searching for the wall to steady him as the boy turned his head.

A crusted hole gaped open where the boy's left ear should have been. His neck was covered with festering blisters. Patches of flesh hung like cobwebs from his arms, revealing charred muscle beneath. He radiated heat.

"You burned my house," the boy said.

"*Your* house…?"

"I watched you do it. It was the middle of the night." The boy stared into the flame, yellow and red and blue dancing off his coal-black eyes. "I woke up. I had a nightmare. But Mommy made me go back to bed. I saw you outside the window in your fireman clothes. You had a red handkerchief in your pocket. You poured water on the bushes. And then you used this."

The boy thrust the lighter toward the man,

"No …" The man's voice was barely audible as he sank to the ground, burying his face in his forearms.

"I was really scared. I hid under my bed."

"Please don't do this," the man whispered. "I did my penance. I just want to be left alone."

"Mama told me that firemen were heroes." A tear streamed down the boy's mottled cheek. "But not you. You're a bad man."

The boy's face scrunched up in a twisted grimace. "I miss my mama," he said. His lower lip quivered, and he squeezed the lighter, as if willing the tears away.

"I miss my mama!"

The boy flung the fireball toward the can of varnish that lay on the floor. It blossomed in a plume of blue heat. Tufts of wallpaper ignited and rained down upon the mismatched furniture. Fire licked at the couch. It pushed across the table in a wave, consuming the plaques. The man's name—*his father's name*—melted away as the wood crinkled into a charred mass.

Fallen heroes.

The man gasped through the billowing smoke that obscured the boy's face. As the heat entombed him, he recalled the heavy, endless weeks before the Walnut Street fire, how he trudged through each day as if dragging a charged line uphill. There were only so many games of Spades a man could play down at the firehouse, so many jokes he could tell, before losing his mind. The summer heat had fueled his hunger for fire; the caged bird raged, yearning for purpose. And that night, as the man walked, he saw an opportunity.

What he hadn't seen was the little boy who pressed his face against the window on the third floor to watch the fireman *watering the bushes* outside his house. The little boy who stood before him, 20 years later, avenging a mother who would always sleep—staring down the nightmare that robbed him of his rest. This brave boy who breathed fire through a gap-toothed smile.

"Please. Forgive me." The man lay on the floor, his body spasming with each cough. Black smoke curled around him like a shroud. "Billy." He reached toward the boy, straining against the effort of breathing.

"No."

"I'm so sorry."

The man gasped his last. The fire he had so craved over the years turned on him, devouring him not in a blaze of glory but of retribution, his death a release for a young boy who had been long trapped, invisible to the world.

Nothing changed here—*nothing ever changed here*—but, perhaps, it had.

The boy walked. He smiled as he pushed onward, through the flame.

AUTHOR'S NOTE

A group of writers and I had been eliminated from the next round of a writing competition, and were upset that we wouldn't have the chance to craft another story for the contest. So we decided to form our own renegade writing team, and write anyway! (Judges be damned!). We picked a random writing genre and character prompt—ghost story, volunteer firefighter—and committed to writing together and critiquing each other's work. I can't quite remember what about this prompt made my mind go to my dad's childhood home, in the middle of coal mining country in Pennsylvania. I've always been fascinated with the town itself—the semi-abandoned nature of it, the dilapidated rowhouses, the mountains of shale in the distance. I thought it would be a great setting for a ghost story.

I knew I wanted to make my main character the one who was haunted and not the ghost himself (though one could argue that my main character, while alive, really functions like a ghost). Which started the questions. Who or what would haunt him? And why? I went to the darkest place I could. What would make a hero not a hero that would haunt him for the rest of his life? My conflict was born. This was the first time I ever attempted a ghost story and I had a tremendous amount of fun writing it. So grateful my fellow writers and I decided to thumb our noses at rejection!

LF

THE STUMPVILLE AFFAIR

JAMES GOODRIDGE

PROLOGUE

THE NEW CYCLE of a full autumn moon cast a cold, icy glow over August Mason's farm. Mason woke at 3:00 AM to the sound of his livestock. While the old farmer hated to venture out at this hour, he needed to find out why the hens were riled. Stepping out into the darkness, thoughts of Deacon Talbert—the local priest who had been recently murdered in the early morning hours—sent a chill through Mason's body as Wellington boots crunched atop the frosted grass as he walked to the barn.

"Something's got these hens worked up," said Mason, buttoning a denim peacoat. Brown earth mixed with manure caked his work boots as he rushed to the hen house. Hatless Mason cupped his eyes, avoiding the moonlight's glare, as its brightness made him nauseous.

Stumbling up to the hen house, Mason blindly felt around the inside wall, eventually locating a pair of dark tinted welders goggles, a memento from his days in the navy during the Great War. He slipped them over his cowlicked auburn hair.

"Now, what are you ladies cackling about ? Where's Mugsy?" Mason wondered aloud, inquiring about his king rooster. He suddenly felt a presence behind him. The hens fell silent in an almost human like terror. Stepping out of the hen house, Mason, a loner with no wife or children, turned around to face what was going to end his life.

The creature snatched at him as razor-sharp fangs bit into Mason's right arm, snapping it off at the elbow. Blood, bone, and muscle mass splattered about in the moonlight. Mason's lower arm sailed end over end into the air, finally landing atop the weathered house roof. As shock set in, August Mason howled in pain, body quivering. His cries reverberated into the village of Stumpville before trauma took him into eternal darkness.

Just before dawn, the day laborers Mason had hired approached in a dirty pickup. As the headlights grew nearer, the creature, which had been feasting upon the Mason's crimson and pink flesh, vanished into a nearby treeline. The hens, which had remained silent, resumed their frenzied cackle as Mugsy the rooster emerged from the crawlspace beneath the hen house.

1

Times were tough, even for occult detectives. Our clientele, those high society moneybags who hired Sue and I to chase ghosts or perform Tarot readings, had dried up as a reliable source of income. Contract work from the city's paranormal Office of Special Concerns had slowed because of budget cuts.

It was Tuesday, 12:35 AM. Dressed in stripped azure PJs and my red smoking jacket, I was in for the night. I sat behind my desk rolling around a nice-sized emerald from our stash on a desk blotter, wondering how much it might fetch. Off in the distance, a tugboat horn mewed deep on the Hudson River. At least the tug captain had work, unlike the occupants of Riverside Drive and 107th Street. A mug of hyssop tea on my desk curtailed my cravings as the silence of the room was suddenly interrupted.

I answered the phone on the first ring.

"Hello Kirkland," I said, aware that only Stuart Kirkland—the young "boy wonder" and head of the OSC—was the only person who would call me at this hour. "How goes it with you?"

"Hey, Madison, old pal. I'm peachy. Listen, I know that times are rough all over with this depression crud going on. so I figured you and Sue might be available for a job."

"Much appreciated," I said.

"Besides, this one's out of our jurisdiction."

"What's the affair? " I asked, intrigued.

"Upstate New York, Sullivan County. Village of Stumpville. The local sheriff, Kilroy Bertrand, has two unsolved murders which he believes were committed by … well … a werewolf."

"The sheriff's a real forward thinking fellow," I chuckled. "How did he decide to reach out to you?"

"You remember *The Life of a Lycan*?"

"The monograph you coauthored with Sue."

"That's right. She'd used the nom de plume *anonymous*. Bertrand read it. He thinks *anonymous* can solve their problem up -there, because *anonymous* 'must be a werewolf to know so much,'" said Kirkland.

To me, that monograph was nothing but trouble. "So what's bub looking for, a Lycan to catch a Lycan?"

"I guess so, Madison. He sounds desperate."

"Yeah, but I'm also desperate for people *not* to know of Sue's propensities," I warned. "Okay, Kirkland, I'll ask Sue. She was under the weather last night and retired to bed a few hours ago. It's her call."

"Fair enough," Kirkland said.

"One question: The village of Stumpville. This a sundown town?"

Persons of mixed heritage like Sue (half native American and half Negro) and I (half Negro and half white) knew better than to work where we weren't wanted, money tight or no money tight.

"I'm ahead of you, Madison. Bertrand says it's an all-American, progressive town. They even have a few farms in the surrounding areas run by people of color," beamed Kirkland.

With that I pulled a yellow legal pad and pencil out of my desk drawer and took down the sheriff's information.

"I'll phone you later in the morning after I speak with Sue. Good morning, Kirkland."

"Good morning, Madison."

I pulled an Old Gold from my cigarette case, lit it with a magenta glow from my left-hand palm, and took a few quick puffs before snuffing it out in my tea mug. I left the smoky room and headed upstairs to Sue's apartment on the second floor, unlocking the door with her spare key.

"Sekhmet, sweetie, what you doing gal?"

Hanging upside down from the ceiling, Sue's pet cat, Sekhmet, meowed. Jet black fur tapered up to five silky black tentacles which held her in place while her forepaws played with a pink ball of yarn that trailed down to the floor among Sue's kaleidoscopic-colored harem pillows. Three innocent, copper-tinted feline eyes blinked at me.

"Come on, gal." I ordered, to which she plopped down on my shoulder, paws and tentacles secure in a piggyback ride to Sue's bedroom with me.

Sue lay sprawled out, face down in a black nightgown, throat rasping, and sniffled a sign of a cold in motion.

"Sue. Sue ? Wake up, love. I think I've got a paying affair for us if you're interested." I knelt by her bed and tapped her arm as Sekhmet hopped on my love's back, doing her best cat shimmy to break Sue's slumber."

"Madison Prescott Cavendish, do we have to talk now?" Sue asked, voice syrupy thanks to her cold.

On more than one occasion my Sue had been mistaken for Harlem starlet Fredi Washington, even being a stand in for the actress during a film shoot. But at this hour, rolling over to see me kneeling beside her and feeling Sekhmet resting atop her stomach, glamor was not on my beloved's mind.

"Job? Wha … what is it? Where? I don't … feel so good. How much does it pay?"

"It's upstate. Stumpville. I have to phone the local sheriff in the morning if we take it," I said.

"What's he want, a seance?" she sniffed.

"He … um … wants us to catch a werewolf."

Sue sat bolt upright.

"Come again?"

"A werewolf," I repeated.

Sue's pupils turned from black to hazel. Even her happy freckles, as I liked to call them, on her beautiful face were becoming inflammatory with anger.

"Seriously?" she asked.

"I kid you not. According to the lawman, this werewolf has already munched two people to death during a full moon. As I'm sure you know, the full moon is in cycle this week. I figure we go up there catch the creature, detain it until morning, then give it a one-way ticket out of town, no sore feelings. I know you were looking to celebrate Halloween, but we need the dough."

Sue frowned. "What if this werewolf is like me?"

My mind flashed back to 1914 and a nameless cosmic horror whose encounter in a lower Manhattan basement had changed our lives in ways we wouldn't have imagined possible.

"I guess we'll see what happens when we get to that bridge, my love. So, how about it?"

"Let me sleep on it, Maddy." Looking around but finding nothing upon which to wipe her runny nose, my Sue playfully ran it across on my pajama sleeve as Sekhmet's tentacle tapped displeasure on Sue's arm.

"Goodnight or good morning, dear," said Sue, rolling over to return to dreamland, with Sekhmet snuggled in her arms. I quietly retreated back downstairs to await her answer.

2

At eight o'clock sharp, Sue stepped into my apartment while I rested in peace. Rousing me awake, she looked fabulous in Halloween-colored attire. An orange bycoket with a black quill pointing out the top adorned her head, while her body was clothed in a black-belted orange sweater dress, black stockings, and semi-heels, all cloaked beneath a black trench coat. The overnight bag in her left hand meant I could phone the sheriff.

I dressed quickly; a gray tweed suit and white shirt matched by a gray fedora with black bowtie and wing tips.

Our first stop was across town to leave Sekhmet in the care of our friends, Zoltar the Magician and Elsa Cranberry, occult detective, both of whom were on idle time. Next we were off to Stumpville.

The concrete and asphalt of New York City in the midst of a depression faded into rural upstate New York, also in economic blues, as we cruised up the Hudson Valley in a dark cherry red 1929 Packard 640 Roadster. After a few hours I swung the Packard onto Stumpville's Lincoln Avenue, the town's main thoroughfare, where Halloween jack-o'-lanterns sat as festive sentinels at the base of lamp posts. Along the avenue, villagers went about their business, looking as if they had recently stepped out of a Norman Rockwell canvas. A few individuals of color confirmed what Kirkland had told me.

While Sue's nose continued its defiance, I parked the Packard in front of Sheriff Bertrand's office. The building was sandwiched between the Stumpville Post Office and an American Legion post that doubled as the mayor's office. I made an educated guess that Stumpville's population hovered around four hundred.

"Hey there, you must be Madison Cavendish and Seneca Sue. If not, I'll have to write you a ticket for parking in front of the sheriff's office in a spot reserved for official business," chuckled Sheriff Kilroy Bertrand, puffing on a pipe, hand outstretched to greet us as we stepped out of our automobile. He was a hearty soul, the kind you'd expect was born to work in law enforcement. Average height, rust-colored wavy hair under a dark felt hat, rosy cheeks, defiant light brown eyes that would rather squint than wear glasses, Bertrand wore a black suit covering a tieless plaid shirt. A badge on his lapel and a Smith and Wesson .38 holstered in a gun belt hanging at an angle below his pants belt were the only indications of Bertrand's occupation.

"Please, come inside. Glad you came," he said, as we entered into a drab pastel green atop Kelly green office with wooden court-room-like barriers; benches on one side, front desk on the other. Bertrand ushered us into his office, past two deputies in khaki uniforms, each wearing surplus New York City police caps and engrossed in a game of chess. Dimly lit holding cells loomed in the back of the building.

"A few introductions are in order," Bertrand said, pointing to the three individuals seated at a table before us. "This is Mayor Douglas, Miss Katherine Liotta, and Doctor Neilson Zellner. They sort of make up the village council. We had a fourth council member, August Mason, but he was killed during the last cycle of the moon."

Sue, Bertrand, and I found empty seats. Mayor Douglas, a rotund man in an expensive navy pinstripe suit, had that old Roman Warren G. Harding look about him. Miss Livotti, a lanky woman with midnight dark hair saturated with pomade, looked tired in her royal blue dress. My impression was that she just wanted this problem to be over with. From the dagger-cold stare he issued, I suspected that the salt-and-pepper bearded Dr. Zellner, decked out in a blueish/gray double-breasted suit, didn't want us here. He wasted no time confirming my suspicion.

"I just want to" Zellner began, "for the record, voice my objection to this whole affair. It's a waste of village time and funds. Meaning no disrespect, what precisely do we know about these two hokum artists anyway?"

"Calm down, Neil," said Mayor Douglas. It was becoming obvious that this council wasn't exactly pleased with our presence. "We've already voted in favor of hiring Mr. Cavendish and his associate to help our village, and by Saxon that's what is going to be done!" The mayor's voice rose to a bellow.

"Please, everyone, let's relax. We are most certainly *not* hokum artists," sniffed Sue, to which the council lightly smiled (though I continued to receive icy looks). After giving them a redacted oral resume Sue asked. "How about letting us and the sheriff work out details and a plan in private."

The council nodded in agreement. Filing out of the sheriff's office, the good doctor seemed to be preoccupied in thought.

"Thank you," whispered Miss Livotti, finally perking up.

Bertrand retrieved a desk a map of the village and surrounding area. Two red pencil-marked X's denoted the recent killings and the time the bodies were found.

"Deacon Talbert died here," said Bertrand, pointing to a church in the south end of the village. "August Mason died here." An X marked his farm, just outside the east end of the village. "I feel the next attack will come in the north end," surmised Bertrand. I made a mental note that the sheriff's prediction seemed odd.

"Okay, sheriff," I said, "we'll need a pair of handcuffs, your map, and some type of anesthesia like diethyl ether."

"That's no problem, Mr. Cavendish. I'll have one of my men catch up to Dr. Zellner for the ether."

"We'll set to work around 11 tonight."

"I've set you up with accommodations. Drive further down Lincoln Avenue and you'll see the Doyle Hotel. Old Paddy Mullins will be behind the front desk, most likely napping. He'll have two rooms ready for you. I didn't know if you two were married or not and we don't do hot sheets up here." chuckled Bertrand. "Across the street is Carmella's Chop House. Put anything you order on Mayor Douglas' tab." Again Bertrand chuckled.

"We'll be sure to do that," Sue sniffed.

We soon headed down Lincoln Avenue. While stopped at a red light, I watched as a woman in a pea-green coat and tam with matching clutch bag chatted with a merchant in front of a sundry storefront. Next to her, a cherubic little girl, dressed as a smaller version of her mother, munched on a shiny scarlet apple. Me and the cornsilk ponytailed child made eye contact. I smiled and turned my green tinted sunglasses that protected my eyes and caught the light as it turned green. The little darling launched the apple into the car like she was on the mound at my beloved Polo Grounds, knocking my fedora off. Sue sat, too into her cold and her eyes closed, to notice. I felt an unexplained, strange vibe about this place, but couldn't understand why.

3

At Doyle's Hotel, we settled into our rooms to freshen up before crossing over to Carmella's Chop House.

"You're having steak. The iron will help with the cold," I explained.

"I'm really not hungry," Sue said.

"A rare steak for the lady. Hot water for me," I told the waitress, as she stood over our table.

"You only want water?" she asked.

"Yes. Hot water. For hyssop tea."

"We don't serve hyssop tea." The indignation was palpable.

"Then I suppose it's a good thing I brought my own."

The raven-haired waitress jotted down the order with Hellenic disdain and stepped away.

At the appointed hour, we got to work. This consisted of driving around the north side of the village, car windows rolled down so that Sue, despite her cold, might pick up the werewolf's scent.

Dawn finally arrived. Low on gas and with nothing to show from our night-long patrol but a shivering Sue, we returned to the Doyle Hotel where I made Sue a hot cup of hyssop tea with lemon.

"Get some rest, love. I'll be back to your room around 11:00 PM," I said, but the tea had already sent Seneca Sue SunMountain to Morpheus. Before turning in, I gassed up the Packard at a Sinclair station. The attendant seemed roiled when I asked him to fill the tank. We were a long way from New York City.

4

"I'm feeling better, sweetie," Sue smiled, as we started our second night of werewolf hunting, just one hour prior to Halloween Day. Similar to the night before, Sue wore only her trench coat, a pair of maroon house slippers, and rose-tinted glasses. This after so many ruined dresses resulting from spontaneous transformations. A change of clothes were in the back seat of the car. Cold gone, Sue enjoyed the night air for a few mundane hours.

"Ooh ... woo!" Sue grabbed my right arm, suddenly. "Maddy!"

"What's wrong? You pick up a scent?" I braked the Packard to a stop.

"Yowzah! This village! I can smell so clearly now! This is ... Maddy, we're in a village of werewolves! I can detect their scents all around me. Feel their blood pumping. One of their pack is sick."

"Well, hot damn this is a problem!" I exclaimed.

Indeed it was a problem, particularly for me, a living vampire. Historically, werewolves and vampires did not coexist well. This explained the vibe I felt earlier, not to mention the apple to my fedora.

"Quick, continue down the road a bit more until I say stop!" ordered Sue.

I drove along until her cue, stopping in front of a pleasant white-washed, two-story house. A well-picked pumpkin patch appeared to be the source of the jack-o'-lanterns lining Lincoln Avenue. Beyond a treeline nearly naked of leaves, a large shadowy figure emerged trudged toward the house. A little girl screamed from inside the house, its lights off and curtains drawn. The minty glow of the moon provided a spotlight for the final act of this affair.

A large, puss-dripping pink mass pushed its way out of one of the dark fur shoulders of the former Lycan. No longer a werewolf, it was in the process of sprouting a second head. The maw of the first head sagged, as if having suffered a stroke. One leg, devoid of fur, was rubbery black skin. Presently, the thing turned in our direction. Sue handed me her eyeglasses before leaving the Packard. She then slipped out of her trench coat, kicked off her slippers, and flicked her head to the moonlight. Knocked to the ground, on hands and knees screaming, her eyes bled as they turned from blackish red to bestial hazel. A grayish-magenta fur rose to cover my love. I issued a vampiric hiss, but before leaving the Packard, checked my Colt .45. Though loaded with silver bullets, I felt it would be lacking, so I removed my suit jacket. If I had to jump in, a vampire versus werewolf encounter would not be pretty. Doubtless it would be more deadly chaotic than a pier six longshoreman's brawl along the Hudson.

A horrid, grappling struggle ensued as Sue and the creature slammed into each other. Claws swiped, dirt flew, and pumpkins were crushed beneath the moon's stoic beam. I glanced quickly back at the house. The curtains, now pulled back, revealed the same apple-throwing little girl, mouth open in horror. A moment later, an unseen person snatched her away. Sue's claws were wrapped tightly around the creature's throat as she struggled to avoid its bite. A deadly tug o' war, which seemed to last forever, played out before my eyes. Sue gained the upper hand by lifting the creature off the ground before eviscerating it with a clawed swipe that dropped the were-thing to its knees. Steaming innards spilled out onto the frosty dark ground. Another swipe from Sue decapitated the beast. Its head spiralled like a football in search of a goalpost, blood misting into the night air. It landed beyond the treeline and rolled into the woods.

—

"Put that shotgun away, man!" I minced oath to the shadowy figure pointing the weapon at me from the second floor window of the house. "I need to use your phone to call Sheriff Bertrand. I also need a sheet to cover the body and water for my gal to wash up. We're working for the sheriff and the village council."

I clutched the were-thing's head, which I'd retrieved from the woods. Sue was bent over the back of the Packard, vomiting. Whomever held the gun likely didn't know that a full side of buckshot wouldn't kill me. After a quiescent few minutes, the door opened. A plump man wearing a nightshirt stood in the doorway.

"Names Culver," he said, handing me a sheet. "I already phoned the sheriff's office. Deputies Trusdale and Issacs are on their way. Your lady friend is welcome to come in and wash up."

In the distance, Sue began transforming back to her sparkling human form. I yanked the sheet from Culver, placed the were-thing's head in the pumpkin patch next to its torso, and covered the remains. I then helped a dazed Sue to the house, before waiting inside the Packard for the deputy sheriffs to arrive and for and sunrise to reveal who rested under the sheet. *Where,* I wondered, *is the good sheriff?*

5

"Help me understand something," I insisted, stepping up to Sheriff Bertrand's desk as he sat behind it with folded hands. "Since Stumpville is a village of werewolves, why didn't you take care of Miss Livotti's situation yourselves?"

Sue stood behind me, dressed from cloche hat to heels in black as if in mourning for Miss Livotti, whose vacant chair was next to Mayor Douglas and Dr. Zellner.

"Mr. Cavendish, I'm sorry," Bertrand said. "The people of this village have, for decades and from around the world, immigrated to Stumpville for a safe haven away from being butchered over lies and folklore. It's no accident that our village is named after Peter Stump of Germany and I myself am a descendant of the Bertrand family of France, so-called infamous names in Lycan history. Our ancestors settled in peace and harmony but with two rules: 1. Do not harm humans. 2. Lycan shall not kill Lycan."

"So, you made me, an outsider, her catspaw executioner?" Sue asked, trying to keep her anger in check.

"She made *you* her own executioner, Sue," said Dr. Zellner, choking back emotion. "I loved Kathy with all my heart. Earlier this year, she made the fatal mistake of picking and cooking wild mushrooms. The variety she picked, while nonpoisonous and delicious to humans, were poisonous to Lycans from souther Italy deluding. She developed rabies. After farmer Mason's death, by her own volition, Kathy decided something had to be done. Sheriff Bertrand stayed with me all night so I wouldn't interfere. How I loved that woman."

Now shaking, Zellner eased into his lover's vacant chair, head in hands, sobbing.

"You loved her? Yet now, Sue, the love of my life, has become infected with that mushroom-triggered rabid illness!" I couldn't help but be tempted to make the doctor his own patient. "You could have told us!"

"Maddy, calm down, you lug. Whatever toxins were in me are long gone, or have you already forgotten the heaving incident behind the Packard? I'm as good as gold and you're still my man," said Sue, planting a kiss on my immortal cheek to the mayor and sheriff's blasphemous gawks. A vampire and a werewolf canoodling, indeed!

"On behalf of the village of Stumpville, I apologize for any duress. Katherine Livotti, rest her soul, is now at peace," said Mayor Douglas, speaking in an official tone as he handed us an envelope containing our wages.

"Madison and Sue," said Bertrand, as he escorted us out of his office to our Packard, a gray leather-bound book under his arm, "don't think what I'm going to give you is quid pro quo. It's from the heart. Tomorrow is All Saints' Day."

Sue and I stared curiously at Bertrand, unsure where he was headed.

"I'll be sending down to the city a truckload of venison meat on ice and apples. Seeing how times are hard down in 'Olde New York,' we in the village figured we could help out."

We nodded appreciatively.

"And look," the sheriff continued, "some nefarious person has placed two bottles of deer blood and a jug of fine applejack in your vehicle. We're still in prohibition, you know, so I hereby order you to drive the applejack out of city limits and enjoy it. Lastly, for you, Sue, a tome on Lycan heritage."

"*Histoire le Famille Bertrand*," Sue said, reading the title.

"I wish vampires had a village like this," I lamented.

"Corcosa," said Bertrand.

"What's that?" I asked.

"Corcosa, New York, up west near Buffalo. Them boys and gals up there like to work the midnight shift on the grain silos and elevators. We reached out to them, even challenged them to a game of baseball once, but they have yet to reply. Maybe they don't know the difference between a winged bat and a baseball bat," chuckled Bertrand.

Sue and I winced at the sheriff's attempt at humor.

After saying our goodbyes, Sue and I headed out of Stumpville. Halloween evening festively encroached. Children in costumes, and others as natural walking-upright wolf cubs, were already trick-or-treating. We were invited to stay for the grown-up activities, which included a Mardi Gras–style bash around midnight, a Lycan run in the surrounding woods, and an oration for Miss Livotti, but we were both missing Sekhmet and wondered what sort of feline mischief she'd been up to.

I stopped for a red light and saw Mrs. Culver with her apple-throwing daughter, Emma, dressed as a pirate and approaching us from Lincoln Avenue. The little darling released her mother's hand and ran up to the Packard. But instead of throwing another apple, she nervously handed me the candied variety before running back to mommy.

"Happy Halloween, Stumpville," I said, as we motored off back down to the Big Apple.

EPILOGUE

The sheriff was good to his word. We donated bags of apples and boxes of venison to folks in Harlem, The Bowery, and Hell's Kitchen. They needed it a lot more than we did.

In the years that followed, Sue and I made an annual October trek to Stumpville, each year growing more appreciative of its small-town charm and the glow of jack-o'-lanterns lined up along Lincoln Avenue.

AUTHOR'S NOTE

The ingredients that make up characters Madison Cavendish and Seneca Sue SunMountain come from various places (e.g., historical, folklore, etc.) infused with my imagination. A lot can be developed by asking, "What if…?" In this case, what if two people, both born in the year 1885, are able to witness world events and historical movement through the 20th and into the 21st centuries, while existing in part of a twilight world of the paranormal and occult due to a horrific Lovecraftian event that takes place in New York as the Great War starts in Europe.

As occult detectives in the pulp tradition, Madison and Sue solve Carnacki-like paranormal incidents and occult crimes, at times in liaison with the New York City Office of Special Concerns and with help from their associates (Cordelia Lovemilk and occultist Rollo Ahmed) both real and imagined. Like Nick and Nora Charles, Jonathan and Jennifer Hart, and with a little *Thomasen & Bushrod* coolness, danger is what these two (he, a living vampire; she, a werewolf) thrive on.

.

JG

THE GRIM, WICKED WOOD

JAMES MICHAEL SHOBERG

Kirk's father said, "Roam and you'll come to no good,
For bloodsuckers lurk in the grim, wicked wood.
This farm's isolated; there's no neighborhood,
And trees swallow screams in the grim, wicked wood."

He frightened the lad, maybe more than he should,
To quell the allure of the grim, wicked wood.

"I know my boy's mind, and he'll come to no good—
He'll get himself lost in the grim, wicked wood.
And frightening him, maybe more than I should,
Will keep him away from the grim, wicked wood."

"Son, they can't cross torrents like you or I could,
The thirsty undead of the grim, wicked wood,
So our stream protects us. Is that understood?
It foils their leaving the grim, wicked wood."

That night brought such snows to the grim, wicked wood,
And soon the creek froze near the grim, wicked wood,
Which ceased any flows 'round the grim, wicked wood.
Then waxen, white toes from the grim, wicked wood,
Belonging to those from the grim, wicked wood,
Crossed ice as they rose from the grim, wicked wood.

The boy and his father both came to no good,
And trees swallowed screams in the grim, wicked wood.

LIZZY DIES FROM A PLANE CRASH AT THE END OF THIS POEM

JAMES MICHAEL SHOBERG

Now, Lizzy Bennett's fear of airplanes wasn't rare, but shared,
With all whom at their mention were from panic quite impaired.
And so when Lizzy's family had made their summer plan,
Of course, they'd chosen airline tickets for the Bennett Clan.
At school year's end, few days partitioned Lizzy from the sky—
She crossed them off her calendar as each one hurried by.
"Why can't we drive?" asked Lizzy in a fretful, nervous plea.
"A long jaunt in a car with you? No way!" snapped Gregory.
Greg was her younger brother, and his humor could be mean,
That's why he tortured Lizzy with his toy flying machine.
Remotely, he controlled his jet from somewhere out of sight,
And feigned a shriek of terror, "No survivors from this height!
The cabin is on fire, turning passengers to ash!"
It wasn't hard for Lizzy to imagine such a crash—
Their mother shouted, "Gregory, your sister's tense enough!
Don't make the matter worse for her with all your vicious guff!"

Greg mumbled, "Sure Mom, I can wait until we're all onboard—
I'll take the seat right next to her where I can't be ignored."
Then Lizzy tailed their mother as she went into the house,
But not before a final notion came to Greg, the louse:
"As she walks past the window, I will take a daring swoop,
And that'll throw the scaredy-cat for one tremendous loop!"
He brought the plaything into range and quickly made a guess,
"She should be passing by in 6…5…4…3…2…1…YES!"
With cruel excitement, Greg pressed down too firmly on the switch.
The lever snapped precisely as Greg growled, "The little witch!"
His plaything struck the window with extraordinary force;
The glass exploded inward and barraged the girl, of course.
The weighty fuselage struck Lizzy squarely in the head.

The right propeller sheared her cheek and sprayed the wall with red.
She fell down on the kitchen floor and gripped her wounded face
(An impulse she regretted with those shards about the place).
Their mother ran to Lizzy, who seemed more afraid than harmed.
Outside, Greg's stomach soured as he, too, became alarmed.
His mom's voice, like a sonic boom, induced his knocking knees—

It thundered through the empty frame,
"Young man, you'd better freeze!"
"Get in here, Greg! I'll deal with you once Lizzy's clean and calm."
She chided him while she pulled glass from Lizzy's bloody palm.
With every cut and bruise addressed, Liz went into her room.
Though dizzy, Lizzy managed still to drone about her doom:
"Mom, my head's throbbing and I'm sore;
the damage may be deep.
I really shouldn't fly." She smirked and pondered,
"Thank you, creep.
Because of you, you nasty thing, your sister will survive—
True, I'm in pain from one small plane,
but now we're bound to drive!"
Her mother kissed her gently, tucked her in, and said goodnight:
"We'll talk tomorrow, honey." Lizzy felt relieved of fright.
Though hazy, bashed, and aching, she did not for slumber strain—

According to her autopsy, she had a swollen brain.

Go on, call me a fibber, but please note my haughty grin:
Review the title closer—it says "from" a crash, not "in."

RUN RED

JAMES MICHAEL SHOBERG

Your lawn's a bit unruly; just a comment, don't get mad.
I only hope that you're not waiting on that Trunzo lad.
I understand he did your yardwork for some extra dough.
That luxury; however, has concluded. YOU DON'T KNOW?!
He ran up at the high school; you know that much, am I right?
And boy, did that kid tame the track whenever he took flight!

Well, I went to a scrimmage there a week ago today.
"Support your local athletes!" Is that not what people say?
Though I was one of many who had taken to the grounds,
The man who drew my notice owned the nastiest of hounds.
You are aware of whom I speak and his rapacious cur,
As well as Trunzo's record with that savage bulk of fur?

It cornered him a dozen times, while cutting grass like yours—
I easily could see it stalking townsfolk on the moors.
And there the massive mongrel sat, next to its master's feet,
Surveying all the passers-by, deciding whom to eat.
Suppress that chuckle, my good man, or else you'll feel regret—
You can't imagine just how bad this story's going to get.

For that's when it saw Trunzo bent into his starting stance,
Before a single pistol-shot cut short its hungry glance.
Propelling himself forward, each young man had joined the race,
And need I even mention Trunzo took the leading place?

With predatory instinct, that wild mutt took off to catch
The single-minded Trunzo, fiercely focused on the match.
He didn't know his canine foe had joined him on the course
And passed between the others as it galloped like a horse.
The boys fanned out in terror, leaving Trunzo all alone,
Oblivious to any threat, while deeply in "the zone."

But screams heard from the bleachers woke him violently at last.
Behind him was a better cause for Trunzo to run fast.

Despite the runner's nimble pace, the creature met his stride,
And even from my distant seat, I saw its eyes grow wide.
It set upon poor Trunzo's leg and sheared the flesh in half,
Which left him tethered to the beast by one unraveled calf.
A tug-of-war to raise the gorge came next between the two,
As shrieking Trunzo pulled the fibrous ropes of gory goo.

Then, naked muscle wetly smacked, the dog began to dine.
The bloody stripe that marked his path
was Trunzo's "finished line."

AUTHOR'S NOTE

"Lizzie Dies From A Plane Crash At Of The End Of This Poem" was composed for my friend and former editor, Liz. She'd worked so diligently to help me polish my poetry (suffering in silence, as I'm admittedly maddening in that regard), and so she'd more than earned her place among my many victims slain in verse. (Yes, this is what passes for a heartfelt display of gratitude in my twisted world.) She revealed to me her fear of dying in a plane crash, and, as it's such a common phobia, I challenged myself to spin it in what I hope is perceived as a fun and clever way.

I composed "Run Red" for my friend Noah. I'd previously written a poem for another friend named Noah, and so, in order not to repeat myself (as eventually the two pieces will appear in the same collection together), I chose to refer to this Noah by his surname, "Trunzo." This also played in well with the high school track theme, as many athletes are addressed in that fashion. Now, more often than not, my horror poems have sprung from the phobias and traumas of my friends and family, but, on occasion, I've also taken one of their prominent attributes, talents, or even beloved hobbies, and distorted it into something … well … okay, there's no real point in sugarcoating it—despicable. For the actual, factual young Trunzo, it was high school track. He excelled at it. In addition, young Trunzo also made (well, "makes") extra money doing yardwork, a service I take advantage of, because I'm extremely lazy and curse the daylight (hiss). One sunny day (hiss), young Trunzo was cutting my grass and was approached and cornered by my neighbor's dog—which *never* would have happened, if they showed me any degree of common courtesy, and which also eventually led to the installation of a "spite fence" between our properties—oh, it was a whole "thing," a horror story of its own, *but*, circling back to the point—cornered by my neighbor's brutish, drooling, ugly dog. The lad handled himself with aplomb, knocked it away, and phoned the police, who, in turn, phoned animal control. And with that, inspiration struck. "Why not marry the two things into a 'track attack,' where poor Trunzo doesn't fare as well?" ("Track Attack." Damn, that would have made a great title, too.)

"The Grim, Wicked Wood" was composed for my friend Kirk, who often reflects fondly on the times he spent with his father when he was young. Kirk also happens to be a steadfast fan of horror, like me, and we have a shared passion for Stephen King's novel *Salem's Lot*. Therefore, I decided to write "The Grim, Wicked Wood" for him, to honor our friendship, celebrate our mutual love of the macabre, and, quite honestly, indulge my sense of "gallows humor" by chilling the warmth of his childhood memories with vampiric carnage—which he loved, by the way. After all, what are friend's for?

JMS

GRAVEYARD

SHUTTA CRUM

Below earth
a hungry wind carves out
            its own space
a grey-green clawing
            of joints and teeth
a thin song for the wind's only child

If we lie with our knees touching
perhaps this lullaby will sing of our names
and we will remember

AUTHOR'S NOTE

I believe each poem will tell you what it needs, and I often set poems aside for decades because they've told me they were not finished yet. "Graveyard" was started years ago. My family has its own burying ground on a mountain in Kentucky. When we lay a loved one down it is with uncles doing the preaching, aunts doing the singing, and everyone bringing food. We mourn, and remember the life of the departed one. In this poem I wondered how those already in the grave-yard could, perhaps, come together to remember as well.

SC

PEARBERRY

BERNIE BROWN

LAST NIGHT, JUST before going to sleep, Sarah heard Linda's voice pass through the wall that divided their bedrooms.

"No. I'll tell you in chem class," Linda's voice said, giggling. "No, I want you to keep guessing."

Guessing.

The word repeated, each repetition growing softer.

Sarah shivered, threw back the covers, and crept next door. Ever since the accident, their mom had kept the door to Linda's room closed in an attempt to shut out the pain. Sarah turned the knob, listening for a giggle or the beep of a cellphone. Her breath came in shallow gulps through a desert dry mouth. She cracked open the door and peeked inside.

Only darkness.

But then, the familiar scent. Pearberry. Linda's favorite fragrance. Sarah felt her eyes widen and her face stiffen. Overcome by cold, she pulled the door shut and raced barefoot back to the safety of her own bedroom and pulled the bedcovers tightly over her head.

Every night before sleep, like a diabolic lullaby, Sarah heard the same sounds. The high-pitched squeal of tires skidding across blacktop, followed by the shriek of metal on metal as the two cars collided. The sounds were followed by the remembrance of pain. The punch of the airbag, as if she'd run full speed into a wall. Grinding pain racing through her ribs and jolting her neck. The accident had occurred two months ago in an instant. For Sarah, that instant recurred daily.

———

Sarah overslept the next morning. No time for breakfast. No time to mentally debate over what to wear. She threw on jeans and a hoodie, jammed a lit book in an already full backpack, and thumped down the stairs and out the front door.

"Bye, Mom," she called, not waiting for an answer.

The silver Corolla was parked at the end of the curb. Jay, who lived next door, sat at the wheel and waited for Sarah to hop in. Sarah's mom liked Jay and had hinted that Sarah consider dating Jay, but Jay had been enamored with Kate Olsen since junior high. Sarah wasn't interested in dating these days anyway.

"No offence, but you look like shit," Jay said. "You sick?"

"Weird night," Sarah said. "Strange dreams."

"Want to talk about it?"

Sarah didn't answer. Jay shrugged, checked for traffic, and pulled into the street to begin the short drive to school.

—

The school halls echoed with the shouts of boys and the giggle of girls. Sarah headed straight for English class as the morning bell rang. She avoided idle chit-chat and other distractions. Sarah felt that the entire day passed in a fog that left her feeling exhausted. It couldn't end soon enough.

After the last class of the day, Sarah walked directly to the west entrance to wait for Jay. She was jostled by the rushing flood of kids pouring out of the school and felt someone tap her on the right shoulder. Sarah looked to the right but no one was there. She looked to the left. No one there either. It was the old shoulder tap trick. Linda used to do that. Sarah's shoulders suddenly burned cold where they had been touched. She brushed repeatedly at her shoulders, trying to rid them of the phantom feeling.

"Hey there," Jay said.

The cold sensation passed and Sarah turned to her friend.

"You daydreaming? I've been talking to you for the past 60 seconds."

Sarah's heart pounded. To her it sounded deafening. "Sorry."

"You look like you're gonna puke," Jay said, as he drove them to their neighboring homes.

"I'm not gonna puke. At least…I hope I'm not."

Throughout the drive Sarah shivered.

"Man, bet you're getting the flu. My brother's got it."

"Yeah, that's probably it. Just the flu."

Jay dropped Sarah off but she neglected to say goodbye. She fumbled her key in the front door lock. After several failed tries the door opened and she flew up the stairs. Sarah slammed closed her bedroom door, threw her backpack to the floor, and buried her face in her pillow. Sobs overtook Sarah. She'd bottled up her emotions since Linda's funeral. Now an emotional torrent racked her body all the way down to her toes.

———

"Sarah." Her mother's voice. Soft knocking at the door. "Sarah, honey. Will you let me in?"

Sarah wiped her face with both hands. Her cellphone chimed a text. She glanced at the message.

tlk2her

Sarah pushed herself from the bed and allowed her mother to enter.

"You're crying?"

Sarah nodded furiously.

Sarah's mom sat on the bed next to her daughter and enveloped her with both arms. "Is it Linda?" she asked, the words barely audible.

"Of course it's Linda!" Sarah shouted, surprised by her own anger. "Linda. Linda. Linda. We never talk about her, Mom. I need to talk about her. So do you."

"I know," her mom sputtered. "I mean, I *should* know. I mean, I … I just don't know what to say."

The rage left Sarah's body and she slumped.

Her mother sighed. Sarah looked back to see her mom weeping, tears sliding down her cheeks, mouth twisted in pain. Sarah held her mom's hand and they both rose. Sarah led her to the closed bedroom door. Linda's door. Mother and daughter exchanged an anxious look.

Sarah threw the door wide open. Releasing her mother's hand, she opened the blinds and pulled them all the way up with a sharp snap. Sunlight poured in. She flung open Linda's closet door and buried her face in her departed sister's shirt, sweaters, and a purple prom dress that would never be worn. Sarah inhaled and exhaled. Pearberry, the sweet scent of Linda. She removed a sweater from its hanger and carried it to her mom.

"It's Pearberry, Mom."

Her mother took the sweater in both hands, bundled it and held it to her nose. She inhaled the scent, slowly at first, then more rapidly, as if drawing in air from a respirator. She wiped her wet cheeks against the fabric. Then she walked to the closet, collected a handful of articles, and brought them to her nose.

Sarah looked on. Her phone chimed and she glanced as the text message appeared.

A trio of kissing heart emojis smiled at her. Linda always closed her text chats with the kissing heart emoji.

Warmly, Sarah replied.

A single tear plopped onto her phone's screen, and Sarah's fingers moved across the touchpad, adding a postscript to her text …

She tapped the SEND arrow, and the message soared out into the universe.

AUTHOR'S NOTE

Many writers excel at successfully incorporating technology into their plots. I don't. I usually prefer to write stories set before the rise of cellphones, smart TVs, and social media. But it occurred to me that writing a story in which a cellphone receives messages from the dead would be a fun challenge.

I wrote about teenage sisters and their mom because I enjoy writing about young people and mother/daughter relationships. Smells are evocative of times and places and people. Most teenage girls have a favorite fragrance, which is why Linda's favorite body spray becomes her totem, so to speak. That and her text messages.

I write ghost stories not because I am an active believer in ghosts. However, I don't disbelieve, either. But I write them because I like playing with the idea of ghosts. What might they do? Where might they be? What unfinished business keeps them from a peaceful death? In her 2014 *The Guardian* commentary, "How to Write a Modern Ghost Story," author Joanna Briscoe suggests that contemporary ghost tales should avoid scenes in which a character sees an actual ghost. She recommends that the story should instead be told with signs that the ghost is present. Following this advice was, for me, proved to be another satisfying challenge.

BB

THE MATRIARCH SIN

DOYLE WELDON KNIGHT

1978

I TASTED BLOOD in my mouth and prayed that all my teeth were intact and not scattered on the filthy asphalt of the parking lot. I looked up through the dim glow to see Delius standing over me with the 2 x 4 in his hand. George and Pinky stood behind him, enjoying the festivities.

"I'm gonna beat your honkie ass, you little shit," Delius said. "I knows it was you dat told ol' man Miley that I took dem speakers."

The 2 x 4 came down across my back. Pain exploded into my brain again. I was flat down on the asphalt, trying to make sense of situation. I wished that I would have left with Mr. Newsom instead of hanging back to make the phone call to Joy.

She'd made it perfectly clear that she only wanted to be friends, but I read between the lines. Any hope of her obtaining any status could not in any way involve someone like me. I hoped she was proud of her flirtatious attitude; it may very well get me killed.

A loud, deep voice reverberated in the distance.

"You gonna let Little Black Sambo talk to you like that?" the man said.

My eyes immediately turned toward the sound. A shadowy outline of a very large man invaded the backdrop of the only dust to dawn light in Newsom's Television and Radio parking lot. He walked at a normal and even pace, straight for Delius.

George stepped in beside Delius and Pinky took off running down the parking lot toward Main Street. I figured he was looking to find backup.

Granny told me that in the 1950s when Miley opened the store, Benton Street carried the best retail locations in Merryville. When the mall opened in '72, it nailed the coffin shut on Benton Street. What remained was almost a slum.

Delius eyed the approaching man. "Whachu say, Honkie?"

"I didn't stutter and your ears didn't flap," the stranger said.

When he got within three feet on the two men, Delius swung the 2 x 4. The man deflected the piece of lumber with a huge left forearm. He nailed Delius squarely in the nose with his right fist. Delius toppled, landing on his stomach.

The man ducked a wild roundhouse from George and planted his knee in George's potbelly. I heard a moan and then a crunch as the man's fist made contact with the side of George's face. George went down like a sack of potatoes as the giant got between me and the two men on the ground.

"You boys need to get on out of here," he said.

Delius rose slowly but still held onto the 2 x 4. He made it up to all fours when the right boot of the big man connected with his jaw. Delius went over on his side and laid still. If George was conscious, he made no attempt to act like it.

The man eased over to me and extended his hand. I reached for it and he brought me to my feet without effort.

"Name's Johnny, but most folks call me Booger," he said.

I sent another prayer upstairs to ask for my mouth to work as I spat a wad of blood onto the asphalt.

"I'm Delbert," I slurred. "Thanks for the help."

"Never did cotton to an unfair fight," he said, smiling. "You gonna be okay?"

"Yes sir, as soon as these tweetie birds quit flying around my head."

Booger laughed. "Come on. Let's get you out of here."

I looked down at Delius and George. They were either out cold or playing possum worthy of an Academy Award nomination. Booger and I started down the parking lot toward my old Pinto.

I felt small in the presence of Booger. He was the biggest man I had ever seen.

"Take care of yourself, little man," Booger said.

I focused on finding the car's keyhole in the dim light. The lock clicked and I opened the door.

"You need a ride, Booger?" I asked.

Receiving no reply, I looked up and all around. The giant of a man had vanished.

I opened the door of ragged out '72 Ford Pinto and slid inside. I found the ignition keyhole, pumped the accelerator three times, jammed the clutch to the floor, and started the motor.

Old Sally kicked off, coughed twice, backfired, and settled into the hum of the engine. The eight-track player started up. *Hair of the Dog* was at full volume as I turned on the headlights and eased out on the clutch.

I gave them a wide berth in the parking lot as Old Sally passed, but I was close enough to see Delius and George stirring a little. While I was glad they weren't dead, I completely understood that be looking over my shoulder for the next few weeks. Delius was not one to be embarrassed.

I turned onto Benton Street and smiled a little.

Delius might be a badass, but he can't hold a candle to the cat named Booger.

I pulled the Nazareth eight-track and slotted Lynyrd Skynyrd.

A short drive later, I arrived home, singing *Free Bird* as if I was part of the band. I noticed the lights were still on in the living room. Granny was up past her bedtime and I wondered what sort of trouble my kid brother had gotten into this time.

Granny, my great grandmother; took care of Timbo and me. She was 87 years old, hard as nails, 90 pounds soaking-wet, and mean as a snake with a razor-sharp tongue. She would never admit it, but she had a soft side to her as well. As I walked into the house, she went into orbit at the sight of my swollen head and busted lip. Timbo got off with a warning. Her attention turned to me. She wanted to know every detail.

When I finished telling my story, Granny took me in the kitchen and doctored me. Timbo laughed and picked at me but took it too far. Without looking, Granny knew when he was close enough and backhanded him. Timbo still smirked at me but he shut up.

"Granny, have you ever heard of a big man named Booger?" The wrinkles on her forehead rose. Her eyes grew wide for a split second and she turned white.

"The man that helped you; he was a big man called Booger?" She asked as she smeared Blue Star ointment across my face.

"Yes ma'am. Said his name was Johnny but folks called him Booger," I said.

Granny's wrinkled faced screwed up into a ball. I wished she would have put her teeth in. She could send young children running and screaming with that face.

"Never heard of him," she said, entirely too fast.

I knew she had lied when she said it, but also knew better than to push the issue. She could probably do more damage than Delius if I riled her up.

The next morning I phoned Mr. Newsom and resigned. Old Miley had heard the mumblings from the rumor mill. He asked if the fight was the reason.

"No, sir," I lied. "I have to watch my little brother. My mama found work and Granny can't handle him."

Watching the squirt was the truth. Mama working was never going to happen.

The socialites on the north side of Benton Street deemed her an unfit mother for abandoning her two boys and leaving them with her grandmother. What society didn't know and would never become aware of was Mama was buried outback by the persimmon tree.

When we found her that night in June, Granny took me out back and handed me a shovel.

"Three-feet wide, six-feet long, and at least five-feet deep. No slacking. Get it done," she'd warned.

We buried Mama that night along with the murder weapons— a cooking spoon and syringe. Granny couldn't afford a funeral on the Social Security crumbs.

That was the one and only time that I ever saw Granny shed a tear. It wasn't much of one, but in the glow of the Coleman lantern I saw the love Granny had held for Mom. She'd wiped her eye and looked straight at me and Timbo.

"Cover her up; it'll be daylight soon," she'd said, and started toward the back door.

Granny concocted a story for the neighbors and gossip seekers. She mainly did it to keep the socialite husbands from sniffing around like dogs in heat. The cock hounds were devastated when they discovered their pretty-little-party-girl had skipped town.

My face was still puffy but, looking in the mirror, some bruising was probably the worst thing the mug would get. My back was a different story. It hurt when I put my jeans on and all I could do was push the pain to the back of my mind.

I decided to venture in the other direction, toward the town of Dexter, to seek employment. I had a much better chance of survival if I stayed out of Merryville for a while, and Delius knew better than to show up anywhere near Granny's.

Within the black community, Granny had a reputation of being a crazy-old-white-woman. She'd pulled a shotgun on the black reverend when he came by to check on her after Pappy died. That put the nail in the sociable coffin. She didn't want any man around her, clergy, salesman, black, white, or polka-dotted. They all got the same treatment.

I stopped at the Dexter Farmer's Coop and asked if they needed help.

"No, but Buford Peacock is looking for help hauling hay," the old man behind the counter said.

He jotted down directions to Mr. Peacock's place and I headed in that direction.

Mr. Peacock put me straight to work. We hauled 2,700 bails over the next two days. Mr. Peacock informed me that Rufus Nugent had a hundred acres cut and drying and that I should go by his place. I did and spent four more days praying my back would hold together and having fun in the sun.

That Friday I gave Granny $250 in cash. She was so grateful that she bought a whole chicken. Fried it for us that Sunday with taters and gravy to boot. Timbo won the wishbone break and Granny actually smiled; this time with her teeth in.

The references from Mr. Peacock and Mr. Nugent got me jobs all over the county during the summer of '78. When I started my senior year at Merryville High in September, I was in the best physical condition of my life. I had actually made enough money over the summer that me and Timbo had a couple or pairs of new jeans to wear. Granny even splurged for Timbo on a pair of Converse All Stars.

Since Granny didn't tolerate long hair on a man, no way, form, or fashion, I stayed clean cut. The popular kids shunned me, but my hair length would not have mattered anyway; white trash is white trash. Joy taught me that lesson.

The school faculty wanted me involved in everything. They wanted to sleep better at night and I was the prime example of how a poverty-level student could rise above it all. Mr. Miller, the principal and lead hypocrite, had me write essays and apply to colleges. My GPA was 3.65; not perfect but admirable. It was a race between me and Debra Carlisle for valedictorian. I did not want anything to do with the ceremony. My ambition was to let my 51 fellow seniors duke it out, as long as I graduated at least third.

When school started, I went to the Howard Brothers Department store and asked for a job. With letters from Mr. Wright and two other respected faculties, Mr. Beason hired me to help with the stocking.

I started inventory stocking with a man named Michael Collins. Mike had retired once from the railroad and couldn't stand the retired life. He'd started his second career, for Howard Brothers, in '72.

I liked the old man. He remembered Pappy and Granny from when they were young. He knew my grandpa and my mama although he never commented on either of them. He had been pals with Pappy's younger brother, Johnny.

Mike was a good storyteller. We were working on Halloween night, and during one of his stories he dropped the name *Booger*.

My heart skipped a beat.

"Booger? That's what you called Johnny?" I asked.

"Yep," he said, "He was Booger from the time I could remember till he passed. Rumor was that his mama named him that because he was so big."

My senses tingled as I remembered the night from last May in Newsom's parking lot.

"There never was a better soul alive on this earth than old Booger," Mike said.

We went to the breakroom at 7:30 and grabbed our packed lunches.

"Tell me more about Booger. How did he pass?" I asked.

"Booger had a heart as big as Texas," Mike began. "He would help anybody; hell, give them the shirt off his back if they asked. The night he passed; he and I were set up to go fishing on Williams Creek the next morning. Booger had a job at the Valdemar Saw Mill out on Pigeon Creek Road. He had to walk back and forth to work like most of us did during those times. We often used the railroad tracks. The story goes that he got in the way of the freight train on the Merryville rail bridge and had to jump. They found him at the bottom of the gorge with a broken neck."

Mike looked up and there was no doubt he was a little misty. He took a bite of his sandwich and glanced at me, perhaps not sure if he wanted to finish the story. After a while he continued.

"I saw him again after that. I haven't shared this with many people, but he came to me. When my Dotty May passed with the cancer in '65, I was already retired from the railroad. I got in a real bad way. I dragged myself into the bottle and stayed there a couple of years."

I nodded silently and listened.

"In '68, I decided that I had had enough and was going to put an end to it. I was on the back porch in the cowhide rocker and was about to put the bad end of a double-barrel shotgun in my mouth. I heard a voice that I thought I would never hear again and it was laughing.

"Booger said, 'How you figure to pull the trigger Mikey? Hell, you can't even reach it on that old long-barrel smoke pole.'" Mike smiled at the memory.

"I saw him sitting beside me in the other chair, gently rocking back and forth; plain as the nose on your face. I told him, 'I don't know, with my toes I reckon,' and we both laughed. The smoke pole got put away and we talked and laughed the better part of the night. He told me the real story of how he died. 'I tell you Mikey,' he'd said, 'old Sheriff Brunson didn't have a clue. Called it accidental death and made it home before supper. Let me tell you what really happened. I was taking the tracks because I wanted to get home and get my gear ready for the fishing trip.'" Mikey paused, trying to recall what Booger had said word for word.

Before he could resume, we both heard the baritone voice. Low at first but then rising to normal range.

"I got close to the bridge and heard screaming and crying down in the creek bottom. I ran to the bridge and looked over with barely any light left in the sky, but enough that I could tell that a young woman was being assaulted," Booger said.

My heart pounded in my chest as I gazed across the table at the big man in the bib overalls sitting there, a wide grin on his face. My intellect assured me that there were no such things as ghosts, but my eyes overruled intellect. Mike smiled, seemed to relax, and took another bite of sandwich.

"Hey, Booger," he said.

"Evening, Mikey," Booger said, and looked at me. "Calm down, Delbert, or you're liable to blow a gasket. Now, where was I? I took off down the creek bank, hollering at a man I'd never seen before. As I got closer, I saw the size of him. This was no ordinary man. He was as big as me." Booger pondered in silence for a moment. "In fact, he was the spittin' image of me, but he wasn't quite right. His eyes glowed red and he was black as the ace of spades. Not Negro black;

charcoal black. It made no difference at the time. I built up speed and tackled him, throwing both of us away from the woman and into the creek."

Booger half-heartedly laughed.

"The creek was only 'bout ankle deep. We squared off and the fight began. Felt like an hour, but I know it was only minutes. I finally got the upper hand and choked him down. I had him in a headlock and he finally went limp. At that moment he started turning to black dust in my hands. In less than a heartbeat he blew away on the wind."

Booger's eyes were serious and stern.

"I prayed to the Good Lord right then and there. I looked and called out for the woman, but she had left in a hurry. I was huffing and blowing and trying to get my strength back when I heard the voice."

Booger altered his voice in attempt to imitate a posh accent.

"'Well John, it seems you were victorious in your altercation. You have squandered the soul of my beloved and faithful Nathaniel. This, dear fellow, cannot go unattended,' the voice stated. I was being addressed by Lucifer himself, in the flesh. I had thought the other demon was big, but Satan was a monster," Booger said, almost giggling before resuming the posh accent.

"'By reason of being a living human soul, you are unassailable with impunity. Not my laws, but I am bound by obligation to obey them. However, might I have cause of wager that could entice you into a contractual obligation? I offer you the same means of conflict that you horrendously displayed with poor Nathaniel. If you can best me in fair combat, you can continue the pitiful path of your life. I will remove the seed planted by Nathaniel, cure your brother of his sterility, and his family will thrive and prosper in the decades to come without interference or curse. If you choose to ignore the challenge, you will go about your meager existence with the knowledge that I will pursue every curse known to man to descend upon you and your brother, Levi. The seed planted by Nathaniel will grow within Levi's family. Shame and pestilence will follow all the days of your family's lives.'"

Booger grew more excited as he continued to recall the encounter. I took another bite of sandwich, hanging on every word.

"Not having much choice, I agreed to the terms with a bloody handshake. I would have agreed to anything to keep Levi and our family safe. Lucifer himself did the honor of the palm slice with a razor-sharp fingernail." Booger crooned as he showed us the scar inside his right hand.

"I got ready and squared off. Satan was grinning at me like he knew something I didn't. The smell of rotten eggs was nauseating. He circled to the right and jabbed me in the chest so hard I thought it was over," Booger said, in reminiscence.

"'Come now, John, you can do better than that,'" Scratch told me.

"Twilight had entered into darkness by this time. I relied more on intuition than physical senses, timing the swing and ducking the next jab. I landed a good one on his jaw. It felt like I had punched a steel plate." Booger trailed to a whisper.

"'Oh, that was a quite well done, but you can still do better,'" the Devil exclaimed, laughing.

"I gave it my best shot and swung for the fences. He ducked and then grabbed for my head, leaving his chin exposed. I took the shot, planting a hard uppercut right in the kisser," Booger said, grinning. "He stumbled backwards and I tackled him, taking him down to the ground and landing directly on top of him. I lit into him with lefts and rights like there was no tomorrow. At the end of the day, there wasn't."

Booger ran a large hand through his hair and looked back at me and Mike with misty eyes. "Lucifer knew he was going down. I could tell he was about out. He opened his bag of tricks. I went to swing a strong right hook and realized I was straddling Levi, who was almost unconscious. I jumped up and off of Levi. Lucifer started laughing and stood up. He was shaky, but he got on both feet and I felt like a putz for having been duped when we squared off again."

"For the next few minutes it was a bona fide exhibition of bare-knuckle brawling," Booger grinned. "I felt winded but would not let up. Pretty soon, I had him on the ropes again, only this time he was still standing. I moved in for a crushing roundhouse when a sudden sharp pain tore through the left side of my back. I turned my head to see a demon holding the end of a long spear. Impaled, I was lifted off the ground and left hanging in midair. Lucifer walked up to me, grabbed my head, and broke my neck. In the blink of an eye, the world went dark."

I finished my lunch and concentrated on Boogers story.

"I remember a bright light and a soft voice that told me to wake up. Lucifer and his sidekick took off running away from the light. The voice said, 'Johnny, come with me now or roam the earth forever.'"

"I thought it over and sat down on a large rock in the creek. The light faded and I still sat there. I had to protect Levi. Whatever the cost, I had to protect him. I started laughing and couldn't stop," Booger said with a giggle. "I yelled into the darkness because I knew Satan could hear me. *'I beat you, you bastard. You'll never get me now because you cheated!'*"

He gathered his thoughts a moment. "I got back on the tracks and walked home."

I locked eyes with Booger and asked, "The girl … it was Granny, wasn't it?"

"Yeah, son, it was. My brother, your great grandpa, had small-pox when we were kids. It left him sterile. Your grandpa was conceived by whatever that thing on the creek bank was. Lucifer called him Na-thaniel. You never knew your grandfather; he was an evil sonuvabitch and was incarcerated before you were born. That evil spilled over into your mama and she fought it the only way she could."

"Am I going to be evil?" I asked.

Mike looked surprised and Booger laughed. "Naw, I don't think so. But keep a close eye on Timbo."

He stood up and stretched. "Guess I had best go, break time is over."

"Thanks for rescuing me in the parking lot of Newsom's," I said.

Booger laughed again. "I wish you would get in trouble more often. That was the most fun I've had in 40 years."

He looked at Mike. "Take care, Mikey, I'll see you soon enough."

Mike nodded in understanding and we watched the giant of a man fade into nothing.

We gathered up our sandwich wrappers and stood up.

"We best get off dead center and get some traction," Mike said.

—

Mike and I continued to work together until one week before Christmas. I arrived at the store to find Everett Hobart in the break-room.

"Where's Mike?" I asked.

"Mike passed away this morning," Everett said, quietly. "From what I heard, it sounds like he tripped, hit a coffee table, and broke his neck."

I didn't say a word. What could I say? I figured me and old Mikey would visit again one Halloween night.

———

Christmas came and went as usual, with no visit from Ol' Saint Nick.

1979

New Year's Day found me taking Granny to the police station at dawn on that morning to pick up Timbo.

Spring arrived with Granny looking somewhat frail. She coughed a lot and was meaner than normal. She mostly took it out on Timbo.

Six weeks before my graduation she was down.

It was apparent that Mr. Miller would once again be disappointed. Fate entwined her golden thread and was not going to allow me to rise above my station. I was not going to attend college. Granny was on her way out and Timbo was only 14.

I brought Granny some soup one evening in late April and sat with her before I had to go to work. It seemed to be one of her better days.

"I'm getting close now, son. You're going to have to be strong and look after Timbo."

"Granny, you want me to get a reverend to come give your soul some peace?" I asked.

She smiled a strained smile. "My destination was determined many years ago. I haven't any need for clergy."

I swallowed a lump. "It was you on the creek bank that night, wasn't it?"

Granny's eyes grew wide and she clutched her chest. Her face started to cloud up like it did whenever she got angry. She took a deep breath and let it out as her eyes got misty.

"Yes, son, it was me on the creek bank. My selfishness and arrogance got Booger killed," she whispered.

"My Levi had smallpox in early life and couldn't have children. I wanted a baby so badly I didn't know what to do. For two weeks while Levi was on a shutdown job in Tulsa, me and Booger met several times under the rail bridge in the evening. I was at the bridge at dusk that evening and me and Booger was going at it hard and heavy. During the act, I smelled burning sulphur and opened my eyes to see glowing red eyes in the black face of Booger. I started screaming but could not get away from him. Booger, came barreling down from the tram and knocked him halfway into the creek. I high-tailed it out of there and turned back to watch a few minutes from behind the rocks. Booger finally got the best of him. I watched that darkie turn to coal dust and I knew then it was a demon."

Granny's eyes were misty with recollection. "I was about to leave when I saw a really large man approach Booger. They talked and then squared off to fight. Booger whooped his ass. He would have won outright, too, if the bastard hadn't cheated. Another demon arose up out of the ground and speared Booger in the back, lifting him up off the ground. I couldn't watch any more. I knew what was coming and got the hell out of there."

I offered Granny a sip of water. She nodded once she had enough and resumed her tale.

"I'd been home for less than ten minutes when Levi came through the door," she said, a tear running down her wrinkles. "I told him everything. How I'd wanted a baby of his blood. How I'd per-suaded Johnny to do it even though he didn't want to. I told him what happened on the creek bank and what I'd seen." Granny closed her eyes tight and was silent for a moment.

"Levi went to the bridge and found his brother. He returned home without telling the sheriff, hoping someone might find him be-fore the wood's creatures got to him. Sure enough, we got word the next morning that Booger had been found beneath the bridge. It was ruled an accidental death, but I knew the truth. Other than Levi, I never told a living soul what happened that evening. Until now. I sur-rendered my soul to the devil and gave birth to his hellion. I haven't been in a Christian way since, and I paid for it tenfold with your grandpa."

I wiped a tear from the wrinkled leather of her face.

"I know what's in store for me. I made my bed, son, and I will sleep in it for eternity."

Timbo walked in and looked at Granny and me. "What are ya'll talking about?"

Granny extended a hand he took it. "Just how much I am going to miss the two of you," she said. Timbo's eyes filled with soft tears.

—

Granny passed two weeks later. It wasn't a heroic scene with heavenly lights and hymnal melodies. Her heart stopped and that was that.

We wrapped her body in a sheet and blanket and buried her next to mama. The only two people there were me and Timbo.

Two weeks later, Sheriff Holloway found out. He came down on me hard but let it go. The deed had already been done and he damn sure didn't want to dig her up.

I made it through graduation and got my diploma. I needed cash and started hauling hay in the daytime while stocking at Howard Brothers at night.

It was an exercise in human stamina, but I got Timbo through high school four years later. By the time Timbo graduated in '82, I was a two-pack-a-day Camel smoker. By age 23, Timbo had two illegitimate sons and had spent six months in jail. I hocked everything I owned to bail him out and pay the court fees. I did all I could to help with his child support.

By the time Timbo hit 25, he was on death row at Langford State Penitentiary and I had filed for Chapter 11.

1990

After pulling an eight hour shift, I arrived home a little past 6:30 on a hot and humid mid-September evening. I had just enough time to grab a quick bite and clean up before I was due at the restaurant. Bucky was a decent enough boss man, but he had little tolerance for late employees. I knew enough to arrive on time.

Before heading into the kitchen, I picked the day's mail up off the floor and discovered a letter from the Langford State Prison. I opened the envelope and unfolded the handwritten letter.

Delburt,

They move my date up to November 12 so I need to see ya.

Call me asap. Wensdy and sundys are the call days from noon to 9pm.

Jim

Tears fell on the parcel. I glanced at my watch and knew I only had time to clean up. No supper again tonight. I fired up another cigarette and headed for the bathroom.

I was glad that they allowed Timbo to send the note. The bank took Pappy and Granny's place when I filed for bankruptcy. I'd tried my best to keep Timbo out of prison but had failed. I guess that I should have been mad at Timbo, but I couldn't help it; I loved him.

—

At 7:30 I asked Bucky if I could use the diner's phone for a quick call. He gave me a stern look and pointed at his watch.

"Make it quick," he said.

I got through to the prison and was placed on hold. Those three minutes felt like three hours. I imagined Bucky busting in at any minute and tapping at his fake Rolex. I was about to hang up when I heard a familiar voice.

"Delbert, is that you?" Timbo sounded stressed.

"Hey Timbo, how are you?

"Yeah, I'm okay. I know you are stretched, but I only got a couple months left. Could you do one thing for me?"

"I'll do whatever I can."

"I know you will. Go and visit the queen bitch, Miss Molly. See if you can bring Little Timothy to visit me. She ain't got no car and you will have to bring her up here. She won't like it none. You're going to have to convince her. Brenda brought Charlie up here a couple of times since I landed on the row, but I haven't seen Little Tim since he was in diapers. He turned five last April and I don't even have a photo of him."

"I have never been to Bogalusa nor met Mollie. She doesn't know me from Adam."

"Please, Delbert. Don't make me beg," he pleaded.

"I didn't say I wouldn't try, Timbo, but don't get your hopes up too much. She'll likely throw me out the door as soon as I tell her my name."

"She is a sho'nuff handful, that's for sure. It's why I ran off the Bogalusa in '85. She moved back to live with her Grandma Bertie May, and I just couldn't stay away from her. Being with Mollie was the happiest time of my life. But she changed. Her behavior changed when she got knocked up. Reminded me of how Granny acted and that's when I split and came back to Dexter. She named me as the father just for pure meanness."

"I'm on the phone at work and the boss is gonna tan my hide if I don't get back to it. Is there anything else you need?"

"Maybe a cutting torch and some dynamite," he laughed.

"If I have an answer about Little Tim on the next call day, I'll phone you again. If you don't hear from me, I'll phone you next Wednesday regardless. How are you holding up with two months left?"

Timbo's voice shook. "Since I got on the row and put in a cell by myself, I'm doing a lot better. Don't get my ass kicked everyday like I used to. My lawyer tells me this and that and not to lose hope. The warden's shrink wants the complete story and has hired someone to ghost write it. They know well and good about the knifing of the reverend and rape and murder of his pretty wife, but that ain't enough. They want to know what I was thinking when it all went down."

"What were you thinking?" I asked.

"I have no idea. The whole night was a strung-out, foggy blur. Didn't know he was a preacher. I only remember being brought to his house for a three-way with his old lady. But when he wanted some fag action, I snapped and, well, here we are." I heard the lighter strike and a large exhale. "Piss on it, Delbert. Let's get this shit over with."

"Do you want me to get pastor Hampton to visit?" I asked. "I remember that you kind of liked him when we were kids."

"You can if you want, but I ain't got no use for him. All I want is to see you and Little Tim one last time and for there to be no pain when the end comes."

"Okay, Timbo, I really gotta go. Take Care."

"Bye, Delbert. Thanks for calling."

I hung up the phone and allowed the waterworks to come, realizing that the state was going to kill my baby brother. I knew the background of why he was a bad seed. I wanted to tell him so bad of how his grandpa was conceived and the agony that our mother endured. I was balling like a three-year-old when the door opened and a stern-faced Bucky looked into the room. When he seen me, his face softened a micro-fraction. He tapped on his watch. "In five minutes, you best have your ass in the kitchen," he said, and closed the door.

I lit a Camel; let the tears come for another minute or two. In four minutes, I was back in the kitchen.

—

The next morning, with the help of the court records and the address where I sent the child support money, I obtained a phone number for Bertha Magdalene "Molly" Harper. Molly didn't live with Grandma Bertie May anymore, and she didn't have a landline.

During my lunch hour I phoned Molly's grandma from the pay phone of the 7-11 on Vinton Street. The phone was on the front of the building, and the street noise made it nearly impossible to hear. The old gal probably thought I was yelling at her. I told Mrs. Harper about Timbo's request and, to my surprise, she didn't hang up on me. I gave her the number of Dexter's Diner.

"I'll be there every night this week from 7:00 to 7:30," I said.

"Molly stops by to visit me almost every day. I'll be sure to have her phone you at the restaurant," Bertie May said

—

It was a typical Saturday night at the restaurant. I bussed tables and felt lost in a train of despair. Molly hadn't phoned the diner. It was becoming clear that I had once again disappointed Timbo. He was weeks away from death by lethal injection. I picked up a tray and turned for the kitchen.

At 9:30 I carried the trash to the outside dumpster and stopped for a break. The restaurant was dwindling now as it always did on Saturday evenings.

Feeling like shit, I sat on the bottom step and lit a cigarette. In the middle of my pity and depression, I heard a baritone voice that I had not heard since a long-ago Halloween night in Howard Brothers.

"You okay, little man?" Booger said, as he walked around the dumpster and squatted in front of me.

"Yeah, I'm okay. You know about Timbo, I reckon?" I asked.

"Yep, sad times indeed. Not your fight though, little man. You have made it to age 30 and have sacrificed everything for your little brother."

Booger moved over and set on the steps beside me.

"Delbert, you ain't a kid anymore. You have to make a move and get out of this rut. You are knocking out 16-plus hours a day at fewer than four bucks an hour. Get off dead center and find a life for yourself. You need a woman, a good woman; someone like Molly."

"You know Molly?" I asked.

"Yep, I know Molly. I know she loved Timbo at one time and I know she loves their son. She is the kind of woman that would not deny Little Tim's father or his uncle of the baby's love."

I lit another cigarette from the butt of the last one. "Well, it's evident that she doesn't want anything to do with any of us. Here it is Saturday and I haven't heard from her."

"How do you know that? How do you know she got the message? How do know that Molly's grandmother didn't jerk your chain? How come you don't know anything? You haven't tried to know is why." His voice elevated. "Let me tell you what I know. Molly is expecting you to be in Bogalusa tomorrow at her grandma's house for lunch. The address is written on the paper that Delilah used when she took the message on Thursday. She forgot to give it to you and it's still under the counter by the cash register. By the way, she wrote the address down as well."

Booger smiled. "You're standing at dead center, my friend. Step away from it."

"Hey, Booger, do you ever see Mr. Mike?" I asked.

"We said our goodbyes and I made sure he made it to the light. He and Dotty May are together again and that's a good thing." Booger looked deep in my eyes.

"I have to go, little man. Dead Center!" He said, pointing at my chest as he faded into nothingness.

I could not see him but I knew the big man was still in front of me. "Thanks, Booger," I said. "Thanks for everything."

2018

All Hallows' Eve. Molly stood downstairs, oohing and awing over the neighborhood kids' scary costumes and handing out goodies.

She checked on me about 5:00, adjusted my bed, and gave me another dose of the precious mother.

Mother Morphine moved in and started chasing the pain. Old Man Pain was stubborn and would not leave, but I must have dozed a little. When I looked up, Booger was seated at the high back chair next to the bed.

He looked at me. "You sure about this, little man?"

"Ain't no way out of this. Molly's been through this once already with her grandma. I've been a burden to her long enough. I also don't want to deal with the pain anymore."

"Well," Booger said, nodding respectfully, "you got off dead center in '90, didn't you? You and Molly made a good life and raised Timothy to be a good man. I'm glad that Timbo got to see his son before the execution." Booger said.

"Ain't a day passes that I don't think about Timbo and the look on his face as those three canisters depressed. When I stared at the man strapped to the table, all I could see was the baby boy, sitting in a dirty diaper, in bad need of a bath, looking up at his big brother with wide and pleading eyes. I was supposed to save him from all the bad things. That was my job and I failed him."

"Weren't your fault. It was mine. I agreed to meet your granny all those years ago and then didn't show up. I figured that would have been the end of it. The big boss man upstairs is fair and kind, but he never meant for your pappy and granny to reproduce. They were to be life mates without heirs. I have had many hours to ponder upon that since."

Booger lowered his voice. "That's why I had to take out Charlie at an early age. He had the symptoms and showed the signs. I couldn't allow any more evil to reproduce. I knew that you, like your grandpa, were sterile, and that Timothy was, too. I am glad that Timothy and his wife have started the adoption process. Molly deserves to be a grandmother."

"I never suspected that Charlie's accident was something you did. It makes sense though. The boy was unparalleled on any type of bike. The jump should have been easy," I said. "I hope Brenda can find peace someday."

"It was the hardest thing that I ever had to do, but he was going through puberty and all the girls were starting to line up for him," Booger said. "I had no choice."

"All the wrongs will be righted tonight. Will the light come for you when I am gone?"

"I've been reflecting on that. I think that because old Satan had to cheat to win against me, the big boss man sent the light. Maybe it was to let me in; maybe it was to run the devil off. I know that he high-tailed it out of there when the light showed up. Satan broke our contract. He can't claim me, and the voice in light told me it was not coming back. I'm afraid my destiny is to roam indefinitely."

He laughed. "It ain't that bad once you get the hang of it. Hell, I might just go shake up old Delius a little. He's always been an ass-hole."

I laughed and then winced as the pain spiked. "Alright Booger, it's time to get off dead center."

"I know, little man, but I can't help you with the hard part. You have that pain and you must struggle to endure it on your own," he said.

He faded into nothing before my eyes.

I took a deep breath and pulled the catheter out of the old plumbing. I paused and I closed my eyes for a minute, allowing time for the morphine to do battle with Old Man Pain as the wetness began to soak me and the bedding increased. I took the oxygen nosepiece out and laid it over to the side. Lowering the bed as far down as it would go, I gripped the retracted rail. I planted both feet on the floor and got ready.

By some miracle I found myself standing on my two feet and eased around the end of the bed. I headed for the door. My feet drug, but I was able to balance. The space between the bed and door was tricky, but I made it to where I could hang onto the doorframe and let the latest round with the pain subside. The wall provided the support necessary to stay upright between the doorframe and the landing to the stairs.

I reached the landing, stood there, and held onto the bannister post. I watched Molly at the front door as she performed an array of acts. The two-year-old Beasley twins reacted accordingly startled. My heart ached; I was going to miss Molly.

"I'm ready." I whispered.

Two hands that felt the size of baseball gloves grabbed my head on each side from behind me.

"I love you little man. Always have," Booger whispered. "Make it to the light."

I remember Molly screamed and the world of color went to a translucent black and white. I stood up. The pain was gone. In the dimness I saw Molly sitting by the floor, cradling my limp and bloody head in her lap and crying. Booger stood behind her and smiled at me.

"So long, Booger," I said. "Take care of my Molly for me."

Booger looked at me. Tears formed in the big man's eyes as he nodded.

An illumination began to appear in the translucence toward my right. My heart longed to stay with Molly, but I ran toward the light with all my might.

AUTHOR'S NOTE

The life of an underprivileged Southern teen in the 1970s often included status prejudices. Delbert evolved from personal experiences and memories of acquaintances from that time period. Some had the stamina to maintain a high moral character, some sank like a rock, and some needed a moral specter to motivate them at different stages of life.

There was a section of the old road that was removed when the new highway was rerouted in the 1950s. There was a bridge on the old road over the bayou. It was probably flashbacking from Three Billy Groats Gruff, but everyone agreed that a booger lived under the bridge. The character, Booger, derived from that dilapidated structure. The bridge is gone now, the forest has reclaimed the real estate, and I am certain that a booger still resides there.

Delbert realizes the nature of Booger's existence and the kinship ties to the family. It takes many, many years to correct the selfish sin perpetrated by the family matriarch. The character of Granny was based on a gentle soul who loved life, never complained, held strong beliefs, was certain of her opinion, and, when riled, became 95 pounds of Tasmanian Devil.

As I rub the inside knuckles of my hands, where once hard calluses resided from endless abuse of hay strings, a bittersweet smile emerges. A wise man once advised me to get "off dead center."

I hope you enjoyed the story and, someday, make it into the light.

DWK

VIOLET'S BLOSSOMS

JOSEPHINE QUEEN

Petals drifting to the table, settling on the polished surface. The faint smell of decay, flowers resting in a vase a day too long. The water starting to discolor. A woman's voice, screaming—an angry cry, not scared. The vase lying on the floor, water puddling between tiles, flowers strewn, stems broken. A child crying.

—

THE BUS THUMPED through a pothole and Jessica woke. The dream licked along the edges of her mind. But the images dissolved quickly, like sherbet in warm water. Soon nothing remained but their aftertaste.

Jessica sat up and rubbed her face, unsure if she was exorcising the dregs of her nightmare or trying to crawl back into its depths.

Memory, Jessica thought, *not a dream.* Not something her mind had created, but something it had recalled.

Rain tapped at the glass. The interior of the bus was hot and stifling. Condensation fogged the windows. The world beyond the glass hovered, suspended in mist.

Jessica wiped at the window with her sleeve. A town beckoned. Shadow Hills.

Jessica recalled a phone conversation from three days earlier when she booked her room and transportation.

"The charter bus stops at Baskerville," the agent had said. "To get to Willow Falls and your hotel, you'll need to take a local bus."

Jessica sat up in the seat and unfolded a sheet of paper she'd been carrying. Her own handwriting was difficult to read, but she made out the scrawl enough to see she was close to where she needed to be. Willow Falls was just one mile distant from Shadow Hills. Much easier to get off here and walk rather than ride ten miles to Baskerville and have to double-back.

She glanced out the window. The clouds looked heavy, but Jessica relished the thought of walking the mile to Willow Falls after being inert for the past 11 hours, rain or shine. It would be a relief to clear her mind of the webs of bad memories and half-remembered dreams.

The bus driver didn't see it that way.

"I can't let you out here, love," he said, a grimace stretched across his aged face. "Shadow Hills isn't a stop. Besides, there's no one here."

Jessica followed the driver's gaze. The town looked deserted, as if everyone had scattered as soon as the rain started, like cockroaches fleeing a flashlight beam.

"But I'm meeting someone in Willow Falls," Jessica held up her scrap of paper as evidence.

"This isn't a stop," the driver said. "I'll drop you at Baskerville and you can get the local from there."

Jessica squinted through the rain-streaked windshield.

"But you're stopped now," she noted. "And Baskerville is ten miles in the wrong direction."

"Yes, but … " he started.

"Willow Falls is a mile away," Jessica persisted. "I can walk it from here."

"It's raining, love," the driver said, pointing at the darkening sky.

"Don't worry, I won't melt."

"Listen, love, you don't want to get out in Shadow Hills. Things happen here."

"What things?"

The driver shook his head. The door of the bus remained closed.

"Just … bad things," he said, but he sounded tired and aware that he was losing the argument. A few passengers began to look annoyed by the delay.

"It's daylight," said Jessica. "What could possibly happen? Can't you just please open the door?"

Jessica was already down the steps. She hoisted her well-worn backpack onto her shoulder and turned to the driver. He issued a look as if Jessica were a bad taste that couldn't be rinsed away. It was the same look her mother had given her on countless occasions. Reluctantly, the driver pulled the lever and the folding doors opened. Jessica stepped out into the rain and watched as the bus slowly pulled away.

The main street was lined with storefronts, most of which were boarded up. Weeds grew through the cracks in the pavement. A cloud of failure drenched the town of Shadow Hills.

Perfect, her mother's voice spoke in her head, *you'll fit in well.*

Jessica felt as if she was being watched, the driver's warning playing with her nerves. She glanced nervously around, looking up and down the main drag, hoping to spot a warm, welcoming coffee shop or general store where she could charge her phone, get directions, grab a latte.

Sunday, it seemed, was not the day to conduct business in Shadow Hills. The rain fell heavier now and Jessica began to feel that departing the bus had been a mistake. Jessica was sure her mom would agree.

Her mom's voice—a grating, nasal, high-pitched tone that narrated so many of Jessica's nightmares—echoed in Jessica's head. *What did you expect? You're so bloody stupid, you've never made a good decision in your life!*

"Not true," Jessica said softly under her breath.

Jessica had made a great decision just two days ago, when she had finally walked away from her mother's stifling rules. Jessica touched her cheek lightly, still tender from being struck by her mother's hand.

"For the last time," Jessica whispered, pressing ahead.

Jessica walked along the street, trying to stay beneath the ripped and moldering awnings. A large, washed-out cactus stood in a store window directly across from her, doubled over as if deflated.

Jessica sighed. She stood, shivering, beneath the meagre shelter, unsure whether to wait for the rain to stop or to risk walking to Willow Falls in the downpour.

A flash of brightness in the grey caused Jessica to look across at the cactus store again. The window was now bursting with colorful flowers. Jessica frowned. The sign above the storefront announced, "Violet's Blossoms."

Jessica was drenched by the time she reached the door of the shop. She pushed open the door and stepped inside.

The humidity hit her first, then the scent of the flowers. It was overpowering, but not unpleasant.

———

They're sitting in the backyard. Her mother smiles at her from beneath the wide brim of a sunhat. Her face covered in shadow, unreadable. She smells the perfume of the peonies that grow like wildfire. Her mother's wine sits unopened between them on the blanket. Jessica tells herself that when she grows up, she won't drink alcohol. A child's promise to protect her older self.

—

The shop boasted roses, lilies, chrysanthemums, and many flowers Jessica didn't recognize. All were stunning in their vibrancy.

"Can I help you?" a woman, voice like honey, spoke from behind her.

Jessica jumped and turned. The woman was young and lovely. Sunflower blonde hair tucked messily into a ponytail. Hunter green eyes peered from beneath thick lashes.

"Oh … I'm sorry to bother you. I was caught in the storm. Do you have an outlet where I can charge my phone?"

"No," the woman smiled. "Can I help with anything else? Some flowers for a special person, perhaps?"

Jessica shook her head.

"Your mother, maybe?" the shopkeeper tilted her head. Jessica noted the fine lines around her mouth.

"My mother and I aren't … that is, she and I don't really get along," Jessica admitted.

"Such a shame," the woman said. "Mother-daughter relationships can be daunting, for sure."

The florist turned her back on Jessica and snipped at some errant leaves in a bouquet with a pair of clippers she pulled from the pocket of her apron.

Jessica glanced at the outlet next to the cash register. *Clearly she doesn't want to help me*, she thought, as she turned to leave.

"Do you love your mother?" the shopkeeper asked. Her back remained toward Jessica, who blanched at the question.

The shop was warm, much warmer than the bus had been. Jessica was suddenly aware of the rivulets of sweat running down the back of her neck.

"Well," she said, starting toward the door, "I should probably be going. Sorry to have wasted your time."

"Oh, don't leave," the merchant said and turned suddenly. Jessica stepped back, almost toppling a pile of pots stacked behind her. "It's such a nasty, gloomy day out there. At least wait out the rain inside."

Jessica wondered how she had mistaken the woman as young. Her hair was streaked with gray and the wrinkles around her mouth were deeply grooved.

"I'm Violet," the woman said, and offered her hand to Jessica.

The skin on her liver-spotted hand felt paper thin and oddly cold given the temperature of the shop.

"I'm Jessica."

"Jess for short?" Violet asked.

"No," said Jessica. "I prefer Jessica."

"Right. Of course you do," Jessica noted the cynicism in Violet's tone and pursed her lips. The same tone her mother used with her. A mocking, passive-aggressive sound that always precluded a tantrum.

"Look, I just want to charge my phone," Jessica said. "Since I can't do that here, can you at least give me directions to Willow Falls?"

"To where?" Violet asked. She was occupied with arranging a flower vase. Jessica didn't notice the petals, which were brown at the edges, or the leaves that drooped, thirsty and dying, from the stems.

"Willow Falls," Jessica repeated.

"I've never heard of it dear." Violet started humming, a whispery tune issuing from her nasal cavities.

"It's the next town over."

"No. The next town over is Bradbury."

"It's Willow Falls. I saw it on the map."

"I once had a daughter you know," Violet said. "She was a tart, too."

Jessica pulled her backpack further onto her shoulder. The door seemed a mile away. Violet now stood between her and the fresh air of the steadily darkening morning.

"Yes," Violet continued. "A tart. Daughters are tricky you know. Slippery things that twist your words and force your demons to the surface."

Violet smiled, brown teeth lined black gums, and not even the hyacinth and lilac could mask the stench of rot that seeped from her. Jessica took another step backward.

"What's your mother's favorite flower?" Violet asked. Her voice was hoarse, like a smoker's rasp.

"Peonies," Jessica said, trembling.

The stench in the shop was now malodorous, but underneath Jessica picked up the faint hint of her mother's perfume. There was a rustle as leaves and petals dropped to the floor. The smell of decay pushed through the perfume and Jessica wrinkled her nose.

Violet skittered across to Jessica and touched its tip.

"Funny little wrinkle-nosed chipmunk," she said. Jessica's

heart lurched.

———

The hazy light of a spring morning. Jessica's mother lying on the couch, a puddle of red glimmering in the bottom of a wine glass. Her mother reaching over, touching the tip of Jessica's nose.

"Be a dear and pour Momma another glass."

Jessica standing, frozen, in the circle of light that dances on the living room rug. Her legs refusing to move. Standing in the sliver of time that shimmers between her mother's happy-buzzed and angry-drunk personas.

"Well, what are you waiting for? Funny little wrinkle-nosed skunk."

The time passing like mercury, the light and mood changing.

"Pour me a glass of fucking wine you little shit."

———

"Mothers can be tricky. Daughters can be slippery," Violet said, in a whispery, sing-song voice. "Tarts and skunks and little shits. All of them need to be dealt with. Put out. Snipped off."

Violet clipped the rotting heads from a bouquet of roses. They fell to the floor. Violet watched with rheumy eyes wide and her mouth stretched in a humorless smile as they rolled, like the heads of small, desiccated animals.

Jessica backed toward the door. All around her, petals and leaves fell with an eerie whispering, decomposing into a rancid heap, then drying to a dust that caught on the wind as her hands finally found the knob and she flung open the door.

Her last glimpse of Violet was of the old crone collapsing to the floor in a pile of sagging skin and crumbling bones.

"Oh, God," Jessica whispered, staggering along through the rain, pace quickening with every beat of her heart.

The cactus in the window bowed down to Jessica as she ran, a mocking gesture to the daughters who lose their way and the mothers whose fingers they slip through, like sand through a sieve. Or grave dust to the wind.

———

The two o'clock bus thrummed into the center of Shadow Hills. The rain was slowing now, but the doors remained tightly closed.

A small hand wiped away the condensation that fogged up the glass of one of the many bus windows. A child's face peered out.

"Look, Mommy. Why is that lady running through the puddles?" The little girl, whose name was Rowan, watched as the young woman, backpack half off her shoulder, ran full pelt up the empty street. It was impossible to tell whether the woman was grinning or screaming silently.

Rowan's mother pulled her daughter away from the window.

"Don't stare darling, it's not polite."

"But she's not even looking at me," Rowan whispered. "She looked scared, Mommy."

Rowan's mother smiled and tapped her, not altogether gently, on the tip of her nose.

"My funny little wrinkle-nosed squirrel," she said. "Do as you're told."

Rowan turned back to the window and traced circles in the fog. Around and around, her finger went, drawing borders over the disappearing figure of the running woman.

AUTHOR'S NOTE

We used to walk by a deserted flower shop on our way to my daughter's preschool. There were yellowed newspapers scattered on the floor, animal droppings on the counters, and a six-foot-tall, bleached-white cactus standing guard in the window. It looked as if someone had let the air out of it. We passed by the shop and the cactus every week for two years. Then one day the shop was empty and the cactus was gone. I'd often lie awake at night, wondering where that cactus had gone.

When I entered a flash fiction contest and one of the prompts was flower shop, I felt that I was being called to write about that cactus. The piece has since gone through a few rewrites and revisions, and Jessica and Violet showed up with their mother-daughter issues. But the cactus is still there, bearing witness to the visitors to Shadow Hills.

JQ

RAZORS AND APPLES FOR MY LOVE

DIANNE PEARCE

Razors and apples, Dear, treats so unique
they carve they some happiness into your cheek.

Kisses of chocolate injected with strychnine
a dearest depart for my sweet valentine.

Another delicious thing cause you to swoon
to be disemboweled by the light of the moon.

So silly, when you said, "You're not in my heart."
when you know, my darling, we never will part.

I love you so truly so deep so sincere
I'll make for you presents of all of your fears.

On Halloween night, so strong and so brave
our true love will take us both right to the grave.

Razors and apples, Dear, dead flowers too—
there's no one alive whom I love more than you.

AUTHOR'S NOTE

When I was a kid, everyone was worried about finding razor blades in their apples. The upside to this is that we stopped getting stupid fruit when we went trick or treating. For this, I remain eternally grateful to the psychopaths of the world.

DP

OUR FATHER

RACHEL M. BROWN

WHEN MY SISTER was abducted six months and 13 days ago, the bracelet I gave her for her twenty-first birthday lay broken on the floor by the front door, next to a badge with the highway Route 66 symbol. Her purse and phone were gone, along with a few clothes. Took me two full days to go to the police. I was only 15 when I was beaten up by some local punks, but *I* was the one they booked for assault. It's the one thing my dad was right about: never trust a cop. When I finally went, I might as well not have bothered. They wrote down the details, but they obviously thought she'd up and left freely. Only I knew she hadn't.

Kyla was the one who took me in the day I turned 18, rescuing me from our father-who-art-in-his-broken-ass-hovel-in-Chelsea. My big sister who stood up for me every time every time he yelled and disciplined me. I lived with her in Roxbury, and I'd go to my job at the Dudley branch of the Boston Public Library every day, getting back right at 5:15 PM. Those were magical days. Plenty of time to prepare things for Kyla. Depending on the date, I prepared a little or a lot.

"Aaron. Come to bed." It's my girlfriend, Heidi, with her thin, whining voice. She's nothing like a Heidi. She's a skinny Japanese girl with multiple tattoos who chain smokes and snorts coke when she can afford it. She says *Heidi, Girl of the Alps* was a popular animated series in Japan that appealed to her mother.

"Be right there," I call back.

I open the twenty-fifth door of my advent calendar and find a chunky star wrapped in golden foil. Kyla bought me my first advent calendar when I was 11, and she warned me to hide it from our father—"he'll say it's Christian crap, but I think it's fun." I didn't hide it well enough though, and our father-who-art-a-tyrant confiscated it on only the twelfth day. Tore it up and put it in the trash, saying there was only one calendar in our house worth a damn. He didn't even let me keep the chocolates. For that reason, 12 is the day of revenge. Even when Kyla was here, it was so.

I've only set foot inside our father's home once since I left. When my Kyla was snatched, I ran straight to Chelsea because I figured the oppressor had her. I ransacked the house, but I didn't find anything. He just stood by and watched, pretending he'd mellowed. Haven't seen him since.

Every day has a purpose. The twenty-fifth is a day for miracles. I don't believe in God; the birth of Christ is literally incredible. So on the twenty-fifth of every month I do something others find amazing. Earlier today I stuffed a twenty-dollar bill into the skirt pocket of a young girl on the subway. She must have been about ten, so I had to be careful in case her mom thought I was groping. I like to think she found the money when she got home and stared at it in wonder.

I go into the bathroom to brush my teeth, lips bared, one at a time. I look older than my 20 years. It's probably all the stubble I let grow. When Kyla was here, I shaved every day. Now, once a week is enough. While I'm brushing, Heidi flounces in without so much as a knock and sits herself down on the toilet to pee. I don't like the way she does that, although I don't complain. Her piss is very loud for such a small person. I met Heidi through Kyla and I'm fond of her, but mainly she's a connection with my sister. None of Kyla's other friends like me much, although I know one or two say I'm hot. Shortly after Kyla was taken, Heidi attached herself to me in a bar, then slipped into my bed. The next day she returned with her backpack, and here she remains.

"It's not a sex day, mind."

As if I would forget. I rinse my mouth. "I know."

"Maybe tomorrow if you're lucky," she croons.

I smile. We both know she's trying to tease me; she'd like sex more often. "We'll see," I say.

"The beauty of the end of the month."

Now she's mocking me, and I don't like that. She knows the untethered days at the end of the month make me uneasy, even though I can do whatever I like. Advent calendars run out after the twenty-fifth, so after that everything is random. Otherwise, the tenth and twentieth are sex days. Heidi's idea. She chose the '0' days, for orgasm. Bizarre, but it's something, a way to organize things now Kyla is gone. It was easy when she was here. One act of kindness for Kyla on day one, two on day two, three on day three and so on, except, of course, for day 12. It didn't have to be anything big. Lord knows, I couldn't think of 25 big things, even for her. So I'd bring her flowers, plump up her cushion just so, give her a foot rub, that kind of thing.

Since she was abducted, I've got new rules. I search constantly—friends, neighbors, work, you name it—but I have other rituals, too. I owe it to Kyla to carry on the tradition. So the first of the month I do something new. The second I speak to a new person—make a friend of sorts. Day three I donate three dollars to a charity, or to a panhandler if I see one who looks genuine. I'd prefer to assign this task to a higher day, but I don't make enough money. I have to be practical. Heidi panhandles sometimes. I don't like it, but she says it's a legitimate transaction without any unwanted baggage: people give money in return for a good feeling. Prostitution with no messy sex. She's compact and plaintive and she probably makes as much as I do at the library.

As we get into bed I stroke Heidi's face, brushing her eyelashes as though they're fine glassware. "Goodnight."

"It's almost midnight," she says.

"Another ten minutes."

She lithely straddles me and waves her long hair in my face. Once I told her I liked the way it tickled. I was humoring her; now she does it all the time.

"Heid, I'm a bit tired."

"Alright."

She leans down and kisses me, then slides onto to her side. Thirty seconds later she is breathing deeply, the sweet purr of sleep. I resent how it's so easy for her. Me, I count. Not sheep, they don't help. I count Kyla. Usually I can drop off around Kyla 171.

Sometimes I did bigger things. Once I gave her a painting of the library that I'd worked on for months. We both agreed we should have had more books growing up. Another time I bought her tickets to *Relatively Close*—I couldn't resist!—when it was playing at the Wang Theater, and a drink afterward. She'd had to buy dinner though, because it was only the second of the month.

The next morning, I show Heidi a different kind of ticket. California. One way.

I've saved up for this and I hoped she'd be surprised, but nothing surprises Heidi. It's the way she is. She merely raises an inquiring eyebrow and asks, "Why are you going all the way over there?"

"Route 66. I think she's on the trail, so I'm walking it. Want to come?"

She'll ignore that. No way she's coming.

"I'd come if I had the money."

She's lying. She's not a west coast girl. "Next time then."

"You're going to walk the whole of Route 66?"

"Maybe."

"You're insane, you know that. In a good way, but you are."

"No. They tested me. *You* know that."

I've been studied by professionals. Not at my behest—I know I'm quirky, but that's not a crime. But some library patrons complained about me at work, and they had to decide where to "place" me—no longer on the public desks, apparently. *Socially awkward*, said one doctor. *On the spectrum*, said another. *Possessive and traumatized*, said a third. *Paranoid and compulsive*, they all agreed, *but not insane*.

It's all right. Some people find my need for order hard. The library patrons didn't understand why I needed to finish one task before turning to the next. They said I ignored them, refused to help. I was happy to serve, but you can't interrupt one thing and leave it messy and undone just so you can attend to the next thing that walks through the door. Nothing would ever get done.

"What about the first of the month?"

She knows how to press my buttons. "I can do it there."

"And on the seventh, when you have to give someone a good luck charm?"

"I'll find someone."

"And the days when you have to help people?"

"So I'll help people."

Three days a month, on the fifteenth, eighteenth, and twenty-second, I do that number of things for random people. I couldn't think of anything better. I'll give them a quarter, tell them they dropped it. I'll slip a postcard in someone's bag saying *I love you* or *You're the best*. Those days are a lot of work, and I know it'll be even harder on the trail, where I won't be able to spare any cash and most people will be in cars.

Heidi butters her toast. "Well, good luck Cowboy," she says. "I'll be waiting." She probably means it. She'll have the place to herself while I'm away, so why would she go anywhere?

I tried in California, I really did, but here I am two weeks later, already on the plane back home. It started out well. Kyla and I always talked about Route 66 when we were kids. A holy grail. The Santa Monica sign was huge in real life, like a grown up version of the badge. *End of the Trail.* It felt right to be there. Kyla had left me a message; she knew I'd follow.

It was all okay until June eleventh. I drove two sticks in the ground, like the number, and speared a piece of paper. Usually I use taped cardboard, but out there I had to make do. I didn't have a picture of Kyla, so I wrote her name and "MISSING" in all caps. I printed my number neatly written at the bottom, as always. Nobody has ever called.

That wasn't the problem. The problem was the next day.

———

My old man is the luckiest alive because for him Father's Day rolls around every month. The twelfth is always entirely devoted to good old Dad.

A smashed window. Stolen mail, especially if it might have money in it, since he robbed Kyla of her childhood. A 2x4 jammed under the front door to imprison him, like he used to do to us. Threatening letters. Phone calls. If I can't think of anything else, I do the phone call. Sometimes I just stay on the line and breathe heavily. Sometimes I play a sinister song. Once I got a helium balloon and squeaked out in falsetto that he was a dead man walking. Just words—I don't have it in me to kill, though I fantasize about it sometimes. I got my gun years back, as a precaution. Just in case. You can get what you need in Chelsea if you ask the right people.

I charged my phone at a gas station and called our father. I checked my watch—9:03 PM, just after midnight on the east coast, so it counted. All I got was an out of service beep. I tried again, but got the same result. Creep must have changed his number. He'd done that before, but I'd always been able to get the new number from Kyla. Couldn't do that anymore.

I knew I had to go back. It wasn't for me. There are other injustices I could right on the twelfth. Hell, I could abandon the ritual altogether. But she was still missing, so I needed to pay tribute to her. I took the Root 66 badge she'd left me and buried it at the side of the road, marking the spot with a cross, then I got a ride to the airport and a standby flight back to Boston. Now I'm on the plane and my hands are sweating. I'm afraid I won't be in time.

I go straight to our father's house. The tiny vinyl ranch incongruously set on a dirt patch amid dilapidated multi-families. I grew up in that house. The gutter still has a dent where I kicked it trying to scramble up on the roof away from our father when I was thirteen.

I sneak into the yard. I haven't decided what I'll do yet. Probably something lame like smash another window. I peer through the Rhododendron flowers that grow stoutly year after year, far too pretty for this place. I hate the smell of them, smells of my youth. It's after 11, but the lights are on. I see a figure inside. It can't be my Dad—this person is half his size. But when it comes into the center of the room, I realize it's him after all. He has transformed in the six months since I last saw him. Those great arms that used to hold me in a death grip hang skinny and shriveled like two desiccated snakeskins. I can see he's gotten more tattoos though, even on that shriveled old flesh. There's a tube coming out of his nose and he's carrying some kind of cylinder. Although he's not that old, his head hangs forward as though the spring holding it up has snapped. When he tries to get out of his chair it takes him three attempts before he can even stand.

I feel an urgent need to urinate. I move into the shadow of the house and relieve myself against the wall, counting slowly to 12. It'll do.

Heidi is asleep when I get home, but she wakes up as I'm getting into bed.

"The traveler has returned." She yawns, rolls over, and gives me a kiss.

"My father's really sick. Maybe dying."

"You went to see him?" She sounds more interested than I had expected.

"It's the twelfth. I had to come back."

"Right."

"You knew I would."

"Well, what are you going do about it? Talk to him?"

I grimace. She knows I won't. "I'll think of something."

"You should go see him. Make amends."

"Heidi, he locked me and Kyla in the basement when we were kids."

"Not for long. Besides, it was the safest place. What was he supposed to do if he needed to go out? Your mom wasn't there."

"And the calendars?"

"Totally   weird,   but   weird   isn't   always   bad." She pauses. "Though, how close did he hold her?"

I turn away and curl into a ball as though I'm about to fall asleep. Heidi doesn't know Kyla that well; how dare she refer so light-heartedly to my sister's torment? "Close," I tell her, my voice muffled by the pillow. "Real close."

Our father-who-art-a-dick ritualized wall calendars. On the first of the month he made us stand next to him as he marked an "X" through the day, then he hugged us, Kyla then me, a whole, full second each. Same thing on the second day, but the hug lasted two seconds, on the third three, and so on. Each day was supposed to symbolize a year of my Mom's life. She died from childbirth complications age 25, after she had me. I know nothing of her other than that she was Egyptian, and I owe her my bronze skin and high cheekbones. In photos she looks almost as a pretty as Kyla. Our father never forgave me, I reckon. On the twenty-sixth day I never got a hug, and it was a huge fucking relief because 25 seconds is way too long for a fatherly embrace, especially when you're a teenager. It was even worse for Kyla, our father held her so tight.

Back then the end of the month was my favorite time. Now that's completely reversed, which shows I'm nothing at all like our father.

I only really talked about the calendars with Kyla once, shortly after I went to live with her. "I was always so glad," I told her, "when we got to the twenty-sixth."

She nodded, and her dark hair rippled like velvet curtains. "I know. I could tell."

"No more of those goddamn hugs," I said.

"Cuddles."

"What do you mean?"

"That's what he called them. Cuddles."

That confused me. It wasn't a word our father used. I should have probed deeper, but I let it go. "Weren't you relieved on the twenty-sixth, too?"

"The months were a little longer for me."

"Do you mean?" I didn't want to say it.

She shrugged. "Just longer, that's all."

She'd been embarrassed, I could tell. But she'd told me enough. It was then that I bought my first adult advent calendar and designated my day of revenge. I could never forgive our father-who-art-depraved for what he did to Kyla.

I go back to him seven days later. It's the day I've chosen for public readings because the Gettysburg Address took place on a nineteenth, and I've always admired the ideal of unity. I've decided that reading may help keep our father alive. He can't die, not with Kyla gone. What kind of revenge can I get then?

I first stop near the window as usual, but what I see floors me. Heidi is there. Heidi! She's standing over him as he eats his soup. Every now and then she passes him a towel, and he wipes his lips. She seems to be speaking to him, because he'll lift his head and nod, or open his mouth as though he's grunting. He never was much of a talker. Watching them, I feel as though I'm fragmenting like ink poured in water. I go away and read a poem to two homeless guys who are sitting near the courthouse.

After that I watch Heidi. I follow her when she leaves the house. I download a tracking app on her phone. I need to know what she's hiding from me. Mostly when she goes out she either panhandles or hangs out with her friends at the skateboard park. I don't see her do coke; I guess she really is recreational. Sometimes she even goes to bookstores. This surprises me. I've never thought of her as a reader. Although, truth be told, I've never thought of her much at all.

I'm thinking of her now as she sits right across the table from Kyla. That's right. There they are, the two of them, sitting bold as brass in a café in Cambridge. I don't know exactly where it is because I never go north of the Charles River, but it's Cambridge. It smells of pretension.

It's as though my brain is being run through a blender. Tears stream down my cheeks and of course my first instinct is to run over and hug my sister. She's alive! She must have escaped. But even as I watch for a few seconds, I feel my cheeks begin to dry. There is no reason for her to see Heidi before me. Why hasn't she come back to me? Has *Heidi* captured my sweet girl? Maybe Heidi is in cahoots with our father-who-art-an-evil-schemer and they're holding Kyla against her will. She must be here under duress.

I rummage through my bag. As usual, I have a few items for disguise. A newspaper, a hat, a wig of shoulder-length blond hair, and a false mustache. For when I need to sink into anonymity.

It's risky, but Kyla needs me, so I purchase tea and slink into the booth directly behind Heidi, which serendipitously is free.

"I feel terrible," says Kyla. Her voice is fresh as spring. "I wish I hadn't neglected him for so long."

"Come on, Kate. There's still time."

I don't know why Heidi is calling my sister Kate, and it makes me want to reach across and punch her, except that I don't punch people.

"I hope so. I'm trying. I'd basically written him off, you know. He didn't deserve that."

Is she talking about me? Why did she write me off? I wish I could see her. Kyla's face is as easy for me to read as a kid's storybook.

"I don't know. From what you and Aaron say I can't blame you. Cuddles every day? Anyway, you're with him now. That's the main thing."

Not me then. Our father.

"Eccentric, for sure. And he was too hard on Aaron, like boot camp sometimes. So I always used to side with Aaron over Dad, but now I'm not so sure. Aaron's impossible to live with. Honestly, Heid, I don't know how you do it."

"I like being with him." Heidi sounds a little icy.

"Well you've stayed well past your due." There's a pause. "How *is* Aaron?"

When Heidi speaks she sounds more emotional than usual. "It's why I needed to talk to you. He's not good. He agonizes over you. He spends all day searching for you and doing his calendars. What did you expect? You've got to tell him you're okay."

"He watched my every move, Heidi. Called me ten times a day. Twenty-five nice things for Kyla means 25 ways to control Kyla. You know what happened when I tried to date. I couldn't even meet my girlfriends. I guess I freaked out."

Kyla's voice is small and I don't know why she's telling such nasty lies. Somebody must be forcing her to say these things.

"You needed a clean break. I get it. But you can't just abandon him. Tell him about your father too. He's convinced you were molested, for fuck's sake."

"It is what it is. I've told him *over and over*. Cuddles, every day of the month, but nothing more."

More lies. Perhaps Kyla has managed to deceive herself. People do that. When things are too hurtful, they spin another story, something that's easier to digest. She doesn't want to think of our father-who-art-truly-a-monster; she prefers our father-who-art-merely-a-freak. I understand.

"Well, I'm not going to lie to him much longer. I'm into him, Kate. I don't like to see him suffer."

I hear Kyla sigh heavily. "I hoped he'd go away, Chicago or California, anywhere on Route 66, set up a new life, get happy, then I could show up in a few months."

"Not happening. Didn't work. *Tell* him."

"Soon. My father might only have a few weeks. I need to focus on him. I can't have Aaron mad right now."

"You're afraid he might hurt you?"

"Nah. He's fucked up and creepy, but he's not violent."

They talk about something else briefly before leaving the café. I finish my tea, fold up my newspaper, and head back home.

It's the twenty-fifth, but I take Heidi in bed, more aggressive than usual. It might be the first time I've really surprised her, and she seems to like it.

"What's got into you, tiger boy?" she says lazily, reaching for a cigarette. "Lose track of time?"

I stay on top of her and stop her before she can light up. "I saw you at my father's place."

She raises both her eyebrows. "Oh."

"Why did you go there?"

She sighs. "I know him from the tattoo parlor. It's how I first met Kyla."

"Don't you mean Kate?"

She flinches, just a little. "What do you mean?"

I reach for a razor I've placed on the bedside table and dangle it in front of her. I explain that because she has brainwashed my sister, she has to answer questions. If she doesn't speak, I'll make a little cut. First one second. Then longer. She knows how it works. But it won't stop at 25.

The months were a bit longer for me. I should have done more. How could I have expected Kyla to forgive me?

Heidi laughs and looks at me sassily. "Come on, Aaron. You're not going to do that."

"No?"

"Kyla said you were weird, but never violent."

"You think Kyla knows everything?"

"She knows you."

I take a deep breath and narrow my eyes to slits, then stab at her left pinky. It's superficial, barely more than a pin-prick, but it's enough to make her yelp.

"Asshole!" she cries.

"She doesn't know everything about me," I say softly. "Tell me who took her."

"Nobody *took* her. She had to get away."

"From what?"

Through halting, broken sentences, Heidi spouts the same lies I heard in the café. *Away from me.* Kyla could never have a normal life with me in the picture. She'd even changed her name. I was like our father, only worse.

I bring the razor close to her ring finger, but I don't jab, just squeeze the finger tight. "I'm nothing like him. I was good to her."

Heidi looks me in the eye. "Was it good to scratch up her boyfriend's laptop? To walk in on them pretending you were sleepwalking?"

"He wasn't right for her."

"And all the others?"

I ignore the question. "Why did you come up to me in that bar when we met?"

"She wanted me to keep an eye on you."

"She *paid* you?"

"Only for a couple of weeks. I stayed because I like you."

She looks proud of herself. Unbelievable. "So you slept with me for money. You're a prostitute."

She shrugs. "Happy coincidence, really. I slept with you because you're gorgeous."

"Is she with our father? Is that why you were there?"

She doesn't answer me and I grab her hand, but I can't make myself hurt her. The problem is she doesn't deserve it. I slash my own finger instead, drawing blood for a full two seconds.

She wriggles out from under me, over to her side of the bed. I wonder if she'll try to run away and if I ought to stop her. I know some people would consider what I did to be assault, even though she gave me no choice. But she doesn't go anywhere.

"We're good together, you and me," she says.

"You're mad."

"Maybe. But we're a couple of misfits. I'd still walk Route 66 with you."

"The whole way?"

"Sure. Until we find somewhere we want to stay."

It's probably some perverted plan to take me away from my sister, but I don't hate it. I realize that I hadn't felt right, being out on the road by myself. I'd been lonely. Maybe Heidi is a west coast girl after all.

"I left something for us out there," I say.

"Can you put down that razor?"

I put it down. She slides back under the sheets and pulls them up around her head. Moments later, she's snoring lightly. I love how it's so easy for her. Next month, on the first of July, I'll do something really big for my Heidi. She's like family now.

But it isn't July yet. It's almost midnight on June 25, so I open the last door of the advent calendar. A wise man. I smile ironically, and eat the chocolate. I don't have to do anything else. There have been enough miracles for one day.

Could Kyla really have run away from me? Could she really be staying with our father-who-art-the-source-of-it-all?

In the small hours of the morning, I gather Kyla's bracelet, my gloves, my shoe covers, and my gun. I'll go back to Route 66 with Heidi, but I need to make a stop in Chelsea first. I hot-wire an old Nissan and drive across Boston, dump it, then head toward our father's house on foot. It's a good thing I'm out here on the twenty-sixth and not the twelfth. On the twelfth I've always avenged Kyla. Tonight I'm out for myself, and anything goes.

AUTHOR'S NOTE

I have been working on a psychological suspense novel for the past few years, and one of the important characters in my novel is a psychopath. She isn't a point-of-view character, so I don't need to write from inside her head, but I often think it would be interesting to do so—albeit difficult for a book-length project. My first idea for *Our Father* was basically a character who had strange rituals around advent calendars. From there, Aaron's character developed—he is in some ways sympathetic and quirky, but he flouts many of the usual norms of human relationships and he has a sinister edge. Writing an unreliable point-of-view character as he reveals more and more about himself was quite challenging for me, but also satisfying and a lot of fun. I don't want to call Aaron a psychopath, and I have more sympathy for him than for the character in my novel, but he definitely became quite disturbing the more I grew to know him!

RMB

THE SEAMSTRESS

RUSSELL REECE

IMAGINE THIS. It is seven o'clock in the evening on October 30, 1975. You are looking into a bungalow in a subdivision near a grimy mill town in western Pennsylvania. The house has a small entrance foyer, two bedrooms, a kitchen, a living-room/dining-room combo, and a bath. There are two entrance doors, one on the side entering into the kitchen and another in front. The house is simply furnished with old, second-hand furniture. It is clean and neat. A calendar hangs in the kitchen with today's date circled in red. There are no knickknacks, no paintings on the walls. A World War II photo of a soldier and a pretty young girl sits atop a bureau in the bedroom where a rented hospital bed has been set up and where a large man lies on his back staring at the ceiling.

—

Mary Bix enters the kitchen. She is a frail, gray-haired woman in her early fifties. Her drab, calf-length housedress hangs loosely on her thin frame. Her hair is tied in a bun, her face is plain, her mouth turned down at the corners. Her eyes are tired and milky from a lifetime working as a seamstress. She looks at the clock on the stove and rubs the palm of her outstretched hand on her hip as she is prone to do when she is nervous. She glances at the small packed suitcase sitting by the front door and then walks into the spare bedroom where her sewing is done and where her pullout bed is tucked against the wall. She picks up a spool of heavy thread, scissors, a needle, and the bag of cosmetics she has just purchased at the local pharmacy. She stops for a moment in front of the window overlooking the drive and recalls the month before when she had seen the police car arrive. Mary knew they had come to arrest her, but she didn't care. Imprisonment would have been preferable to being with John again. But rather than an arrest warrant, the officers had brought news. John had been in an accident.

She would smile about it now if that were her way.

Mary walks into the bedroom where John lies immobilized by a spinal cord injury. His eyes follow Mary as she checks the IV drip and then places the sewing material and the bag on the table next to the bed. John's bottom lip quivers as it has done since he was brought home from the hospital only three days ago. The visiting nurse said the trembling was to be expected.

Mary picks up the photograph of their wedding day. She was 19, John 23. They had met and married when John was home on leave. Whenever she looks at the portrait she tries to remember how it was then. She had been happy, she remembered that. Her love for John had grown while he was away at the war in the Pacific. She was so relieved when he made it safely home. Joy had surrounded those first days after his return, and for many years she was able to recall that, at least in part. Even when the drinking and the abuse had started, she used to be able to take solace in those feelings, pull them in when needed. That was a long time ago. Nothing remained of that life but the photograph.

She glances down and catches John's gaze. He is done with the slapping and manhandling, done with the demeaning insults and the booze. Done with everything.

Mary continues to stare at John, no change in expression, as she recalls Darla—dark hair, made-up eyes, and scarlet lipstick. Mary remembers all too well the night when John had done the unthinkable and brought the stranger to their home. Had forced Mary into her sewing room, threatening to kill her if she ventured out. Soon Darla's giggle and John's deep voice rose and fell in fits of passion. Drunken taunts followed.

"You're an ugly smudge of a woman," John had said. "You belong in that goddamned room. Sewing is all you're good for."

John and Darla had laughed and stayed in the bedroom for hours. Mary buried her face in her pillow as her fear of John turned to unchecked hatred. She knew that nothing would ever be the same again.

John gazes around the room and then stares up at Mary, a sudden realization in his eyes. "It was you," he whispers, breathlessly.

Mary thinks back to the night in front of Rapa's Tavern, one month earlier, as John walked across the street toward his car. He was alone, perhaps too drunk for Darla. Mary had hoped to run them both down but it was just John, moving slowly in the cool evening. His car was parked beyond the wash of the streetlight and she had timed it perfectly, her car upon him before he could react. She had delighted in his terrified expression, the way his hands had slowly reached toward the front of her speeding car like a frightened child. She wanted John to know it had been her, hoped that in the half-second before her car snuffed out his life he would have seen her and would have known.

Only John hadn't died.

At first Mary felt delighted. It had worked out better than she could have hoped. No one suspected her, and John had no memory of the event. He would be confined to a hospital bed for the rest of his life, nurses rolling him over twice a day to change his diapers, nothing for him to do but stare at the ceiling. John's would be an empty life, just like the one She had lived for the past 30 years—a fitting end for a cruel, heartless man.

It soon became apparent that John would require constant care, the kind provided in a home for invalids. He had no insurance and there was no other money. Mary's job as a seamstress barely left her with enough to survive. The state agencies were little help. Her church offered to fund a visiting nurse a few days a week but the rest would fall to her. She felt as if John were abusing her all over again.

John was transported from the hospital to the home he and Mary shared. Upon reflection, Mary was happy. The hit and run had been impulsive. It would have been too kind, too abrupt a payback for everything John had put her through. *This will be much more satisfying,* she thought. *I won't get away with it this time, but I don't care.*

Mary sits down on the tall stool next to John's bed, leans on his chest, and stares into his eyes.

———

Imagine that you are John looking up at Mary, the timid mouse of a woman you have ruled over for the last 30 years, the skinny hag you were embarrassed to be with, who has always shied away avoiding contact, who has been so meek and subservient it sickened you and drove you to dole out even more abuse. Here she is daring to lean against you, staring down with some weird expression that should be slapped off her ugly face.

"Get off me," you say.

Mary pounds your forehead with a closed fist. You grit your teeth. You want to grab her scrawny neck and throw her to the floor, grind her face with the sole of your shoe … but you can't move. You'll never be able to move. Your lip quivers. You squeeze your eyes closed as she whacks you again. You have no way to avoid her blows. You open your eyes. Your heart races.

She opens the bag of cosmetics and retrieves a lipstick and a small plastic pallet of black eyeshadow. "This is what you like, isn't it?" she says. She gouges out a clump of eyeshadow with her fingertips. It crumbles onto your white undershirt as she smears it in one stroke, like a child finger painting, over her closed lids and into the arches of her brow. She wipes her fingers on your chest. She removes the lipstick cap and, still staring at you, applies it to her lower lip and upper lips. You've never seen Mary with lipstick, and then you recognize the color. Darla's color. Your heartbeat quickens.

"What are you doing?" you say, but Mary clenches her jaw and whacks you again. You glimpse her teeth through the scarlet lipstick which looks bloody against her pasty skin. She smears it beyond the lip line past the corners of her mouth into a jagged ghoul's mask from a house of horrors.

A frightened, sinking feeling runs through you as you gasp for air. "Crazy bitch," you say, lips trembling.

Mary raises her shadowy brow and nods agreement. "Are you worried?" she asks.

You *are* worried but you don't answer. You won't give this hag the satisfaction.

"You *should* be," she says.

Mary swipes the bag and makeup containers with the back of her hand. They clatter against the wall and onto the floor. Her eyes flare and her teeth show again as she glares down at you.

Your pulse sounds in the back of your head as you watch Mary unwind a length of thick thread from a spool, cut it expertly with a pair of small scissors, and thread it onto a needle. You see her practiced finger and thumb pull a knot into the end of the thread.

"What … are you doing?" you whisper.

With the needle poised in her right hand, Mary pinches your trembling lip with her left thumb and index finger. Imagine the wasp sting of the needle, the sound as the coarse thread pulls through the flesh of your lip, and then the tug, and the needle coming down again, the tip of Mary's tongue in the corner of her painted mouth as she pierces your upper lip and pulls the thread taut. And then into the lower lip again and through the upper. She repeats this action seven more times until your mouth is sewn completely closed. She finishing with a double stitch and a hard tug. The force jerks your head from the pillow. She snips the thread.

"I've wanted to do this for years," she says.

Your heart is pounding so hard you think it will break through your skin. Tears stream down the side of your face and your chest heaves as you breathe heavily through your nose. Mary looks down, appears to admire her work. She wipes trickles of blood off your chin with her open hand and then cleans it on your undershirt. Mary's fore-finger and thumb grasp your nose. She squeezes. Her eyes are wide again, lips parted in anticipation. Your chest tightens, your eyes bulge and your head begins to pound as you strain for breath. You want to scream, to beg her to stop. You can't speak. You grunt and whine like a whimpering dog. Mary releases her grip and you draw a long raspy breath. She smiles.

You've haven't seen Mary smile in years. This frightens you even more. For a fleeting second you look past the madness and see the pretty girl of 30 years ago, the moment you arrived home from the war, when she met you at the front door and momentarily collapsed in her excitement.

A second later the hag is back and Mary's scarlet lips part in concentration as her thin fingers reach toward your left eye. You moan a scream, blink, squeeze your eyes closed. She roughly pinches your eyelid and stretches it open before releasing it. You blink away tears and whimper for her to stop. She looks at you and nods.

"I understand, John. Really, I understand. But I've more sew-ing to do before this is over. That's all I'm good for. Isn't that what you said?"

Mary knots the thread in the needle again.

—

Hours later Mary stands by the living room window awaiting a taxi. She'd finished with John 45 minutes ago, after sewing his second nostril closed and watching his head quiver and his face turn blue against the bedsheet. With his final heartbeat, the anguish of 30 years was gone. Mary felt overcome with a rush of peace and calm. She showered and dressed for her trip to San Diego. She'd always wanted to visit San Diego, to see the world-famous zoo and the California beaches. It was something that John had promised they'd do after they were married. A promise unfulfilled. She would go now, enjoy a few days before she was located and brought her back to stand trial.

Mary glances across the street at Mrs. Daniel's house where a candle gutters within a carved pumpkin. She realizes that tomorrow is

October 31. Kids will be out with their costumes, knocking on doors, consumed with the spirit of witches and goblins, and delighting at things that frighten them in the spooky night. Mary recalls how John never enjoyed Halloween and would actually chase away would-be trick or treaters. Mary checks her watch. Plenty of time before her flight. She is struck with a sudden inspiration.

A while later headlights approach as her taxi arrives. With overcoat and suitcase in hand, Mary walks to the curb and gets into the back seat. As the taxi pulls away she stares back at her front porch where her husband's severed head has been carefully propped upon the top step. "Happy Halloween, John," she whispers under her breath. She fights back a grin and settles in for the ride.

AUTHOR'S NOTE

I had just read Stephen King's 2015 short story collection, *The Bazaar of Bad Dreams*. I'd never written anything in the horror genre and thought it would be fun to give it a try. I decided to avoid the supernatural, keep it plausible, but push the creepiness factor as much as possible hoping for a horrifying result. I also wanted to make the story somewhat theatrical to capture the intimate connection theatergoers often feel with actors. Thus, I began by describing the setting, as if the reader were in a theater observing the set and watching the main actress take the stage. I wrote the first paragraph and most of the second before I even knew what my story would be about. I also shifted the point of view halfway through the tale, so the reader "experiences" the awful business at hand. Finally, the story had been so over-the-top I opted to finish with an over-the-top ending.

RR

THE MAN IN THE HOTEL

BERNIE BROWN

THE REEDS PLAYED the mellow theme to Glenn Miller's "Moonlight Serenade" and Peter Abercrombie held Ginny close. Her hair smelled of lilacs. He buried his nose in Ginny's soft, dark locks and inhaled the fragrance.

"I've got something for you," he whispered.

Ginny pulled her head back. Her eyes, blue with brown flecks, eyes met Peter's.

"What is it?" she asked, impatience adding a lift to her voice. Ginny loved presents.

"Come outside and I'll show you."

They stood on the steps of the Tylerville Lion's Club in the clear September night, the air as crisp as a cracker. Other couples were there, stealing a kiss or gazing at the moon. Peter pulled a small box from his jacket pocket and placed it in her hand.

Ginny eyes widened, and she sucked in her breath. "Can I open it?"

"Of course, silly. It's for you."

She lifted the lid, eyes aglow with excitement. She glanced up at Peter. "It's lovely. Help me with the clasp." With her back to Peter, Ginny lifted her hair away from her neck.

Peter fumbled the clasp in the pale moonlight, but got it on the second try.

Ginny turned to face him again and held the silver and gold locket away from her neck to admire it. "It's beautiful."

"Look inside."

She opened the locket and smiled her bright smile at the small photo that had been placed on one side. "It's you."

"Don't forget me, Ginny." Peter placed his arms around Ginny, already jealous of any man who might look at her while he was gone.

"Never." She squeezed him tight, a squeeze he wanted to last forever. Ginny kissed Peter. Her lips tasted of spearmint. Her eyes, always expressive, glowed. "We've been together for over two years and ...well ... let's get married," she said with quick breath.

"You mean when I return?"

"No, I mean right now. Tonight."

"Are you serious?" Peter felt his face go hot with excitement.

"Yes. We can find a minister or justice of the peace or a sheriff or somebody to do it."

"A *sheriff*?" He laughed.

"Well, somebody."

—

Peter and Ginny spent their honeymoon night in Room 10 of the Scranton Hotel.

Peter shipped out at dawn. Ginny's brown hair spread out on the pillow like a cloak as she slept soundly. The heart locket she'd been given rested atop the delicate skin of her even more delicate neck. Lightly, Peter kissed Ginny's forehead. He longed to stay with her, but couldn't. He had served in the army during the early 1930s and had been honorably discharged in 1937. But the world was at war now, and he responded to the call.

At 8:00 AM on September 8, 1941, Peter Abercrombie boarded an outbound train headed for the coast. He was soon en route to London to join a ground forces division charged with defending naval and air bases as part of the War Department's RAINBOW 5 plan. He was soon transferred to the coast of Italy.

While Peter was abroad, Ginny wrote to him several times per week. At times, Peter would receive up to six or more letters at once due to the inconsistency of the mail services.

"You lucky stiff," his fellow soldiers often remarked. At times, Peter shared parts of the letters with his troop, but never the entire letter. There were parts he read over and over meant for his eyes only. In December of 1941, Ginny wrote to tell Peter he was going to be a father.

The letters stopped three months later.

His buddies liked him too much to tease Peter, but they'd seen it before. Peter heard the whispers about the "Dear John" letter that was probably going to arrive any day now. The men stole sideways glances at Peter's face when mail call ended and he was left empty-handed. Finally, toward the end of April, a letter arrived. Not from Ginny, but from her mom. Peter read the words through tear-stained eyes. Ginny had miscarried, lost the baby, and suffered a fatal hemorrhage.

In the letter, Ginny's mom had included the heart locket he had given to Ginny. Peter opened the locket and saw that Ginny had placed a photo of herself on the opposite side of his photo. They had been alone together in the locket around Ginny's neck the entire time he was away, the entire time before she died. Peter sobbed, lost and empty.

The irony of Ginny's death was not lost on Peter. *What kind of sick joke is it that the soldier gets the sad message about the loss of a civilian?* he pondered. *If anyone should die, it's me. I'm the one at war.* Peter felt an urge to throw the locket as far away as he could. Perhaps, he thought, the locket would carry his pain away with it. But he couldn't do it. The locket was all he had left of Ginny now.

—

The war ended for Peter three weeks after he'd learned of Ginny's death during a skirmish with an enemy battalion. Shrapnel from a grenade shattered Peter's right leg. Although medics repaired the broken bones, the injury was too extreme. After being confined to a Red Cross hospital for several weeks of recovery, Peter was shipped home with a Purple Heart and a walking cane.

When Peter returned home to Iowa in June of 1942, he checked in to room 10 of the Scranton Hotel,.

The hotel room was unchanged from the year before when he and Ginny had spent their first and only night together as husband and wife. An ornate Turkish rug extended within a few feet of the walls, exposing solid hardwood floors gone dark with age. The window treatments drifted languidly in the summer breeze. The bed, an ornate black Art Deco frame was covered with a red chenille spread, threadbare in spots. Off the interior wall was a tiny bathroom with pre-war fixtures and a cast iron, double-ended clawfoot tub. The black and white tiled floor, cracked and in need of new grout, had, like Peter, seen better days.

Peter awoke that night to the scent of lilacs. He licked his lips and tasted spearmint. He decided to remain in room 10 indefinitely.

He had no real life outside of his daily routine. Peter survived on a small inheritance and his military pension. Always the early riser, he dressed neatly in pants, jacket, and tie. Every morning he ate ham and eggs for breakfast in the hotel restaurant. A post-meal walk took him a few blocks in one direction and then back again if his leg began to throb. During the late mornings and early afternoons, Peter read the newspapers in the hotel lobby.

The lobby had high-back, comfortable chairs and floor-to-ceiling windows. Plenty of sun exposure. Peter watched as people came and went on sunny days. Salesmen arriving or departing by train, college students walking to and from school, housewives shopping for goods. Peter felt inspired to take the train somewhere, but couldn't quite commit to packing a suitcase or buying a ticket.

On most evenings he awoke to the taste of Ginny's lips and the scent of her hair. He enjoyed Ginny's presence and was reluctant to leave it behind.

———

Late one morning, when he returned to his room to freshen up for lunch, Peter saw a flash of light on the bed. Just a trick of sunshine, he told himself, but he stepped closer to be sure. A heart locket lay there twinkling, the light like sunshine through fog. Peter gasped. It appeared to be Ginny's locket. *That's impossible,* he thought. *It's always in the pocket of my dress uniform, and my dress uniform in the suitcase on my closet shelf.* He extended a hand to grasp the chain, only to touch the rough fabric of the bedspread pulled as tight as an army cot by the hotel maid. There was no locket, but the air around Peter's extended hand felt unusually cool. He sensed a soft pressure as if his fingers were being grasped by an invisible presence. *I know you're here,* he thought.

Peter walked to the closet, opened the suitcase, and checked the pocket of his dress uniform to confirm the locket's whereabouts.

Peter hobbled to the bathroom, washed his hands and brushed his hair. Collecting his cane from the bedside chair, Peter limped down to lunch. He was particularly expert at descending the stairs with his cane.

At the hotel restaurant, the lunch waitress, who Peter had learned was named Connie, pulled Peter's chair out for him as she did each afternoon. He wasn't sure whether Connie did this out of courtesy to his injury or because she genuinely liked him. Peter liked to think he was Connie's favorite customer. She was young and pretty and reminded him of Ginny, but only in her youth and beauty. The waitress was short and blonde, whereas Ginny had been tall and dark.

Connie brought Peter a steaming bowl of tomato soup. She babbled happily as she fussed over him.

"I'm so excited. I'm taking the train to Westfield to visit my aunt." A flush colored Connie's cheeks with the pleasure of anticipation. "Do you like to ride the train?"

"I've only ridden it twice. Once to the war. And once back." He took a spoonful of soup.

"You should take it now. My mom says it's much nicer than it used to be. I love to eat in the dining car. There's a white tablecloth and a rose on the table, and it's nice to be waited on for a change." Connie laughed at her own joke.

"I haven't any place to go."

She topped off his coffee. "Go to Westfield. It's a pretty town. You could ride with me. We could dine together."

"Oh, no. I'm not the best company these days."

"I don't mean the whole trip. Just on the train. You would be on your own when you got there. I would be with my aunt. They have a nice hotel much like this one where you can stay. There are band concerts in city hall on Wednesday nights."

Connie disappeared for a moment. She soon returned with Peter's entrée, a chicken pot pie. She placed it in front of him. Its steam rose temptingly. Through the steam Peter glimpsed the young woman's necklace. It was exactly like Ginny's locket. He stared for a moment and then dropped his eyes. Staring was impolite, and he didn't want to appear rude.

Upon finishing his meal, Connie stopped at Peter's table to take away his plates. Peter looked at the necklace again and realized it wasn't like Ginny's at all. It was clearly a cross with a pearl, not a heart.

Twice in one day he had seen, or thought he'd seen, Ginny's locket. *Perhaps,* he thought, *I'm going mad.*

———

On most afternoons Peter met up with another former soldier, an older veteran from the First World War. Occasionally they played chess, though neither played it well. They often forgot how the different pieces moved and spent much time checking the rule book. More often they played checkers. When the weather was cold, like today, they played inside Herman's Bar and Grill, making one beer last the entire afternoon.

"You ever been to Westfield?" Peter asked the old guy, who he knew only as McGuire, as he set up the board.

"Went there one time with the wife before she died. Pretty little town. We took the train. Why do you ask?"

"Oh, I don't know. Somebody told me they had weekly band concerts in city hall."

"They've got a movie theater. I know that. The wife and I saw *Ma and Pa Kettle* there. You ever go to the movies?"

"Sometimes," Peter said.

"You know anybody who lives in Westfield?" McGuire asked.

Although Peter had brought up the subject, he was tired of talking about Westfield and the train. He feared Ginny would know and feel abandoned. Betrayed. Peter quickly changed the subject. "There was this guy I knew once. Believed in ghosts."

"You don't say?" McGuire said.

Peter had expected the old soldier to laugh, but he seemed interested.

"You never know," the older said. "My wife saw her mother several times after she died. Or saw things her mother owned, like a handkerchief or a pair of lace gloves."

"I don't know, either," Peter feigned a casual attitude and shrugged. "I was afraid the guy might be crazy."

McGuire eyed Peter as if he knew Peter was talking about himself.

Uncomfortable, Peter looked down at the board, jumped two black pieces, and said, "King me," with a laugh.

"How'd I miss that?" McGuire took a swig of his beer.

Peter easily won after that, and they called it a day.

"If you don't show up one day, I'll know you went to West-field."

"Probably won't happen."

"Maybe we'll go together." The old guy cleared the checkerboard.

Peter was half way out the door. "I'll think about it."

———

That night the train's whistle woke Peter as the 451 Local pulled into the station shortly after midnight. Peter's thoughts again turned to Westfield.

Could he do it? Could he willingly let go of the hold Ginny had on him?

Moonlight shone through the window. It reminded Peter of the moonlight on his last night together with Ginny outside the Lion's Club—soft, eerie, romantic. The train whistle broke the morning silence again as it pulled out of the station. Ginny's locket hung suspended in the light from the window, swinging back and forth, tantalizing Peter. It faded away with the waning train whistle.

In his half-awake state, Peter thought about retrieving his suitcase once more to make sure the locket was still there, but exhaustion overtook Peter and he drifted back to sleep.

—

Peter awoke in the morning, and for the first time since he'd taken residence in room 10 he did not smell the scent of lilacs in the air, did not taste spearmint on his breath. The room itself looked different. Books that he'd left haphazardly on the coffee table were now neatly arranged. The bedside wastepaper basket was empty. He looked across the hotel room and saw his suitcase next to the door.

Peter felt a cold chill stretch across his spine as he stepped out of bed and walked toward the door. As he looked more closely, he saw Ginny's locket lying atop of the suitcase. The locket was opened. He took the locket in his hand and stared at the photographs within it.

"I understand," he said. "It's time for me to let go. Time to start living again."

Peter stared at Ginny's photo once more and it began to fade away. Within seconds, it was gone. The two halves of the locket then folded together and snapped shut.

"All these months I thought I'd been cherishing your memory. Instead, I'd used it to keep from living. I'm sorry."

At that moment, Peter knew now he would take the train to Westfield or to anywhere. He would bring Ginny's memory along with him. Peter smiled, finally understanding that Ginny's memory didn't live in this hotel or in the locket. It lived in his heart.

AUTHOR'S NOTE

The hotel in "The Man in the Hotel" was inspired by the Whitney Hotel in Atlantic, Iowa. Like the Scranton in my story, the Whitney sat within a short distance from the railroad station. Both the station and the hotel were no longer in their heyday when I went there. By that time, the Whitney functioned only as a restaurant, but some of the sleeping rooms upstairs were maintained for historical purposes. As an adult on home visits to Iowa, I often ate at the Whitney with family who lived in Atlantic. After one lunch, curiosity drove me up the stairs to visit the hotel rooms. The rooms, with their vintage décor, captured my imagination. I wondered about the people who had stayed there, maybe even lived there. Even after I returned to North Carolina, I thought about those people. You might say they haunted me.

I knew I had to write about the hotel and a war veteran who I imagined had lived there. I tried to write a novel in which he was a minor, but important, character. The novel just didn't click, and I abandoned it; but the man who lived in the hotel stayed with me. He finally found his place in this story, and he no longer haunts me. We are both at peace.

BB

ALL HALLOWS' EVE: FULL DARK

CATHARINE CLARK-SAYLES

Inky water flows the Sound, refracting light
into a sequined show. Marilyn and Elvis
running drinks, The Little Tramp hitches pants

and a tray of dirty plates, wobbles off past video
flickers on the wall: a Busby Berkeley chorus line
morphs to Judy Garland putting on a show.

I place my vote on the jack-o-lantern parade,
decide I'll stay in place, let trick or treat come to me,
in my disguise as the sort of woman who leans on bars.

The bartender in rolled white sleeves, black tie
and thick black glasses frames hums a bar:
"Buddy Holly" I laugh, he smiles, strains vodka

stained red with pomegranate, named, tonight,
a "Vampire's Kiss." I sip sweetness, turn to watch
Spider-Man hit on the guy in Bogey's trench coat and fedora.

On the wall Gene Kelly waltzes with a mouse
Jane Fonda floats through space and Tippi
Hedren flails at a winged and blackened sky

At midnight on All Hallows' Eve the dead
are given leave and we, the living, dance
again with those who taught us how.

MONSTER LOVE

CATHARINE CLARK-SAYLES

I worry about the monsters, the ones we loved
on the Saturday Creature Feature in black and white.
Will Godzilla ever get enough to eat?
Is King Kong still pining for his tiny blonde?

On the Saturday *Creature Feature* in black and white–
Mostly they were trying to find love.
Is King Kong still pining for his tiny blonde?
Frankenstein never meant his creation to cause harm

Mostly he was trying to find love,
Not the pitchforks, the torches, the angry mob.
Frankenstein's monster never meant to create harm
His outstretched hand making a silent plea

Instead it was pitchforks, torches, the angry mob.
Howling after the Wolfman, lying broken on the ground
His outstretched hand made a silent plea–
The blind woman promised love could break the curse

Howling after the Wolfman, lying broken on the ground.
Listen! The children of the night, how they sing–
The blind woman promised love could break the curse:
Eternal thirst for blood, yes, and Dracula wants his bride.

Listen to the children of the night, how they sing.
Will Godzilla ever get enough to eat?
Eternal thirst for blood, yes, but Dracula needs his bride.
I worry about the monsters, the ones we loved

CREATURE FEATURE

CATHARINE CLARK-SAYLES

On Saturday afternoons I dressed Barbie
in her wedding gown, screamed "Alive.
She's alive!" lurching Barbie, her arms
extended straight across the bed.

On the rolling picture of the black and white TV,
on snowed-in Colorado afternoons—The Bride
with lightning-bolt bouffant, tiny face
too-large eyes, and kewpie lips looked neither horrible

nor bad—only new and tottery, unsure; bird-like
darting of her head. Bridal bandages, swaddled
from neck to floor, left to imagination:
lines of stitches in pallid flesh.

Eve made for Adam, sewn from stolen bits,
for the bolt-necked creature clumping
down the dungeon stairs. But when he reached to touch,
trembled out a questioned "Friend?"

my fingers stretched, unconscious, to take his hand,
The Bride began to screech, his hand pulled back;
love becoming rage and even Barbie and I could not create
a happy ending for this stitched-together pair.

AUTHOR'S NOTE

A few years ago I spent Halloween evening at the Edgewater
Inn in Seattle. The waitstaff dressed as dead celebrities and a video
montage flickered on the wall. I had the feeling of floating out of time.

I wrote a few poems about the evening and then rather obsessively began writing poems about the classic monster movies of my childhood. Eventually I discovered that I was viewing them from the perspective of the lessons an adolescent girl might take from Frankenstein's monster or Norman Bates as she wrestled with her own monstrosity of a gawky, clumsy body suddenly sprouting acne, hair, and inconvenient bleeding.

So many of our monsters were just looking for love, and my sympathies seemed to be more with the creature than with the frightened townsfolk and their torches. As a child, I would replay the script with a happier ending for the creatures, sometimes enacting the story with Barbie dolls. In "Creature Feature" the key scene of Elsa Lancaster with her baby bird awkwardness recoiling from Boris Karloff seems to encompass a lot of the missed connections in bad first dates.

"Monster Love" continues the theme of looking for love. I like writing in form and find the puzzle-making sometimes distracts my left brain to allow surprising things to slip through from my right brain. The pantoum form gives a lovely obsessiveness to the poem as it considers the ways of love.

"All Hallows' Eve: Full Dark" is one of the poems in the group that sets a frame of the experience of spending Halloween in this bar with the re-created icons of my adolescence: musicians, actors, and a few of the monsters. The perspective is more adult and reflective with Buddy Holly serving as my guide. I often imagined different endings. What if he had missed the plane and continued writing music?

CC-S

ERATO'S ASSISTANT

PAUL MILENSKI

And to each dark night intrepidly he comes
      With searching amber eyes.
He magnifies his stealth with padding foot pads –
      An ambivalent crush of leaves.
Blame his mischief on the night, blame it on the languor
      Of mist and mottled moon.
Imagine his innocence—dreams will dissipate,
      Innocence is coincident with doom.
Stay wakeful then and wish the day the clarity
      It promises. It's the hoarder
Of the dark released. Its measure is the sight
      Of reluctant ignorant light.
Toward the gloom, a sentient gleam appears.
Man awakes and hears what he should hear.

AUTHOR'S NOTE

  Unless one is the reincarnation of Keats, the writing of poetry, even the rule-based types is difficult. But if just before sleep a poetic idea arrives, slumber is visited by the muse or her male assistant, the latter a sneaky sort who like a Halloween spook disappears at dawn. The poet then awakes with his idea transformed, and in daylight the terrifying reconstitution of the idea begins. How often has this happened to all who write—good idea at bedtime, better idea in the morn, but near impossible to capture in writing? Darn muse's assistant!

PM

MUNCHERS

DAN ALLEN

THE STAIRS WERE narrow. Each step took them further from the entrance and into the darkness. Loud thumping shook the house and the walls vibrated with a rhythmic pulse. Buck covered his ears and froze, unable to take the next step.

"I don't want to," he said, in a quiet voice that had yet to turn hysterical.

Buck's father squeezed in behind and gently coaxed his son along. Behind them the stairwell filled with people pushing and crowding, desperate to reach the top.

"Come on, Buck. We have to go."

"I don't want to. I want to go back."

"We can't now. There are too many people behind us. We need to keep going, little bear. We're blocking the way."

Buck took another step; his tiny knees shook like a trembling rabbit. Ahead, someone screamed, and Buck turned back.

"Keep going, buddy."

Buck wrapped his arms around his dad's leg and held on with a firm grip. Jake lifted his son and carried him.

At the top floor of the haunted house, they waded through knee-deep green fog. Sounds of a swamp ricocheted off the walls and an owl's screech competed with a thumping jungle drumbeat. The orange glow of a fire cut through the mist and a large black kettle boiled over, clearly the source of the fog.

A witch jumped from the shadows pressed her face close to Buck and Jake. "Well, what do we have here?"

Jake Underwood felt his son's body stiffen as he clung tighter. "It's okay," he whispered.

"What's your name little boy?" The witch paused, giving Buck a chance to respond and perhaps save himself. Seeing that fear paralyzed the child's ability to speak, she stomped her foot, demanding an answer.

"Go ahead," Jake said. "Tell her your name, son. It's okay."

The witch reached for Buck, her fingers unnaturally long, nails curled in a hideous gnarl. The wart, bent nose, and crooked hat completed a vision that leapt from the pages of a haunted storybook. Buck buried his face in his father's shoulder, arms locked tightly around the neck.

"I'm going to throw you in my stew." The witch cackled and let them pass, content to torment the next child in line.

"I told you I didn't want to come here. I told you." Buck's bottom lip quivered as small pools gathered below his eyes.

Funneled through a hanging gauntlet of severed legs, Jake hurried toward a crack of sunlight marking the exit. Car headlights flashed on and raced toward them, a horn blared, and Jake held his breath as he instinctively jumped back. Buck lost his grip and slipped from his father. The boy slumped to the floor where he sat, flopped on one side like a ragdoll.

Most of the visitors to the haunted house remarked that the firefighters outdid themselves with the headlight gag. The annual attraction received rave reviews from everyone, with one exception.. Solemn and defeated, Buck's life would never be the same.

Buck sat in the backseat and refused to speak during the ride home. Later that evening, Jake entered his room to tuck him in.

"Want to give your dad a hug goodnight?"

"I do. But I don't," said Buck, pulling the covers over his head.

———

Night crept toward dawn. Jake awoke to sobbing coming from his son's bedroom.

"I told you not to take him," Sandra said, clearly displeased. "I knew he wasn't old enough to handle a haunted house."

"Alright, already."

"No, it's not alright. He's only seven. Do you know he told me a witch wanted to throw him in the stew? He had tears in his eyes, Jake. Not smiles. Tears."

"C'mon, Sandy. He loves Halloween. Spooky stuff is part of the festivities. He's old enough to handle it."

"Just like he was old enough to watch *Die Hard?* Because you insisted it was a Christmas movie?"

Jake had honestly forgotten about the film's violence and language when he suggested the movie, but he knew better than to make excuses. Whenever Sandra was upset, it was always best to smile, nod, and keep his mouth shut.

Jake found the boy sitting on the floor beside the bed, hiccup-like sobs punctuating awkward sniffles.

"What's wrong, little bear?"

"The Munchers are coming." Buck stared at the wall. His pupils remained undilated when Jake waved a hand in his face.

"Did you have a bad dream, buddy? You know there are no *Munchers*, right?"

"There *are* Munchers, Dad. Mortaki told me all about them."

———

A two-foot-wide ribbon of morning sun cut through the kitchen and brightened the room. The cat positioned herself perfectly to allow both her head and tail to fit inside the yellow strip of light.

"Honeycombs?" Jake asked, handing the cereal box to his son.

"Yes, please," replied Buck, the trauma of the previous day apparently over.

"Trick-or-Treat is this weekend. Have you decided what you want to be? I could paint your face and make you a vampire."

"Dad, are vampires real?"

"No, buddy. They're make believe."

"Do you think maybe *some* of them are real?"

"Nope. They're only pretend."

"I don't like vampires. Too scary. I want to be something happy."

"Happy, eh? How about I put a big yellow ball over your head and paint a happy face on it." Jake grabbed the boy under his armpit and squeezed his giggle spot. Buck squirmed away laughing.

"No, Dad. I want to be a good guy; a superhero!"

"A superhero? We can do that. Which one?"

"The movie guy. I want to be the Black Panther."

Jake nodded. "T'Challa, the king of Wakanda. Sounds like a good choice."

———

That evening, Sandra Underwood stood in the hallway with a finger over her lips. Her head was slightly cocked as she squinted.

"Jake, come here. Quick."

"What is it?"

"Shhh. Quiet."

Jake, in a pair of striped boxers, tiptoed across the cold hard-wood floor, chilled by the late October weather. He heard talking and shook his head, certain he heard two voices.

"No, Mortaki, No … I don't want to. But what about the Munchers? Yes. Yes. Okay. Do you promise?"

Sandra nudged the bedroom door open to find. Buck standing in the corner, bare chested and wearing only his Spiderman pajama bottoms. He faced the wall with his hands behind his back. His eyes were closed. His head was tilted at an impossible angle toward the ceiling. Buck's mouth stayed open and created the perfect illusion of a sleepwalker.

"No, Mortaki!" he screamed, arms flying and little clenched fists swatting at the air.

Jake flinched at the sudden outburst, his knee smashing against the half-opened door. Buck turned, arms falling to his sides. His eyes opened and he looked at his father.

"I'm late for school." Buck said, distantly. He climbed into his bed and snuggled down under the covers. His soft breathing and the gentle rise and fall of the sheets confirmed he was asleep.

"What the hell was that about?" Jake looked at Sandra for an answer.

"You know what that's about, mister. That's about you forcing a frightened child into a scary haunted house."

"I didn't exactly make him."

"Do not go there. You dragged him in and carried him out."

———

Sandra laid overlapping sheets of newspaper on the kitchen floor while Jake washed dirt off a basketball-sized pumpkin.

"Buck, bring your drawings, it's time to cut this puppy open."

Buck presented a crayon sketch of a classic pumpkin face—triangle eyes and nose, jagged teeth. Jake handed his son a cheap steak knife.

"Carve away."

"Oh, no you don't," said Sandra, taking away the knife and gritting at Jake. "You carve, Buck directs."

Jake worked his magic and created a perfect Halloween jack-o'-lantern. He went off the menu with the eyes, curving them up in the corners, more cat-like than triangular, and the overabundant teeth ended up resembling pointed fangs.

"What do you think, Buck ol' boy? Is that scary or what?"

"I like it, Dad. It looks just like my drawing."

"What say you clean up all the pumpkin guts and I'll get us a candle."

"Ew, pumpkin guts! Gross, Dad."

Jake returned with a candle minutes later and his mouth fell open. He held the doorframe for support, inhaled deeply, and let out a sigh as Buck, grasping the knife in a firm overhand grip, slashed away at the pumpkin. He stabbed and hacked repeatedly at what remained of the face.

"Stop!" Sandra pushed into the kitchen and grabbed Buck's arm. "Why, Buck? Why did you do this?" She snatched the knife away and tossed it in the sink.

"He said the Munchers wouldn't like it. He said it was too scary," explained Buck.

Sandra felt her son's head, checking for a fever. "Is this enough festive fun for you, Jake?"

Jake ignored her question. "Who, Buck? Who told you this?"

"Mortaki. Jeez, Dad."

"Buck, you destroyed all of our work. Now we won't have a jack-o'-lantern for Halloween."

Buck shrugged. He jumped up and scurried away, leaving shredded pieces of a masterpiece for Jake to clean up.

"Dad," Buck called from the next room, "what's a turnip?"

"It's a vegetable, son," Jake mumbled, his mind not on the question.

"They're no good either," said Buck.

———

Buck shifted from one foot to the other and checked the street for the tenth time. He moved around with the anxious fidgeting of a little boy who needs to pee.

"Come on, Dad. Let's go. I see kids out already."

Buck, wearing a faux black Spandex shirt and pants, ankle-high boots, and gloves with plastic claws, dressed as the Black Panther as planned. Jake thought he looked more like Batman but he wasn't about to spoil the kid's fun.

An impossibly large harvest moon illuminated the annual game of dress-up and blackmail. Jake and Buck hit the streets while a smidgen of pale blue sky clung to the western horizon. Buck was determined to accumulate the world's biggest pile of candy. Jake zipped up his jacket and kept his hands in his pockets, regretting that he hadn't dressed in warmer clothes.

The first hour passed quickly, as dusk surrendered to evening.

"Your bag getting too heavy?" Jake asked.

"No way. Not even close. Anyway, I'm not giving in until we visit the big houses up the hill."

Oak Street twisted and turned as it rose to the crest, an unforgiving climb but well worth the effort. The estate homes ranking the ascent offered far better candy than the townhouses below. The barren trees, their leaves having fallen off weeks earlier, looked dead. But their emptiness provided Jake a glimpse into backyards normally camouflaged by foliage He spied multitier decks and inground pools with envy.

An unusual gust of cold air swept through the street. Buck stopped suddenly, frozen in the center of the sidewalk. Tumbling leaves spun around his feet, switching directions at will.

"I'm big enough," Buck said. "I can do it, Mortaki. I promise."

"Mortaki?" Jake asked. "Your imaginary friend?" He wanted to grab ahold of Buck and head home, but the boy sprung forward and ran toward a darkened house. The driveway held no cars and the property bore no decorations. Buck reached the door within seconds where a little clown, holding a semi-deflated balloon, waited patiently for someone to answer.

"Nobody home there, Buck. Go to the Wilsons. It's the next one over."

A miniature Spider-Man and an even smaller Ninja followed Buck to the Wilson driveway. A group of teenagers, in minimal costumes and without masks, busily gorged themselves on treats from their booty. They stepped aside to allow the little ones a clear path to the door where a scarecrow sat propped up in an adjacent lawn chair. Weathered straw hung from his boot tops, the waist of his denim jeans, and the sleeves of his red lumberman's jacket. Jake felt suspicious about the scarecrow and he moved in closer. The teenagers, aware of what was about to happen, shuffled positions for a better view. Hidden speakers began to play an off-key version of the tension-inducing jack-in-the-box song, about a monkey chasing a weasel. The eerie music further unnerved Jake.

Mrs. Wilson answered the door. She took one look at Buck and dropped the candy bowl.

"You're not supposed to be here," she said in a deep, angry voice, much unlike her own.

"Trick or treat," said Spider-Man.

"Oh, my. I don't know what came over me," Mrs. Wilson said in her normal, pleasant voice while bending over to retrieve a dozen tiny bags of chips. "Now, who do we have here?"

The kids added to their haul and said thanks. Jake flinched at the movement of a gloved hand and, still too distant to warn the children, watched as the scarecrow abruptly stood.

"Happy Halloween, you little rascals!" said Mr. Wilson, removing his scarecrow hat.

The Ninja cried, but Buck held it together and remained composed. "Gee whiz, Mr. Wilson. You really scared us good."

"You kids have fun tonight. And be safe."

As Jake and Buck headed up the hill toward the next house, Jake noticed a boy approaching. He was the same size as Buck, but his face looked much older. He wore a burlap bag like a dress. His eyes were dark and sunken. Long dirty hair flowed down the sides of his face and over his shoulders.

Creepy costume, Jake thought.

The boy drew closer and Jake saw the dirty bare feet, stained fingers, and unclipped nails.

"Hey, it's too chilly to be walking around with bare feet. You're gonna catch a cold," said Jake.

The boy stopped a few feet in front of them. A small gust ruffled his hair, accompanied by swirling leaves and the smell of rotten apples. He carried no candy sack but held a cloth doll by the arm, dragging the rest of it across the ground behind him.

"You live in this neighborhood?" Jake asked.

Although he felt the urgent tug on his pant leg, Jake ignored little Buck and stayed focused on the urchin-like stranger. The urchin said nothing but slowly opened a black, toothless mouth and smiled. He raised a hand with four equally long fingers and no thumb. The strange child pointed over Jake's head and down the hill.

A black curtain crept out of the shrinking horizon and slowly began to absorb everything in its path. Sidewalks and houses, lawns and driveways, all flickered like a heat mirage and were swallowed up. The curtain was not exactly a black hole, but more like an all-consuming entity that left nothing behind but an imageless void. Jake heard the distant sucking sound, the slurping and crunching. Underground pipes moaned and twisted as they were rendered from their housings. Electrical wires sparked for a brief second before vanishing into the advancing emptiness. A whiff of ozone hung in the air for only a moment longer before it, too, was consumed and sanitized into nihility.

Jake stood frozen in place, mouth agape, and watched the void creep closer. He wanted to run, but he couldn't decide where to go. Buck remained uncharacteristically calm, as if watching a city bus approach instead of the end of the world. He tugged harder on his father's pant leg and Jake finally looked down at his son.

"Munchers," Buck said, with the seriousness of someone much older. He squeezed his father's hand. "Come on, Dad."

The urchin blocked their path. He began taking exaggerated steps backward, easily outpacing Jake and Buck. He smiled, and his lips curved over his gums creating the illusion of an exceptionally long chin. He slowed so the father and son could close the distance. As soon as the duo were within an arm's reach, the urchin spat on young Buck.

"Hey, kid. What the hell are you doing?" Jake lunged for the guttersnipe, but the urchin fled, darting up the hill and dissipating into the night. His laughter trailed behind, forced and exaggerated, bouncing from one side of the street to the other, until it, too, faded away with one last whisper and an echo.

The streetlights blinked dim, then bright, and finally faded out completely. The lights in the homes lining the hill shut off in a rolling sequence. A dark purple glow covered the neighborhood in a silent dome. No leaves rustled on the sidewalk. The air remained still.

Jake looked pale and stumbled near collapse. The blood drained from his face and his shirt stuck to his back. A cold breeze rippled over his arm hair and he could hear his own pulse.

Not now, damn it. Keep it together, keep it together. He talked himself out of the panic attack and focused on his son.

"You okay, Buck?" Jake saw his own breath. A damp chill stung his cheek.

"We don't have much time, Dad."

The silence was uncanny. No traffic. No excited cries of children trick or treating. It all disappeared with the house lights. Only the orange glow from candles in carefully carved pumpkins escaped the blackout. An eerie contrast to the purple air.

"Where did everybody go?" Jake, stunned and confused, dragged his feet and looked heavenward. The oversized moon no longer brightened the sky. Even the stars refused to show themselves.

Buck tugged on his dad's wrist and tried to keep him moving along. Crunching sounds, stomping like an industrial press, chattered the silence and startled Jake back into action. He realized that he needed to ignore the insanity unravelling around him and focus on saving his son.

They walked uphill, following the orange glow shining from the pumpkins standing sentry on each doorstep. Their carved faces, no longer smiling, now appeared sinister and snarling. As Buck and his dad passed each driveway, the flame inside the jack-o'-lantern bent itself between crooked teeth and stretched downhill, creating a long thread of fire. The void sucked it in, stealing the heat and light. Each extinguished pumpkin rolled itself to the curb in preparation for the imminent black curtain.

"Pick up your feet, Buck. We need to go faster," said Jake, finally aware of the danger bearing down on them.

A beacon glowed from the crest of the hill. A lone flame waved from a candle propped in the grand window of the Millar mansion. The house predated the rest of the subdivision by a century and its position above the valley commanded a powerful view.

"This way, Dad. Run!"

Cement crumbled and broke apart, releasing billowing clouds of toxic dust that nipped at their heels. The driveway pitched and rolled like an ocean wave. Jake hoisted his boy up with one arm. He struggled to keep his balance and ascended the front steps with a drunken stagger. Not an eyelash of light escaped from the slightly open double French doors. Jake dove headfirst into the unknown. Buck landed atop him as they slid over the marble floor.

Once across the threshold, the foyer sparkled to life under the umbrella of a fabulous chandelier. At the bottom of the grand staircase stood an old man dressed in a tailed tuxedo with a maroon ascot in place of a tie. His white hair cascaded over his shoulders and his long arms bent back awkwardly at the elbows. He was tall and hovered over

Buck and his dad. An image of a praying mantis flashed through Jake's mind.

"I am Mortaki, master of this humble abode. You are Jake Underwood, I presume. Buck, I have met. I must say, governor, you spared no time getting here. Cut it mighty damn close if you ask me."

Mortaki closed the thick oak doors and turned the center deadbolt. The world eater paused its advance and the blackness waited at the edge of the property line. Before Jake could ask how Mortaki knew his name, and where he'd met Buck, storm clouds formed and circled the mansion. Gale-force winds whistled as they revved up and ripped at the outer walls. The front picture window rattled in its old wooden frame and a small crack skated from a corner, sliced across the glass, and threatened to spill out a waterfall of shards. The lonely candle flame, still burning, flickered and swayed in a dance all its own.

"What have you done, Jake? Look at the destruction you have caused." Mortaki offered Jake a hand and pulled him from the floor.

Mortaki's grip was strong for an old man and Jake felt uncomfortable in his presence. Despite the sanctuary of his home, Jake disliked the lanky elder and was suspicious, maybe even jealous, of Buck's apparent infatuation with him.

Jake studied his son and watched as the boy removed his panther costume and placed it neatly on a wingback chair.

"Why'd you take off your costume, Buck?"

"It's not time for trick or treats, Dad. Isn't that right, Mortaki?"

In the far corner a familiar rag doll sat slumped leaning head-first against the baseboard. Buck scurried over and retrieved it. A panel slid open and a four-fingered hand grabbed the boy's collar and pulled him behind the wall.

Jake charged to the spot and examined the panel, desperate to locate a point of entry. Finding nothing, he pounded on the wood and screamed.

"Mortaki! Where is my son, Mortaki?" Veins in Jake's neck bulged as he spat out the words. He turned to face the white-haired man, but Mortaki was gone.

"You torment your children with stories of monsters." Mortaki's voice came from above and echoed in the empty room.

Jake stood alone, staring at the ceiling and heard a second voice.

"I'm here, Dad. Over here."

Jake ran into the adjoining room, a study with a double wide fireplace. The hearth was cold and unused.

"You *entertain* them with programs depicting violence and slaughter." Mortaki's voice again came from above but it sounded even further away than the ceiling.

"Buck, can you hear me?" called Jake.

"You dress them up and take them to dark places of make-believe, exposing them to cult-like activities."

"I'm here, Dad. Help me!"

"Activities that worship the dead and celebrate evil."

Jake watched the contours of the ceiling and followed them into a library, the walls lined with leather-bound books and the shelf edges lined with dust.

"How much can their little minds sustain, Mr. Underwood? How much, I ask you?"

"Here, Dad. This way." Buck's voice called from further away and Jake backtracked to a sitting room beyond the front hall.

"You exposed your boy to powerful entities, dark and evil forces. Honestly, you humans are so reckless with your children."

"It's only Halloween," whispered Jake.

"Your son prayed to them. In his fear, he begged them to take it away, the costumes, the haunted houses, and wicked jack-o'-lanterns, all of it, Mr. Underwood, all of Halloween. The people, the buildings, everything."

Mortaki's voice sounded closer now and Jake followed it back into the great foyer. He found the conjurer standing exactly where he saw him last. The mantis-like man approached with an awkward jerk, as if his legs slightly preceded his body. The rest of him struggled to catch up before his legs moved again. He slinked from the corner and stood by the bannister, his old wrinkled eyes now twinkling and boring directly into Jake.

"Give me my son," demanded Jake.

Mortaki raised a hand and gestured to the front yard.

"This is his wish, his world, but you created it, Mr. Underwood. You set it in motion and enabled it to happen."

"I'm sure you had a part to play, you bastard."

Mortaki shrugged and lowered his head to hide a smile.

"There must be something I can do." Jake spoke aloud and to himself, but his words carried.

"You can do nothing. Only your son has the power to send them away. But he must do it alone, without you."

"Fair enough," said Jake, not knowing for sure what he intended to do and not willing to promise anything to the mantis.

The gale picked up to hurricane force and the windows imploded, spraying needles of glass into Victorian-era wallpaper. The candle, its flame extinguished, fell to the floor sliced in half. The storm rumbled louder than anything Jake had experienced, and the sound left him concussed. Lightning flashed within the house, directly above the grand staircase. Buck materialized on the steps and tumbled the rest of the way down. He came to a rest at his father's feet, none the worse for wear.

"Thanks for finding me, Dad."

Jake smiled and nodded. *I didn't find you, not really*, he thought.

Buck marched toward the exit, fully confident in what he was about to do. The French doors split and opened themselves. Freezing air blasted into the room. The force pinned Jake to the wall. He could only watch as his little boy fought his way down the driveway. The wind pulled at his clothes and squeezed the skin flat on his cheeks.

Jake's heart ripped open and he made a move to chase after his son.

"Come back, Buck!"

Fingers pinched Jake's shoulder, the nails pressing through his jacket and holding him firm. A shadow loomed above him and Jake felt warm breath upon his neck.

"He must go alone, governor!" Mortaki shouted in his ear loud enough to be heard over the gale.

Buck stood in front of the endless void, hands on hips. Unintimidated, he pointed to the left and then the right. Jake could that Buck was speaking, but the wind obscured any meaning. The boy threw his hands in the air as if he was releasing invisible doves. A chill crept around Jake's collar and spread across his back. He shivered with fear. Dread weighed him down, anchoring him in place. Buck turned his head toward his father and shrugged.

"No, Jake. Don't do it!"

Buck either couldn't hear or chose not to. Eyes closed, he raised his arm and punctured the wall with a single finger. An explosion of light ripped apart the dark fabric of the curtain, shredding it into specs of stardust, scattering it like a Fourth of July flare. The violent winds continued to circle and rose above the mansion, twisting themselves into a tight funnel and vanishing into the atmosphere.

Buck opened his eyes to see the full moon overhead. It illuminated a street filled with children dressed in colorful costumes. Pirates, witches, and zombies crisscrossed the road to carry out their candy-collecting chores. A stream of leaves chased one other over the pavement and swirled around Jake's legs. He smiled and exhaled heavily. All was right in the world.

Buck ran to Jake who dropped to his knees to embrace his son. Jake's eyes watered and threatened to leak, his emotions overflowed with pride and relief. Buck bypassed his dad, heading instead toward the open French doors.

"What are you doing? Don't go back in there, Buck. Come back!"

"I have to go, Dad. I forgot my costume."

The doors snapped shut behind the boy. Jake remained unmoving and held his head. He mumbled a mantra, *come back, come back, come back,* and prayed for his son's return. Moments later, the doors opened and Jake's happy little Black Panther appeared, dressed and ready to resume the evening's festivities. Buck bounced around and shifted from foot to foot. He tugged on Jake's pant leg and pointed to a whimsical group of princesses decked out in flowing pastel-colored dresses with matching ribbons in their hair.

Jake looked back at the Millar Estate, silhouetted by the yellow glow of the impossibly large harvest moon, and glimpsed something in an upstairs window. He thought maybe the curtain moved and a hand slapped the glass, or maybe it only waved.

"Did you see that?" he asked Buck, but the boy shook his head.

Beneath the super-hero costume, sunken eyes glowed like embers and sharp claws from a thumbless hand poked through the black jungle cat gloves.

"Trick or treat," whispered the urchin.

AUTHOR'S NOTE

First, you need to know that everything I write is true … up until a point, then exaggeration and imagination take over. *Munchers* is no exception. I enjoy writing dark, speculative fiction and I lose interest if the danger can be easily explained. Horror stories open unlimited possibilities that keep me entertained both as a reader and a writer.

Of course, horror authors have a kinship with Halloween, and many feel their body of work should include at least one tale set around that specific date. I'm one of those people and, up until *Munchers*, I had not written anything that included the traditions of jack-o-lanterns, disguises, and training children to blackmail their neighbors with threats of *trick or treat*.

I came up with an idea of a revenge story where a father is punished for being too careless pushing the holiday on his children and I started with the truth. Buck is loosely modeled around one of my children and the opening scene at the fireman's haunted house occurred pretty much exactly as written (even the part where the witch threatens to put him in the stew). The experience traumatized the little guy and I was in the doghouse at home. Buck didn't destroy the pumpkin, but he did refuse the good night kiss with the wonderful line *"I do but I don't."*

Buck didn't dress as the Black Panther that year. (The movie was still 20 years from release.) He went as a vampire and I specifically remember him asking if vampires were real and then asking again, *"Do you think maybe some of them are real?"* In hindsight, he was terrified.

The urchin came from a dark corner of my imagination and the rest of the story is every parent's worst nightmare—losing a child. I wanted Buck to succeed, I really did. But I had to throw that twist in at the end. Don't blame me. It's in my nature. I'm a horror writer.

I almost forgot. There is one more creepy detail to share with you. One night around the same time, Buck really did mumble the name Mortaki. Whom he was talking about remains a mystery.

DA

...AND ALL THE TRIMMINGS

J.C. RAYE

PROFESSOR NORMAN Tack sat very still inside the oversized tow sack as the little creatures bore him away across the frosty, December evening sky, surely bound for what would be a grave, if not unpleasant, incomprehensible fate. While other abductees might have shouted and flailed or set about ingeniously transforming a stainless-steel pen into an improvised weapon in preparation for a daring Hollywoodesque escape, such was not the case with Norman. It simply was not in Norman's makeup to do so. He was a thinker. A theorist. Not so much a coward. The details were always such a distraction for the man, always inhibiting any decisive or compelling action on his part. Instead of worrying *where* they might be taking him, or *what* actually took him, at this moment, the professor was genuinely trying to place the pungent odor of the scratchy fabric surrounding him. An endless ride of jolts and jerks in complete and terrifying blackness, the assurance of yet another herniated disc in the near future, while Norman inhaled big whiffs of air, trying to decide between paint varnish or graham crackers.

Professor Tack was lovingly referred to by both students and colleagues alike as *Tic-Tack*. He'd inherited the nickname either because of an unmistakable, square, pale head, or the irritating but reliable chatter of boxed breath mints that emanated from the pocket of his tan corduroy jacket on any given day. Presently he was not even leaning toward the casting of blame, as most would in this scenario. Certainly, a dramatic, rather supernatural–and very public–kidnapping on a medium-sized college campus like Carroll University might not have occurred if the school grounds been equipped with adequate lighting, or if a single security officer had been present on the long path back to the west faculty lot. And yes, there were others on the walkway who might have served as more enchanting victims. Several attractive yet unattached coeds had been milling about, cluelessly texting on their cells, each no doubt capable of emitting a blood-curdling scream. There had also been older, tenured, more cadaverous colleagues tottering out to their strategically parked Audis in the furthest regions of the lot. These, the creatures might have swept away with ease and, conceivably, procured a booty of greenbacks and a Rolex in the process. Norman, therefore, concluded that the little *jabbas* must have wanted *him*, specifically, as they scooped him up and plunked him into their sack. He didn't fuss then, and he wasn't fussing now. Unwisely perhaps, he was more curious than anything else.

Jabbas. Norman's first impression. Firing into his grey matter the instant they effortlessly floated down from the foliage in wooly three-piece suits, to surround him on the gravel. Indeed, they reminded him of the repulsive alien-gangster from the *Star Wars* mythos. Noggins shaped like slowly melting chocolate kisses, and wide slit-eyes, gleaming golden, which erupted from thick folds of moist amphibian skin. In all honestly, these were far less intimidating than the movie character, as not a one of the creatures rose over two and a half feet tall. There was also that added, innocuous, sugar-plum coloring which made them almost doll-like. Dolls with the strength of sumo wrestlers who had mastered the power of flight.

—

Hands clasped behind his back, bedecked in a velvet, burgundy dressing gown with a quilted emerald green silk collar, Norman turned circles on the tufted rug in front of a crackling fire in the great reading room. As he travelled, he stared down and scowled at twin idiotic snowman faces crocheted into the slipper socks the jabbas had bestowed upon him. Seven pairs in all. These, the least emasculating. Norman's patience waned. It was a new and altogether disturbing emotion for the 60-year-old humanities lit professor.

It seemed to Norman that the Christmas elves (he knew this now) had kept him captive a little more than two weeks. *Certainly, the remaining days until the holiday must be few,* Norman thought. Yet to his great dismay, this unspecific supposition was the very limit of how certain he could be about the passage of time during his captivity. Norman was losing track of the days. Not at all surprising and completely forgivable, when one's surroundings no longer included the customary, recognizable patterns and mechanisms that parceled out normal human existence. The rooms he was allowed to see were bereft of clocks and calendars. From what Norman could fathom, his pint-sized captors, (beyond numbering in the hundreds) also bore no timepieces, whether wrapped around chubby eggplant wrists or dangling from a fob chained to a cherry-red waistcoat. And, though all the rooms featured towering windows, as befitting a Gothic Santa Clausian estate, none were transparent. Norman noted that the windows were not glass but a type of iron-hard colored ice, which never indicated any change of light outside, whether dawn or dusk. Each window a unique stained glass depiction that included colorful background details–decorations, lights, and all the trimmings. Strategic shards weaving the glory of Santa. Flying the sled over a beaming yellow moon. Feeding reindeer. Descending from a chimney. Visiting joyful children in faraway lands. The renderings reminded Norman of the stained glass Stations of the Cross he'd seen portrayed in churches.

These creatures, Norman concluded, seemed to have power over ice, snow, and water. He did not really notice it when they appropriated him against his will. Too much to take in then. He had assumed they were floating or flying. At closer inspection later, he observed their power of flight to be manufactured by a steady spool of churning ice crystals beneath their feet. Infinitesimal. Soundless. Serving any whim, at any speed, and in any direction. The unbreakable windows, many of the door locks, and even the fireplace were mystifying and fantastic examples of this strange technology. The fire looked and acted like a fire. It emanated heat and dispensed the traditional blend of colors, pops and sizzles. Yet, it was made entirely of ice and, therefore, required neither a refreshment of logs nor supervision. Norman assumed that Santa and the elves had avoided detection by utilizing this same unnerving skill. *Perhaps this entire estate is safely tucked inside an ice mirage of some kind*, he thought.

Norman was allowed unlimited access to this space, a great reading room, via a connecting door to his bedroom. This room, undoubtedly the man cave of Old Saint Nick. It was by the far the grandest part of the compound. The enormous rectangular room was filled floor to ceiling with bookshelves containing several thousand hardcovers that were inserted into an ocean of shining Italian walnut linenfold panels. In the center of each panel, an emblem of holly had been etched. A brightly painted fresco of fir branches adorned the 15-foot-high ceiling. Norman felt that it provided the room with a kind of *protected* feeling, and a sense of comfort and warmth, despite the fearsome tempests beyond the walls which howled constantly. At least Norman *assumed* it was a storm outside, and not an insistent chorus of hungry wolves requesting a raw elf dinner, but he had no way of knowing.

Eight interior columns flanked the longer walls. Exquisite carvings of poinsettia garlands were twisted around each like the stripe on a candy cane. The leather chairs were wide and comfortably broken in. Drapes and their tiebacks, however, were noticeably absent, perhaps to prevent detainees from inflicting self-harm.

The focal point of the space was the massive fireplace at one end of the vast chamber. Reliefs of toys were hand-carved into the yellow marble. Norman counted four dozen in all. Each figure was so punctiliously sculpted into the stone, that from afar, it seemed the toys might snap to life at any moment and leap down from their station to freedom. The mantle reached well above 12 feet, above which hung a strange coat of arms that appeared to have been constructed of a mixed media rather than pure metal. A trickle of dried skins hung from the coat, and from this Norman could only assume that Santa, in his spare time, was a small game hunter. *Everyone's got their vices,* he mused.

Reading was a most powerful distraction from Norman's piteous circumstance. Norman attributed his constant physical pain and the increasing ache in his scalp to be the result of an allergic reaction or blossoming infection caused by either the plucking of all his native sandy brown hair or the expedited ten thousand hair grafts of white llama hair which followed, expedited over his first four agonizing days in captivity. The elves, it seems, were unaware of ibuprofen. They did, however, recognize suffering, and were quick to provide their custom icepacks following any of Norman's many surgeries.

The library books were Norman's means to self-heal. He soon discovered that the library collection was more than just eclectic, it was astonishing. Among the many delightful items on its ledges were a 15th century *Book of Lismore*, a *Gutenberg Bible*, and the *Codex Leicester* by Leonardo Da Vinci. Norman almost mistook Leonardo's rose-colored tome for a placemat while looking to set down his daily mug of mulled cider. A colleague at Carroll had shared with him years ago that only one such copy existed, the original, penned single-handedly by the mathematician himself, and acquired by Bill Gates in the 1990s. Norman had no idea whether any of these books were copies or originals, obtained legally or criminally. For all he knew, Santa was a closet biblioklept.

In the early days of this compulsory call, farthest from the fireplace, and deep in shadows at the back of the great library, Norman found a section of books that seemed a mismatch, a subdivision of sorts, almost at odds with the room itself. These shelves were a disorganized mess, and clearly a signpost of steady activity outside of his peaceful visiting hours. Here, books were tipped over onto their sides or half pulled away from their ledges. Large piles stacked haphazardly crowded the floor, surrounded by others splayed open with pages bent or torn, looking as if they had been carelessly lobbed from several feet away.

The professor picked up one of these and scanned its cover. Upon inspection, Norman noticed that these were not bound books, but leather journals with buckle closures, though many of the straps were missing as a result of their apparent abuse. The brown leather was hard and thick, perhaps buffalo rather than goat or cowhide. The front of the journal contained a rendering of a toy soldier that had been meticulously embossed into the grain. Inside the journal, Norman found step-by-step instructions describing how to make the toy. No words or text. No table of contents. Only diagrams and drawings. The last few pages featured color palettes and strokes specific to the painting of eyes, shoes, and uniform. Norman tucked the journal neatly back onto a shelf and selected one that teetered on a ledge.

Norman looked over his shoulder to confirm that he was still alone, uncertain how his little *friends* might respond to an outsider spying on trade secrets. Then again, Norman reasoned, creatures who trimmed their toenails with their teeth were not likely beleaguered by the concept of intellectual property being stolen out from under them. This second journal was much chunkier. Spinning tops in tin and wood, and a vast array of painted design samples. Everything from cowboys to ballerinas to astronauts to dinosaurs. Other journals he found, on higher shelves and coated in dust, were those of what Norman assumed to be toy concepts that had lost their popularity, such as wind-up racecars or wooden horses with wheeled feet.

Norman concluded that these journals had been prepared by Santa. He now made a rather exhilarating connection. Norman recalled that several days ago, face deep in *Arabian Nights*, he heard a breathy exhalation behind him. He'd looked up to see an elf, rather lanky, but with a slightly oversized cranium, just inside the paneled door, observing him quite strangely. Norman had smiled at the creature, nodded and held his book aloft as if to express his enjoyment of it. The elf regarded him for a moment more, then placed his hands on his hips, shook his head, and left the room. *That was it.* The jabba did not seem to understand the concept of reading. Perhaps Claus quietly suppressed this skill, fearing it would result in reduced productivity.

—

Two days after they removed his nose and replaced it with that of a crimson-faced uakari monkey, the combination of itch and throb in Norman's snout could not be satiated by another afternoon of Melville, Austin, Tolstoy. Norman headed over to the north wing with a hankering for Yorkshire pudding, and maybe a bit of treacle sponge cake. If there were any benefits at all to being slowly torn asunder, body part by body part, and *Frankensteined* into a Santa Claus (which he now assumed was happening) it was the food. A feast was ongoing at any time of day. Not a meal. A *feast*. The likes of which King Henry Tudor might have drooled over. Trifle, custards, cookies, and cakes. Duchess potatoes soaked in butter. Roasted brussels sprouts. Cranberry and chestnut salad. Glazed ham and beef Wellington. Roast duckling. Stuffed capons.

Apparently, the elves worked in rotating shifts to ensure that Santa's dining hall was always set for a scrumptious repast. The creatures also seemed to eat in shifts as well. Day and night, the hall was jammed with their smelly purple selves, elbow to elbow, deafeningly blabbering away in their slushy, phlegmy, undecipherable mother tongue. Norman usually prepared a tray to take back to his bedroom, after spending a good deal of time searching for unmolested portions on the large serving platters, since the creatures were seemingly unaware of silverware or the decorum of chewing with lips zipped. The professor could have eaten 24 hours a day if he so fancied. Portion control supervision did not exist. No surprise there. Unless they were planning to use a tire inflator on his belly in the last hours before Christmas.

As he passed through the connecting hallway lined with thick timber beams and reindeer portraits, two of the jabbas burst out of the toy shop which was immediately to his right. One had a chisel handle protruding from his eye socket. His eye gushed purple elf juice all over the damn place. He chased the other with large red hand saw. Norman literally dove out of their way. Losing his balance, he painfully thumped his funnybone on the corner of Donner's likeness. His presence was unnoticed by the elves. The elf being chased shrieked in fear, and the other, unbelievably, still functioning with the business end of a metal chisel driven deeply into his skull, growled like a deranged hound. They soon disappeared down the hall.

But now, the toy shop, which Norman had never been allowed to see, was open. Consumed with their Two Stooges cabaret, neither elf had bothered to closed and lock the door. It was far too tempting.

———

A deep disappointment to be sure. Even though his rather lofty expectations of Santa's famous toy shop might very well have been pieced together from childhood memories of Rankin/Bass stop-motion animation. This was a mess. This was *wrong*. Overturned tables. Tools scattered along the floor. Spilled paint cans. Norman treaded carefully to avoid tripping. Near one of the many spills, little purple hands had finger painted a reindeer with three heads and a long penis with holly berries growing on it.

There were no complete toys to be found at all, only parts in progress, though some of the instructional journals from the library lay about as well. The finger painter seemed to have been working on these, too, penis theme persisting. Someone had painted a crooked checkerboard directly onto a table and used a hoard of doll's eyes as the pieces. Several shelves were cramped with rag dolls, piled and pushed onto each other in twos and threes. The dolls were missing arms, legs, and dresses and had been placed in disturbing positions. One had been crucified with pencils, a painted tear beneath one of her eyes. At the far end of the room, nails had been carefully driven into the wall in the shape of an elf's face that resembled Norman's lanky, cranium-endowed friend. It appeared as the nail outline was used for a game of rasp file darts. Someone had even thrown an axe.

Norman slipped on a paint can lid and lost his balance. Midflight, he caught the vision of a chisel hanging off a bench seat, fast approaching his face. His decision to attempt an army roll came late and failed for a several reasons, not the least of which was the fact that Norman knew precious little about actually performing the maneuver. He fell hard and his shoulder landed directly inside an open box of tacks. A few of them stuck. His first thought was not registering new pain, but the fear he had somehow damaged his nose. He lifted his hand to check. All good. He then started to remove the little silver thumbtacks embedded in his flesh, using plyers to extract the stubborn ones. There was a bit of bleeding, and Norman spotted an overturned journal just under the table near him. Though not ideal, the loose pages would, Norman determined, be useful in blotting the blood.

———

It was not a mislaid instructional journal from the library at all. And it was *clearly* not authored by Santa. Jabba hand. Norman was quite sure it was a never meant for his eyes. The first three-quarter cluster of pages was meticulously rendered; vivid colors, exquisite lines. This illuminated manuscript might have rivaled any medieval monk's sketchbook, stretching back in the elves' history to the time when Santa first brought them here. The renderings upon the weathered pages depicted hundreds of elves, chained together and attached to the tail of a very large beast, against a landscape that matched their coloring. If the professor had to liken the monster-jailor portrayed to any earthly animal, he might settle on the capybara, a South American desert rodent, but one that was over 80 feet long and weighed 300,000 pounds. Clearly under duress, the elves were churning up the ice under their feet to keep the beast cool. Drawings depicted other beasts scuttling about too. Skinnier ones, toothier ones, eating smaller jabbas, possibly elf children.

Turning the pages, Norman learned how Santa, under cover of night and in small groups, had chauffeured the elves away through the stars to bring them to his snowy sanctuary. The years that followed looked very happy, with elves being clothed, learning to cook, and blissfully crafting beautiful teddy bears and model trains while always, *always,* maintaining a blind deference to, and passionate admiration for, the man who had rescued them from space rodents. It was here, Norman noticed, that the pages had become dislodged. The leaves were handled. Crumpled. Stuffed in. The art chaotic, shoddy, with a touch of rage.

Apparently, Santa had gone through a change. Alzheimer's? Mental illness? Norman could not be sure. Illustrations showed the man wandering off naked into the hills and often breaking toys in anger. Pages and pages of elves being slapped, kicked, and pummeled. As the violence increased, so did the weapons of choice; whips, belts, mallets. A bloody scene laid out like a pornographic centerfold recounted the night Santa murdered all of the reindeer with an augur.

Norman did not really need to see the final pages, a helly, holly, wholly predictable, *'Twas the Night,* surefire sequel, in which hundreds of jabbas finally maxed out on a life of pain, over *two* planets nonetheless. However, like any worthwhile literature professor, he felt compelled to read the story to its end.

Norman dropped the journal and raced back to the library, his craving for Yorkshire pudding or other nourishment utterly forgotten.

Norman pushed the chair closer to the fireplace. He felt the heat intensify on his knees as he stood atop the chair. Not that it mattered. He needed a closer look.

Yes, they had done it. What he had mistaken for a rabbit or martin carcass slung over the coat of arms were, in fact, slices of dried human skin and century-old tangles of white curly hair. They had killed him. Killed him long ago. And had evidently enjoyed the killing. Had taken their time with each ritualistic slice of the vicious tyrant. Had reveled in the newfound freedom and the end to their endless nightmare.

Norman's mind worked quickly to assemble a puzzle that forming in his mind but still lacking various pieces. After a time, he deduced, one of the elves, possibly the one with the large cranium, must have realized that the world might *miss* Santa or look for him. Maybe the elves thought everyone on Earth behaved like Santa and they'd be horribly punished. Maybe they feared the world would send another oppressor to take his place. In any case, Norman concluded that this was why they needed him. And others. Probably others too. *Each year.* They needed a Santa.

For the first time in weeks, Norman felt real fear. He also felt terribly decisive. Norman hopped down off the chair, resolving, for the first time in his life, to take a compelling action. *Of course*, Norman thought, *taking a compelling action is easier said than done when 12 purple chocolate kiss creatures topple you to the ground.* Because that's exactly what they did.

When they finally seated him in the wooden sleigh, Norman lacked even an ounce of resistance. Not that it mattered since he was outnumbered at least fifty to one. Norman knew without any doubt that his hour of reckoning was approaching. It seemed as if every resident had put down their figgy pudding pops and red-handled saws to see him off. Many helped load the countless toy sacks onto the sleigh. As the tears streamed down Norman's face–absorbed into the thick white llama beard only recently sewn into the fleshy part of his lower cheeks–he moaned horribly and pleaded for release. Of course, many of his words now were mostly unintelligible due to a current lack of dental fricatives. The elves then shoved a translucent rubber mouthpiece, slathered with a gelatinous and sticky goo, into his yowling mouth. A wide hole in the rubber enabled breathing between his gums.

Now Norman understood last night's dental visit, which had resulted in the removal of his teeth, one by excruciating one. His choppers would chatter and break when his face was being mercilessly pounded by the icy gale. A Santa with a bleeding mouth might be quite a shock for anyone possessing a telescope with an aperture of 70 mm or higher. Rosy cheeks were fully expected. Bloody shattered fangs, not so much. While some of the jabbas snapped Norman's boots into the clamps bolted to the sleigh floor, others tightly belted in his body and pushed his right arm into the iron brace. This gave the appearance that Norman was waving. Waving forever.

—

As the sleigh launched into the sky, the elves had the audacity to wave goodbye to him. They cheered as if he were a champion, as if they did not expect him to return from his trip an unrecognizable skeleton murdered by their own purply selves. As he rose, their figures became tinier and tinier, yet Norman could still see the celebratory dance which broke out in their ardent merriment. A devilish and floating Do-Si-Do.

—

Occasionally the reindeer, crafted entirely of hoarfrost, would sharply accelerate upward, climbing above the cloud rim. This was most likely done to avoid impact with obstacles and transmitted by slushy sonar inserted into their lifeless skulls. These motions jerked Norman blindly through long and terrifying veils of white. The seat pushing against his back, and his back muscles pushing against loosely connected organs inside his body. His eyes shut tightly, fully anticipating collision with a flock of wayward geese or the razor-sharp propellers of a helicopter. Perhaps he just waited to hear the piercing snap of the harness breaking off, as he and his jingling red coffin tumbled backward into the night sky. At other times, and again, without warning, the team would plummet downward on a 90-degree angle. Frightening though these dips were, screaming was out of the question, as during this zero-G air time, Norman had to focus all his energy on remembering to breathe.

As the reindeer team straightened out once again, Norman saw the lights of cities below begin to lessen and then disappear altogether. He knew that vast carpet of blackness which now appeared beneath him was an ocean. Norman heard a rustle behind him. Unmistakably, a toy sack, shifting. Though his body was locked in place, Norman's head was not. It took more effort than expected to twist his face sideways and he could hear and feel a crackling on his neck where frost had accumulated. But now Norman was finally able to identify the source of the sound, and his heart thumped with life anew.

The lanky elf had freed itself from a sack and was now clambering over the back of the bench to reach him. Had Norman any tears left to cry, he would have cried them. The elf immediately set to freeing him from his Yuletide bonds. First, he unstrapped the professor's belting and his arm from the bar. It was numb as hell, and there'd be a ruthless outbreak of pins and needles to follow, but at least, Norman acknowledged, he still had full function of the appendage. Now the elf moved to the floor, breaking the locks which held the boot clamps in place. Once unfettered, the elf freed each foot from its black rubber boot. Producing the red wool slipper socks like a magician pulling a dove from the air, he helped Norman slide his feet into them. The elf bore other surprising gifts, such as a warm and wonderful patchwork quilt adorned with fir trees. He placed it around Norman's shoulders. He also presented a small thermos steaming with hot mulled cider.

After gulping down half of the warm liquid, Norman placed both hands on the elf's shoulders, looked deeply into the creature's eyes, and nodded. Norman hoped the elf with the large cranium would understand how grateful he was for having saved his life, and the kinship he now felt for the creature. And when the professor was sure the lanky elf had received the message loud and clear, he let go.

The valiant little jabba assisted Norman in climbing out of the bench chair, motioning for him move toward the back, among the sacks, perhaps to have more room up front to untie the reigns and regain control of the sleigh. Norman's will to take direction from his new hero was fervent, but his body could only navigate sluggishly, muscles sending irritating pain memorandums to the spine. At that moment, Norman felt his entire body being lifted. Just under the shoulders, vertically first, then horizontally, at the hands of a gentle, purple sumo wrestler. Elevated effortlessly, as if he wasn't stuffed tight with coconut rum balls and eggnog cheesecake.

—

The archipelago of the Lakshadweep Islands sits approximately 250 miles off the west coast of India. Had Pitti Island been inhabited, had it not been declared a tern sanctuary by the government in the 1960s, perhaps someone might have been lounging on the empty beach and spotted the Santa Claus, who tumbled out of a bank of clouds in the direction of Antarctica. At first, the Santa appeared as a giant red snowflake, butt and belly rotating, arms and legs flailing in all directions. But he quickly modified into more of a shuttlecock, body mass down, picking up speed as he screamed toward the Indian Ocean. To the surprise of the little jabba with the oversized cranium, Norman did not churn up the ice crystals under his feet to break his fall.

AUTHOR'S NOTE

I was raised to imagine and fully expect a worst-case-scenario for every action I take. Anticipate the vilest, nastiest outcome possible, so anything better feels like a joyous miracle, like a party worth celebrating. It's a twisted way to live, I admit. But then of course, I didn't raise me, someone else did. I suppose this deeply embedded, quite disturbing canon spills over onto many of my poor main characters. Terrifying realizations just one second after it is much too late to do anything about it. Maybe one day they'll wreak their dreadful revenge upon me for not providing them with any hope of escape. I certainly deserve no less. See? There I go again. I'm damaged goods to be sure.

JCR

THE DOGGONE GHOST

BERNIE BROWN

MARVIN TRUELOVE prided himself on his small feet. In fact, he fussed over every detail of his appearance. As head salesman in men's suits at Clark's Department Store, Marvin maintained a high standard, the likes to which he hoped his clientele would aspire.

Attention to detail also marked the care Marvin took within his department. Each morning, Marvin arrived early to ensure that each suit was properly buttoned. He also arranged stray suits, making certain that they all faced the same way on the rack and hung in ascending order of size. The morning of May 31 was no different. Marvin surveyed his sartorial kingdom with a pride seldom scene at the store.

Everything in men's suits stood ready and waiting for a banner sales day. Or did it?

Marvin's instincts twitched. Like beacons, his eyes scanned the sales floor. Not one speck of dust remained on the rack top displays. The shoes were polished and shone like mirrors. The socks display created a rainbow of color. Yet, despite this perfection, the thin hairs on the back of Marvin's slender neck stood at cautionary attention. Something was amiss.

Marvin checked the aisle that separated suits from athletic wear. He swiveled his neat little neck all the way down to outerwear and back to the changing rooms. Nothing unusual to be found.

He slowly walked up and down each aisle, checking between racks. All was well. At last he reached the aisle that led to the elevators. His inner alarm sounded loud and clear. Something was not quite right. In a moment he knew what it was.

"Oh, doggone it," Marvin said. This was the harshest expletive he would allow himself. "Doggone it. Doggone it. Doggone it." He ran a finger under his shirt collar, which suddenly felt too tight. It had happened again. Alarm mounting, he hurried to the display next to the elevator bays.

For the third time this year, the suit on the meticulously dressed mannequin—a double-breasted Yves Saint Laurent cotton-wool blend adorned with matching shirt and tie—had been replaced with something entirely inappropriate.

A bikini.

It was, in fact, the yellow polka dot variety popularized in that dreadful Brian Hyland song from Marvin's youth. The prankster had even stuffed several pairs of Calvin Klein socks—one of the most expensive lines— into the top to provide the mannequin a most unwelcome bustline. Marvin rushed to the storeroom to fetch the stepladder and undo the culprit's handiwork.

Marvin hastily redressed the mannequin. He was desperate to complete the task before the store opened and before Mr. Derleth, the tightly wound display manager, made his morning rounds. Marvin recalled the pranks from earlier in the year. In February, the mannequin had been dressed in a sequined thong, the type Marvin thought were completely inappropriate and ought to be declared illegal. In early April, it had been a skirted design.

"I'll bet the stock boy, Weaslie, is to blame," Marvin had complained to management following the second incident. "I did scold him for his sloppy unpacking, to which he told me to go to…" Marvin hesitated. "H-E double hockey sticks."

"Couldn't have been Weaslie. HR sacked him a week ago. You weren't the only one to complain about him."

Marvin couldn't imagine that anyone else would hold a grudge against him. He barely socialized with his coworkers. He ate his lunch in the breakroom, alone and away from the others, and abstained from caffeine, thus having no reason to socialize on a coffee break.

He had only ever quarreled with one other person at Clark's, though that was years ago, back when Marvin was a lowly stock boy. He didn't like to think about that. It had ended badly.

———

There. Finished. And with no time to spare. Marvin patted the elevator mannequin's expertly tied necktie, descended the stepladder, and hurried to return it to the stockroom.

Marvin hated the stockroom. Mysterious pipes and cables crisscrossed the cavernous ceiling. Metal lamps hung up there amidst all the apparatus. *Probably as dusty as the Sahara*, Marvin thought. *The doggone place is just plain spooky.*

A scraping sound emerged from behind a stack of boxes. Marvin shivered. He quickly hung the stepladder on its hook and turned to return to the comfort of the sales floor. *Clang!* He jumped and then turned to see that the ladder had fallen. *Must not have secured it.* He rehung it, this time making certain it was secure. Marvin rushed to leave. *Clang! Clatter!* The stepladder fell again. Marvin glanced over his shoulder.

"Tattle tale. Tattle tale. Hanging from a bull's tail." The voice came from behind those boxes and sounded vaguely familiar.

"Who's there?" Marvin called. His query was met with silence. *Oh, just leave the doggone ladder on the floor,* he thought. Perspiration gathered on his forehead. Marvin patted it with his neatly folded pocket square and quickly left the room.

—

Marvin nearly skidded to a halt by the elevator mannequin just as Mr. Derleth made his rounds. "I like this suit, Truelove. Might buy one for myself."

"You would look very distinguished in it, sir." Marvin hoped Mr. Derleth didn't notice that he was panting like a marathon runner. Stress made Marvin's heart beat irregularly, too. He took quinidine for arrhythmia.

—

The day passed without further incident. The store's Memorial Day sale didn't break any records, but a nice stack of receipts filled the accordion folder under the counter. At nine o'clock, Marvin checked the dressing rooms for merchandise, turned off the lights, and hoped that the elevator mannequin would remain properly dressed overnight.

Thoughts of the one man who might hold a grudge, might wish him ill, crept into Marvin's head. Marvin Truelove's mind was too tired to keep them out.

On several occasions in the early 1960s, during Marvin's years as a stock boy, he had encountered Harvey Busterd, the head salesman of men's suits at that time, behaving inappropriately with Ethel Fairwether of formal wear. On numerous occasions, Marvin had nearly tripped over them in the stockroom, their arms wrapped around each other like twin boa constrictors. Marvin recalled the time the staff elevator doors opened to reveal Busterd's disgustingly pimpled backside, Ms. Fairwether pressed against the wall. Then there was the time when he'd heard their passionate cries, moans, and grunts escape from one of the toilet stalls in the men's room. By late 1967, Marvin could take no more.

Marvin had reported his observations to the human resources manager—a most uncomfortable conversation. It happened that that the brother of the HR manager was engaged to Ms. Fairwether. Word got around and both Fairwether and Busterd were let go "to pursue other opportunities."

But all that was so long ago, Marvin reasoned. *Water under the bridge, bygones being bygones, forgotten down memory lane.* Or was it?

Marvin suddenly recalled the long-forgotten handful of anonymous letters he'd received in the mail almost immediately following Busterd's termination. Each note, hand written on Clark's Department Store stationary…

TATTLE TALE. TATTLE TALE. HANGING FROM A BULL'S TAIL.

A chill shot through Marvin's body as another realization surfaced from the recesses of his mind. *He's dead. Ms. Fairwether's fiancee shot and killed Busterd, point blank, only weeks after learning about the affair.*

At that moment, Marvin turned as a shadow caught his attention. He stared, dumbfounded, as the tweed three-piece suit he was about to rehang, a Martin Brothers design with suede elbow patches, puffed up as if Griffen himself, the ill-fated protagonist in H.G. Wells' *The Invisible Man*, had stepped into it. The chest expanded and the arms took shape, flexing to display the elbow patches. Soon after, those arms pushed aside the gabardine navy and the gray twill. The legs took form and the entire suit stood tall to stretch its tweedy arms. It had shape and bulk like a man, but was devoid of flesh. No bespectacled professor's head gave the garment dignity. No hands extended from the sleeves to sport an old school class ring. Only floor existed where brogues might have completed the look. Marvin stared, half-convinced he was dreaming, but the fluttering rhythm of his faulty heart convinced him otherwise.

The living garment approached Marvin and swatted his cheek, the wool scratchy and dry. Marvin backed away, staring, a fierce flush rising where he had been struck. He was struck again, harder this time but still little more than a slap. Still, the force surprised Marvin and he stumbled backward and nearly fell to the floor. His weak heart responded. *Guh thump thumpitty thump guh thump thump.*

The suit lunged for Marvin. He turned and ran. He ran past the socks display, disrupting its orderly arrangement. He careened past sport coats, toppling the belts perched in the center of the rack. He rounded the corner into the stockroom. The dreaded stockroom. He imagined the dusty light fixtures laughing at him.

The suit, now quite the animated inanimate object, was at his heels, snatching at Marvin.

Marvin ducked in and out of the stacked boxes and discarded display racks. One rack tipped over with a resounding clang.

The suit continued its pursuit.

Marvin headed for the back stairs. He despised the back stairs, so littered with cigarette butts and dead insects. Carelessly, Marvin's toe struck the metal guard on the top step. The suit gave him a mighty push in the center of his back.

He tumbled for what seemed an eternity, bouncing.

Crack.

There went a rib.

He tumbled further.

His left arm popped out of its joint.

And further still.

One ankle folded under him. Excruciating pain shot up his leg and back. Marvin landed hard on his head, and a fearsome wrench shot through his neck. Now semi-conscious, Marvin wondered if the demonic suit would follow him down the stairs to finish the job it had started.

"Who…are you?" he managed, voice trembling.

Over the sound of his irregular heartbeat, Marvin heard a reply.

"Why, doggone it. I think he's dead. Tattle tale. Tattle tale. Hanging from a bull's tail."

Martin winced at the high-pitched cackle that echoed in the stairwell as a shadow fell over him.

Marvin Truelove heard no more.

AUTHOR'S NOTE

I found humor creeping into some personal essays I'd written, and it is an important element in the novel I am currently writing. Those essays and the novel led me to wonder if I could write a ghost story that had an element of humor. "The Doggone Ghost" is my attempt at creating a humorous ghost story.

The setting is derived from a job I held in the late 1960s. I worked in the display department at Gold's Department Store in Omaha, Nebraska. There I learned about mannequins (how to assemble and disassemble them) and how to arrange an attractive tabletop display. But the most interesting thing I learned was that behind the tempting sales areas in attractive department stores exist creepy back rooms akin to neglected attics. A ghost could happily thrive in those rooms and emerge when the sales floors were deserted. It is in this type of storeroom that the ghost of Harvey Busterd waited to seek its revenge upon Marvin Truelove one fateful May evening.

BB

WAVES

ROBIN HILL-PAGE GLANDEN

"COME ON, MOMMY, take me to the beach, seven-year-old Dylan begged. "Daddy's busy and he can't take me. I wanna go make a sand castle!"

Maggie sighed. She closed the romance novel she'd been reading and set down a half-empty glass of Pinot Blanc. "Dylan, you know I don't enjoy sitting on the beach. Wait until your dad's finished, then go with him."

"He said he's gonna be working for a really long time. By the time he's done it'll be dark. I wanna go *now!*"

Maggie stood up and walked to the kitchen where Gerald was halfway under the sink repairing a leaky pipe. Leaning down, Maggie asked, "How long you going to be?"

"A while," Gerald replied.

"Can you take Dylan down to the beach when you're done?"

"It'll be too late by the time I finish here. Why don't you take him this time? It's a nice day, not too hot. Can you please hand me the wrench?"

Maggie removed the pipe wrench from Gerald's toolbox and passed it to him. "All right, but we're not staying long."

"Okay Dylan," Maggie said, returning to the living room, "we'll go for a little while. Go get your sand pail and shovel and grab me a beach chair." Maggie downed the rest of her wine.

"And can we go to Dolle's and get a box of saltwater taffy?"

"Sure, Dylan. We can get some taffy."

"Yay!" Dylan ran off to the laundry room to fetch the beach gear.

Maggie walked back to the kitchen and pulled the chilled Pinot Blanc from the refrigerator. She filled her stainless steel travel mug and placed the bottle back in the refrigerator. "We're going, Gerald. Be back soon."

"Okie doke," Gerald mumbled from under the sink.

Maggie grabbed a flowered silk scarf from the hallway table and tied it over her dark brown curls. Then she walked with Dylan the three blocks from their house down to the beach at the far north end of the Rehoboth boardwalk. It was early September. The tourist season was over and school was about to resume. The beach was deserted, much to Maggie's delight. She settled down in the weathered beach chair just shy of the shoreline as Dylan started happily digging in the wet sand. Maggie watched her young son as he laid the foundation for a sand castle. Designing and building sand castles was Dylan's passion. Gerald said their son would grow up to be an architect.

The sun was warm and a gentle breeze came off the ocean as high tide arrived. Maggie typically didn't enjoy sitting on the beach. Her fair complexion tended to bake in the sun. Gerald, on the other hand, enjoyed the beach and always took Dylan along. But today's weather was pleasant and comfortable. Maggie unscrewed the lid of her travel mug and sipped the cool wine before resuming her novel.

Despite the steamy romance that was developing between the book's main characters, Maggie began to feel drowsy. The warm sun, the cool breeze, the sound of the ocean—all of these elements were like a lullaby. Maggie's eyes grew heavy.

—

She woke with a start. Maggie felt disoriented as she tried to remember why she was resting on the beach. She had no idea how long she had been asleep. The sun hid behind clouds and the wind had picked up. Maggie looked to her right where Dylan had been crafting a sand castle. The base of the castle and his shovel were there, but Dylan was gone. A moment later, she heard Dylan's voice. Looking up, she saw him out in the ocean—head barely above water and crying for help. Maggie panicked. She jumped up, but stood frozen with terror. Maggie felt helpless—she didn't know how to swim. She looked around frantically, but there was no lifeguard presence during the off-season. There was no one in sight.

Dylan screamed again before he vanished beneath a huge wave.

Suddenly, Gerald sprinted past Maggie, stripping off his shirt and kicking off both shoes. He dove into the water and started swimming toward the spot where Dylan went under.

Maggie watched as Gerald dove beneath the water, resurfaced, then dove again. He continued to search for his son. Finally, he resurfaced with Dylan and started swimming toward the shore. Gerald gently placed Dylan on the sand and started examining him as Maggie ran toward them.

"Is he all right?" she asked, breathlessly.

Gerald didn't answer. His face was tense as he applied chest compressions. Maggie started to cry, sobs shaking her body.

She turned at the sound of distant sirens. *Someone must have seen what happened and phoned 9-1-1*, she thought, relieved that help was so close now. Two paramedics appeared and tended to Dylan. Gerald fell back onto the sand, soaking wet and exhausted. The paramedics placed Dylan on a stretcher.

"I'll ride in the ambulance," Gerald barked at Maggie. "You get the truck and meet us at the hospital."

"I want to go with you," Maggie cried.

Teeth clenched, Gerald ordered, "Get the truck and follow us."

He ran to catch up with the paramedics. Moments later the emergency vehicle sped off toward the hospital. Trembling with fear, Maggie quickly gathered up their belongings and ran back to the house.

———

She arrived at the emergency room 15 minutes later and found Gerald sitting in a chair, staring out the window.

"Is he okay?" Maggie asked.

"I don't know," Gerald replied, his voice shaking. "They're working on him now. Good thing I came down to tell you that I'd finished the job. You were gone a long time."

Maggie put her arm around Gerald's shoulders, "I'm so sorry. I fell asleep. I should have been watching him."

Gerald looked up at Maggie. His eyes flashed with an anger she had never seen before. "That's right. You *should* have been watching him. Dammit Maggie, you had one thing to do—watch our son. Were you drinking? I really don't have to ask, do I? Of course you were."

Twin doors opened and an ER doctor emerged. With a weary expression, he approached the couple and shook his head sadly.

"I'm terribly sorry. We did everything possible, but we lost him." The seasoned physician paused for a moment, knowing his words would take time to sink in. "You can go inside and see your boy in a few minutes. I'll have a nurse come get you. Again, I'm so very sorry."

Maggie burst into tears and stumbled, falling onto a chair as the doctor walked away. Gerald stood frozen. Finally, he turned to Maggie.

"You never wanted a child. Even after Dylan was born–you didn't want him. You always treated him more like a bother, an annoyance."

Maggie gasped at the accusations. "That's not true, Gerald. No, it's true that I didn't really want children, not at first, but you wanted a son. And I wanted to give you a son because I love you. I always loved Dylan."

"Well, we no longer *have* a son," Gerald said. "So you should be happy now."

"That's a terrible thing to say, Gerald," Maggie said, tearfully.

The couple stood silently for several minutes until a nurse escorted them into a room where Dylan lay lifeless on a cold, metal table. A white sheet covered his entire body. The nurse gently pulled the sheet down to reveal the boy's face. Maggie sobbed quietly. Silent tears streamed down Gerald's cheeks.

When they returned to the waiting area, Gerald grabbed the truck keys from Maggie. Without a word, he turned and headed for the parking lot. Maggie followed behind him, trying to keep up.

—

Maggie walked alone toward the water. It was cloudy and cold for early September. The chilly wind blew Maggie's long, white hair back away from her face. She stopped, scanning the ocean, remembering that afternoon exactly 15 years ago. She continued down toward the water's edge, moving slowly. The arthritis in her left knee was bothering her more than usual. As the waves washed over her feet, soaking her bedroom slippers, Maggie heard a voice call out.

"Hey, Mom, what are you doing?"

Maggie turned and gasped at the sight of her tall, handsome son. "Dylan, you're here!"

Dylan grinned. "Of course I'm here. Where else would I be? What are you doing in the water? You don't like the beach. And look, your slippers are all sandy and wet. Dad has breakfast ready. Blueberry pancakes–our favorite. Come on now. Let's walk back to the house."

"Your Dad made breakfast?"

"Yeah. He makes breakfast every Saturday morning. You know that. He even made that French roast coffee you like so much."

Maggie walked toward Dylan slowly, confused. "Dylan, you drowned 15 years ago. And your father, two weeks later he followed you into the sea. Told me he was going out for a walk, but never returned. His body washed up onshore the next day. You were both gone. I was left alone. So alone."

"Mom, did you have that dream again?" Dylan asked. "Like I've suggested before, maybe you should see a therapist for a while. You keep having that same horrible dream."

"Yes. Yes, I guess I *did* have that dream again," Maggie affirmed.

Dylan motioned for Maggie to follow him. "Come on, Mom, let's go home."

Maggie turned and headed back up the beach toward the boardwalk. Back at the house, as she walked up the back steps to the kitchen, she felt a familiar sensation of dread.

Her chest tightened. She felt lightheaded. She braced herself, opened the door, and stepped into the kitchen. The stove was cold. The coffee pot was empty. The breakfast table was set with one plate, one glass, one coffee mug, one spoon, one knife, one fork.

Maggie leaned wearily against the kitchen counter. Another day, starting like so many others had started for the past 15 years. She sighed, then took the coffee carafe to the sink and filled it with water. She scooped French roast into the filter, then poured the water into the machine's reservoir. She pressed the ON button. The machine sputtered into action. As Maggie watched the dark liquid trickle down, tears streamed over her cheeks.

She was so tired of it all. Dylan and Gerald would not let her follow them into the sea. She had tried and tried, but they refused to let her go. Maggie poured a cup of coffee and added half and half. The first sip in the morning always tasted so good. Something about a steaming hot cup of coffee always brought Maggie a cozy, comforted feeling. *Caffeine always seems to clear the cobwebs out of my head,* she thought. Maggie sipped slowly, savoring the beverage. She cupped both hands around the mug to feel its warmth. Usually she would go back for a second cup, but this time when she finished, she rinsed the cup and set it in the sink. Then she went to the drawer in the pantry and, after rummaging around a bit, retrieved a small box. She sat down at the kitchen table and struck a match. Maggie touched the flame to the edge of the flowered linen table cloth, which quickly spread to an adjacent stack of newspapers. For the first time in so long, Maggie felt a wave of calm wash over her, followed by a quiet sense of blessed peace.

AUTHOR'S NOTE

"Waves" was originally written with a happy ending in mind. I'm mostly a "happy ending" kind of writer. As I neared the end, to my surprise, the story took a dark turn. And then it got really dark. I honestly did not see this ending coming. But I figured if it surprised me, it would probably surprise the reader, and that would be great! I'm especially proud of this story, and I am so pleased with the way it wrote itself for me!

RH-PG

THE SEA CEMETERY

ANDREA GOYAN

"IZMIR TO LESBOS, port to port, 30 minutes," Lonan said, fastening the clips on Raahel's life vest. "Like we never leave land."

"Only we do," Raahel said.

"It's safe, my love." Lonan tucked the ends of her scarf beneath her straps.

"Aegean's full of the restless dead," she said and made the sign of the cross.

Her husband laughed. "You sound like an old woman." H held her head between his hands, "The dead are dead."

She'd twisted from his hold. "It isn't safe."

"Which is why I bought you this," Lonan said, as he lifted Yawsep from where the baby lay supported inside the donut hole of a foam safety ring. Lonan held his son aloft, high over his head. "You're as big as a two-year-old in your vest! You are."

Yawsep giggled, and for a few seconds, Raahel too laughed and forgot where they were, what the night held in store. The moment ended when a burly man approached Lonan and leaned in close. Raahel watched as her husband slipped the man a handful of lira, saw the sneer that painted the man's face before he swaggered away. Lonan motioned her over to the boat. There was a tightness in her chest. A life's savings poured into this one hope.

"Our time," Lonan said. Raahel took his hand, and together they waded knee-deep to the waiting boat. "We die if we stay."

Raahel nodded, and Lonan, holding Yawsep in one arm, helped her onto the boat with his other. The rubbery surface was wet, and her feet sought purchase on the wobbly deck. She took Yawsep from Lonan's arms so he could board. He helped her to the rounded edge of the vessel where she took the seat she knew he'd paid extra to procure.

"Hold here," Lonan said. He'd grabbed the thin rope that ran along the perimeter of the craft.

Raahel nodded, even though she knew what he asked of her was impossible. She needed both arms to hold Yawsep. He was too small to hold himself and too big to secure with just one arm, especially in his life vest. Lonan nestled the safety ring beneath the crooks of her knees. As other passengers clambered aboard, the boat tipped and shook. Raahel gasped.

Lonan kissed her head. "I'm going to the back of the boat to help."

Raahel grabbed his hand. "Stay."

"The sooner everyone boards, the sooner we arrive in our new home."

Raahel knew he was right, and she released her hold, though the thought of Lonan leaving her side nearly paralyzed her.

The moon was bright enough to see the other travelers as they crowded on deck, but Raahel wished she couldn't. They looked like washed-out remnants of human beings lacking any flush of life, and Raahel wondered if their hearts still beat inside their chest. Hers did. It pounded so hard she felt it in her throat and temples, in the arms that cradled Yawsep. The refugees crammed aboard until every square inch was occupied by anxious families. Raahel reached an arm over the edge and wetted the tips of her fingers. The boat sat much lower in the water than when she'd first stepped onto the vessel. A horde of strangers stood over Raahel, their feet stepping on her toes. Raahel felt like every breath she took was another person's exhalation, containing all their fears as well as her own. She struggled to take even shallow breaths. Worse, Lonan was stuck on the other side of the dinghy. He waved to her, face largely a silhouette in the darkness. She clenched her jaw and looked the other way.

The band of smugglers started the engine and pushed off away from shore. The man at the helm then jumped off the vessel into the waist-deep water and shouted vague instructions about how to operate the outboard motor. The dinghy circled aimlessly, and the pale refugees cried out. Raahel held Yawsep closer, afraid he'd be hurt in the endless jostling. Finally, Lonan took the helm. Raahel knew he'd never piloted a boat, but after a few moments, he turned the vessel and headed away from shore, toward refuge.

The wind whipped against Raahel's face. It stung her eyes and cut through her wet clothes, chilling her further. She clutched her son close against her chest. Cupping his head with her hand, Raahel shielded Yawsep's face against her body. For the first time since boarding, she was grateful for the crush of others and the bit of warmth they provided. The roaring outboard motor and sound of the hull as it skipped and slapped against the waves drowned out any chatter around her. Lonan, stood at the back of the boat helming their journey, but she could barely see him through the throng of fellow refugees—Christian and Muslim alike—that separated them.

Raahel touched the tiny jar of strawberry jam she'd hidden beneath her blouse, a treat she'd brought aboard for Yawsep. She knew that a spoonful would calm him down under any circumstance. Lonan wouldn't approve. His instructions had been specific: pack only essentials. But for Raahel, the preserves *were* essential. Made a year ago from her mother's recipe while Yawsep quickened in her womb, the jam was more than a sweet treat. It was promise. It was hope. Canned and labeled before trucks filled with corpses began to roll through the streets, it was the taste she remembered before the metallic grit of the first of the bombs polluted the town's air with a rancid metallic tang. Raahel was happy that Lonan hadn't discovered her precious stash; this one small object that brought comfort—a taste of the home she once knew and would never see again.

Dark water splashed over the edge of the dinghy, drenching Raahel, punishing her for being a land creature, a foreigner in its surf. She sighed. It wasn't the sea that made her feel like an outsider. It was life. Despite the cold, her face burned. She wondered if people would ever stop shouting, *go home*. Raahel thought, *if only I could*. She regarded the ache deep in her bones as a sign that she'd never see Syria again.

Raahel sought to catch her husband's eye. She shouldn't have looked away before. In Lonan's gaze, she found solace, but now he was turned away from her, looking toward Greece, hand tilling the rudder like a man plowing the fields for their future. She squeezed Yawsep and thought, *it's okay—as long as they're with me, I'm home."*

The vessel turned sharply, and one of the passengers fell against Raahel. Yawsep started to cry. The dinghy skipped over the swells, bouncing as its propeller howled.

"Shh," Raahel said, but Yawsep couldn't hear her over the keening engine, couldn't feel his mother's gentle bounces over the harsh waves that tossed the boat.

Metal on glass. Raahel felt the hull connect and strike a solid object. The engine cut out and they were airborne. The dinghy glided above the water. Its own momentum pushed the craft forward until it slammed back into the water with a massive crash. Everyone aboard the dinghy was pelted by an onslaught of water Raahel lost her hold on Yawsep. He slid from her arms onto the body of one of the many passengers who'd fallen.

A moment's silence was followed by cacophony. Yawsep wailed. Everyone on the boat spoke at once.

"Yawsep!" Raahel said. She reached down she caught hold of his vest and pulled him back onto the relative safety of her lap.

"Another boat," someone shouted.

"We're going to die."

"Djinn."

Raahel searched the night, convinced they'd collided with something. She saw only dark swells. No signs of another vessel or evil demons riding the surf.

She kissed Yawsep repeatedly. "My love, my baby boy."

"Start the boat!"

"I'm trying!" Lonan yelled.

The engine clicked and whined but refused to turn over.

The wind howled.

Raahel loosened her vest, wriggled her fingers beneath and procured the hidden treat, only realizing in the moment she turned the lid that she'd forgotten to pack a spoon. Raahel quickly dipped two fingers into the jam, stashed the jar away, and then pressed her fingers to Yawsep's lips.

"Strawberry," she whispered.

Yawsep's cries abated as he sucked the sweetness. Raahel, lost in the moment and already soaked to the bone, didn't notice she was knee-deep in water until the shrieking began. Raahel's neck and arms turned to gooseflesh as she realized her fellow passengers were not producing the screams. Instead, the sounds arose from the water that enveloped them. The confused passengers huddled closer together, pushing toward the center of the dinghy, as it took on more water. A female passenger yanked Raahel's arm, dragging her away from the edge of the boat.

"Look out," she said, eyes wild.

Raahel pulled away from the stranger and fell to her knees. Still clutching Yawsep, she cried out for her husband. "Lonan! Lonan!"

Raahel felt a pinch upon her arm from the woman who had dragged her moments earlier. She pointed, and Raahel turned in the direction of the woman's gesture, to where Raahel had only just been seated. Hands that may have once been human rose from the sea and gripped the boat's rubber fender with fingernails resembling the talons of a mythological harpy. The hands were attached to arms, arms attached to bodies, and bodies attached to heads that rose up over the sides of the boat. The creatures, for none aboard would dare call them human, looked upon the bewildered passengers with hollow interest. Rather, they seemed intent upon taking refuge aboard the boat, their sharp nails puncturing the rubber fender as they climbed out of their watery grave.

Raahel backed away from the specters, whose faces and garments bore such a resemblance to her fellow passengers that she could only distinguish one from the other by the pallor of their skin. She retreated until she could go no further. The living pressed tightly against one another like interlocking puzzle pieces.

The dead continued to board.

Raahel turned and shoved against the other refugees, forcing a space open where she could squeeze and hide Yawsep.

Then the dead moaned. Voices erupted from mouths frozen in rictuses.

"Save me." The dead woman wore a hijab. Its tattered fabric exposed her lank, algae-covered hair.

"Mama!" The deceased boy couldn't have been more than five, but his tiny fingers were as powerful and damaging as all the rest, shredding the boat's outer core as he boarded.

Raahel squeezed Yawsep, aware that the boy could easily be hers.

"Please, God!" another lifeless voice cried. "Spare us."

The boat listed, heeling portside as the living fled the dead. The sudden shift in weight proved too much for the flimsy vessel, and it began to sink. Waves as big as houses slammed into the boat. Raahel was thrown backward and washed overboard, Yawsep torn from her arms.

"Yawsep!" she shrieked, swallowing seawater. "Yawsep!"

Crashing, flailing bodies tumbled into the water around Raahel. She could no longer tell the pleas of the living from those of the dead.

Something nearby caught Raahel's attention. The flotation safety ring, and next to it, Yawsep floating on his back.

"Yawsep!"

Kicking her shoes off, Raahel swam toward her son. Her life jacket hobbled her effort, and she lost sight of Yawsep with each passing swell. Finally, he was at arm's length.

"Mama's here," she called out.

Inches from grasping hold of his vest, a gurgled voice, more water than words, spoke. "My … baby."

Bone-white fingers wrapped around Yawsep's torso and pulled him beneath the water, tight toward an empty bosom.

"No!" Raahel screamed. "He's not yours!"

Raahel clawed at the hands, peeling away icy flesh that didn't bleed until she wrested Yawsep away and pulled him to the surface. Yawsep choked and coughed up saltwater. The wraith rose high above the sea. It held its arms like a woman cradling a baby and began to rock them back and forth. Then, a wild, guttural animal sound loud as an exploding barrel bomb poured from the creature's open mouth as though its soul was being disgorged. There was no time to comfort Yawsep. Raahel lunged for the safety ring, tucked Yawsep inside, and pushed the ring ahead of her as she swam, feet kicking away from the thunderous howls overhead. Raahel did not stop until her lungs burned and she could no longer see or hear the wraith. Moving Yawsep to lay atop the safety-ring, out of the water, she ducked under and slipped into its center. The temporary warmth the burst of exercise had given Raahel eked back into the water. Her teeth chattered, and though she placed her arms around Yawsep, he also shivered.

Raahel checked his fingers, toes, and face, crying as she kissed him over and over, swallowing her sobs. If anything happened to him, she would allow the water to take her too.

At first, the night was loud. Cries for help rang out all around Raahel, but since she couldn't distinguish the dead from the living, Raahel remained silent. She floated, quietly, afraid to make the slightest sound that might draw unwanted attention from the wandering spirits. The moon set, the night darkened, and the sea fell silent.

Bodies bobbed all around Raahel. Many more than ten dinghies—much less a single vessel—would carry. Raahel whispered a prayer for the dead. When Raahel's grandfather died, her mother hastened to bury him in consecrated ground. "Otherwise he cannot rest," she'd told Raahel. "He might not even realize he's dead."

Raahel made the sign of the cross. She couldn't let Yawsep die here. Over and over, Raahel whispered the opening verses of Psalm 27. "The Lord is my light and my salvation; I will fear no one. The Lord protects me from all danger; I will never be afraid. When evil people attack me and try to kill me, they stumble and fall. Even if a whole army surrounds me, I will not be afraid; even if enemies attack me, I will still trust God."

Though she knew they still dangled beneath her in the murky water at the ends of her tingling legs, Raahel no longer felt her feet.

Numb is good, she thought, *it comes after pins and needles, it deadens the pain.* She hummed a hymn, cradling Yawsep against her bosom, but had no warmth to offer. Occasionally he opened his eyes or whimpered. Raahel dipped her fingers back into the jam jar. As she filled Yawsep's belly, her hopes and promises converged as she realized the jam's real value: it could save her son.

Movement caught her eye as a body she recognized rose from the water.

"Lonan!"

Even as she spoke his name, Raahel knew her husband was gone. She thought she saw a spark of recognition in his eyes before he slid back beneath the brackish water.

"Husband ..." the word stuck in her throat.

Moments later, something grabbed her feet. Raahel tried to free herself but then felt the strangest sensation. Warmth. Where before she'd had *no* sensation, the flush of warmth flooded through her, traveling up her legs, saturating her body with the greatest sense of peace. She draped over Yawsep, feeling the love flow to him.

"Daddy's with us now," she whispered.

———

Startled awake when Lonan released his hold, Raahel opened her eyes to a gray world. Night was over. Soon the sun would rise. Yawsep was already awake, or maybe he'd never slept. He began to fuss as soon as he realized Raahel was watching him. Lonan, now among the sea's undead populace, emerged a short distance away and watched Raahel scrape the bottom of the jar with her fingers.

She fed the last bits, more syrup than fruit, to Yawsep, then looked at Lonan. "My little secret," she said.

Yawsep giggled and wriggled his fingers toward the being that, only hours ago, had been his father.

Raahel closed her eyes and said a prayer for Lonan that he might find peace in this his final resting place. She reopened her eyes just as the sun crested the horizon. Lonan dove beneath the surface of the water, fleeing the shimmering sunlight that skittered across the surface like skipping rocks.

Raahel gasped. Her tears were a thimble of grief in an ocean of sorrow, but they were warm, thanks to Lonan.

A horn blared, and Raahel scanned the water. A fishing boat headed their way. She recognized the Greek lettering on its hull.

"We did it, my love," she whispered. Giving Yawsep a quick squeeze, Raahel began to call for help.

AUTHOR'S NOTE

"The Sea Cemetery" began with prompts I received in a short story competition. I was tasked with writing a ghost story that was supposed to take place in a port. I began to brainstorm about the ocean and shipwrecks as I searched for a way to incorporate the prompts into an engaging story.

At the time, the headlines were filled with tales about Syrian refugees. Boats filled with people desperate to make new lives kept capsizing in the Aegean Sea. Thousands perished. The human toll haunted me, and I was reminded of a quote by British-Somali poet Warsan Shire: "No one puts their children in a boat unless the water is safer than the land." The story's seeds were sown.

The sea is full of the dead.

Though I couldn't quite find a way to set the story in a port, I decided to write it anyway. After completing my first draft, where I'd written the family as Muslim, I performed some additional research. That's when I learned that Muslims generally don't believe in ghosts, so I needed to rethink everything. After some angst, the solution ended up being pretty simple. I decided my main characters could be members of a Christian family who also fled Syria. I adjusted what I'd written to reflect this.

I wish the crisis had ended since I wrote this story. It hasn't. As Dina Nayeri, award-winning author and refugee, stated in a 2017 interview, "It is the obligation of every person born in a safer room to open the door when someone in danger knocks."

AG

PUMPKIN SEED SPIT

R. DAVID FULCHER

BRIAN AND RIA waited near the stop sign at the intersection of Wofford Lane and Marlboro Way. Brian wore black and white face paint and a skeleton shirt. Ria wore a pointy witch hat and cape. The pillowcases in their hands for collecting candy were empty.

"Where is he?" Brian asked, impatiently.

"He'll be out soon; chill out. You know how mean his father is," Ria replied.

A door slammed and Matt ran out of his house. Sniffling, he wiped tears from his eyes. Matt wore green sweats and green dishwashing gloves. He carried an alien mask in his hands.

"Are you okay, Matt?" Ria asked.

Matt put on a good face. "Yeah, just another fight between my parents," he said stoically, taking Ria's hand when she offered it to him. She always made him feel better.

"Alright then," said Brian, the unspoken leader of the group, "let's get this show on the road."

"Sorry for the delay, guys," Matt said, apologetically. "I bet the good candy is already gone."

Brian slapped him on the shoulder. "You're in luck, buddy. This year it's not about candy. This year we have a shot at eating lunch with the eighth graders."

"What are you talking about?" Matt asked.

Ria interjected. "The eighth graders made some stupid dare with Brian that if we see The Pumpkin Tree they will let us eat lunch at their table."

"You guys can't be serious!" Matt asked. "That thing is a myth. I say we go trick-or-treating like every year."

Ria squeezed Matt's hand and smiled at him in agreement.

"Nope, this time they'll be forced to take us seriously," Brian asserted. "You two can act like grade schoolers if you want, I'm going for The Pumpkin Tree." Brian took off down Marlboro Way. Ria shrugged before she and Matt followed their friend down the street.

The trio received odd looks as it marched determinedly past parents and the other trick-or-treaters, never once stopping at any of the houses to amass confections. Brian's pace was brisk and the others struggled to keep up with him.

"Slow down, Brian!" Ria said.

"What's the rush?" Matt asked.

Brian turned around and glared at them. "Do you guys actually want to walk through the woods in the dark? Not me. We probably have a half hour of daylight left."

"How would we even prove we found The Pumpkin Tree?" asked Ria.

Without answering, Brian held up his cellphone, pointed at it for emphasis, and marched on.

They walked and walked. Matt and Ria looked longingly at the yards and porches decorated with garish orange lights, plastic tombstones, and inflatable ghouls.

It was unusually warm for October, and they were all sweating as Marlboro Way became an uphill climb. Finally, they reached the dead end of the road and began following a small dirt trail into the woods. Soon the narrow path widened to a gravel road where a great clearing stretched out in both directions. Every several hundred yards metal support structures held up powerlines like ancient gods pleading to the heavens.

After the clearing, the small dirt path resumed. Eventually, the three friends emerged from the woods and reached the parking lot of the high school.

"Let's rest here," Brian said.

They all sat down on the curb. Ria shared a package of M&M's she had brought from home.

For several moments, the gang was content to rest and munch.

Matt finally spoke. "Brian, what if this is all a joke? What if the eighth graders are playing us? Not only will we be harassed all year, but we'll totally miss out on Halloween."

"Don't you think I've thought about that?" Brian fired back. "Man, you guys must think I'm an idiot. I'm hoping it *is* a joke. I plan to go in there, take a photo of some creepy looking tree, and tell them we found The Pumpkin Tree. The joke will be on them when they try to find it!"

"I don't know, Brian," Ria said. "I think they're smarter than that."

"Remember, I'm a year older and wiser than both of you," Brian countered.

"That's only because you were held back a grade," Matt replied.

Brian raised a fist as if to punch Matt. The younger boy shrunk back against the curb.

"Alright, let's get moving. The woods get really thick beyond the sewer pipe." Brian stood up and brushed dirt from his jeans.

"The sewer pipe?" Ria gulped.

"Yes, the sewer pipe," Brian replied. "It's tall enough that we won't even have to hunch down as we walk. Relax, I've gone through it a hundred times."

Brain hurried across the parking lot. Ria and Matt reluctantly followed. Soon they entered the woods on the opposite side of the lot.

It was getting later and darker. There was no path. The branches and brambles scratched and stung them. Matt looked back at Ria and shook his head as they continued on.

The sewer pipe was nearly six feet in circumference. Brian activated the flashlight on his iPhone, though it did little to cut through the enveloping darkness. They tried to straddle the concrete pipe as much as possible to avoid the stream of murky water, but inevitably with soaked shoes and socks.

Finally they reached the other side and were relieved, although the daylight was dying and only provided meager light in the deep woods.

Brian scrambled up one of the muddy banks of the stream that was fed by the pipe and squinted into the darkness ahead.

"I think I see something," Brian exclaimed.

"Ha ha," Ria replied. She felt dirty and exhausted as she climbed the slippery bank.

"Good one, Brian," echoed Matt. "You really got us that time."

"No, I'm serious! Come here!" he ordered.

They joined him on the bank and followed his outstretched hand. At first the light was so subtle as to be insignificant, but after staring at it for several moments, none could deny the orange flickering glow in the distance.

"Okay," said Ria, "I've seen enough horror movies to know that a campfire in the middle of the woods on Halloween night is never a good thing. We should get out of here now," she urged.

"You two can sissy out if you want," Brian said. "I didn't walk all this way for nothing." He stormed ahead, oblivious to the noise he made while crashing through the undergrowth.

"He's like a bull in a china closet!" Matt exclaimed. "So much for the element of surprise."

Ria gripped Matt's hand again. "C'mon, let's go see this tree."

"Guys, c'mon! You won't believe this," they heard Brian say in the distance.

Bumbling through the last thicket of branches, they joined Brian in a small clearing.

An ancient, colossal tree stood before them, limbs stretching in every direction. Dozens of jack-o-lanterns, lit by candles that flickered in the breeze, hung from countless branches.

For several long minutes they stood in silent awe before The Pumpkin Tree.

"Who did this?" Matt asked in disbelief.

"The eighth graders," whispered Ria.

"No. I don't give them that much credit," said Brian. "Probably some local college kids set this up."

"I don't know. Seems like an awful lot of work," Matt replied.

Suddenly the limbs creaked and the tree twisted and bent over them. The jack-o-lanterns rocked violently from side to side.

Matt, Ria, and Matt stood frozen with fear.

"Silence!" a guttural voice cried from a dark jagged opening in in the tree's trunk. "I am not some parlor trick here to frighten school children. I am The Pumpkin Tree. I've been here for countless generations. I will be here long after your children's children have turned to dust."

They instinctively stepped back from the tree, but were met by a network of branches that felt as strong as steel cables against their backs.

"There is no escaping me," the tree answered. The voice made their skin crawl, and its breath reeked of decay and death.

"Wh-what do you want?" Brian asked.

"I ask that you simply return to your night's activities, passing out my seeds as you go. Open your pillowcases and approach me," the tree demanded.

The branches against their backs pushed the kids forward, right in front of the awful maw of the tree.

Brian and Matt held out their open pillowcases. Ria stood in a daze.

"Ria!" Matt insisted. "Ria! We have to do what it says!"

Finally Ria held her out her bag, but she turned her face away from The Pumpkin Tree as she did so.

The Pumpkin Tree inhaled with such force that Ria had to grab her pointed hat to avoid it being sucked into the gaping hole of its mouth. An awful exhalation followed as the tree rapidly spat several dozen seeds into each bag. Despite the bags being largely empty, they soon became so weighty that the friends had to hold on to their pillowcases with white knuckles to avoid dropping the heavy loads.

The tree then breathed over them with a sickly, intoxicating breath that smelled of gourds and earth.

"Go!" it demanded, loosening the network of branches that held them prisoner.

Brian, Ria, and Matt quickly retraced their steps as they made the long journey home, remembering little of the details. The sewer pipe, the powerlines, the path in the woods—it all seemed effortless as the moon watched their trek from high above. It was well past seven o'clock, and they were in full darkness, but even that seemed more of a comfort than a hindrance.

When they reached the first house near the dead end, they knocked and said in unison, "Trick-or-Treat!" As Henry Armitage opened the door, Brian opened his bag. The middle-aged man frowned at them before starting to mutter something about the lateness of the hour. Armitage gazed into Brian's bag of seeds and was immediately mesmerized. An orange energy tendril spiraled upward, carrying a single seed into Armitage's mouth.

Brian, Matt, and Ria wanted to scream, but found it impossible. While their souls were wrenched into knots by the horror they witnessed, outwardly they were emotionless, even tranquil, as layers of skin and flesh melted away until all that remained of Henry Armitage was a living skeleton.

When the transformation was complete, they went to the next house. Ria shared the seeds, and Asenath Waite, a young mother of two, was hideously transformed into a witch with boils and green teeth.

Matt received his chance as well, and didn't hesitate to share three seeds with a couple and their young baby, leaving behind a family of giant pale, eyeless larvae that oozed and squiggled out of their clothes.

The kids continued in this manner late into the night, all the way down Marlboro Way, up Wofford Lane, and across the great loop of Limestone Place. They then visited the homes on Metzerott Road that stretched almost to the interstate.

They continued until they were left with only three empty pillow cases.

Just before midnight, they were dragged, spellbound, back through the woods and the creek to The Pumpkin Tree.

As before, the tree greeted them with its awful, thorny embrace.

"Excellent, children. Excellent!" the tree croaked, clasping two short branches together like hands. "Tonight, we have ushered in a new age of monsters, the likes of which the world has not seen since the last time I was visited, centuries ago."

"You think your bags are empty, but I am not such an unkind fellow as that. Please open your sacks and see," the tree urged.

Still entranced, they each looked inside their bags. Orange tendrils of light like vines reached up and forced open their throats, bringing with the light a single seed for each of them.

The Pumpkin Tree shook and laughed deeply as the children changed. Its limbs clicked together like the cracking of teeth.

Moments later, the tree bent over the skeleton, witch, and swamp creature approvingly.

"Fly from this place. You have a head start, but I fear your friends and neighbors are doomed. You have become monsters in the purest sense. As such, you must exist on the edge of shadow and darkness. Never forget that you are, and shall forever be, in my debt. Never forget me, especially on All Hallows' Eve"

The creatures that had been Matt, Ria, and Brian nodded, understanding and embracing their fate.

"Flee!" the tree roared, and three new monsters escaped into the darkness.

AUTHOR'S NOTE

As a child growing up in College Park Woods, Halloween was a magic and mysterious time. Our neighborhood was surrounded by woods. Behind the woods, powerlines stretched in either direction as far as the eye could see. The older kids always dared us to go into the woods on Halloween night, but as young children we never chanced it. "Pumpkin Seed Spit" evolved from this memory. I was intrigued by the idea of young treat-or-treaters being dared to enter the woods on Halloween night and returning transformed into something horrible. In my 2007 story, "Pumpkin Night at the Pinkstons," pumpkin people had the ability to rapidly spit seeds at their victims, and this idea from my earlier work also was used in the story. These concepts, along with the common horror literary device of a haunted tree, congealed together to form "Pumpkin Seed Spit."

RDF

THE CREEPY DANCE OF RED CURLY HAIR

AMIRAH AL WASSIF

HER RED CURLY HAIR has joined me in my grave. I try my best to touch my bones with my fingers to make sure that what I see is real. There can be no doubt, it is real. The red curly hair moves toward me, the creepiest dancer I ever saw in my whole life.

As a horror aficionado, I'd seen hundreds of hours of horror films, and read countless horror stories. I visited the horror tree, threw myself in both abandoned houses and haunted hotels. I wanted to experience fear.

Nothing scared me.

I longed to be made afraid, if only for a moment. Although my friends tried many times to frighten me, to bring the horror to me, no one had ever succeeded.

One October evening a weird idea floated into my head and whispered, "The graves." I realized that I might experience genuine fear by spending my nights in a grave among other graves with my dead friends. So I officially became one of the half-dead, wandering in the wide forests by day and sleeping quietly in a terrific grave by night.

I spent many long evenings in the cemetery without a bit of fear, until this particular night when I heard whispering coming from outside my comfortable grave.

The voices quietly related a story about the terrible crime of a girl.

"She was 12 years old when they found her body in the wooden cave," a male voice explained. "Her mother said, 'My daughter was a very brave girl. She never ever experienced fear, not even in death.'"

A female spoke. "Why would anyone kill a child in this terrible way?"

A deep male voice answered, "Nobody knows. When they found the girl dead, they discovered that her head had been completely shaved!"

The trio fell suddenly silent. I pressed my ear to the inside wall my grave, trying my best to hear them. Fortunately, they soon resumed their discussion.

The first voice said, "The child's mom was shocked and terrified when she saw the body of her little girl sinking in a lake of blood." He added with a voice full of fear, "The poor mother fainted when she later saw the shaved head of her dead daughter. The crowd thought it was a normal reaction because she was, after all, her mother. But I noticed something odd that scared me."

"What scared you?" the female voice asked.

"When I stood close to the mother, her mouth moved quickly and she murmured, 'She told me that she wanted to be scared until her hair danced.'"

The first voice fell silent and then the second voice asked him, "What was the color of the missing hair?"

Before the first fellow could answer, something entered my grave. It felt soft against my skin. It moved right and left underneath my body. I fumbled for the matchbook always nearby and struck a match. As light cut through the darkness of my grave, and as I saw what was next to me, the voice outside suddenly answered, "Red curly hair!"

AUTHOR'S NOTE

I had this idea of a man who feels bored of traditional horror themes and concepts. He's watched horror movies his whole life. He feels extremely bored and wants to find something that will terrify him. His solution—to sleep in a grave at night—is unorthodox. It produces the result he'd hoped for, but not in the way he expected, as he suddenly finds he's not alone in his confined tomb.

AAW

NEW MEAT

ROBERT LEWIS HERON

YOU'VE PROBABLY known kids like me. My dad was military, and like all kids, I was hauled here, there, and everywhere. Never anywhere fun like New York or LA. Just one boring town after another. Not easy making friends when moving from school to school every two years.

Dad died in a car wreck two years ago. Some asshole fell asleep at the wheel—a tractor trailer against a beat-up Ford—no contest. Last month we moved here, to Dunwich, an unimpressive east coast seaside town. My mom tries her best. Works two jobs. I also work, part-time, as a waiter at the Dunwich Diner, famed for its juicy burgers.

Dunwich is larger than the small towns we typically moved to before Dad's death. I don't stand out as much at Dunwich High, so at least there's that.

—

I'm working the afternoon diner shift when Brody calls out to me.

"Stop daydreaming, Zee, and get back inside. We have customers."

"I'm on a five-minute smoke break."

"Well get the hell out of my sight. If you gotta smoke, take it around back. And five minutes is five. Not six, five."

"Sure, Mr. Brody. No problem."

"And empty the trash. I've told you to buckle down to hard work if you want to be my assistant manager."

I don't want to be Brody's assistant manager, but the money is better than cleaning dishes so we'll see. Besides, he skims half of my tips. I try to pocket them quick, but he's always looking over my shoulder. Does the same to Pam, his daughter. She's sweet as can be. Sometimes I think she must be adopted. No way she can be Brody's. No way. She's way too sweet.

—

Lately, I've noticed a group of local teens hanging out by the rancid dumpster in the alley behind the diner. Tonight is no exception. I walk toward the dumpster, a trash bag in each hand. I've seen them at school. Jake, Molly, and Mandy. Leather jackets and boots. Goths.

"Hi there, new meat. You bringing us snacks?" Molly says.

The others laugh.

"You're free to trash dive. The burgers are really good tonight. Real juicy." I heave the trash bags into the dumpster. "Looks to me you'd probably feel right at home crawling through garbage."

Mandy flicks her long black hair over her shoulder, "Smart boy. You think you're smart?"

"Thinks he's funny," Molly says. "What's your name, new meat?"

"Zee."

Molly shoulder bumps Mandy. "Stupid name. Rhymes with pee. You, uh, pee your pants much, new meat?"

"Fuck you, bitch."

Jake moves toward me. "Shut your mouth, Zee. No one fuck's with my gang, except me. Comprende amigo?"

Both girls curl their arms around Jake's waist and purr like cats.

Mandy points a long, red, perfectly manicured fingernail toward me. "As it happens, our gang is one male short. You man enough to fill the bill?"

"Gang? What *gang* might that be?"

"We're the Death Squad." All three turn around to show off the backs of their letter jackets. Each proudly display the gang's name.

"What the hell?" I reply, more perplexed than impressed.

Mandy walks closer and wraps her pale arms around my neck. "We have lots of cool fun." She licks my left earlobe then my right. Her hips gyrate against mine. "What do you think, Zee? Want to join our lil' ol' gang?"

The moment is broken as the back door to the kitchen flies open and light floods the alley.

"Zee, get your fat ass back to work," Brody says. "Your five minutes are long over. People to serve. Now!"

"On my way, Mr. Brody," I answer.

"As for you three creeps, how many times have I told you to stop hanging out back here. You're nothing but shit. Next time you assholes show your degenerate faces I won't be responsible for what happens. Comprende?" Brody turns, enters the kitchen and slams the door shut.

"Wait a minute," Jake says, as I head back to the diner. "Are you in or not?"

"Your gang. Sure, why not. I'm in."

All three smirk. Mandy shows off her pierced tongue, revealing a silver skull and crossbones charm. "Not so fast. First, there's the initiation test."

"What test?" I ask.

Jake pulls a gun from his pocket and hands it to me. "You've got to kill someone."

I recognize the weapon as a Glock G42, capable of holding seven, .380 auto ACP caliber rounds. Before he'd died behind the wheel, Dad taught me about firearms. Spent a lot of time together on the firing range. It was the only thing about his military work I admired.

"Where the hell did you get this?"

"Never mind. You in or out?"

"No joke?"

"No joke," Jake replies. "You kill someone, you're in. We've all done it. There's a reason we're called the Death Squad.

"You have 24 hours," Mandy adds.

"Meet here tomorrow night, 11:00 PM. If you haven't done the deed by then, consider the offer withdrawn, and consider yourself a chicken shit."

———

At 11:05 PM the following night, long past closing time, I exit the diner by the kitchen door and approach the dumpster. Jack, Molly, and Mandy stand in the shadows by the dumpster.

"Over here, Zee," Mandy calls. "We've been waiting."

"I can hardly see you guys."

Jake stands in front of the girls. "So?" he asks.

"It's done," I answer.

"What do you mean, *it's done*?"

"I mean it's done. I killed my fat slob of a boss tonight. Clean headshot right between his unsuspecting eyes. Should have seen him squirm. Felt so good."

"Okay, macho man. Sounds like a pile of bullshit," Jake replies. "I'll take back the gun now."

"No bullshit, Jake. You can look if you want. The body's in the diner kitchen. Actually, I could use some help buying his fat ass."

"Bullshit. The gun was loaded with blanks, Zee."

"About that … I took the gun to the range today. Wanted to get used to it. I know about handguns, but that's another story. I shot your stupid blanks and reloaded with live bullets."

Mandy and Molly take a step back, mouths agape. Jake follows. "You're telling me you put real bullets in my gun and shot Mr. Brody?"

The girls back up further. Mandy leans against the metal dumpster's side. They gasp and start to cry.

I'm livid. "Wait one friggin' minute here. Are you telling me this whole gang initiation shit was a hoax?"

"Of course it was a hoax!" Jake says. "Who the fuck goes around shooting people?"

I step back, facing all three figures, Jake out front and Molly hiding behind Mandy.

"Now we have a problem, kids," I say.

"Not *we*—*you* have a problem," Jake answers.

"The way I see it, Jake, is like this. I have a gun and you three bitches don't. You know I killed that fat slob, Brody. So correct me if I'm mistaken, but my problem goes away if you three go away. Right here, right now."

"Wow … wow … wait a minute, amigo," Jake pleads. "We won't say anything. You're in the gang, and gang members don't snitch on other gang members."

Molly and Mandy's sobs increase. Black mascara streaks run down both their cheeks.

"Zee, it's our fault," Mandy says. "We should never have tried to trick you like this. It's just a misunderstanding. I think … I think you're real cute. You can be my, ya know, boyfriend. Look, I'm real hot for you. You can kiss me if you want." Her voice cracks with distress, like a condemned prisoner asking the hangman for a reprieve.

Molly, equally desperate, adds, "You can kiss me too. Any time you want. Just please, please don't hurt us."

———

Three 9-millimeter bullets is all it takes.

The first bullet pierces Jake's eye and explodes through the back of his skull. The second strikes Mandy's forehead and she slams back against the dumpster before dropping to the ground. Molly screams, but those cries quickly end as her jaw is ripped apart, the bullet continuing through her upper carotid artery.

And just like that, the Death Squad is history.

The kitchen door opens, casting a revealing light over the bodies.

"Excellent, Zee" Mr. Brody says. "Job well done. Looks like you are assistant manager material after all."

"Thanks, Mr. Brody."

"Call me Brody. You deserve it. Let's get this meat into the grinder. We've got juicy burgers to make."

———

In the dark basement of the diner, Brody oversees as I grind bone and sinew into pink burger meat. I'm intrigued by this new unfolding reality, an eager student embarking on a dark career path.

"Brody, what do you want me to do next?"

"As assistant manager, I expect you to provide a steady supply of burger and hot dog filler. Plenty of sources to be found in this town. You've got homeless sleeping under the boardwalk at the beach. Tourists, and student types I call June bugs. Always plenty of June bugs around here. And, of course, the schools are full of young meat. You figure out the rest."

"Excellent, and thank you for my promotion. Can I ask, what happened to your previous assistant manager?"

A high-pitched whine resonates from the grinder.

"What do you *think* happened to him, Zee?" Brody grins, patting his round belly. "You won't have to worry about that. Long as you keep that sweet meat coming. Everyone loves June bugs. So young and juicy."

I nod, understanding. The whining increases as skull bones are shredded by the grinder's whirling blades. Skull bone is so, so hard.

———

Everything is great for the next year or so. I bring home more money to help Mom and become quite adept at the finer points of assistant management and meat grinding. However, nothing in life is certain. For example, when Hurricane Jasper devastates our cute little seaside town, the June bugs stop coming around. The homeless relocated to Seagull Island. Security at the schools is tighter than ever since the most recent mass shooting. The only real juicy meat left around these parts is me. I'm largely to blame. I just love burgers and fries and have gained nearly one hundred pounds in the past 12 months.

Which is why I'm going to die tonight. The likelihood is high, as in one hundred percent high. As high as June bugs in June.

They say shit happens when you least expect it. I knew this might happen. What the heck. As I said, it's nobody's fault but mine. Then again, some folks are real sick in the head. Know what I mean?

The thing is, I thought Brody and I were tight. Allies with the same objectives. Although I had noticed, quite recently, that he'd begun looking at me a bit …hungrily … I sure as hell didn't expect him to attack me. I suppose that when inventory is low, 275 pounds of juicy flesh is difficult to resist … for a madman.

His first deep stab wound (of many) tore through my shoulder, and as I turned he plunged a meat hook through my groin. The pain is almost gone now. I'm bleeding out, and it's now just a matter of time. Brody, meanwhile, won't be finishing the job. He lies at my feet, poisoned. I thought it would act much faster. Didn't expect the attack. Guess I've lost my promotion. To think I had ambitions of managing a place of my own.

Nothing to do now but wait. Yep, looks like I'm dead meat.

AUTHOR'S NOTE

Scotland's capital, Edinburgh, has many true sordid tales to tell. I combined one such tale, with another fictional tale of cannibalism, to pen my own horrific take on the criminal mind. Deacon Brodie was a respectable Scottish businessman by day and a thief by night. This dichotomy of respectability and real evil nature was the paradox which inspired Robert Louis Stevenson to write *The Strange case of Dr. Jekyll And Mr. Hyde*. Also the paradox which inspired my story.

In addition to Mr. Brodie there is the terrible fictional tale of Sweeny Todd who slit the throats of his hirsute customers and ground their carcasses into meat pies. Relocate the aforementioned scenario to a small American diner, and voila, *New Meat* is born.

In terms of plot, I believe that all short stories must grab and hold until the death. I have tried both full plot structures and "by the seat of your pants" plotting. I enjoy writing without knowing where I am being led. Let the muse lead me to wherever.

I love the unknown.

RLH

ALICE'S HAT

TERRI CLIFTON

THE BELL TOWER atop the Innsmouth Museum of History had remained boarded up for nearly a century. The building, which had originally been a church, was nearly destroyed in 1927 when half the town was consumed by a fire, the origins of which were never discovered. Deemed unsafe for human occupancy, the building was abandoned by the church and sat vacant for long decades until the town council of Innsmouth opted to renovate the damaged structure to commemorate the town's upcoming bicentennial. Work on the main structure was completed in 20 months, at which point the bell tower was assessed.

Inspectors deemed the tower to be salvageable. On October 30, metal scaffolding was erected and soon surrounded the tall structure. From a distance it resembled a geometric spider's web. The next morning, while the town readied for its annual Halloween festival, workers began the arduous task of removing the hundreds of planks that enveloped the tower, unsure what to expect underneath.

Amidst the foggy morning and the dust that filled the air as the barrier separating the workers from the bell tower was torn asunder, none of the crew noticed the small cloth object. Black and dust covered, preserved for countless years within the tower, the black article was carried into the air by an errant wind that arose suddenly on an otherwise windless morn.

It tumbled through the air, spiraling above the town until the wind that carried it aloft dissipated as quickly as it had begun. It landed in the middle of Innsmouth Park, where the town's annual Halloween festival was in the early stages of commencement. Alice Woodly's hat was free.

For quite a while, no one noticed the hat at all, and it was just past noon before Madeline Usher first picked it up. She examined the vintage piece, the jet beads of the hat pin glinting as she turned it in her hands, then looked around to see to whom it might belong among the zombies and witches and their kindred strolling the festival grounds. Madeline placed it on a stack of apple crates next to the ticket table and left it for its owner to find.

William Wilson picked up the hat next. A beer in one hand, Wilson sat the hat askew on his bald head and ambled across the grounds.

In the ensuing hours, more than a dozen festival goers tried on the hat. It was finally placed atop a pumpkin next to a vendor selling cold beverages. Later still, the hat was liberated by a group of adolescents who played a game keep away while taking turns trying it on. Any tingling sensations or odd sounds were immediately lost to the noise and excitement all around.

Gabriel Glendinning first noticed the hat at dusk atop a pylon along the river. By this time, the town was bustling and the Halloween festival was in full swing. The brilliant orange sunset reflected from the hatpin and caught Gabriel's eye. He appropriated the hat and handed it to Krysta Camille.

"This looks like your style," Gabriel said, grinning. "Put it on and I'll take our photo. A perfect souvenir of our first date."

"If I get head lice, this'll be our *last* date, too."

The hat fit, so Krysta wore it as she and Gabriel followed the sound of a funk band beginning its set. Music thumped out over the streets and darkness, adding to the atmosphere of Halloween fun. A laser light show projected flashing images over the walls of the library, theatre, and museum to the crowd's amazement. Jack-o'-lanterns faced the night, while dancer's glowsticks bobbed with the music.

As Krysta started to dance in the bright lights from the stage, Gabriel had the startling sensation that he could see through her. He reasoned it was an illusion produced by the haze generator, until others began to comment.

"This is so cool," a hippie girl said. She wore a long skirt and zombie paint with a shirt that read "The Ungrateful Dead." "I can see through myself! How are they doing that?"

Others looked around, trying to locate the technology responsible for the bizarre effect. Gabriel looked back at Krysta and saw a hazy blue glow surrounding the hat. A sense of dread and doom washed across Gabriel. *This is not part of the show*, he thought. The hair on Gabriel's arms stood up. He gazed at Krysta's hat and the caerulean hue surrounding it.

"What are you doing?" Krysta asked, as Gabriel suddenly removed her hat. He whirled away to find the hippie girl who was still dancing nearby.

"Is this your hat?" Gabriel asked.

"No."

"But you had it on?"

"Yeah, I just found it. Not mine though."

Gabriel asked others who'd worn the hat these same questions. Their skin filmy and faded, each admitted to having worn the hat. Those who hadn't worn it appeared unchanged. Gabriel hurried back to Krysta.

"There's something wrong with this hat," he said, aware of the almost comical nature of his words.

"Wrong?"

"I think it's cursed or ..." Catching sight of Krysta's expression and raised eyebrows. Gabriel trailed off. He then quickly offered a theory and observations, wanting to be ridiculous. "I hope I'm wrong," he said. "I'd love to be wrong, but I don't think I am."

Krysta glanced around, trying to decide whether Gabriel was crazy or astute.

"You know, one of the reasons I wasn't sure about going out with you is I thought you might be lacking in imagination. But now ..."

"I know you don't know me well, but I always rely on facts. I never trust instinct. But I'm telling you, everything about this feels wrong." *And I was the one who had asked you to on the hat*, Gabriel thought, guilt forming a lump in his throat. He took another photo of Krysta, two hours since she'd last worn the hat. He turned the screen toward her. Krysta stared at the near ghost image of herself, before looking at Gabriel with a horrified understanding.

They found the spell an hour later, on a weathered strip of parchment folded tight and tucked under the inner brim of the mysterious black hat.

I DID NONE OF WHAT WAS SWORN AGAINST ME.
FOR THEIR LIES LEAVE THIS CURSE.
FADE AWAY YOUR PRETTY CHILDREN,
FADE AWAY YOUR DANCING MAIDS.
FADE TO NOTHING AND ALL HAS ENDED.
BEFORE THE DAWN THIS CURSE IS LAID.

BY EARTH AND AIR I SEAL THIS SPELL.
SO MOTE IT BE.

ALICE WOODLY, 1921

There was no logical place to seek help, but as they walked across the festival grounds, Gabriel and Krysta stopped at a booth where a medium named Madam Liegia sat. From her crystal ball to her colorful, flowing robes, Liegia was the stereotypical fortune teller. Next to her sat an unassuming elderly woman in black attire. Her eyes were fixated on a worn hardcover. She ignored the exchange between Gabriel, Krysta, and Liegia until the psychic tapped her arm.

"Wanda, you may want to see this," Liegia said, presenting the hat and parchment and then pointing at a nearly transparent Krysta. Liegia turned to the young couple. "If anyone can help you, it's Wanda. This is witchcraft. Wanda is an elementalist."

After a few moments, Wanda gazed at Krysta and frowned. "You're under a powerful spell. Arcane magic. This hat belongs to Alice Wooly."

"A witch?" Gabriel asked.

"She was. Decades ago. It was rumored that she spent most of her nights perched in the bell tower right behind us. I recall reading that she vanished shortly after the great fire. Some members of the town council believed Alice had started that fire, and they wanted her gone. The last anyone saw of Alice, she was being chased through the woods by Archibald Baxter and his cronies by Cypress River, just beyond that clearing." Wanda pointed to the north where the moon reflected in the distant pond. "By their reckoning, Alice dove head first into the water and was never seen again. Most peculiar her hat would appear today."

"What's going to happen if we can't undo the spell?" Krysta asked, her voice quiet and desperate.

"This sort of incantation works quickly," Wanda said. "If this isn't resolved by sunrise …."

"What can we do?" Gabriel asked.

"We can't do anything here. Too many people. Too distracting We need to find a quiet place."

"My place is within walking distance," Krysta said.

Wanda nodded. "Let's go."

—

Within Krysta's modest, second-story apartment, Gabriel boiled water for herbal tea. Wanda handed a cup to Krysta.

"I'm not thirsty."

"It'll help slow the spell," Wanda said. "Time is not on our side."

Wanda removed a Conté crayon from her bag and scratched a large pentagram on Krysta's hardwood floor.

"Sit within the circle," she instructed. "Do you have any paper to write with?"

Krysta pointed to a nearby desk. Gabriel fetched the paper and a fountain pen.

"Your best chance of beating this is to write a counter-spell."

"Can you write it? I thought witches were good at this sort of thing," Krysta said.

"It has to be written by someone who has been touched by the spell. Unless you'd like your friend her to go back to the festival grounds to find another of its victims ...."

"No," Krysta said, sighing. "There's no time."

She scribbled on the paper, erasing and then starting anew. Finally, she looked to Wanda and read the spell.

"Restore the children and the dancing maids. Restore all that life has gifted. Back the wholeness, keep them living. By midnight the curse is lifted. By fire and water I seal this spell. So mote it be."

"Very good," Wanda said. "Sign and date it."

While Krysta did as instructed, Wanda grasped the girl's write and hand cut across her palm with a small knife.

"What the hell are you doing?" Krysta cried, pulling her hand away as blood dripped onto the counter-spell."

"It was necessary. Only one thing left to do."

"What's that?" Gabriel asked.

"A quick stop at Cypress River."

—

It was a short walk to the river. Wanda gazed into the blackness of the water, aware that there were many ways a witch of Alice Wooly's skill might easily have survived her pursuit.

"We're going to return Alice's hat to her," she said. "Place your spell inside the hat.

Krysta folded her paper and pressed it inside the hat's brim. The hat pin resisted reinsertion into the thick material so Krysta gave it a hard push. It passed through the hat and sank deep into the palm of her Krysta's left hand, which now was all but invisible.

"That's twice tonight I've bled," she said, wrapping the fresh wound in a bandana she'd been wearing around her neck.

"All the better," Wanda reassured her. "You may want to recite your spell again as well."

Krysta did as instructed. She then dropped the hat onto the water and the current slowly carried it away. Wanda handed Krysta a book of matches and the original spell.

"Burn it," she said.

The parchment ignited quickly. Ash rose into the air before falling onto the water.

"I feel like that worked," Krysta said. "I feel … different."

"That's good," Wanda said. "We've done all we can. I should get back to the festival and help Liegia pack up."

"Thank you, Wanda," Krysta said. "I really don't know how to repay you."

"Just … try to avoid magic and witchcraft," Wanda said, departing.

"I don't know about you, but I could use a drink," Gabriel said to Krysta as they stood alone by the water. Krysta nodded and they walked toward the festival and the Innsmouth Pub. Heavy clouds covered the moon and the walk was especially dark. As they approached the bright lights of the pub, Gabriel glanced at Krysta. To his relief, she was no longer fading away.

"Looks like you're back," he said.

Krysta gazed down at her formerly translucent hands and beamed. As they approached the pub's door, they were met by the hippie girl they'd seen earlier in the evening. She also looked normal.

"Hey!" she exclaimed. "Did you find they owner of the hat."

Krysta smiled. "We did."

"Cool! Happy Halloween!" She hurried away to catch up with her.

"How do you feel?" Gabriel asked.

"Brand new," Krysta said.

"If you'll go out with me again, I promise it'll be much more boring date."

Krysta hugged Gabriel tightly. "I was sorta hoping we might raise the dead, but sure. Okay."

Over Gabriel's shoulder, Krysta saw her reflection, young and alive, in the pub window. She smiled slowly. Gabriel couldn't see the odd glitter that came into her eyes, or that under the bandana, the hole in her hand had already healed completely.

AUTHOR'S NOTE

At the 2018 Zombie Fest (held in Milton, DE), I saw an abandoned witch's hat. My writing brain immediately took over. I imagined all sorts of people passing around the hat, and began to wonder what magic might linger inside. Good magic? Bad Magic? Would it stay with the wearer, or stay with the hat? It then occurred to me that every witch's hat must have a witch, and every witch has a story. So I took little pieces of local history and places and began to stitch one, which is how I met Alice and, subsequently, learned how she got her hat back.

TC

A HOUSE HAUNTED

DAVID W. DUTTON

ANDREA PADGENT sipped her martini and then looked at us and smiled. "I hope I'm not being too presumptuous."

"Hardly." My wife, Susan, laughed, and reached for a water chestnut wrapped in bacon.

Andrea was the current girlfriend of friend and attorney, Jacob Reynolds, who had lived next door to us for the last three years. Pre-dinner cocktails had become somewhat of a regular thing with Jacob and whomever he was dating at the moment. Andrea took another sip of her drink and looked from Jake, seated in the chair next to her, to us, seated on the sofa across from them. She paused. Whether it was for effect or simply a measure of her uncertainty was unclear. In the scheme of things and it made no difference.

"Are you aware that you have a ghost?"

My wife and I looked at one another and smiled.

Andrea Padgent mirrored our smiles and set her martini glass on the coffee table. "I can see that I've hit a nerve."

I chuckled and looked at Jacob. "Yeah. I guess you could say that."

Jacob laughed. "Sorry guys. I should have warned you that Andrea is somewhat of a psychic."

My wife rallied and took another sip of her cocktail. "Really? How fascinating."

Jacob continued. "I hope you aren't offended."

I laughed. "No. Not at all." I turned to Andrea. "You're right, and we've experienced a lot of strange occurrences over the last year or so. I could tell you a story or two."

—

Susan and I have always entertained an interest in the occult, particularly ghosts and their hauntings. Initially, this intrigue was fostered by published works and an occasional TV special. In that, the whole concept was simply a matter of curiosity generated by our imaginations.

Were ghosts real? Were they actually unsettled spirits who prowled the halls and vacant rooms of empty mansions? Who knew? To us, the possibility was fascinating.

We'd been raised in big, drafty old houses. We were well-accustomed to the proverbial "bumps in the night" and delighted in scaring one another as we contemplated their source.

Susan and I had been married for six years when we relocated from the city to the small, coastal village of Endbrooke, a town steeped in history. Endbrooke was picture-book lovely, and the house we had chosen fulfilled our sense of adventure and romance. The huge, brooding, stone structure dominated the corner of the block on which it sat. Its four floors were filled with large, gracious rooms, a massive staircase, and many leaded and stained glass windows.

By this time in our marriage, Susan and I were the proud parents of two children, Cheryl (age seven) and Michael (age five). Reilly, our second son, was born a year after we moved to Endbrooke. Shortly afterward, the weirdness began.

I was at work when my phone rang. It was Susan, and I could tell that she was upset.

"I just fell down the front stairs." She tried to stifle a sob.

"Are you okay? Did you hurt yourself?" I rose from my desk, prepared to head home.

"No … no, I'm fine. I think I twisted my knee, but we're okay."

"*We're* okay?"

Susan took a deep breath. "I was carrying Reilly."

"Is he okay?" Panic began to grip me.

"He's fine. I was able to grab the banister and break most of the fall." She paused. "It scared me though."

I sat down again. "I'm sure it did. How on earth did it happen?"

Susan took another breath before she continued. "I don't know. I didn't catch my foot on the stair runner or anything like that." She paused again. "It … it was almost as if someone pushed me."

"What?"

"I … I thought I felt a pressure on my shoulder. I don't know. Don't listen to me. I'm not making any sense."

"You're both really okay? Do you need me to come home?"

"No. There's no need for that. I'm just a bit shaken is all. We're fine."

"You're sure?"

She paused. "Yes. But could you please stop by the pharmacy on your way home and pick me up a topical? Aspercreme or Icy Hot? I have a feeling my knee is going to be hurting."

———

We put the staircase incident behind us and lapsed into a comfortable life in the big, old house. A couple of months passed without further incident, and Susan's fall was shelved as a mere accident.

The next occurrence happened during Cheryl's ninth birthday party. The house was filled with her friends and schoolmates. The girls found great delight in chasing one another up the front stair, along the second floor hallway, and then down the narrow rear stair to the kitchen. Whoops of laughter echoed throughout the house.

The joy of the moment was suddenly interrupted by a young girl's scream followed by the loud thuds of a falling body. Susan and I, seated at the kitchen table, jumped up and ran toward the rear staircase. We reached the staircase and found a young girl lying in a heap at the bottom of the stairs, her carefully curled locks a fright and the skirt of her pretty party dress up around her waist. She looked at us and burst into tears.

Susan gathered the girl in her arms and rocked her back and forth. "Oh, sweet child, are you all right? Are you hurt, dear?"

The little girl snuggled close and shook her head.

"You're okay?"

The little girl nodded.

Susan held her and kissed the top of her blonde head. "What happened? Did you trip?"

She shook her head left to right. "I was pushed."

We both looked up the narrow stairway. At the top, in the shadow of the upstairs hallway, several girls stared down at their friend.

I sighed. I hated the role of disciplinarian. "Did one of you girls push her?"

The girls shook their heads, denying any role in the incident.

Cheryl looked down at me. "No, Dad. She was way ahead of us. We didn't know she had fallen until we got here."

"Cheryl, are you sure?"

She nodded seriously.

And that was that. No further incidents, thank God, and the

fun of the party resumed unabated.

———

Things were fairly quiet at home after the second staircase incident. Life went on as normal, and none of us felt the least bit uncomfortable. Weeks passed without further drama.

The next strange happening involved Cheryl's glasses. She was readying for school and becoming frantic. "Daddy, I left them on my nightstand when I went to bed."

Skeptical, I looked at her and smiled. "You're sure of that?"

In her nine-year-old way, Cheryl placed her hands on her hips and glared at me. "Yes, Daddy, I set them right there on the nightstand."

"They're not there now?"

"No."

"Did you look under the bed? They may have fallen."

Her exasperation reached an apex. "Of course! I looked under the bed. I looked in the nightstand drawer, on my dresser, and in my closet."

Susan interceded. "I have one of your old pairs here." She opened a kitchen drawer and withdrew the eyeglasses, smiling as she handed them to Cheryl. "These will do for today, sweetie. I'm sure we'll find the other pair. Now, off to school with you."

When I arrived home that evening, I opened the kitchen door and stepped into a heated debate between my wife and daughter. Something was obviously amiss.

"You're sure you didn't leave them in the laundry when you went down to get your school clothes?" Susan waved the missing glasses in front of her.

Cheryl sighed, her frustration clearly evident. "No, Mom. I was still wearing them when I went down to the get my clothes. I didn't take them off until I was upstairs in my room."

They paused and glared at my intrusion.

I managed a weak smile. "Glasses found?"

Susan sighed. "Yes, buried under a pile of clean clothes that have been there for three days."

What could I say?

———

Andrea Padgent laughed.

Susan glared at her askance. "Why is that funny?"

Andrea hoisted her martini glass, and I poured her another from a crystal pitcher. "The behavior you've described is quite typical of young spirits. She's playing with you."

I looked from Jacob to Andrea. She obviously knew more than she was sharing with us. "*Young spirit?* How can you tell?"

My wife intervened before Andrea could answer. "*She?* Is it a woman?"

Andrea paused to sip her drink and shook her head. "No. Your ghost is a young girl. As I said, she's having fun with you."

I was becoming perplexed and impatient. "Why in hell would she do that?"

Andrea's laugh was a bit jaded. "Shes a *child*. She obviously likes you and enjoys being a part of your family."

"Hell of a way to show it," I muttered.

"Spirits often attach themselves to families. They want the relationship they had when they were alive. Apparently, your family has provided that, and it would seem that she is very comfortable with you. You have children, don't you?"

I nodded. "Three."

"That's part of the attraction."

I looked at Andrea and frowned. "Well, that's hardly reassuring."

———

The missing glasses were the tip of the iceberg. While I was at work and the children were at school, Susan was outside collecting firewood for our woodstove. Sensing something, she paused and looked up at the rear facade of the house. Cheryl's bedroom was at the back of the house and faced the driveway where the firewood was stacked.

Susan was surprised to see that the drape over the window had been drawn aside and a shadowy form stood behind it. Susan's initial reaction was that Cheryl had been watching her mom gather firewood.

It wasn't until the drape fell back into place and the silhouette disappeared that Susan remembered that Cheryl wasn't at home. She was at school.

Andrea looked surprised. "That's rather remarkable. An actual apparition is quite rare."

Usually, their presence is much more subtle." Andrea paused to devour another hor d'oeuvre. "Have you ever noticed her in any of your family photographs?"

Susan finished her cocktail and set the glass on the coffee table. "No, I don't think so." She looked questioningly at me. "Have we?"

I shook my head. "You're asking me if I've seen the spirit of a young girl in our family photos? I've never seen anything like that. Then again, how would I know?"

Andrea smiled. "Spirits, especially children, love to be part of a family. They miss what they had in life. They often show themselves during celebrations ... Christmas, birthday parties, those sorts of things. They tend to manifest themselves as a mist or a fog that may appear to be an imperfection of the film."

Her words caused me to gasp inwardly. I *had* seen that. In many of our family photos, there was often a hazy area off to one side or the other. I had always dismissed that phenomenon as a consequence of my smoking. The truth was shocking.

I nodded somberly. "Yes. I've seen that."

Andrea smiled. "Always at happy times, I suspect."

I nodded again.

—

The next incident happened soon after in our bedroom. I was changing clothes in preparation for a meeting I was obligated to attend. Nothing seemed unusual. I stood in front of my high chest, searching for the proper tie. A sudden movement caught my attention. I turned to the left, viewing my wife's dressing table. The white leather box that held her collection of rings suddenly became airborne. It hovered in mid-air before falling to the carpeted floor.

Shortly thereafter, Susan and I were watching television in our living room. The children were long in bed, and the house was quiet. Suddenly, the tinkle of breaking glass diverted our attention from the screen.

Susan looked at me in surprise. "What was that?"

I shrugged in response and rose from my chair to investigate.

Our wet bar was clearly visible from our seats in the living room, and the floor in front of it now sparkled with broken glass. I took one step toward the bar, when a martini glass flew from its stemware rack, paused in mid-air, and then exploded in a shower of crystal.

Susan jumped from her seat. "Oh, my God, those were a wedding gift. They were handblown."

Another glass followed suit, its shards joining those of its partners on the oak floor in front of the bar.

—

Andrea's eyebrows arched alarmingly. "Oh, my dear, you've apparently alarmed her. I would say she's quite angry."

"Why would that be?"

"Have you noticed any pattern to her aggressive behavior?"

I looked at Susan and shrugged.

There was a pause as we took time to think. Andrea and Jacob sipped their beverages and watched us closely.

Andrea popped another hor d'oeuvre into her mouth. "Think of anything?"

Susan hesitated and then looked at me. "Well … it seems as if there is always more activity whenever we put the house on the market. We've been thinking about selling and moving to a property with more acreage."

Andrea nodded. "That explains a lot. This spirit obviously likes your family and doesn't want to see you leave. Her increased activity is a reflection of that."

—

As time will, it passed quickly. There were other occurrences, but once we had a viable offer to sell the house, the activity seemed to wane. Our life entered the fast track as we packed and made ready to move to our new home.

The new owners seemed thrilled with the big, old house. We supplied them with many photographs of the house in its earlier years and a detailed accounting of the birds that came with regularity to be fed. It was a bittersweet time for us. We had lived there for 12 years, and leaving was more difficult than we expected. The new owners invited us to a celebratory cocktail party on the day of settlement. Neither of us felt inclined to accept. That chapter of our life was behind us … or though we thought.

—

A few months later, an old acquaintance phoned me.

"You're a difficult man to find. I didn't know you guys had moved."

I laughed. "Sorry, Kevin. We haven't had a chance to send out announcements. It's been crazy. You know how moving can be. How'd you find out?"

"I stopped by your house … your old house … two weeks ago. I knocked on the kitchen door and a kid answered it. Sixteen maybe. He looked terrified."

"Really?"

"I asked for you. He said you had moved, so I asked if he knew your new address. He looked frantic and told me he couldn't talk. He was waiting for an ambulance because his dad had fallen down the stairs."

I gasped. "Oh, my God." A feeling of fear and panic swept over me.

"Yes. He was quite distraught."

"Was his father okay?"

"No idea. I left and drove away before the ambulance ever arrived."

"What a mess."

"Yeah, well, it was just one of those things."

When I learned, days later, that the new owner had died, I couldn't help but feel a sense of guilt and dread.

Should we have warned them about the stairs? About the ghost? It was too late now for those regrets.

Life had wound itself down. What was done was done.

—

Several months later, I received a phone call from a local historian named Harriet Simpkins. I had known Harriet for years; she was a close friend of my Aunt Mildred.

"Hi! This is Harriet. Do you remember me?"

I laughed. "Of course, Harriet. How could I not remember you?"

"You're too sweet to an old lady."

"Nonsense. What can I do for you?"

She paused. "I'm trying to help the Clark's, the young couple who just purchased your old house on Atlanta Boulevard."

"Really?"

"Yes. They're a lovely couple."

I hesitated, unsure of how to proceed. "That's nice. It's a wonderful house. I hope they're happy with it."

Harriet did not respond. The gulf of silence stretched between us. "Harriet? Are you there?"

There was a muffled "yes" and then silence.

I knew Harriet was getting along in years, but this hesitation was more than a result of old age.

She obviously had some concerns.

"Harriet? Is there something wrong?"

I heard her inhale deeply. "Well … yes … apparently so."

I shrugged off a sudden feeling of anxiety. I knew and dreaded what was coming next. I did my best to lend a cheerful lilt to my voice before responding. "And what might that be?"

Her pause was accompanied with a deep sigh. "Well, they seem to feel there are problems with the house."

I laughed. "It's an old house. There are bound to be problems."

"I suppose so, but these are of a somewhat different nature."

"Really?" The chill was back, but I wasn't ready to acquiesce.

Harriet hesitated again. I could sense the conversation was becoming difficult for her. The pause continued.

"What is it, Harriet?"

"Well … they're somewhat concerned about various things that have happened."

Inwardly, I sighed, but I kept my voice light. "Such as?"

Harriet paused again. "This may sound rather peculiar, but they've experienced strange occurrences."

I finally took a deep breath and plunged into the murky depths of the matter. "Ghosts?"

Harriet's gasp was audible. "You … know?"

I sighed. "We lived there for 12 years. I think we saw most of what the house had to offer."

Harriet was breathless. "Did you ever tell anyone?"

"A few people … family, mostly. I can't say it ever became a matter of public knowledge."

"Well … that makes me feel a bit better."

"I did phone one of the previous owners"

"That was brave of you."

I laughed. "Brave but stupid. I think he thought I was out of my mind."

I went on to tell Harriet much of what had happened during our residence, as well as Andrea Padgent's opinions. Harriet murmured a few times during my recounting but never offered a value judgment or opinion. When I had finished, I paused, awaiting some sort of response. None came.

"Harriet? Are you there?"

"Goodness, yes. I'm simply trying to digest everything you've told me."

"I hope it was of some help."

"I certainly know much more than before I made this phone call."

"Will you keep me in the loop?" I asked.

"What?"

"Will you let me know if you discover anything?"

"Oh, of course, certainly. At least, now I have something to work with."

———

Several weeks passed before I heard from Harriet again. In fact, I had almost given up on her finding anything of interest. Whatever had happened had happened a long time ago.

I picked up the ringing phone but was unable to even give a greeting before Harriet spoke. Her dialogue was preceded by a deep, audible breath. "I've found your ghost."

"Really?" Needless to say, I was taken aback.

"Yes. Her name was Cynthia Camfield. She was the daughter of the family who built the house back in 1916. She was a Down syndrome child who only lived to 11."

"That's tragic. I always thought Down syndrome children lived long, full lives."

"Most do."

I could sense that her response was open-ended. "But?"

"You will appreciate this."

She was baiting me, plain and simple. "What is it, Harriet?"

"She died from a fall down the stairs."

"Good God, Harriet. How did you find that out?"

She laughed. "I may be old, but I do have my sources."

"You're remarkable."

"Thank you for that. An old woman can use all the compliments she can get."

"You don't need any help from me."

"You're too sweet."

"Did you find anything else?" I asked.

She chuckled. "Oh, yes. There's quite a bit of documentation regarding the Camfield family. They were quite prominent, you know."

"No, I didn't."

"Well, they were." Harriet paused. "Are you ready for this?"

I laughed. "Let me have it."

I could almost see the sly smile on her face. "You know the Presbyterian church down the block from the house?"

"Of course."

"They've a stained glass window dedicated to her memory."

"You're kidding."

"Nope. It's there as plain as day. 'In memory of our special child. May she rest in peace.'"

I almost choked. "So much for that."

AUTHOR'S NOTE

Although the above story is a work of fiction, I must admit to a degree of veracity. My family and I have had the dubious honor of inhabiting two haunted houses within a 24-year period. The first residence covered 11 years and the second, 12 years. Fortunately, we were granted a one-year respite between the two while we enjoyed a townhouse on Lewes Beach. Even with that, the time spent cohabitating with spirits was, periodically, exhausting. To say that those times were interesting and exciting would be an understatement.

As a reader, you may scoff at such claims. You are welcome to do so. Prior to our experiences, I would have probably been skeptical as well. All I can say is, at times, life has a funny way of changing one's perspective. For me, this was one of those times.

DWD

MARY WU

DIANNE PEARCE

ON A PARTICULAR night in early October, Mary Wu returned home from class loaded down with grading, walked through the back door of her row home, past the laundry waiting in the cellar for her to do in the morning, up the stairs to what was normally a darkened kitchen, to find the lights on and both Ted and Jenny awake and waiting at the kitchen table. Ted looked as if he was about to drift off any second, but Jenny was clearly upset.

"What's wrong?" Mary moved to set her bookbag on the bookcase next to the table, and turned and hung her coat up on the cellar door.

Ted gestured at Jenny. "She won't go to sleep. Not even with me."

"What? Jenny what's wrong?"

Jenny burst into tears.

"She said the kids told her about some woman in the bathroom who was gonna get her at Halloween."

"What? Jenny there's no woman in our bathroom, honey."

Mary crouched next to her and put an arm around her, pulled Jenny gently off of the chair and into her bony, but sturdy, lap.

"What did they say? Mom and Dad are not going to let anyone get you. You can't believe in the crap kids say."

"Mom! You said crap!" Jenny sat up, and she and Mary tumbled onto the floor. Mary began tickling Jenny as Ted yawned in his chair, watching them.

"You *did* say crap," said Ted.

"Well, call it what it is. Jenny, Honey, it's crap. It's crap that kids say, especially at Halloween, and especially city kids, and they probably have older brothers and stuff who tell them these stories to be mean."

"Kennedy said her mom believes it, and she is afraid and won't ever try it. But Karen turned off the lights in the girls' room and did it while Shavonne and I were peeing, and now she said we're all gonna die from it. But Genai said it's 'bullshit,' and it won't work anyway without it being nighttime and that you need a candle."

Mary sat back and looked at Jenny. "Okay, wait, what *is* it, exactly?"

"I don't want to say it."

"See," said Ted, "we're not getting any sleep tonight, and I have a conference with Dr. Franks at 7:00 AM." He sat back in his chair, exasperated.

"Alright," said Mary. "Jenny, get to bed, and I don't want to see or hear you until morning, and I don't care what happens, you stay in that room."

"No, Mom! I can't!"

"Uh, uh, uh! Don't you cry, or you'll be in more trouble. If you don't want to go to bed then you better tell me now, what the hell those girls said."

"Mary Worth. She comes and gets you."

"What?" said Ted and Mary in unison.

"Mary Worth."

"Uh, we need more than that, kiddo," said Mary.

"Her name is Mary Worth. You go into the bathroom in the dark with a candle. And you say her name three times. And she comes in the mirror and she pulls you into the mirror or she comes out and bites your face off and you die. And no one ever sees you again!" Jenny started crying again.

"That's not real," said Ted. "That can't happen."

"Of course not," said Mary.

"Kennedy's mom said it is real, and Bey said her cousin fainted when she tried it because a hand came out and grabbed her."

"Well, get up, and let's go do this thing."

"Really?" said Ted, sitting up in his chair.

"C'mon, get me a candle, somebody, and let's go do it and see what happens."

"But, Mom …"

"It's the only way you'll know it's not real, Jenny."

"What if Mary Worth gets you?"

"She can't get me because she's not real, this is not a true story, and I am not afraid. But I *am* tired, so let's do this thing and get to bed."

Jenny found an emergency candle in the kitchen drawer and a pack of matches. The trio walked upstairs to the small bathroom.

The room was still like it had been when the old row home was first built. Tiny white half-inch square tiles with black accent tiles covered the walls and floor. The ceiling was plaster lathe and had a huge skylight in it that operated on a long chain that hung down, so you could ventilate the steam from a bath or shower. The old deep cast iron tub was against the back wall. Then came the toilet on the right side, large and porcelain, and on the left a wide pedestal sink with an old mirrored medicine cabinet above it that was mounted into the wall. The mirror in the door was losing its silvering in places, which gave the image in it a streaky and warped look, but it was good enough to use to apply mascara, which is about all that was ever done with it.

"I hate this mirror," said Ted, "it's useless."

"Me too," said Jenny.

"Well I don't hate it, though it is pretty useless," said Mary. "But I like how the bathroom is so retro. Anyway, Jenny, let's light the candle."

Jenny lit the candle and Ted turned off the lights.

"Alright now, honey, hold the candle up so you can see in the mirror and let's do this thing."

"*What?* No way!"

"Yeah, I think we thought *you* were going to do this," said Ted.

"Oh sure, I can do it. Okay, give me the candle and let me be up front. Now, what do I do?"

"You say 'Mary Worth' three times."

"I think that's an old newspaper comic," Ted said.

"Okay Jenny, I say it three times and anything else?"

"Nope, just three times and she gets you. Should we hold onto you in case she pulls you into the mirror?"

"No, honey, it's not real," insisted Mary.

She turned and squared off her shoulders, leaned over the candle flame to put her face close to the mirror, and spoke slowly and dramatically.

"Mary Worth, Mary Worth, Mary Worth."

They waited.

Ted touched his Apple Watch to check the time.

They waited.

"I don't know," said Ted, "it's been two minutes Jenny. I don't think anyone is coming."

Mary tapped the mirror. "Me either, Jenny. It's just me in there, looking tired."

Ted walked over and flicked on the light. "I think we're good here."

"Wow," said Jenny, "thanks Mom."

"Sure. Anything in life you're afraid of, you've just got to look at it, Jenny. Just look at it and see if you really need to be afraid or not. And find a nicer group of girls to hang out with. Aren't there any other Asian girls in school?"

"Just the super snotty Korean girls. I'm not rich enough for them."

"Ha! Neither am I, I guess."

"I'm definitely not," said Ted.

"Alright, well, go tell those bastards tomorrow that you are not afraid of Mary Worth." Mary looked into the mirror, "This Mary is not afraid of you, Mary, because I'm real, and you're not."

"Thanks, Mom." Jenny gave her a big hug.

"Okay, can we sleep now?" said Ted.

—

Mary was asleep and dreaming. She was in a huge pit, or cavern. It was dank and dark and muddy, and she was at the bottom of a hill. She walked and walked, uphill through the humid, fetid air. Then—WHAM—her foot hit a step, carved out of rock. In fact, she could now see, because of phosphorescent lichen on the wet walls, that she had reached a stone staircase that went up, with no end in sight. She began to climb.

As she climbed, she felt herself becoming angry, angry that she had to climb these stairs, angry at all the people in the world who were outside in the light, angry about the cold and the ache in her bones, and the sweat of the hard work to climb these stairs.

Looking up up up to where the end of the staircase would never be she yelled out suddenly, "These goddamn stairs!"

Mary awoke to find Ted snoring next to her in bed. *It was just a crazy dream.* She turned onto her other side and sat bolt upright in bed. There, standing next to her bed, was Jenny. Her eyes and mouth were open and hollow looking. Her long black hair, which reached her shoulders usually, now reached the floor, and appeared to have some of the phosphorescent lichen tangled in it.

"What the hell, Jenny, are you okay?" She switched on the bedside light. Jenny was there, but she was regular Jenny, small, and sweet.

"Mom? Is it time for school?"

"What? No." Mary looked at the clock. "It's 4:00 AM, Jenny. Are you okay?"

"I thought you called me for school."

"No. Let's go back to bed, honey."

Mary walked Jenny back to her room and lay next to her until Jenny was softly snoring.

Mary stopped off to pee on her way back to bed, and as she stood washing her hands, she heard a voice.

"You didn't wait very long. You know I can't get up those god-damn steps as fast as I used to. I'm three hundred years old."

There was an old woman in the mirror, with grey hair and a mob cap on her head. She looked lined, and dirty, and angry.

Mary opened the medicine cabinet. It looked normal inside. She closed it. The woman was still there.

"What the hell?"

"It's all about Hell, isn't it? Yes, Hell."

"Okay, this is bonkers. I must still be asleep. Ted! Ted!"

Ted came running into the bathroom, his boxers crooked and his hair wild. "What, what is it? You okay?"

"Oh my god, am I awake?"

"What?"

"Do you see anything in this mirror?" The woman was scowling at Mary.

"C'mon," said Ted.

"I am serious," said Mary. "Do you see anything?"

"I don't have my glasses on, but no." He flicked on the light.

The face disappeared. Mary didn't see it anymore.

"Ted, am I awake?"

"We both are, unfortunately." He scratched his butt and yawned.

"Ted there was an old lady in the mirror. She spoke to me. She was colonial or perhaps something medieval. She had on one of those hats …" Mary trailed off, looking at the floor, thinking.

"You're just tired. You had a dream, or something, and it hung on because you're teaching too many classes this semester." Ted put his arm around Mary and led her back to bed. He wrapped his body around her, and they fell asleep.

———

The next night as Mary was pulling into the driveway behind their house, she noticed that the dwelling looked taller than normal. It seemed to curve and reach up and up. The ground had all been cut away from the row homes at the back, so that the cellar could be accessed and there could be a driveway. This meant they were three stories high in the back, as opposed to two in the front. Mary paused the car, half in and half out of the driveway, and craned her neck to see. Up at the top was Jenny's window. There was a soft glow there. Mary thought she saw Jenny—not real Jenny, but Jenny from the dream, with the long terrible hair all around her. Her mouth was open, and it looked as if she was screaming; her hands banged at the window.

Mary parked haphazardly and started frantically pushing buttons on her cell to try and reach Ted. The call kept coming back as "No cell service."

She leapt from the car without her bookbag and slammed at the back door with her key, trying to get the old lock to turn. There was a thud behind her, and she turned to see one of Jenny's stuffed animals, a giraffe, lying on the ground behind her. The lock turned. Mary jumped to grab the giraffe, and then ran into the house, across the dirt floor of the cellar, up the stairs into the darkened kitchen, through the kitchen into the narrow, windowless dining room, up the stairs to the top floor, and into Jenny's room where she threw on the light.

Jenny stood by her open bedroom window and held a stuffed turtle out of it. Mary ran to her, and grabbed her, dropping the giraffe on the floor. Jenny slumped into her mother's arms, going limp, asleep. The stuffed turtle tumbled out of the bedroom window and down, down. Jenny's nightgown was damp and she smelled like the woods from when it had rained that one time they had camped.

Mary half-walked and half-dragged Jenny back to bed and tucked her in. Jenny never stirred. Mary turned to close the window, but it was already closed. She went and looked, and even the screen, inside, was down.

She walked out of Jenny's room and took her coat off and draped it over the bannister. She went into the bathroom, ran the sink and cupped her hands to bring the cold water up over her face. She held her face in her hands a minute, sighed, and stood up.

"Fuck!" She jumped back.

"Eee hee hee hee, you'll fit right in down there with that dirty mouth." It was the woman in the mob cap. She was less spectral than last time.

"Ted! Help!"

"Shut your lips now, shrew!"

"I don't believe in you, hag! TED!"

"Fine, it's no mind to me if you believe in me today. When your baby comes to me, you will."

Ted smashed in through the door and flicked the light switch.

"Are you okay?"

"Yes, I think so." Mary looked into the mirror and only saw herself. "I saw a woman in here, Ted."

"Oh my gosh." Ted took a step back, "Mary, are you okay?"

"Yes, she didn't get me, but I think she wants to."

"That's not what I meant. I meant, *are you okay?*" Ted looked her up and down.

"What? What are you saying?"

"Mary, it's 2:00 AM. Did you know that? I have to meet with the study funders tomorrow. This is the second night in a row you have woken me up screaming over the mirror. And there's nothing there, babe. Nothing."

"Oh, real nice, Ted; real nice. There's nothing there? There's a freaking crazy colonial lady in that damn mirror, and she wants to hurt me. We should go back to San Fran, to our people, away from this history-ridden town. For all I know it's Betsy Ross coming after me because we don't put a damn flag on our front lawn every June 14th."

"Well, we should put out a flag. I say it every year."

"We're Chinese, Ted. We built the railroads, and we were the last people in the country to get the right to vote. We're not putting out the flag of racists."

"Mary, babe, it's so late. You need to rest. You shouldn't be in the bathroom in the middle of the night worried that a colonist wants to kill you. C'mon now." Ted put his arms around Mary, turned her toward the door. "Come to bed with me, with Teddy bear; c'mon."

"I haven't brushed my teeth."

"Mmmmm, that's okay. I love the way you stink. Come and get what's yours, and then let's go to sleep. C'mon. I'll give you a little something to make you relax. Well, not *that* little."

"Ted, I'm not gonna have sex. I'm being stalked by a demon from a cave underground."

"And from a bear above ground. C'mon now, come with me. You know you want to."

Ted started posing in front of her, showing off muscles that he didn't have. Mary couldn't help but laugh and let herself be led off to bed. She didn't hear the small cackle that escaped the mirror in a little puff of fog and went up and out the skylight.

———

The next day, as soon as Jenny and Ted were out the door, Mary was at the kitchen table on her computer researching Mary Worth. There wasn't a lot. It was an urban legend, had been around for at least 50 years, was passed around by kids. She learned it didn't have to be nighttime to call Mary, it just had to be dark, candlelit, in the room. And, according to everything she read, Mary couldn't get you because:

A: She wasn't real.
B: She could only attack, maim, or take away entirely (her crimes varied based on who told the story) the person who summoned her.

That was a huge relief.

After her second cup of coffee and her second hour of reading all things Mary Worth, Mary went upstairs to shower and dress for school. After she showered she went in her room to dress, then went back to the bathroom to do her hair and makeup. In the bathroom she screamed involuntarily at the words written in the steam on the mirror:

I AM REAL.

"Jesus Christ!"

"Eh heh heh heh. Don't bring Him into it. He's got nothin' to do with the likes of me."

The words came out of the mirror in a harsh whisper on a little trail of fog.

"That is it!" Mary grabbed the bar from next to the toilet that was used to close the blinds over the skylight and blocked out the sun. Then she closed the door, switched off the lights, and grabbed the candle and matches that were still sitting below the mirror on the sink. She pulled out a match violently, struck it, and lit the candle.

The woman, staring at her from the mirror, was the same as

before—old, wizened, dirty, scratched, matted hair sticking out from under the mob cap jammed down tightly on her head, and smiling a gap-toothed smile.

"What the hell are you?" Mary gasped.

"I'm Mary Worth."

"You're not real. I read about you."

"I don't know about that cause I never learned to do no reading, cause I never had no books. But I feel real to me."

"Well, get the hell out of here or I'll …" Mary looked around desperately and grabbed the hair dryer that was on the back of the toilet. "… I'll smash this mirror!"

"Oh yes," the old woman whispered back, "smash the glass, smash the glass. I want to get out. Smash the glass and let me out. I want to go outside and find all the children. Smash the glass, Mary. Smash it. Smash the glass. Smash the glass."

The hairdryer clattered to the floor. Wax dripped from the candle onto Mary's left hand.

"Just. Go. Away."

"I ain't going away, Mary. I'm tired o' this job. I got old bones. But the demon in Hell won't let me go until I bring him a replacement. What's your name? Mary Wu is what I hear in my head. So close to my name, though you look so different. I never saw people like you, but the demon won't mind. He's seen them all. Smash the glass, Mary. Smash the glass."

"You can't get Jenny. She never called you here. You leave her alone and get away from us!"

"Jenny can't come with me, no, you're right. She never called me to her. But Jenny can be hurt. Jenny can die. Ted can die, too. I am too old to climb that hill and all those hard steps when people call me. I need to stop toiling. You come and do it for me, Mary, Mary Wu. Smash the glass and let me out."

"No!" Mary threw the burning candle into the sink, turned on the bathroom light, and flung open the door. She ran downstairs and gathered up her things and ran down the cellar stairs, through the dank earthy cellar, and out the back door to her car. She sped out of the driveway, headed for the coffee shop, trying to dial Ted on her phone, but the call would not go through. The sky was getting dark, and when she looked at the dash clock she realized the day had gotten away from her. She had just enough time to get to her 5:30 class. No coffee tonight.

—

Mary was exhausted, mentally and physically, when she finally steered her quiet electric car into the alley that night. Though the sky was without moon or stars, she could see the glowing in front of her house. As she drove closer, her gaze rose up to the glow. There, in the air outside her window, was Jenny. She was in her My Little Pony nightgown, and her hair was long, reaching down past her feet, and matted around her like a web. In her hair was the glowing lichen from Mary's dream. From her hand dangled the stuffed giraffe.

Mary didn't even pull into the driveway, and she didn't try to phone Ted. She stopped the car in the alley without turning it off, and climbed out. Eyes on her daughter, she slowly walked to the house and went inside. As the door closed behind her, the toy giraffe dropped to the ground and landed next to the turtle that had been dropped the night before.

The cellar was transformed. It was a dark dank cave, all rock and deep dark dirt for walls, glowing lichen showing the way to the hewn rock steps. The steps went directly to the third floor. There was no way to get out in the kitchen. There was only up, up to the bathroom. Mary walked up the stairs. When she reached to top she went not into Jenny's room, but into the bedroom to get Ted. He was asleep, but as Mary reached for him she could see that his hair, too, had grown long and matted, and was wrapped around his neck. When she leaned toward him the hair tightened around his throat, and his gentle snore turned ragged. When she touched his arm the hair pulled tighter, and some wrapped around his face, over his mouth. She pulled her fingers away and went into the bathroom.

The candle she'd dropped in the sink was still there, and still lit. The light switch didn't work. A little dank swirl of fog was coming from the mirror. It carried a small raspy sound.

"Smash the glass. Smash the glass. Smash the glass. Smash the glass. Smash the glass. Smash the glass."

"Stop it, just stop it."

"Smash the glass. Smash the glass. Smash the glass. Smash the glass. Smash the glass. Smash the glass. Smash the glass. Smash the glass. Smash the glass. Smash the glass. Smash the glass. Smash the glass. Smash the glass. Smash the glass. Smash the glass. Smash the glass. Smash the glass. Smash the glass."

"Let them go, just let them go! You're not real! I don't believe in you!"

"Smash the glass! Smash the glass! Smash the glass! Smash the glass! Smash the glass! Smash the glass! Smash the glass! Smash the glass! Smash the glass! Smash the glass! Smash the glass! Smash the glass!"

"Shut up you hag! Leave us alone!"

The voice shrieked through the glass now, the fog carrying it and the spittle from the old woman's lips.

"MARY WU, MARY WU! CALL HER NAME THRICE SHE'LL COME FOR YOU! MARY WU, MARY WU, THIRD TIME YOU SAY IT YOU MAKE IT TRUE! DIE FOR ME NOW, MARY WU. OPEN THE GLASS. I'M HERE FOR YOU! SMASH THE GLASS! SMASH THE GLASS! SMASH THE GLASS! SMASH THE GLASS! SMASH THE GLASS! SMASH THE GLASS! SMASH THE GLASS! SMASH THE GLASS! SMASH THE GLASS! SMASH THE GLASS! SMASH THE GLASS! SMASH THE GLASS!"

———

No one quite understood what had happened with the Wu family. They had seemed a nice enough couple. Both worked at the college, and the college had given them the house to live in because the husband was doing important research. But, one early morning in fall, the ladies who did a morning powerwalk each day saw Ted walk Jenny down to the car out front as usual, but then he went back inside and came out with two suitcases which he slammed into the trunk without so much as a nod at the women walking by. The car jerked to life and sped off, much faster than the allotted speed limit. Then the police came, because Mary's car was still running, and still in the alley, and Kevin, the fireman who lived next door, couldn't get out to go on his shift. When the cops arrived, because the car had been left there, and the back door to the house was ajar, they went inside. They found the house was clean and neat and orderly except that the mirror to the medicine cabinet in the bathroom was broken and the floor covered with shards from it. The walking women told the police they had seen Ted leave with Jenny, but the police couldn't find him. He didn't show up at his research job. They checked with Ted's coworkers and with his family in San Fran, but no one had seen nor heard from them.

As for Mary, no one had seen her leave the house, and no one ever saw her again.

Well, not no one, actually. Kids saw her sometimes, those who were brave—or stupid—enough to stand before a mirror in the dark by candlelight and call her name.

Mary Wu

Mary Wu

Third time you say it you make it true.

So say it again.

Call Mary Wu.

AUTHOR'S NOTE

My daughter came home from school one day, worried about Bloody Mary, also known as Mary Worth. I knew all about Mary, because I remembered trying to call her out of a mirror at slumber parties from when I was a kid, but she never came.

This time, when I called her, she did.

DP

THE GHOST OF CHILLINGHAM MANOR

PATSY PRATT-HERZOG

EVELYN WAS STARTLED out of an uneasy sleep by a pervasive cold that gripped her with icy fingers. She sat up, pulling the thick woolen quilt more tightly around her but it did nothing to shelter her from the chill.

It was here.

Her gaze darted wildly around the room. The fire burned low in the hearth casting flickering shadows that writhed like agonized spirits in the semidarkness. With trembling fingers, she lit the bedside lamp, but its paltry glow did little to push back the oppressive dark.

For propriety's sake, hers was the only occupied room in the East Wing of the manor. David and the children slept in the West Wing and the servants had their own wing on the ground floor. Evelyn shuddered. Not for the first time she wished propriety had not demanded she be so isolated.

She had come to Chillingham Manor three months ago as a tutor to Lord David's children. Michael, aged five, and little Mary, aged three, were sweet, gentle children, eager to learn and craving her attention.

The huge old mansion and extensive grounds were well tended, but the moors beyond were dangerous and untamed. The staff still whispered of the children's mother, Lucinda, who had vanished one night to be lost forever in the wilderness. Despite its surroundings, Evelyn had been made to feel immediately at home by the staff and his lordship.

It hadn't taken long for David to win her heart for he was handsome and charming. But the closer they became, the more these strange happenings seemed to plague her. At first, it had been little things, like objects in her room moved from place to place—things that could easily be attributed to the children or the servants. But then the cold had come—waking her at night with its icy clutch, and Evelyn started to feel eyes upon her no matter where she went in the house.

It seemed this restless spirit was her cross alone to bear, as it bothered no one but her. David didn't believe in ghosts and had laughed when she'd spoken to him of her fears, even joking of moldering skeletons in the walls. Chillingham Manor had stood for a century, and in that time the old house had accumulated many tales of murder and woe. "Falderal and poppycock," David had called them.

David may have been skeptical, but Evelyn knew what she had felt and seen—there was something here, and that something did not like her.

Tonight on the terrace beneath a beautiful harvest moon, David had asked her to be his forever, but her happiness was in imminent danger of turning to nightmare. As soon as he placed the ring on her finger, she felt the icy prick of *its* presence against her skin. David had dismissed it as a chill wind and taken her inside, but she knew better. She knew what she must do–tonight she had to confront *it* once and for all when it came.

The heavy drapes billowed outward from the closed windows, the fire flaring and crackling in a nonexistent wind. Evelyn's heart pounded as the sweet scent of lilacs, so heavy it was almost suffocating, pervaded the room. The manifestations often came with the smell of lilacs, and Evelyn had grown to hate the flower.

"I feel your eyes upon me where ever I go," she said, shivering. The cold had intensified to the point where she could see her own breath. "But I don't know what you want of me."

As if in answer, her bedroom door jerked open, letting in a rush of warm air. The empty door gaped into the darkened hallway beyond, erasing her hopes that a human hand had turned the knob.\

"I am not leaving," she said, glaring defiantly into the darkness. "This is my home."

The vase of scarlet roses David had given her that evening skittered across fireplace mantle and dropped to shatter upon the floor.

It was more aggressive tonight than ever before.

"Why are you doing this?" Evelyn asked though she feared she already knew the answer. She self-consciously twisted the large diamond ring upon the third finger of her left hand. "Don't you think I deserve him?"

She repressed a shriek as the doors to her wardrobe exploded open. Her gowns came flying out and went swirling around the room in a virtual tornado of colorful fabric. The bureau drawers were next, one-by-one disgorging her undergarments into the maelstrom. Her traveling trunk sprang open and then as if by magic, the tornado of clothing sorted itself into place and the lid slammed shut.

"I am not leaving," Evelyn repeated, her voice trembling, "and no matter what you do, you cannot make me."

The blankets were ripped from her hands and flung to the ground. She drew her knees to her chest, huddling beneath her long sleeping gown as if it were a protective shroud, the braid of her hair coiled around her feet like the tail of a cat.

The bed vibrated against the floor, rattling and jumping like a living thing.

"Why are you doing this?" Evelyn shouted, clutching the crucifix around her neck so tightly it cut into her palm. "I've done nothing to you. Leave me in peace!"

The bed stopped shaking and Evelyn sat there, trembling and gasping. She knew it hadn't gone—she could still feel it in the room, watching her. "Show yourself!" she challenged and then stared, mesmerized as a ball of white light formed, hovering in the air before her. From its actions, she had expected some hideous, terrifying beast, not this beautiful, delicate orb.

"Spirit, why do you plague me?" she asked. "What must I do to appease you?"

The bright globe glided toward the door and stopped, hovering expectantly.

Evelyn lowered her feet tentatively to the ground and then hesitated. Dare she follow it? The light floated gently toward her, and then away again to hover by the door.

"If I go with you, do you promise this will stop?" she asked.

After a long moment, the ball of light bobbed once in the air.

"You will plague me no more," she demanded, raising her chin.

It bobbed insistently.

If she wanted answers to this mystery, she could not keep to the safety of her bed. Gathering her nerve, Evelyn stood and pulled her dressing gown from the tangled blankets on the floor. Donning it, she tiptoed after the bobbing light on bare feet as it glided down the hall and up the stairs.

She had never been to Chillingham's attics. It was a place the children were forbidden to go, and the staff seemed oddly reluctant to venture there as well. She couldn't imagine what the spirit wanted to show her in the topmost rooms of the house, but she followed it ever upward until they came to a narrow scarlet door.

The ball of light passed through the door and Evelyn hesitated with her hand upon the handle. If it were to somehow lock her in, it might be a long, cold time before she was found. Finally, curiosity won out over her better judgment and she tried the knob. The door opened reluctantly, creaking with disuse. The attic was dark, but her glowing guide waited for her, hovering patiently just beyond the threshold.

The rough floor was cold beneath her bare feet, but she followed the orb as it glided between rows of dusty crates, leading her toward the rose window that graced the front of the house. The full moon glowed brightly through the colored glass, beckoning her like a moth to a flame. She looked expectantly back to the ghost hovering there amongst the cobwebs.

I don't understand. Why have you brought me here?"

The globe of light swelled in size and began to take on color and form and features. Before long, Evelyn stood opposite a tall, willowy blonde with penetrating blue eyes. Her glowing gown was the same shade of lavender as the lilac that graced her coiffed hair.

Evelyn's breath left her in a rush. "Lucinda," she gasped.

A portrait of the children's mother hung above the hearth in their playroom. Michael sometimes spoke to it as if he was speaking to a living person. He had been only three, and Mary just a baby when Lucinda vanished . . . but perhaps she had never truly left her family after all. Evelyn's fear was replaced by pity as she stared at the glowing ghost.

"I know you still care for them," she said gently. "I care for them too. Can't we come to some kind of an understanding?"

The brightness of the ghost flared painfully, whether in anger, or some other strong emotion, Evelyn wasn't sure.

"Then why did you bring me here?" Evelyn asked.

Lucinda raised her hand, directing Evelyn's attention to the left. In an attic composed largely of wood and plaster, the spirit pointed to a bare wall of brick.

Evelyn looked back to the ghost in confusion. "I don't understand."

Lucinda drifted past her and vanished through the center of the brick wall.

She waited for a long breathless moment, but Lucinda did not reappear. Evelyn laid her hands against the rough surface. The wall was crudely constructed; it shouldn't take much to pry out a brick. Curiosity got the better of her, and she looked around the attic for something to use as a tool. After a few moments of searching, one of the dusty boxes yielded an old kitchen knife. Evelyn set to work determinedly.

The sprinkling of mortar falling to the floor was eerily reminiscent of the sound dirt made when striking the lid of a coffin in the grave.

She shuddered. Doing her best to put aside the morbid thought, she continued her work. After ten minutes of digging, she pried out one brick, and then another. She sawed away at the lumps of mortar with her knife, enlarging the hole until it was big enough to look through.

At first, all she could see was Lucinda's glowing back, but then the spirit moved aside, and a scream tore from Evelyn's throat.

In the small room beyond, a pair of empty eye sockets stared back at her from a nest of faded blonde hair. Dressed in the remains of a lavender gown, the skeleton slumped on a small cot, a manacle on one bony wrist anchored to a chain in the wall.

"You shouldn't be here, Evelyn."

She spun like a scalded cat at the sound of David's voice. He stood behind her, his dark eyes glinting in the light of the candles he held.

He shook his head sadly as he placed the candelabra on a stack of boxes. "I had such a life planned for us, and you had to go and ruin it."

Her heart shattered at his admission of guilt. "You buried her alive. How could you?"

He shrugged. "It was her fault, really. A good wife would have forgiven me a few little . . . indiscretions, but she was going to leave me, and take all her father's money with her." He laughed. "I couldn't allow that, now could I?"

His eyes glinted as he took a step toward her, and she took a step to the side to keep the distance between them.

"A man gets used to living a certain way, and I wasn't about to give all this up." His handsome features bunched into a scowl. "But she wouldn't listen to reason."

Evelyn looked at the man before her and didn't recognize him. Gone was the romantic, attentive gentleman who had won her heart . . . in his place stood an icy, calculating monster.

He stared down at her, his expression cold as the grave. "Are you going to listen to reason, Evelyn?"

He was going to kill her. Evelyn clutched the handle of the rusty knife with sweat-slick fingers that were folded into her dressing gown; she didn't think David had noticed it in her hand.

"I . . . I can be reasonable," she stammered.

He laughed. "Oh, my sweet, Evelyn. You're a terrible liar."

He lunged toward her, and she raised the knife, slashing it across his face before he knocked it from her hand. David cast her to the ground with a hard shove.

Evelyn rolled with the blow, protecting her head with her arms as she hit the ground. She sat up, cradling her bruised shoulder.

David stood before the rose window, the moon's glow bathing him in a ruddy light. He raised his hand to his bloody cheek.

"You'll pay for that," he snarled. "I was going to make this quick, but now you'll join Lucinda."

His face went ashen as his gaze shifted up and behind her. Evelyn turned, knowing what she would see. Lucinda stood behind her, her face darkened with choler, her blue eyes enraged. A corona of light flared around her with the brilliance of a sun. Her gown and her long blonde hair billowed around her as a cold wind surged through the attic.

"Lucinda," he gasped.

Evelyn felt a rush of energy as Lucinda surged through her. In the blink of an eye, Lucinda had moved to stand between her and David like an avenging angel.

Evelyn scrambled backward as the floor beneath her trembled and bucked. The bricks in the wall concealing Lucinda's body blew out, pelting the room with stone fragments. Stacks of boxes toppled and spilled, their contents swirling around the room in an angry vortex of freezing wind.

"Never Again!" Lucinda shouted.

Evelyn watched wide-eyed as Lucinda's spectral hands flew up and a shockwave of power ripped through the room, pitching David backward into the window. Eyes wide with terror, hands grasping at empty air, he screamed as he plunged through the glass and vanished from sight.

The swirling wind ceased, sending debris crashing to the ground all over the attic.

Evelyn came shakily to her feet as Lucinda turned slowly to face her. The avenging spirit's new-found power crackled across Evelyn's skin in an icy kiss.

Evelyn shook her head. "All this time you were trying to save me, and I didn't understand. I promise you, I will take good care of the children. I'll be here for them always."

Between one blink and the next, Lucinda was mere inches away, her blue eyes burning. "I know."

Cold fire poured into Evelyn's body through their locked gaze. Lucinda's spirit filled her up as Evelyn's consciousness splashed out upon the attic floor like water spilling over the brim of a too-full glass. Evelyn tried to fight...to scream, but she had no hands...no voice. Only a gossamer thread tethered her to her own body. Evelyn watched helplessly as her body moved toward the attic door, pulling the thread taught...until it snapped.

AUTHOR'S NOTE

This story started life as a contest entry for NYC Midnight. I enjoy participating in their flash fiction and short story contests. Authors are given three writing prompts and a few days in which to demonstrate their writing magic. The prompts I received for this story were: a ghost story/a private tutor/a love affair.

In the version I submitted to the contest, the story had a more romantic ending in which David saves Evelyn from the vengeful ghost of his first wife, Lucinda. I revision, I took the story in a darker direction, and *The Ghost of Chillingham Manor* was born.

PP-H

THE DARK AUGUR

ELIZABETH VEGVARY

THE WATER IS lukewarm, all the way through. Down to the bottom of the bathtub where her knuckles brush the smooth enamel, and back up to the top, breaking the surface. The temperate consistency of it is comforting. Languidly she swirls clockwise and counterclockwise eddies with her hand as the bath fills. She has opened the faucet mid-way; tepid she thinks and then wonders if she knows precisely the meaning of the word.

The stoppered drain is a mouth she has closed. She is seated on the rim of the body of the tub, staring seeing and unseeing into and through the bathwater.

There are things she cannot remember—remembrance a river in her mind, the depths hazardous with the threat of submerged debris, carrying her forward never backward. She allows herself to recall standing very still on a narrow sand and gravel bank. The smell of sun-warmed fennel and bay and something else beneath that, sour and foretelling. The shadowy woods at her back, the sunlight ricocheting off the currents in front of her. The water moving too erratically ever to be a mirror. And she, the living girl, opening on the cusp, the sharpened curving arc of her that will cut away childhood.

Her flesh and bones recollect bare feet, gravel beneath tender soles, the chill of a cool stream wicking up her legs. Denim shorts and a simple cotton top, the warmth of the sun on the crown of her head.

A memory, like a body, surfaces from up out of the depths, it rolls then sinks again.

The small inlet is a swimming hole of neighborhood repute. You and Marissa know how to get there. You follow Peach Drive down to Rose Road where the construction on the new houses has churned up the meadow, transforming flowers into dirt. You keep walking, teaching yourselves how to whistle with a bent index finger and thumb in between your lips until the pavement ends and a footpath continues through the long and smelly weeds. Down a swale, up a swell and then back down into the trees. A forbidden hike.

Transients, your mother warns. Stay away.

Scumbags and dangerous, your father says. Don't let me catch you.

The neighborhood boys swim there from time to time, but most days the boys stay inside their houses, playing video games and drinking endless cans of soda. Neither of you has brothers. Marissa has an older sister; you have two younger.

The day it happens you have been sneaking down to the river for weeks. To kick off your Converses, wade upstream and back downstream and then lie your young bodies down on the August-hot gravel shore, eyes shaded with the backs of your hand. You talk about horses, wild and corralled.

It is the end of summer; you are both 12 years old, standing together in the water nearly up to your knees, practicing your whistles.

You don't hear him approach. He is not there, and then he is there. Standing at the tree line, the thin rocky border of land lying ragged and useless from the toes of his battered cowboy boots to where both of you are wading barefooted.

That's something to see, that is, he says.

The sound of his voice jerks your head up. You are not familiar with the taste of adrenaline or the experience of how fear skips through the body, a poorly thrown stone. Just an arm's reach away, Marissa's eyelids shutter then open. You hold her gaze, a lifeline.

Come on out of there, come on over here, he instructs.

You can only move your eyes. The knife is the scariest thing you have ever seen in your life. It glints in sharp sunbursts. It is long and tight in his fist. The world narrows to this man and his weapon. His sheer presence is a dark command completely foreign to you.

Now, one of you girls is going to do exactly what I tell you to do. He is wheedling. Or else you're both going to regret it sorely. I'm sorry to tell you that. But I am fully able to hurt you bad. So, be good girls and do what I say.

You begin to cry. Your shoulders are shaking.

And then what? Marissa asks, calling across to him.

Then what nothing. I'll go on that way, he points with the knife upstream, and you two go on back to your mammy's and pappy's where you belong. You ain't supposed to be out here, I'm betting. Isn't that right? This surely is not the place for two young girls. You even bleedin' yet?

He laughs, and the laughter becomes a cough and wracks through his torso until he puts his weaponless hand up inside his t-shirt and thumps at his chest. Never mind that. One of you is going to do a man a favor.

You think you might faint. You have once before, at the clinic. The nurse merely held up the hypodermic needle, and all the blood left your head, and you swayed forward into your mother's arms, darkness embracing you. It is the same feeling but where is your mother now.

What's the favor? asks Marissa and her voice is small but without a tremble. I'll do it if you promise you won't hurt us.

Marissa, don't, you tell her, but no sound comes out of your mouth.

It's okay, Marissa nods, a small movement barely perceptible. It'll be okay, she says.

That's right, Marissa, he says in an approving voice. I promise you. Come on up here now.

He waves her out of the water, and she obeys.

You reach out, but she is already stepping gingerly onto the rock and gravel, walking on the outer edges of her feet, towards him.

He points past Marissa and right at you with the tip of his knife, working the tongue of his belt through his buckle. Now you stay right where I can see you. I know secrets about you, girl. I'm looking at you and I know things.

What things, you whisper.

I'm going to tell them to you right after your friend here does me that favor. I'm watching you, girl. You'd run home by yourself, wouldn't you, now? Leave her here, huh.

Marissa is only slightly shorter than he is. You can see the shape of his body as though he is a corona outlining the shape of her body. He puts a hand on her shoulder, urges her down to her knees, and then puts his hand on the top of her head. He says something you can't hear.

You don't want to run; you want to sink to the bottom of the river, your skeleton becoming a perilous snag. Instead, you squat down in the water and it laps at your skin. You hug your legs tight and press your face into your knees to keep from seeing. Then you cover your ears with your wet hands.

He whistles for you. You look up. He has Marissa by her ponytail, pulling her to the edge of the water. He lets her loose with a shove and walks into the water, walks right up close to you.

He reaches for your shoulder and pulls you to your feet with fingers like claws. His lips are at your ear. You're going to drown your third born in the bathtub, he tells you. His breath reeks of something unknown. That's what I know about you.

He steps away from you, smiling through cracked lips, three of his front teeth are gone completely. His mouth is a black void. He shuts it and grins.

He turns and sweeps his arms wide; the knife calls all the daylight and swallows it down whole. Now you two get them sneakers and get ready to run, he tells you both. I might follow you. I might not. You better hope you girls are smart enough not to tell anyone nothing about this. I'll find you. I'll kill your mommas slow-like right in front of you, and you can't even imagine what I'll do to you then. He waits, tucks his thumbs into the belt loops of his trousers, the knife, a loosely dangling afterthought, in one sweat-grimed hand.

You reach down for your shoes, and then you run.

She dials off the water, wipes her hands dry on her jeans. She moves with deliberation. Out in the front room, her two oldest are on the sofa, snacking on a tube of Ritz crackers, the baby is standing unsteady in the playpen, waving a gnawed cracker in her chubby fist.

You two behave now, she tells them. She leans down to lift her youngest up and out and onto her hip. The child melts into the motherly shape of her body, arms fast around her.

What are you doing, what are you doing? the two older girls sing-song in unison. Their attention glued to the television screen.

Just giving the baby a bath. Now hush.

AUTHOR'S NOTE

I wanted to explore an otherworldly possibility, a disturbing and darkly sinister reason behind infanticide. It's such a betraying crime. The child victims are already victims of projection. As with many horrifically unexplainable murders, we are told about voices and psychotic reasoning. What if … these explanations were true? As to the setting, there's always a simmering rage about the safety of girls and young women living in a youthful freedom.

EV

HAPPY FUCKING BIRTHDAY

JOHN DAVIS

If you want to talk about Washington, why not mention
Donald's birthday bash in the machine shop
on Halloween and the rednecks proud to be rednecks
screaming at the band to play Skynyrd and Ted Nugent.
How about the long legs of his daughter balanced
on stilted heels. Under the birthday streamer
she keeps inching up her dress strap that slides
off her shoulder —little black strap thin as yarn.
And Erskine who sets up a stand beside the band
and rolls cigarettes. And Andrew who wears a shit-
eating grin for a costume. And the dog who sits
on the grandmother's lap and yaps at Dinosaur Man.

You think I'm talking about White House Washington
with museums, Supreme Court and monuments.
This is Washington State in the woods. Monuments
to chainsaws and axes. A woman in blue scrubs
beats up two men. Her wife miscarried yesterday.
Anger spills out of her like fake blood on the birthday cake.
Only this isn't fake. The moonshine she passes to me
smells of cinnamon with a turpentine aftertaste.
Saws and sanders hang on the wall. Wedged against
the drill press, the bulldozer holds its silent growl,
waits for Sasquatch to suck a joint, start up the dozer.
I fit right in. Coast to coast the bull begins.

HALLOWEEN DANCE

JOHN DAVIS

The hamster and the frantic surfer
wanted to land the mermaid.
Even Freddy Kreuger was willing to unwind
the white wrapping from his face
and lace his lips around
two abalone shells that formed her bra.
A medfly drank sangria, spun her wings
at skeletons while Doris Day danced with St. Augustine
or Aristotle or whoever her robed date was.
She eyed the on-stage guitarist, fully ready to gut-punch her lust
into his G minor chords knowing why a man
strokes the blond neck of a Telecaster.
Outside, brown corn-stalks waltzed in a cool wind
and caramel-colored spiders crawled
the warped cardboard
of campaign signs.

AUTHOR'S NOTE

I have played in bands for many years. The events from
"Happy Fucking Birthday" stem from a party at which my band performed for a Halloween/birthday celebration. It was a surreal experience jammed into a garage/workshop. I was wedged between a drill
press and table saw playing my guitar. Oil was smeared on the concrete
floor. Hammers, wrenches, vise grips and screwdrivers hung on the
walls. The crowd was wild drunk on moonshine or stoned from the
ever-present smell of weed. Dogs barked. Fighters fought. Rain poured
outside. The poem practically wrote itself right off the grease stains in
the sliding door.

"Halloween Dance" originated from an earlier Halloween gig. Careful attention to costumes gave way to the tequila shooters bar. After half an hour someone stole two bottles of tequila, but by then the dance floor was crowded, and no one was feeling any pain. Hats, scarves, and waistbands were thrown on the floor, and dancers grinded as the tequila worked its charm the week before Al Gore challenged George W. Bush in the 2000 election.

JD

TEACHER'S PETS

LINDA RUMNEY

MONDAY MORNING. Mr. Wilkie braces himself for class. He stares at his own reflection in the men's washroom mirror. A few more grey hairs and a little patch of stubble he missed shaving earlier this morning. He needs an eye exam. He's noticed his eyesight fading for weeks now. Mr. Wilkie realizes it's nothing more than the effects of aging but he is disappointed all the same.

He straightens his tie, grape green, a poor match with his sky blue shirt, but who cares? He flattens the cowlick on his right side. The barber had not listened when he requested that it remain a little longer than on the left side so it would lie down, and now it stuck up as if he'd been sleeping on his face. A memory of his youth prickles at the back of Mr. Wilkie's neck, the awkwardness of his goofy hair, military style with a twist. That damned cowlick.

Mr. Nelson sits in a stall, a running commentary accompanying his various bodily sounds.

"I swear to God, if I have to eat one more freakin' cooking experiment I'll shoot myself. My wife ought to tell Cynthia we're not vegetarians. Who in the hell eats bulgur wheat anyway? Isn't that what aid agencies feed the poor in the Sudan? Jesus. I'm sorry ... I should tell Cynthia myself, but it would only come out wrong, upset her."

"I have a class," offers Mr. Wilkie as he stealthily leaves the washroom.

"... her husband's not been dead five minutes," Mr. Nelson continues. "Carol, that's my wife, says the cooking class is therapeutic for Cynthia. Perhaps, but not for me. You know what I'm saying? Ah, god. You still there?"

Mr. Wilkie hears the noise from his class from the corridor. Twenty-eight teenagers who could care less about positive integers and will never appreciate the beauty of quadratic formula. He places a hand on the doorknob, takes a deep breath, and pushes into the room, back straight, eyes on his desk. The kids fall silent until some smart-ass starts to hum the theme tune to *Star Trek*, a running quip in reference to Mr. Wilkie's pointy ears. The kids erupt into sniggers and exchange fist bumps.

Mr. Wilkie has heard it all a million times and remains calm and quiet, waits for the hullaballoo to fizzle out.

"Turn to page 69."

More sniggering, but either the reference escapes Mr. Wilkie or he's heard it too many times to care. Without a beat, he turns to the blackboard and scratches out a math problem.

The kids fall silent again, rifling through textbook pages and protesting weakly. Peter, a Polish boy the size of a legendary linebacker, snoozes at the back of the classroom. Moonlighting for his father's trucking business keeps him up all night, so the classroom is but a resting place.

"Try to solve the problem in pairs and then we'll work through it. You have …"

Mr. Wilkie checks the classroom clock against his wristwatch. He adjusts the time on the wristwatch.

"… 15 minutes."

The students huddle in pairs and hushed negotiations ensue. A hand goes up, Heather Givens.

"Sir, I don't have a teammate. Chloe isn't here … again."

"Well now," Mr. Wilkie searches, "join Clare and Eve."

Heather pouts, gets up out of her chair and drags it, noisily, across the room, dumps her books on Eve's desk as Eve and Clare huddle closer together, rolling their eyes. Peter stirs at the back of the classroom but, thankfully, the disruption isn't enough to wake him.

Mr. Wilkie folds his arms across his chest, his tweed blazer a little tight across the shoulders. The leather patch on his left elbow has begun to pull at the stitching.

His mind wanders as he contemplates a trip to The Home Store over the weekend. He will purchase a few things for his guest arriving on Sunday, maybe a new tablecloth if he can find one, and some pretty plates or a centerpiece to make the visit fancier. He already has the menu thought out. Pork chops the way his mom used to make them, a little baked apple on the side, mashed potatoes and gravy, nothing that would break the bank.

Mr. Wilkie checks the clock, watches the second hand as it hits the 12.

"Okay. Who has an answer?"

———

Tuesday morning. Mr. Wilkie walks Skip, his aging Golden Retriever, before school. They take the same route every morning, a route that has become shorter as the dog's years have progressed and his rheumatoid arthritis has worsened. This morning Skip is slower than ever and Mr. Wilkie contemplates making the route shorter still or, perhaps, starting earlier. He scoops up Skips poop, inspects it for worms, and deposits it in a trashcan designated for animal waste amidst a frenzy of flies.

The bright morning has drawn out other dogwalkers, earlier than usual. On most mornings Mr. Wilkie has the quiet streets to himself. A blonde woman with a well-groomed, antiallergenic, nonshedding, crossbreed heads in his direction. Mr. Wilkie swiftly attaches Skip to his lead to avoid any canine interaction that might trigger a conversation. He avoids eye contact as the woman approaches. He chances enough of a glance at her to see that she is smiling, all lipstick and cheek implant.

"Well, hello there. Beautiful morning," she chirps.

Unable to ignore her, Mr. Wilkie nods and smiles pleasantly as they pass one another.

"Mr. Wilkie, isn't it?"

It's unavoidable, he must respond in case it's a parent. He doesn't recognize her, but after a while all parents look alike, sound alike, make the same jokes, and assume their kid is the brightest and best.

"Yes. Good morning. How are you?"

She laughs. "It's okay. You can drop the pretence. I'm not a parent. I'm Carol."

Mr. Wilkie stares blankly, strains to remember whom Carol might be.

"Ted's wife. Ted Nelson, from school."

The penny drops.

"Right. Yes, sorry. Ted, yes."

"Ted tells me you're single. No lady friend?"

Mr. Wilkie reels from the intimacy of the question, having only just met this up-to-now total stranger.

"Oh, don't mind me. I'm just a little Miss Busybody. I like to think it helps me look out for folks."

Mr. Wilkie does mind, but he tries hard not to show it.

"Well, it was nice to finally meet you. Ted talks about you all the time."

Carol throws her head back and expels a cackle that makes Mr. Wilkie's cowlick spring up like a startled cartoon cat's fur.

"I'd like to be a fly on the wall for those conversations."

"Oh no, it's all good."

Mr. Wilkie surprises himself with his social ability. Carol taps him on the arm with a well-manicured hand.

"I'm so glad we bumped into one another. I have a favor to ask."

Who the hell does she think she is? Mr. Wilkie wonders, a fixed smile on his face. She moves in closer and continues without taking a breath.

"We have a friend, Cynthia. She lost her husband last year and … well … we try to support her as much as possible, and God bless her, she's doing the best she can to overcome her loss. Cooking classes and whatnot. The thing is, she has been gifting us with the most delicious food from one of her classes, vegetarian cuisine, and Ted and I … as much as we look forward to these delights, simply don't always have time to appreciate them."

Mr. Wilkie knows she's lying. His smile starts to fade, anticipating her request.

"I was thinking it might work rather well for you both if, perhaps, she gave you the occasional dish."

"Oh, I don't …" Mr Wilkie checks his watch, seven minutes fast after the adjustment he made the day before.

"Okay, good. It's settled. I'll tell Cynthia."

Carol strides away before Mr. Wilkie has time to rebut.

"You don't know where I live," he calls after her.

"Oh, don't be silly," she laughs.

———

Wednesday morning. Mr. Wilkie walks Skip around the block. It is 5:00 AM. The street is quiet and only half-lit by an early-rising sun. No other dog or its owner walks the streets at this hour, which is exactly the way Mr. Wilkie likes it. He has enjoyed Skip getting older, less exposure to the risk of fellow dog lovers asking the statutory questions of others of their ilk. *How old? What's his name? Have you had him since he was a puppy? Is he a rescue?* Now 14, Skip came to him as a happy accident, as a puppy, yes. The woman in the pet store had told him, while he was collecting hay for Charlie, that someone had left Skip in the dumpster out back. He took to Skip straight away, the same color as Charlie, and hoped they would get along. At home, when he introduced him to Charlie, the chinchilla had seemed to take to Skip as well, much to Mr. Wilkie's delight.

Back at the house Mr. Wilkie feeds Skip and whispers a hello to Charlie, still hidden in his nesting box inside the large, tall cage in the living room.

"That wasn't so bad, eh Skip? I could get used to heading out that early every morning."

Skip chows down, a little deaf now, too, he only senses the one-way conversation and looks at Mr. Wilkie with a well-rehearsed gaze of acknowledgement that he knows will satisfy.

—

Thursday evening. Mr. Wilkie marks test papers. The neat piles stacked to match up with the checks on the blue gingham tablecloth. He does not add smiley faces or praise. His neat hand simply notes the answers as correct or incorrect with a uniform tick or cross and the total in the bottom right-hand corner. His final paper, perfectly timed, concludes with a knock at his door, the arrival of the take-out delivery boy.

When he swings the door open, wallet in hand, Mr. Wilke is surprised to find a shy, homely woman wielding a casserole dish.

"Mr. Wilkie, I presume," she jokes. "Stanley," she continues weakly, extending a hand.

Mr. Wilkie checks up and down the street for the delivery boy.

"I was expecting someone else."

"Oh, well. I'm not *really* Stanley, of course. I'm Cynthia."

"Oh?"

"Carol's neighbor. She said to come over. I brought you an eggplant cassoulet."

Mr. Wilkie eyes the dish cautiously, uncertain how to proceed. Cynthia extends the dish toward him, almost thrusting it into his belly, now embarrassed and close to tears. To Mr. Wilkie's relief the take-out delivery boy arrives and the distraction of exchanging payment for food lightens the tension and awkwardness of the moment.

Cynthia steps down from the porch and starts to back away.

"It will keep in the fridge for a couple of days. I can come back for the dish another time."

Skip appears at Mr. Wilkie's side and Cynthia seizes the opportunity for another attempt at conversation.

"Well now, who's this? Hello."

Skip waddles toward Cynthia to get a better look, completely blind in one eye. He sniffs at her for a moment. Mr. Wilkie, loaded with the casserole dish and the paper sack with his Kung Pao chicken and rice, shuffles on his feet, anxious to retreat inside.

"Skip."

"Ah, well, nice to meet you, Skip," Cynthia says, as she strokes the dog beneath the chin, the place he likes to be stroked best.

"It must be nice to have the company of a pet. My late husband …" Cynthia pauses, then begins to cry. "Oh dear, how embarrassing," she says. "I'm terribly sorry."

Mr. Wilkie surveys the street for a possible audience then re-signs himself to inviting her in, lest the neighbors spot her and gossip ensues.

"Please, won't you come in for a moment?" he offers. "Just until you gather yourself."

"Thank you." Cynthia steps up onto the porch and pushes past Mr. Wilkie, a little cheered by the unintentional kindness.

Mr. Wilkie follows with the food and kicks the door closed with his left foot. He sets the food down atop the kitchen counter as Cynthia stands, awaiting the invitation to sit.

"Can I fetch you a glass of water?" he calls, through a 1950s-era serving hatch.

"No, thank you. I'll be alright."

When the invitation to sit fails to materialize, Cynthia wipes her face with a sleeve and takes a deep breath. She notices the cage.

"What's in there?"

Mr. Wilkie cranes his neck to look in the direction Cynthia is pointing, then appears beside her to offer her an explanation.

"That's Charlie. He's a chinchilla. He's nocturnal and very old."

"Sounds like me," Cynthia jokes. "I seem to come alive at night these days. Have trouble sleeping, you see."

Her pain is lost on Mr. Wilkie who eyes the paper sack hungrily.

"Well, you must be hungry," Cynthia says. "I should soon as well."

"Would you care for some?" The words escape from his mouth before he realizes it. "It's Chinese, from the new place at the end of …"

"Yes, I've seen it. I'll maybe just have a bite or two."

Mr. Wilkie moves his test papers and returns to the kitchen to divide the take-out between two small plates. He places one on the table and offers Cynthia a chair.

"Oh, that's far too much," she protests, but tucks in even before Mr. Wilkie joins her at the table.

"I didn't realize how hungry I was," Cynthia says, satiated.

"Isn't that always the way?" Mr. Wilkie comments, unsatisfied.

Cynthia twitters along like a dawn chorus as Mr. Wilkie pretends to listen. He thinks about Sunday and spending time with his guest and smiles to himself. Cynthia smiles back at him, mistaking this for an expression of pleasure, impressed that Mr. Wilkie is such a good listener.

Finally Mr. Wilkie pretends to suppress a yawn.

"Forgive me," he says, "I was up quite early this morning. It's been rather a long day."

"Of course, I don't know how you do it. I could never be a teacher. Speaking of which, is there any word on that missing student? Chrissie, was it?"

"Chloe. Runaway, according to the parents."

"Ah. Ran away once myself when I was young. Well, I should let you get to bed."

Mr. Wilkie accompanies Cynthia to the door and she thanks him for a pleasant evening,

"I'm sorry for going on so," she adds "It's so nice to have someone to talk to."

She leans in unexpectedly and plants a light kiss on Mr. Wilkie's cheek. He catches a brief waft of lemon and pomegranates.

"Till next time."

"What?"

"I'll stop by for the dish over the weekend."

"Yes, yes," Mr. Wilkie says, narrowing the gap between himself and Cynthia with the door until she is gone.

———

Friday morning. Mr. Wilkie washes his hands at the men's washroom sink beside Mr. Nelson who is talking about his golf game in a language completely alien to Mr. Wilkie.

"It's a bit of a dream, but to play at St. Andrew's would be amazing. Too bad about the weather, though I guess that's why the course is so green, hah! And you, you dark horse, I never knew you had it in you."

"Excuse me?"

"You know. Cyn-thi-yah. She was on the phone this morning telling Carol how sweet you are. Sweet!"

"I ... she showed up at my door with a stew or something. I think I made her cry so I invited her in."

"And?"

"And what? And nothing."

Mr. Nelson nudges Mr. Wilkie sharply in the ribs. "Hey, your secret's safe with me. Men of the world, right?" He smiles conspiratorially and makes an annoying clicking noise with his tongue in synch with a wink.

Mr. Wilkie raises an eyebrow,

"I have a class to teach."

"Sure, buddy." Mr. Nelson slaps Mr. Wilkie on the back, tosses his paper towel in the trash, and walks away.

"Catch up with you later."

"Yes, later."

Mr. Wilkie surveys his face in the mirror. *"Men of the world?"*

—

Saturday morning. The weekend finally arrives. Mr. Wilkie holds a list of desired items in one hand and pushes the cart around the charity store with the other. Already resting in the cart is a nice china bowl which he plans to use for the salad. He sees a stack of complementary plates on the other side of the open shelf display and maneuvers around two Asian women in a heated dispute about a copper pan, both tugging at it fiercely. He places two of the plates in the cart and moves, quickly, away from the intensifying debate. The women wrestle to the ground and a child, sitting in a cart, wails hysterically. Amidst the commotion, Mr. Wilkie makes a dash for the checkout, pays with cash, and disappears from the store.

In the parking lot he sees Cynthia leaning into the trunk of her car. Without missing a beat, he jumps into his ancient Nissan and starts her up. He flips down the sun visor and startles at a sudden rap on the passenger-side window. He barely has time to think before Cynthia opens the door and squeezes into the seat beside him.

"Hi," she says, all smiles and warmth.

"Hello. How are you?"

"I'm good actually," she tells him, "I haven't felt this good since ... well, I can hardly remember when."

"I'm very happy for you. That's ... swell."

"Swell?" Cynthia laughs, "That's cute. I didn't think anyone used that word anymore."

Mr. Wilkie lets out a sigh and appears wounded.

"I'm not poking fun," she apologizes, misinterpreting annoyance for hurt.

"No, I'm sure," he asserts, irritated beyond words.

"Oh God, I've hurt your feelings, I'm so sorry. It's been such a long time since I've done anything like this."

"Like what?" He doesn't have time for this.

"Dating, of course."

Mr. Wilkie turns to Cynthia with a forced smile. He's prepared to do whatever it takes to get her out of his car so that he can carry on with his business.

"I'm not upset," he assures her. "I should apologize. I'm in rather a hurry, you see, and there was a disturbance in the store that set me back a bit."

"Oh dear." Cynthia reaches for the door handle. "I won't keep you."

She pushes the door open and clambers out. More than just a few pounds overweight, she is lacking in agility. Cynthia leans in as Mr. Wilkie starts to pull away.

"I'll come by and get that dish."

"Yes, fine." He steps on the gas and the door closes. Cynthia, an object in the rearview mirror that looks closer than it appears, fades.

—

Sunday morning. Mr. Wilkie awakes to Skip lapping his tongue over his face. He has grown accustomed to the early start to the day already, disproving the adage about old dogs and new tricks.

Mr. Wilkie pulls on a pair of casual pants and a pair of hush-puppies, too worn for school but still clinging to life. A dress shirt finishes his ensemble.

The morning walk is pleasant, if a little short due to Mr. Wilkie's eagerness to start the preparations for his guest. He cuts across Willow Avenue to Hope and through the back alley behind Gideon to bring them back to Albion and home. This early on a Sunday morning guarantees deserted streets, and this heightens Mr. Wilkie's excitement for the day ahead.

He feeds Skip and says hello to Charlie, as elusive as ever, hiding away in his nesting box. He takes a light breakfast of cereal and toast with strawberry preserves and washes the few dishes, a normal day in most respects except today he will have to ensure the air conditioning is set at its coldest and Charlie is removed to the spare bedroom so as not to feel too cold.

Mr. Wilkie drags the cage down the hall and throws a plaid blanket on it, the kind you might use for an impromptu beach picnic, not that lunch on the beach has ever been an option for Mr. Wilkie.

He scrapes the untouched eggplant cassoulet from the casserole dish into the garbage, washes and dries the dish, and places it on the porch should Cynthia happen by to collect it. He places a polite note in the dish:

Delicious.
Skip and I enjoyed it very much. Sorry I'm not home to thank you in person.
Regards –

The note hints at him feeding the stew to his dog. A cunning plan to discourage any further offerings. *A clever one*, he thinks.

Mr. Wilkie turns on the oven, cores the apples, seasons the pork chops and peels the potatoes. Once the oven reaches the required temperature he throws in the tray of meat and apples, boils the potatoes, and prepares the instant gravy.

He showers and dresses in a clean, casual but smart shirt, unseasonably warm sweater and khaki pants, with pockets at the knee, a purchase from the outdoor recreation equipment store where he bought the extra-large cooler used by fishermen for transporting their catches.

The kitchen is arctic, save for the heat from the stove, which Mr. Wilkie hopes, will not alter the overall temperature and cause problems for his perfect lunch date. He sets the table for two and prepares the salad in the bowl bought from the charity store. The plates really do go well and he congratulates himself while admiring the arrangement. Skip wanders down the hall to the spare bedroom, the kitchen far to cool for his taste, and jumps up onto the bed, nestling into the comforter for warmth.

Mr. Wilkie unlocks the basement door, flicks on the light, and takes the stairs to the small space below the house. He retrieves a key from its hiding place under a half-empty can of Magnolia, eggshell finish paint, and unlocks the padlock on the chest freezer.

Cynthia arrives in her little red sports car, a gift to herself, the grieving widow, outside Mr. Wilkie's house. She has made a special effort today, her hair newly trimmed and her voluptuous figure squeezed into a summer frock, two sizes too small. She wears a pair of heels that her feet are attempting to escape from, swollen flesh oozing between the straps, and hobbles inelegantly onto the porch.

She sees the dish and frowns with disappointment. She smiles at the cute note and the sweetness of sharing with man's best friend.

"Well now, that is adorable," she sighs, and walks round the porch to peer into the house in the vain hope that he has not yet left, heels click-clacking in Morse code—*I'm here, it's me, yoo-hoo.*

Mr. Wilkie hears the approaching footsteps from the basement and freezes to the spot, cursing uncharacteristically beneath his breath.

"Gosh, darn it."

He holds very still, suspending the large object he's semi-retrieved from the deepfreeze, half in and half out. Plastic wrap squeaks in his moist hands.

Cynthia taps on the spare bedroom window, spotting Skip on the bed.

"Skip, hello, Skip. Is your daddy still home?"

Skip, deaf and oblivious to Cynthia's presence, sleeps on.

"Skip. Skip!" Cynthia, concerned, calls out. "Oh dear, I hope he's alright." She moves to the back of the house and shoves her face up to the glass in the back door. She sees the table set for two and blushes with embarrassment.

"He's entertaining. He's having lunch with another woman."

Cynthia hammers on the door. "Mr. Wilkie, I know you're in there." She raises her nose to the air. "I can smell pork chops." She hammers again and leans in, listening for movement or lowered voices.

Mr. Wilkie stands firm, his hands start to feel the chill of the deepfreeze and the moisture has fastened them to the plastic. He wiggles his fingers loose and encourages the circulation back to regain feeling. His spine feels a twinge as he hangs over the freezer. Noiselessly he grimaces.

Cynthia persists. "Carol warned me about you. She said you were secretive. Well, don't think I'll be coming around again with any of my cooking, you … you creep." Unsatisfied by her own words, Cynthia offers a word of warning to Mr. Wilkie's lunch guest. "Watch out lady, you're probably not the only one."

She stomps round to the porch steps then peels off the heels, marked horrifically by the straps. She hurls the shoes at the sportscar then retrieves them and inspects the vehicle's bodywork for damage.

"Damn and blast it, Cynthia, he simply isn't worth it."

She throws the heels onto the passenger seat through the open window, forces her plump body behind the wheel, and starts the engine, revving the accelerator for dramatic effect. She throws the car into drive and speeds off down the street, startling a jogger on the sidewalk.

Mr. Wilkie waits for several moments until he hears the engine roar. He sighs with relief. "I thought she'd never leave," he whispers to the large object that emerges in his arms from the freezer.

He carries the object up to the kitchen and sits it at the dining table, frozen to fit perfectly on a dining chair.

"I hope the chops aren't spoiled," he says, pulling down the oven door, excited and back on track. "Ah, they're okay. Not burnt at all. That would be so embarrassing."

He drains the potatoes, adds lashings of butter and cream to the pan, and mashes them to a smooth mush. He boils the kettle and adds water to the instant gravy powder.

Mr. Wilkie serves the meat and potatoes onto two plates and places them on the dining table, one for him and one for Chloe, his chilled guest, who smiles coldly back at him.

AUTHOR'S NOTE

In my final year at school, before expulsion and my apparent disappearance, I had the most unusual math teacher. Not unlike Mr. Wilkie, he wore tweed and corduroy and was a dead ringer for Mr. Spock, of *Star Trek* fame. It's true we mocked him with the theme to *Star Trek* as he lumbered into class, a brown leather briefcase with goodness only knows what inside. He seemed to take something of a dislike to me, sending me, on most days. to the back of the class until I simply stopped showing up. I left school, ran away from home, and disappeared (my superpower of invisibility had been truly honed by this time). I often wondered if anyone thought about me. This story is where my imagination went in posing that question.

LR

THROWN OUT OF THE CHURCH BY MY FATHER — A BAPTIST DEACON, 1964

ALICE MORRIS

after James Tyner's *Attacked by a Pitbull, 1989*

You're herded up the steps, his hands gripping your mother's throat,
and his gold tooth glinting now, and his lips go tight

with snarls, with hisses, and you're thinking no one
is going to get home in good shape tonight, and now you won't have
　　your homework

ready, and it's amazing how strong your father is and you
wonder what has driven him into such a frenzy, maybe your brothers
　　laughed

too loud during his upstairs deacon's meeting, sent him racing to the
　　church basement
and now he's throwing his family into minus 40 degree wind chills

telling them, *You'd better not leave that car!* And in the distance the glow
　　of a
house light, and you dare and triple dare each other to leave the car,
　　ring that bell

but no one dares, and there's only metallic darkness
brothers hunched on floorboards, and now the cold's going for your
　　belly

and in your mind, you're telling your father you're pissed, you've
　　worked
six months bringing your grades up, trying to get somewhere, and it's
　　bleak

as hell out here, and you flick that fucking thought back,
and no one is moving now, it's silent, breath slipping

away like serpents, and your fingers frozen like fangs at his throat.

SHE WAITS FOR A SEASON OF HOPE

ALICE MORRIS

1

Spectacles now thick as magnifying glasses perched
On the bridge of her nose
Where will this aging take her —
Will her children send letters
Will she be taken to the old folks home, or at 74
Buy a place of her own, with windows
That open, and close

2

She once had long black hair in a braid down her back
She once looked to Buddha
Had gardening tools, gloves dirty from working among
Tomatoes and garlic
A bowl of fresh eggs from the chicken coop placed on the counter
Each morning, the news delivered
By bicycle

3

Wind gusts, and lightning
Blow her house into flashes of purple, chartreuse,
Egg yellow
She puts on her classical music, paints
Bold strokes into the night, freed
Of the blackness
That has gripped her

4

For 24 years she wintered at The Grand Hotel of Paris
Each morning precisely at seven
Took the same table and ornate white metal chair
Under the same green and white awning, looked toward the same
    sidewalk
Alone, always dripping
In gold

Sophisticated attire, manicured nails, a slim brown cigarette between
    fingers
Wondered how she would amuse herself until noon when she would
    meet
Dominique at his yacht
A long drag, and—another smoke-filled meditation —
Will there be time for all the places, all those places she wishes to
    go…
Her mother died just a month ago

An exhale
Another Draw
Her mind blank, and from some far-off place
A string of sparrows saying
> *Give us six reasons why you neglect your art*

> *Fear*
> *The family won't like it*
> *They'll disown me*
> *I've kept it to myself this long*
> *It forces me to look back*
> *I'm not up to completing the task*

5
Sunlight fractures sky
She wonders, did she remember to lock her back door?

6
Hidden in shadows except to those who knew her café habits
She looked up, saw the aging but lithe Pierre approaching, his strut
His only constant
She was such a fool back then, so willing to confuse illusion for truth
One night he didn't return to their apartment
Had been with his new lover
Later she learned his name was Francisco
She studies her blood-red nails
These days, she considers herself a much wiser woman

7
Her life has been a string of recriminations

They pass through walls and time to follow her
The air thick with the meaningless banter of ancestors lost
Long ago among ruins
She has walked the aisles of dark towns seeking
Envelopes of pale blue — filled with hope

8

The Human Genome Project, she reads, as she sips her steaming espresso
Has not yet decoded which chromosomes mutated, causing early man
To seek light
The blue string of DNA, representing the urge to experience joy
Was somehow destroyed
Replaced
By strands of
Scarlet anger

9

The birds, when she woke that morning hid in the elderberries
The light was still and dove-grey
By six, a murky yellow began to break through
Wrens, sparrows, and martins began singing —
Their songs welcome

10

Dust has settled
Everywhere

SPIRIT OF THE EVENING, PRAY FOR US ALL

ALICE MORRIS

a wandering daughter dreams in fear—
a broken plate   a horse's head

waterfalls through rocks
old men   weary souls mutter and choke

lean toward an emptiness
in late September wind

blades of grass   plants   slowly dying
atoms   bones   hair combine

to nothing
wrapped and mummified in fog

the thinnest lines connect the world
of shadow   clouds of smoke

her future sealed in whispers

AUTHOR'S NOTE

"Thrown Out of the Church…" When I first read James Tyner's poem, *Attacked by a Pitbull, 1989*, I knew I had found the model for a poem I had been trying to write. I knew I would follow James Tyner's form closely. His form would be the vehicle that would provide the necessary parameters, it would give me word markers—like road signs, it would dictate the speed of the poem, maybe even give me the actual permission to go on what felt like a very dangerous and risky ride.

Perhaps I can only speak of this poem in metaphor, rather than try to use words to speak outside of the poem itself.

I love the words of Richard Hugo in *The Triggering Town*. He says, as a poet, "You owe reality nothing and the truth about your feelings everything."

I think *Thrown Out* … is a "truth about your feelings" poem.

"She Waits for a Season of Hope" was inspired by several images that had been on my mind, and by a notebook of my responses to free writes, some responses from a free write based on artwork.

But to go back a step, before writing this poem I had been thinking I had never done anything with my free write work, and I had notebooks filled with it. I decided one morning to choose one of these notebooks and try to write a poem based on the prompts and responses, but I would also allow myself the freedom to add newly prompted material as I went along. I decided to go through the notebook page by page, in order, trusting that I would find fragments that would somehow speak to each other. I would let my instincts lead the way and accept that no matter what appeared on the page, all of it was some expression of something I either needed or wanted, on some level, to say—as had been the case when I had initially responded to each prompt.

By the end of a long day, when I came to the last notebook entry, I had the rough draft of this poem, "Sister of the Evening Pray for Us All." During a week-long poetry challenge, I realized I was coming across some very strange images contained in less than five words. These strange, gothic, absurd images were prompting my own thoughts, ideas, and images. I knew I had to write this all down and try to write a poem because there seemed to be something deeper that I was feeling. I had to try to get to the bottom of that. This poem went through several drafts as images were dropped or distilled to make this rather eerie poem.

AM

WHY THE WRITER CANNOT REST

PAUL MILENSKI

AFTER A DAY OF fictive torment, manic word searches, and tempestuous keyboard fingertip strikes, I staggered to the brook and sat on my bench hoping to observe the benign chipmunks scamper in and out of the cracks of the large boulders that serve as retaining wall for my lawn.

I carried a quart thermos of dark-and-stormies, with the blackest rum, the most bitter ginger beer, and sour lime wedges. My aim was to get twisted and abstracted, forgetting the demented theory of mind required to earn a living from the scourge of my day's weary narrative pique.

Often I fall asleep, head back, mouth agape, arms unheedfully distended from sloped burdened shoulders.

How often have your fingertips feathered blades of grass? Your fingertips are the gentlest part of you—feel them.

I first saw the fisher at Gray Summer's End. More frightening than ghost or goblin, the fisher is a member of the weasel family, known for its ferocity. He poked out of a hole between the two largest boulders and stared me down, eyes beady and vexatious, mouth a grimace of shearing fangs that eviscerated gray squirrels and domestic cats, their excoriated carcasses too gruesome to peruse.

In my life, I've had my share of unpleasant, shaky, terrifying moments. When not writing fiction, I wear the uniform of a US Marine and work as a trial court investigator. On assignment, I climb steep dark stairways and pound on the doors of gang members. I have faced the jaws of enraged pit bulls. Twice I have been shot at close range.

The fisher is an animal created to intimidate.

He stared demonically, made a spitting noise, and turned on a dime back between the boulders.

Round one, the recognition stare-off, was mine.

Soon there was the reappearance. The fisher's fur sinfully black, his eyes two penetrating lasers. He assumed the high ground on the topmost boulder and stared downward, a dark-furred specter.

He spit, gave one contemptuous look, and scurried 50 yards downstream, sinuously like a black rope yanked over rock and flotsam.

I was impelled to retreat up my drive, back to my office, but then a thought occurred:

I am writer; do I not hold dominion over all?

I unscrewed the top of my thermos and chugged my dark-and-stormies. The sugary mixture struck like a hot iron fist

My face twisted into a sardonic smile. Now self-sedated, I dropped my hand to the cool grass to reaffirm:

You are writer. Nature is your sanctuary.

The black beast returned suddenly, like a dervish, his teeth attached to my fingers at the first set of knuckles. He lurched forward for a firmer hold, then backward with a twist to rend away my fingertips.

Shock!

Diminution of digits.

Extremity loss.

Fingers to the knuckles without fingertips, I wobbled upward and stared blurrily into the water. Beside me was the reflection of the dark sinister fisher. My fingers were now bloodied, knob-knuckled remnants of the physical and mental anguish derived from the fictive effort in the creation of the perfidious.

It was my reflection and the delirium of my writer's rest.

Cerebral anguish.

The fisher's attack.

The ignominy of having to pound out stories brutishly, without grace and touch, with just a single facial appendage—the blunt uncompromising nose.

AUTHOR'S NOTE

The creative act requires time away from the mundane. Once that is accomplished, the craft requires yet additional time. As a piece nears completion, ruthless cuts are required to find its center, which at best must be amorphous so that readers can add their own meaning. So here we have the terror of post-creation, the fisher cat eating one's digits which receive messages from the brain that translate to keyboard strokes and ghostly images. When a writer finds time to rest, he has been made fingerless, with just the waft of newer stories coming in his direction. Given he has a caring and able editor and publisher, then, yes, the fisher cat is fictive, not a menace.

PM

MR. GIBB'S BANNER YEAR

HEIDI J. LOBECKER

THE KIDS OF Stonebridge High School always crossed their fingers when they were in the gym. On the wall a commemorative photograph of Old Coach Rogers glared at them. The iron-grey eyes gave Kevin, the quarterback for the Wildcats, tingles on the back of his neck.

"What's he so mad at?" asked the new kid.

"He's pissed we keep losing," said Kev. "His teams won a ton of championships, and now we just suck."

"Chin up, Kevin," Principal Dugan said. "This year, we'll turn it around. I'm recruiting a different coach. One with a history of winning."

When the final bell rang, Principal Dugan watched the stream of people leave. He fingered an old black whistle in his pocket. He was looking for the new algebra teacher, Mr. Gibb; Mr. Gibb, with his lame handshake and doormat demeanor.

Ahhh, there he is, Principal Dugan recognized Mr. Gibb's shuffling gait. *That man's shadow is more noticeable than he is.*

"Take a walk with me," Principal Dugan said, grabbing Mr. Gibb by the elbow.

"Oh, okay," shrugged Mr. Gibb.

The two men stood in the gym, the photograph of Coach Rogers hanging on the wall before them. The rank smell of old sweat and damp concrete hung heavy in the air. High above them, keeping company with the dust motes, hung 11 Division 1 State Championship banners—the glory years of the legendary Coach Rogers. The faded red and black banners proved that though Rogers' memory lived on, his winning streak was as neglected as the academic standards of Stonebridge High.

Coach Rogers was an old-school, hawk-faced man. Twenty years ago, when Coach spoke, his team listened. Even now, his picture commanded respect; in it, he wore his starched shirt, black tie, horn-rimmed glasses, and a tweed hat.

"That man gave his life for football," said Principal Dugan.

Mr. Gibb mumbled a response and chewed his lower lip. His dull brown eyes glanced at the picture.

Principal Dugan resigned himself to talking to this dud of a man. He told the story of Coach Rogers with the reverence it deserved:

"We were playing the Vikings. Our men played sloppy, and old Coach Rogers couldn't stand sloppy. He was pacing the sidelines. He had just given Ed 'The Tank' #19 the next play, and then he grabbed his right arm in pain. He knelt on the grass, just six minutes into the game, he collapsed on the 50-yard line. Ed quickly called a time-out and rushed to Coach Rogers' side. No heartbeat. He died on the field right on the sidelines."

"Huh," said Mr. Gibb; he tried to look suitably solemn.

"He worked here right up until the day he died," said Principal Dugan. "That field is sacred ground." He gave Mr. Gibb a side-eye.

"Sacred ground," repeated Mr. Gibb dully. Mr. Gibb figured he'd die playing video games on his couch—his default pastime as he limped along through life. He hoped his neighbors found him before his dog, Woody, ate his face. He wouldn't mind if that happened though; Woody was the only one ever really happy to see him.

Prompted by the jock-talk, Mr. Gibb said the burliest thing he could think of: "I used to be a volunteer referee for my nephew's football team." It sounded suitably athletic.

"Oh? You got family around here?" asked Principal Dugan.

"Not really. My sister's in the Army. They're in Germany now."

Principal Dugan, always grasping and pawing at things, nodded eagerly. His big hands pushed Mr. Gibb forward into a dim office, situated at the back of the locker rooms.

"Yes, yes. I saw you were a referee on your resume," the principal said. "You have so much potential. We need a football coach to start summer training for the Wildcats right away." White globs of spit gathered at the edges of his mouth in his excitement.

"C-coach?" Mr. Gibb stammered, wanting to avoid responsibility. "Oh no, no. I couldn't do that."

"It's an extra $4,500 for the season," said Principal Dugan.

"Okay, then show me where to sit," said Mr. Gibb.

Principal Dugan gestured to the cracked black Naugahyde covered chair, patched with duct tape. It went with the worn, metal desk, at least 20 years old.

"Great, great," Principal Dugan said. "I'll leave you to it. Good luck." He hung the black whistle around Mr. Gibb's neck. He quickly closed the door and scuttled off before Mr. Gibb could change his mind.

Principal Dugan walked out of the empty locker room. The dingy pipes leaked slow drip-drip-drips into shallow puddles on the floor. The walls curled off strips of gray-green paint. The lockers hung half-open like dark mouths, squeaking on rusted hinges.

Principal Dugan stood in the gym, stared at Coach Rogers' picture and yelled, "He's perfect."

Eleven red and black banners fluttered in a foul breeze.

———

Even in the full heat of a sweltering August, in the small office, Mr. Gibb felt a cold chill. To distract himself from the decay, Mr. Gibb did a quick search for "How to coach high school football."

The gym stink condensed around him. Five minutes into reading "15 Tips for a Great Practice", Mr. Gibb felt light-headed. Needing fresh air, he got up to open the door. It was stuck, the rotting frame had swollen in the humidity. He grabbed and pulled at the doorknob with wet, sweaty hands. The dull metal slipped around in his slick palms. The door would not open.

Heavy pressure in the air pushed down on his shoulders. He could not move. A fast wind slammed musty, mildewed playbooks off the shelves. The same wind, full of fists, pounded him BAM BAM BAM like players going after a running back at the bottom of a fumble pile.

He desperately tried the door again; his hands scrabbling and clawing at the knob. A foul breath pressed his face.

Frantic to get the door open, he pushed and pushed, harder and harder. The air was dense and dank; the room shrunk around him.

He pushed, pushed, PUSHED!

The door slammed open. Breath uneven and short, he stumbled out. A helmet, full of teen boy smell, flew at Mr. Gibb's head. A solid hit. Mr. Gibb fell to the ground, unconscious.

When he came to, he was dragging a two-man sled from under the bleachers. He looked over, and three more sleds were lined up on the ten-yard line. His shirt was sweatier and smellier than it had ever been in his whole life. He realized he'd moved 300 pounds of steel all on his own. He stood a little taller and smoothed his hair down across his balding scalp. He tried jogging as he went by the 50-yard line, blowing the old whistle as he went by.

That night Woody sniffed and snorted at him when he arrived home. The dog wouldn't come near him until he showered twice, in extra hot water. He had to scrub hard to remove the fusty tang that clung to his body.

———

It was one month before school, and the Wildcat's prowled the field.

"All right, boys, let's get started." Mr. Gibb tried to command the team's attention, but they were much more invested in the phones they'd snuck onto the field.

"Boys," he tried again, "I need you to listen!"

"He's just a boring old dude with bad B.O.," said Kev, the quarterback, when the team gathered in the huddle, "I wanna work on my short game. Let's do some passing drills."

Tired of insta-lurking the cheerleaders, the boys practiced a shotgun formation they knew. The ball arced hard and fast in the crisp fall air. Mr. Gibb, ineffectual as ever, decided to end practice early when the dank smell rushed at him again.

He sniffed the rot in the air and raised his puffy arms to wave it off, but he was too slow to stop the speeding football. The ball headed right for his temple; that pigskin missile didn't miss.

Mr. Gibb woke up, smelling of jock itch, sitting at Coach Rogers' beat-up metal desk. Mr. Gibb's weak fingers pushed at the sore on his head. The boys were finishing up their showers, and he caught bits of their conversations.

"Mr. Gibb was no joke at practice today. He ran our asses off."

"That way he showed us how to use a sideline to stop a running back was cool."

"Never would've guessed that old guy had it in him."

The side of Mr. Gibb's head may have been tender, but for the first time in his life, his ego was full. His ego liked that.

He stared at a well-worn red leather notebook placed in the middle of the desk.

Written in the careful cursive, and proper penmanship taught by nuns, were years of experience from Coach Rogers on what turns a boy into a football player. Mr. Gibb read what it took to transform an unfocused 100-pound 15-year-old into an All-State quarterback. How football makes men of boys. How to form those men into a team. How to lead that team to three consecutive state championships.

Mr. Gibb pulled out his own notebook and began to take notes. Notes on making sure the boys took care of their uniforms. Notes on how to build a team and how to let the boys find their strengths and weaknesses.

He learned the importance of knowing how to act. He had a new game plan for practice. He would start by reminding the boys they needed to be class acts—not only playing football the right way but how they conducted themselves.

Mr. Gibb absorbed page after page of sage, straightforward advice; the old Coach whispered in his ear.

After he read a good 50 pages, Mr. Gibb gathered up his things and said goodbye to the boys. He noticed the team covered their noses when they talked to him, breathed through their mouths to avoid his scent. A nasty draft followed him out, pushed between his shoulder blades, making sure he stood up straight.

He stopped at the store, loaded up on odor-removing laundry detergent, room spray, and extra strength deodorant.

He picked up extra treats for Woody; they were having a hard time living together. When he got home this night, his usually happy mutt rumbled and barked at him, circling around him with his hackles raised aggressively. Woody spent the night in the garage.

Practices started going well, and when the Wildcats walked in the hall of the math wing, they growled, low and deep. The normally apathetic students yelled hallway chants, "Go Cats, Fight Cats!" Stonebridge hadn't shown this much school spirit in decades. Principal Dugan proudly told his wife the whole place sounded like the tiger house at the zoo.

At the front of his class, Mr. Gibb stood tall. He now wore button-down shirts and a black tie. The snarling, howling boys were his. Showing up, digging deep. They came by to get him, to escort him to practice, the coach of their team. They didn't walk too close though.

They wanted more of his wisdom, more offensive plays, more strategies like using a short passing game to move down the field successfully. He liked the respect. He could never remember what he did to deserve it.

"Glad to see you brought back the short passing game," said Principal Duggan, "that's how we would win, back in the day."

Mr. Gibb nodded. The attention and compliments felt good; he hung onto them to cover the taste of vomit in his mouth. He had pine tree fresheners in the pockets of his blazer to hide his rotten egg smell. No one dared say it to his face, but he heard the offensive line call him "Dank Stank."

He was sad when Woody ran away, his only real friend in life. He put up LOST DOG signs in the neighborhood, featuring a big picture of the brown and white mutt. He spent a week looking for him. But in his heart of hearts, he knew Woody needed to be gone. Woody's frantic whining, pawing, and clawing at the door to get out, get out, GET OUT when feeding time came just about broke Mr. Gibb. At that moment, he wished he could run away with Woody, leave his sour milk stink back at the school. When Mr. Gibb inhaled deep to relax, he smelled what had permeated his soul.

———

It was early September, and the new and improved Wildcats were ready for their first game of the season. Mr. Gibb led them onto the field, looking especially dapper in a new tweed hat.

"How do you feel we'll do against the Vikings?" Principal Dugan asked. He was standing upwind from Mr. Gibb.

"Our team is ready. They know what to do. It's time we beat this team."

"Look what I found," Principal Dugan said. He held up a #19 football jersey, properly cared for just like Coach had taught him. "I remember climbing into my pads for my first game and putting on this jersey. It was the best and worst day of my life. The first day I played in a game. The day you died."

Coach looked at the jersey and nodded to the man before him. He'd always had high hopes for Ed "The Tank" Dugan; it was no surprise the boy had grown up to become principal of Stonebridge High School.

"Good to have you back, Coach," said Principal Dugan.

Coach walked towards the 50-yard line, his iron-grey eyes focused on his players, his mind already planning his next move.

"Good to be back," said Coach.

He blew the old black whistle hard and sure. The players turned to him, fired up, ready to go.

"Best make room for another banner, Ed," yelled Coach over his shoulder to Dugan. "After all, there are no championships when you're dead."

AUTHOR'S NOTE

"Mr. Gibb's Banner Year" was inspired by ghost stories that I was reading to my son. We talked about what would make a ghost angry, and I remembered a legendary high school football coach in my home town who had died several years ago. None of his replacements have been able to stir their teams onto victories as he did. That lead me to think about a dark, smelly, empty gym locker room at the end of the day. It's such a wonderfully creepy setting; it makes my stomach hurt just to think about it.

HJL

ACHE

MARK ALAN POLO

SAMMY RAN through the worn door that had no bell no lock and no glass. The tilted stairs in front of him were little match for his speed when he was this excited. As fast as a bird takes to the air, Sammy ran up five flights of stairs, his feet hardly hitting the worn marble steps of the old building. Every turn of the stairwell caught Sammy off guard as he hit each landing with his shoulder, making the usual turns sharper but shorter. He yelped with protection and delight, taking care that his large bag of Halloween candy was not compromised from his rapid movement. He captured each floor on automatic pilot, negotiating one more dimly lit hallway than the last because of random broken lights and absent maintenance. This was the home Sammy knew now.

"Dad, wait'll you see how much I got!" Daniel heard his son yell as he approached.

Daniel opened the apartment door as Sammy's voice grew louder. He walked out of his paint-starved doorway and stood at the top banister watching down the twist of steps to see his son's happiness. This was the first year Daniel had allowed Sammy to go trick or treating, as the odds were that there would be more tricks— with the possibility of danger—than treats in the bag. Sammy's happiness assured Daniel that this would be a regular Halloween event. Happiness like this was rare, and Daniel needed to see it, remember it, somehow absorb it and, most of all, take risks to let it happen. Still, it was one more potential danger, adding to the list of exposures his son would endure, including trips to the store, the daily walk to school past broken and abandoned buildings, corner drug deals, and the piercing sounds of random gunshots. Daniel tried to set safeguards and enforce rules, but Sammy was getting older and needed increased independence. Sammy listened to his father, but it was always a leap of Daniel's faith that his son would adhere to the rules. He basically trusted Sammy, but there were so many variables in this end of town, so many frightening obstacles, so many traps that could turn a simple fun afternoon into a scary permanent calamity.

They had struggled as a family for the past 15 months, after Sammy's mother was killed by a stray bullet that punctuated an argument she never heard. It had pierced the night air in a neighborhood deemed safer than the one they now called home. The bullet had struck the back of the head as she walked home following the evening shift at the Dollar King. Until that day, finances had been tight but manageable. Now those same tight numbers squeezed their motherless family even tighter. A new neighborhood, worse than before, and a new apartment, older and more tired, became their home. Neither Sammy nor his two younger sisters wished for anything on any day aside from their mother's return. It would be a wish never granted to them. They knew it. Daniel knew it.

But for one day, that terrible moment would be wiped from his sight. For just a few hours, a bag of candy would bring Sammy back to the child he was before the click of the hammer changed the direction of their lives. Just one bullet, just one thing, just one moment.

On this Halloween, Sammy rushed home from school to put on his costume. He fashioned it out of his dad's plaid shirt, all padded out, and a pair of old ripped pants that fit snugly. He smeared white makeup on his face and painted blood-red drippings on the corners of his mouth with his mother's old lipstick. He was a zombie. He'd thought about being a zombie for two months, knowing this day would eventually arrive. He was so excited. Sammy and his friends commiserated, planned, and convinced their parents they were old enough and would stay together for safety just to have these few hours of Halloween fun. Sammy had grown a lot this year. Last year's clown costume would not do, even though it was the final thing his mother made him before her death.

He and his friends grew bolder and more confident with age. They went into building after building, mingling with younger and older kids, passing them in the dank hallways and overly painted walls of the tenements in which they lived. He and his friends knocked on every door in every apartment house for ten blocks, one worse than the next.

"Stay in a group and I won't follow you. Got it? That's the deal," his dad repeated over and over as Halloween approached. "That's the deal, or you can't go."

The deal was an easy one to make, but as much as Daniel said it, Sammy wanted to make it look as if he struggled with it a bit. It was the game they played. Sammy loved his dad, and didn't want to make his worry worse, but he still was a kid who stretched his independence as much as he could. After all, young people live forever.

Sammy hit the top landing of his apartment and pushed his dad aside as he ran to the kitchen table and dumped the bag of candy onto its stained wood top.

"Daddy, look at all the candy I got today!" Sammy exclaimed, as he checked the now-empty sack for any stray prizes. He stood back, proudly his dad's inspection of the goods.

"You know the deal. I check it all out, and then I'll give it back to you," Sammy's dad said. "It won't take long." Everything became a worry for Daniel since Emily's death. "There's pizza in the oven. Grab a slice and I'll get to work."

Daniel sifted through the stash. He spread the contents of Sammy's sack out, candies of all shapes and sizes tumbled out: Paydays and Reese's, Mounds and Double Bubble, coins and small boxes of Juicy Fruit and malted balls. He spread it out further, tossing aside the pieces of fruit, unwrapped hard candies, and cookies.

"With all the rest, it's a small price to pay for a little bit of safety." Daniel said aloud, as Sammy tore at the slice of pizza in his hand.

"Don't throw away too much!" Sammy shouted, in defiant protest. "I worked hard for all of that."

"Cool your jets," Daniel shot back. "It's my job."

Nearly done, Daniel removed one another large, flat cookie from the pile. Only then did he notice a small box. It was Tiffany blue. He remembered his Tiffany nights with Emily. They would walk the nicer parts of town on warm summer evenings, past the corner where the blue boxes lived. They would stop and dream of life inside those boxes. He would kiss her in front of every window and promise her a future filled with Tiffany blue surprises.

Daniel held the box, inspecting it for an owner's name to help him decide what to do with it, but found no inscription. Although he tried to open it, the cover was solidly attached and would not come off. Sammy munched loudly as he read a comic book about zombies, patiently waiting for his dad to complete the inspection. With his back turned, he didn't notice as Daniel hid the box. He slipped it into his pocket, determined to inspect it further after Sammy went to bed.

"Okay, sport, you can have three pieces tonight."

"… Aw, Dad, only three?"

"Yup, three. Pick 'em and get off to bed. School tomorrow."

Sammy grabbed quickly and sped off to his room. His sisters were already asleep, having not gone trick or treating this year. To their disappointment, Daniel had insisted that they wait until next year when they would be a little older. However, Sammy would share his stash with his younger siblings.

The house soon quieted down. Daniel hit the sofa hard, knowing the day was over and the long night would begin, the long night yet again without Emily. Fifteen months, three days, 14 hours since Emily's death. He was stuck missing her, despite having tried to move on. He'd recently started to date again, but it hadn't gone well. Daniel wore his loss, his Emily's death, in every pore of his being. He felt he had nothing to offer. He decided to close that chapter of his life for a while, hoping time might heal the open wounds within his soul.

"When the kids are older. Maybe, then," he said softly.

Daniel switched the TV and settled in. Flickering shadows bounced and danced on the shabby walls. The monotonous flashes and sounds lulled him to sleep this night, every night, the same as the night before and the same, he assumed, as the next night and the night after that. The sofa was his bed, as he could no longer afford a bigger apartment in which everyone could have their own nest. They had moved in here shortly after Emily's death. It never felt like home, just a way station, waiting for this chapter to change.

As Daniel lay back to begin the stare of passing night, he felt a lump in his pocket that made it uncomfortable to settle in. He remembered the box and fished it out. It felt oddly warm. Once more Daniel attempted to open it, but it would not come apart. He shook it, then held it close to his eyes. Nothing moved or jingled inside. He placed the box on the cushion next to him. Determined to pry open the box, he rose to fetch a knife from the kitchen. When he returned, the box was on the floor, next to his shoes. Confused, Daniel paused before picking up the box and starting his attack.

He slid the knife down the side under the tightly sealed cover and punctured its weak spot. A groan and a shudder escaped from within. Daniel dropped the box, startled by the movement and sound. It fell to the floor and he instinctively lifted his feet to the sofa. The box shook and a sudden gush of steam escaped, accompanied by a light, constant hissing. The steam filled the room in an oddly contained perimeter, as if a larger box of wet mist needed to be opened.

The hissing stopped and the steam began to coagulate into a thick fog. The fog rolled and formed, twisted and turned, and settled into the chair across from the sofa on which he sat. Captivated, Daniel rubbed his eyes from the dew that the fog created. It seared his skin and burned his eyes like onion cut with a dull knife. He pulled his knees to his torso for protection.

As the fog evaporated, the form of a man in a wrinkled gray suit sat in the chair across from him lit by the acid glow of a nearby streetlamp. Flashes of light hit the side of the figure's deeply wrinkled face, catching the crevices and tops of these wrinkles, and the messy tangle of long, wiry hair. Daniel's eyes narrowed, trying to determine if he was dreaming. He felt convinced that he was awake, but wasn't sure why, then, he wasn't frightened.

As the fog lifted, the being in the dull gray suit looked around, unsure of its freedom. It carefully smoothed out its wrinkles, starting at its ankles. Slowly its hands pushed the wrinkles aside on its legs, then its knees. It smoothed out the wrinkles of its jacket and bow tie, extending it out to its edges. It lifted its head and stretched the skin of its neck to shiny smoothness as the streetlamp from outside spread over its newly refreshed skin. It breathed in deeply as if filling its body for the first time. Its hands pushed up against the wrinkles of its face and the wrinkles quickly disappeared. Lastly, it smoothed its hair and sat still for a moment, surveying a newfound freedom. It was pleased. It glanced down at its hands on its lap and grabbed at the skin to smooth out a missing piece of itself, as if an afterthought. It breathed in again and then looked at Daniel, smiling with faint recognition.

"Hello, Daniel," it said.

"Wh-what are you? How do you know my name?" Daniel stuttered.

"It's my job, friend. I've known you for … forever."

"I don't understand."

"You're not supposed to. Simply know that I am here for you."

"For me? Why for me?"

"Your mind and body have not rested for quite a while. When Sammy came to the right apartment in the right building on the right street earlier tonight, I was summoned to be given to you."

"What apartment? Who did this?"

"The details are unimportant. I am here for you."

"Do you … have a name?" Daniel asked as if a name would legitimize the entity.

"Call me … Ache," the being said, staring curiously at its fingernails.

"What kind of a name is Ache?" Daniel asked wryly. He leaned forward, no longer fearful of the apparition.

"I am the hole in a man's soul. The space ripped open by life's unfortunate combination of events."

"What hole do I have?" Daniel teetered on disbelief, his attention held by the bizarre notion that he was, in fact, conversing with a fog.

"A bullet pierced your Emily and then your soul." Ache continued to inspect its nails.

"How did you know?" Daniel asked, stunned.

"Seriously, Daniel? I materialized from within a Tiffany box. There's little I don't know." Ache spoke in a tone that indicated a shortness of temper. "I haven't much time. I'm here to help you. Tell me what you want. Name it. Whatever it is. One thing."

"A genie in a box? You're kidding, right?"

"I haven't time for this. Want it or not, it is yours. One desire, one piece of your life to change. I need to move on. With this one change, you are also entitled to a reversal. A retraction, should you need it."

Still skeptical, Daniel nonetheless played along. "You're saying that if I ask you for a million dollars, and then have a change of heart, I can instead ask for … my own island in the Pacific?"

"Correct. One wish, one retraction if you deem. Do not waste this chance. Think it through. So many have wasted this chance on the obvious, the least important, the immediate. Remember, everything fits with a reason and a purpose. Don't be shortsighted."

With this warning, Ache opened its jacket and the fog pushed out from its chest, enshrouding him once again, piercing the light from the streetlamps. Ache diminished. The fog thinned to a ribbon and reentered the misty box from whence it came. The last edges of the steam found the blue box lying on the floor, sucked back into and under the cover. The hissing waned and the room cleared. The air, again, still holding back the peeling paint on the wall.

Daniel sat alone, gazing at the chair where Ache had appeared. He thought about what he'd been told, but shook his head in disbelief. After some time, Daniel drifted off to sleep.

Sleep offered no respite. Dreams assaulted Daniel throughout the night. He twisted and turned on the cushions of the sofa, mind filled with visions of Emily. Shifting locales. Different times. Alone with Emily. Together with their family. Daniel awoke, body sweating, as the sun tore through the bottom edge of the tenement window. He sat up, recalling Ache, the man-like being with wrinkles and the bow tie.

"Shit, what a dream," he smirked at the memory.

As Daniel stood up, hit foot bumped against something on the floor. The blue box was empty and open. He stared at it curiously until his concentration was broken by the morning alarm clock. He went to rouse the kids for school.

—

Throughout the day, Daniel thought about Ache and the blue box.

Assuming it was real and not a dream, assuming I really do have one wish, what now? What do I wish for?

He thought about how much he missed Emily. Would he want her back, now that he may have the chance? The answer seemed obvious. His own pain would be gone. His children would have a mother again. Everything would be as it was before the stranger's argument, before the gunshot.

He spent all day at work in the garage, disturbed by the decision he had to make and the warning he'd been issued about the decision he'd been gifted. Sammy and his sisters arrived home from school and dove into the candy.

"You'll ruin your dinner." Daniel reprimanded them. "We're having chicken tonight." He was tired of ready-made meals, made ready by someone else. He remembered the meals he and Emily used to cook together. They were tedious intrusions on long days until they weren't. He longed to have the tedium back again.

Daniel watched his kids as they sat around the table, staring at a shared Game Boy and eating chicken legs. Talking and pulling at french fries, some hitting their plates, some not. He knew right then what he had to do.

Sammy interrupted Daniel's determined thoughts. "Dad, I gotta run across the street and get my basketball from Freddie. I need it for gym class tomorrow."

"Yeah, okay, but you're not staying there to play. Got it?"

"Fine, no problem," Sammy said, and was out the door within seconds.

Daniel glanced out the window and watched as Sammy darted across the street toward Freddie's house. He thought of Emily and spoke. "My kids need their mother. Now."

At that very moment, steam filled the room and a groan murmured then roared. The air grew thick and cold. The girls stared, dumbfounded, and for the first time in longer than he could remember, Daniel smiled.

The moment was broken by the screech of tires on blacktop and an audible thud. Daniel sprinted to window to see Sammy's body lying unmoving against a sidewalk stained with blood as a horrified middle-aged driver exited her sedan.

"Sammy! Sammy!" Daniel screamed.

The fog in the apartment thickened and an apparition formed in the same chair as the night before. Daniel pushed through the fog as the form came into focus. He stopped for a moment, stunned, but remembered the bloody sidewalk and ran out the door.

Within seconds Daniel was on the street. He pushed past the driver and the crowd gathering around his son.

"It's my son! Let me through! Let me through!"

Daniel fell to his knees, Sammy's blood quickly soaking into the material of his pants. He reached out to embrace his son, pulling on his shoulders from behind.

"Sammy, Sammy."

"I didn't see the car, Daddy. I'm sorry. I'm sorry, Daddy."

Sammy started to fade. Sirens echoed as an ambulance screeched to a halt. The EMTs rushed to Sammy's aid, applying pressure to slow the bleeding, working to stabilize his vitals, pushing and pulling him onto a stretcher.

"Stay with me," the lead EMT said. He looked at Daniel, "What's the boy's name? What's his name?"

"Sammy. His name is Sammy!" Daniel cried out. "Save him. You have to save him!"

"We'll do our best. Start the IV," the EMT told his partner. "Sammy, stay with us, guy. You can do this. Stay with me, Sammy! Shit."

They rolled him into the ambulance. Daniel panicked, desperate to ride along with his son, oblivious that his daughters were alone in the apartment. The siren wailed as the ambulance backed up, about to begin its panicked ride to the hospital.

Daniel held Sammy's hand and stroked his head, wiping blood from his little boy's eyes. Daniel gazed down at the blue box. Blood stained, it started its haze of steam.

Through the ambulance window, Daniel glanced up at their

apartment and saw Emily standing in the window, surrounded by a cloud of steam. She touched the glass, knowing that their longing, Daniel's wish, would not be satisfied now. There was another decision to make.

A retraction, Ache had called it.

Daniel felt the ache pierce his soul. An ache different from Sammy's, different from his situation now.

Different.

AUTHOR'S NOTE

It is tradition that all things beautiful come in the tiny blue box. All things loving come in that little blue box as well. We are sure that all things magical come in that beautiful blue box.

It is the sign of a future and a promise. All things, no matter what they are, come with a price.

MAP

O' DEATH, YOU SONNET!

DANTE J. SILICATO

O' Death! The Earth rejoices at your coming,
Swallowing up old flesh and fallen leaves;
A newfound energy returning something,
Supplying vital minerals by bowing down unto your needs;
Although all living beings fear the song you sing,
Our natural Mother welcomes you home to fertilize her seeds…

O' Death! You foul smelling villain, O' Death, You Sonnet!

O' Death! The Earth rejoices at your coming,
Swallowing up old flesh and fallen leaves;
A newfound energy returning something,
Supplying vital minerals by bowing down unto your needs;
Although all living beings fear the song you sing,
Our natural Mother welcomes you home to fertilize her seeds…

O' Death! You foul smelling villain,
I smite thee while I search for fountains of youth;
My fear of you dissipates at the thought of your ruin,
But your daily chorus reminds me of the horror like sayers of
sooth;
The uncertainty you reap torments my thoughts towards
oblivion,
Puncturing my heart with your slow sinking tooth…

If love were your mistress, she might change your face,
Until then we wait with crossed fingers when she's sent in your
place.

AUTHOR'S NOTE

I wrote "O' Death, You Sonnet" in the form of a love sonnet as a way to deal with my fear and perception of death. While people perceive death as a frightening and horrifying occurrence, the earth and her lifecycles view it as a natural and necessary process. I wanted to contrast these opposing positions within the structure of a sonnet.

DJS

TICK TOCK

BAYNE NORTHERN

OUT OF THE DARKNESS of the night, Missy walked up the driveway and into the bright, shining light at the entrance to her home. She yanked the screen door open, stepped into the vestibule and unlocked the back door. The ceiling light revealed her caramel-colored tresses that gently transitioned toward her dark chestnut crown. A sigh escaped from her lips as she glanced at the wall clock confirming she'd beat the 11:00 PM curfew with ten minutes to spare. She opened the coat closet to hang up her hobo bag, surprised to see her sister's hook empty. Her sister, Francine, usually came home first. For every ten minutes late, their curfew moved up one hour earlier the next weekend night. The requirement to return home before their peers resulted in no invitation to parties, no underage drinking, and no heavy petting when parking with their boyfriends—a severe punishment. The creative consequences were the brainchild of their mother.

Missy walked back out the kitchen door expecting Francine's arrival. Her eyes squinted from the glare of the blazing exterior light mounted on the wall of white siding. She scanned the long driveway to see if she was walking toward the house, but there was nothing to see.

She returned to the kitchen and threw some crackers and cheese slices on a small plate, grabbed a can of Coke out of the fridge, and sat down at the kitchen table. A pile of catalogs was stacked neatly in the corner of the laminated wooden surface. She pulled the top one toward her and flipped through the pages displaying photos of young women in skirts, sweater sets, and casual slacks with matching tops. When she finished eating, she closed the booklet and tossed it back on top of the pile. She rinsed her dish over the kitchen sink and glanced up at the clock. 11:35 PM. That would be bad for Francine. Missy poked her head out the door and peered down the driveway again. Fog was developing as the warm spring day cooled into night. A figure moved toward her in the darkness.

"Francine? Is that you?" The moist air altered the sound of her voice. Missy discerned an outline of a human form walking up the driveway. Footsteps could be heard scraping the rough gravel. A silhouette emerged into the light. A young man stood in front of her. She didn't recognize him but assumed the guy was part of her sister's crowd.

"Hey." An athletic, attractive, well-built male with light brown wavy hair sticking out from under his cap acknowledged her. He shivered and jammed both hands deep into the pockets of his coat. He cocked his head and smiled. "Is this Peterson Drive?"

"Oh, cute. Very clever." Their last name was Peterson. Missy realized he was attempting to be cool.

"Am I on Peterson Drive?" His question seemed genuine. This guy was apparently a good actor.

Missy decided to spar with him. "Yes, you are. But Francine isn't home yet. You should come back tomorrow. It's getting late."

A very confused look clouded the man's face. "I am supposed to report to Peterson Drive today."

"You can knock it off. It was only funny the first time." Missy noticed his glazed eyes. Maybe he was high. "Sorry, but it's too late tonight. You'll have to catch up with Francine tomorrow." She pulled the screen door closed, walked back through the small vestibule, and shut the wooden door. Her hand instinctively reached up to turn out the lights, then she remembered her sister should be home any minute and dropped her arm back down. Missy glanced back toward the door and was startled to see the guy still standing there. The cast of the bright exterior light made him visible through the filmy, shear curtains covering the glass panes on the wooden kitchen door. He had placed himself squarely in front of the screen door. His black eyes stared at her. His handsome face appeared blank, expressionless. If Francine arrived now she'd run right into him.

Missy ran upstairs to alert her parents. She whipped around the upstairs hallway and suddenly plunged into darkness. Her eyes struggled to adjust after leaving the brightly lit kitchen. Her left hand guided her down the hallway as it glided along the curved banister. Her parent's bedroom door creaked as she pushed it open.

Her mother, an incredibly light sleeper, instantly awoke. Her head popped up from the pillow "Missy? What's the matter?"

Her father's quiet snore could be heard beside her.

"There's a guy standing outside by our back door. I was peeking out to see if Francine was coming up the driveway and …"

Her mother interrupted. "Your sister called earlier this evening. She's sleeping over at the Daugherty's tonight."

"Oh, good. I was worried about her being late. Anyway, this guy outside is creepy and I thought ..."

"Donald, wake up." Missy's mother pushed her hand against her husband's side. "Get up. It's important."

"What?" His voice sounded groggy.

"There's a young man hovering on our driveway."

He glanced at the alarm clock. The neon colored numbers displayed 11:45 PM. "I'll stop this bullshit right now!" Donald leapt to his feet. Although he stood a tall 6 feet 2 inches, his once, taut, bulging muscles were now soft and sagging. Nonetheless, his size and girth could still intimidate. He slipped on his robe and jammed his feet into his slippers. His long legs took giant strides down the hallway and pounded down the stairs.

Missy followed her dad. Fear rose from deep within her and caused her heart to hammer inside the walls of her chest.

Her dad pushed open the swinging door into the kitchen, stopped with a jolt and yelled. "What the hell?!"

The young man stood in the kitchen. He opened and closed the kitchen drawers, but some of them still hung open a bit. He was now onto the cabinets. In the bright light, Missy could see that he wore a double-breasted, woolen peacoat, way too heavy for the time of year. The standard, white Navy Dixie Cup hat cocked sideways on his head. Small, light tan ring curls poked out from under the brim.

"Reporting for duty, sir." His bloodshot, watery, blank eyes peered at her father. "I'm sorry I'm late. I had trouble finding the location." He turned and suddenly yanked open another kitchen drawer and slowly removed a large, serrated cutting knife. A sneer curled at the corner of his lips as he laid it on the counter.

Missy's dad pulled her toward him and whispered. "Tell your mother to call the police. Don't come back down until they're here."

His daughter bounded up the stairs taking two at a time. When she entered the bedroom, she found her mother sitting on the edge of the bed completely dressed and wide awake. The bongs of the grandfather clock in the living room rang eerily through the house signaling the midnight hour. They could hear muffled conversation coming up from the kitchen.

Missy grabbed her mother's hand. "Dad wants you to call the

police. The weirdo let himself in. It's all my fault. I left the door unlocked."

"Don't worry about that, now," Mom said, patting Missy's arm
reassuringly. Then she picked up the phone on the end table and
quickly dialed 9-1-1.

Although Missy knew she shouldn't go downstairs, she did it
anyway. The guy was obviously unstable and might hurt her dad. She
slipped into the foyer and quietly positioned her body against the wall.
The scene unfolding was clearly visible from the opening between the
dining room and foyer. Her cheek pressed hard against the wooden
trim. She could feel her heart beats throb fast and furious. Her breath
escaped from her lips in rapid little bursts as she watched and listened.

The troubled young man continually opened and closed cabinets. He seemed completely unaware of his surroundings and oblivious
to the inappropriateness of his actions.

Missy's dad, nervous but trying to sound normal, asked, "What
are you looking for?"

The question startled the stranger. He spun around on his heels
and looked bewildered, surprised that someone else was in the room
with him.

Attempting to stay calm and in control, Missy's dad repeated
the question. "What are you looking for?"

Missy sensed the fear in her dad's voice from her distant perch
in the foyer.

The intruder froze. Then his head slowly turned, to the right
and then to the left, in the tick-tocking motion of a metronome. Back
and forth. Right and left. He stared into space completely baffled by
the inquiry. Missy found the bizarre, repetitive head cocking pro-
foundly disturbing.

"Why don't you sit down, son?" Her dad gestured to a kitchen
chair. "Let me wait on you. I know where everything is. I'll fix whatever
you want."

The exaggerated tick-tocking of the head continued as he appeared to contemplate the question. The repetitive movement became
more rapid and developed a mechanical quality to it. Yet even with his
cranium bobbling, he pawed through the pantry shelves. He grabbed
a coffee mug from a cabinet and placed it on the counter next to the
serrated utility knife. Next he rifled through the corner cabinet, spinning the interior turntable around and around, back and forth, mim-

icking the motion of his head, and finally removed a jar of instant coffee. The glass container cracked as he slammed on the counter surface beside the sharp metal blade. It seemed like a thought suddenly popped into his head. He whirled around to face Missy's dad.

"Got any skags?" His head bounced from side to side. His voice sounded anxious and urgent.

"I'm sorry, I don't understand," Dad replied, always consummately polite.

"Skags. Butts. Got any butts?" His black eyes looked expressionless. His tone became demanding and insistent.

Nausea rose from Missy's stomach as she stood watching, fixated on his skull swinging back and forth.

"Oh, cigarettes. No, I'm afraid I don't."

His blank look suddenly changed to one of anger. Rage engulfed him. He turned around and wrenched a kitchen drawer completely out of the cabinet, noisily dumping kitchen utensils all over the floor.

As the clatter of metal hit the ground, Missy's mother ran down the steps and stood against the wall across from her daughter. She quietly whispered, "I wish the police would get here. It's been ten minutes since I called, but it seems like an hour." Her mother's eyes grew as big as saucers as she observed the action taking place in the kitchen.

Missy nodded.

The stranger, unaware of the clutter of knives, spoons, and spatulas strewn all around him, walked awkwardly across the room. He slipped on an aluminum potato masher and kicked it away. His foot lashed out again and again and metal and wooden instruments ricocheted against the baseboards and bounced right back in his path. He turned back to the counter and grabbed the jar holding the coffee granules, twisted off the lid. Then he pulled at cabinet doors until he grasped a saucepan from the lower kitchen cabinet, filled it with water, and placed in on the range. He repeatedly tried to turn on the gas burner, rotating the knob over and over again, but it wouldn't light. As the burner was clicking and clicking, his head began ticking and tocking again. Her father quietly observed the deranged man's actions but said nothing, choosing to remain silent and standing very still but in a state of high alert. The man finally gave up trying to start the flame but the failure agitated him. He suddenly grabbed the pot of water off of the stove and threw it into the kitchen sink. Water sloshed up and over the stainless steel sides and spilled onto the floor.

He cranked the hot water handle as far as it would go. Warm water burst out of the mouth of the faucet in a vast stream that rapidly emptied into the sink. His left hand lifted the coffee mug off the counter, the right grabbed the open instant coffee jar next to the knife. He poured the dark brown crystals into the cup then held it under the hot running water filling it until the murky brown liquid splashed over the rim. He placed the ceramic mug back on the counter. To Missy and her mother's horror, he picked up the large, serrated knife and slowly stirred the brew with its long, razor-edged aluminum blade. He grinned. His head rocking slowed to a steady, even pace. He grasped the sharp instrument with his left hand, raised the cup to his lips with his right and made a loud sucking sound as he swallowed a big swig of the gritty, muddy liquid. His pupils dilated. His eyes deepened into glossy black coals. He turned and stared angrily at Missy's father. Keeping his glare focused on him, he slowly lowered the coffee cup and placed it on the counter. He stood, staring, glaring, and tick-ticking his head.

Missy's dad was still. Missy and her mother were frozen in place. Everyone seemed to be trying not to breathe.

Without warning, the stranger agilely leapt across the room, grabbed Missy's dad, and slammed his body hard against the wall. The women watched as Missy's dad struggled with all his might. The attacker had the advantage of youth and athleticism. He swiftly pinned her father up against the plaster surface, lifting him off the floor and completely incapacitating him. The doorbell rang just as the knife plunged deep into her dad's abdomen. Missy and her mother screamed as blood squirted out from beneath his pajamas, saturating the material and puddling on the floor. Her mother ran to the front door, and struggled frantically with the lock trying to open it. Finally the big wooden door succumbed and swung wide open. She whispered to the two policemen and pointed toward the kitchen. Both officers immediately drew their weapons and burst into the crime scene.

Missy's father lay crumbled on the floor in a pool of blood. His attacker stood over him, still holding the knife that was dripping red droplets onto the light beige speckled linoleum. His head jerked from side to side like a bird looking for worms. A big smile spread across his face.

The first cop pointed his gun and immediately recognized him. "It's Tick Tock!" He slowly moved forward in his direction. "Stand back! Stand back! Drop the weapon. Hands in the air!" An audible click emitted from his gun as the trigger moved into position.

Instead of moving away, Tick Tock jumped and landed his feet in the puddle of blood surrounding Dad's slumped body. He then began stamping all around the kitchen admiring his trail of moist, dark red footprints. He threw his head back, snapping it up and down now and howled. "Miller, Miller, he's a killer! If you're not dead today, Reed will come and get his way!"

The cop lunged then, wrestled him to the ground and handcuffed his sticky, bloody wrists behind his back. As he yanked Reed to his feet, his head slowly began to move from side to side again. His skull became a human pendulum. Tick tock. Tick tock. His eyes were glassy and vacant.

"Turn around." The policeman commanded.

The other officer had bent over her dad and pressed against the knife injury in his belly to slow the bleeding. His chin leaned into his chest as he spoke tersely into the walkie-talkie attached to his shirt pocket. "Ambulance needed at 1123 Winding Way. Man bleeding from stab wound in abdominal area. Still conscious and breathing."

Within minutes, the sound of a siren could be heard in the distance. Missy and her mom held onto each other trembling with fear. They both found the distant wail comforting knowing help was on the way. The first policeman guided Tick Tock out the front door, past several nosy neighbors that had gathered on the lawn, and pushed him down into the back seat of his vehicle. A muffled voice could be heard from the automobile as the patrolman leaned into the front seat and talked into its loud speaker.

An ambulance careened up the driveway in the back of the house. Missy held the door wide open for the emergency crew. The officer released his bloodied hand from the stab wound as the paramedics took over. They quickly took vitals and hooked up IVs. Dad's body was carefully placed on a stretcher, and swiftly carried to the waiting van. Missy's mom followed them and hopped into the back beside her injured husband. She grasped his hand in hers and squeezed it tightly as tears rolled down her face.

"I'll meet you at the hospital!" Missy called out to her mother right before the doors slammed shut.

The ambulance sped away with lights flashing and siren screaming. Missy watched until the blue and red blinking dots disappeared in the distance, then turned and walked inside.

When she was in the house, the cop stopped speaking into his walkie-talkie and addressed her. "Excuse me, miss, but can you tell me what happened here?"

Missy, shaking and crying, recounted how Tick Tock had gotten into their home, his rambling speech, odd behavior, and his final act of stabbing her father. The uniformed man quickly took notes.

"That's very helpful. I will need you and your mom to come down to the station within 24 hours to give your official statements and fill out some paperwork so that we can keep Miller from hurting anyone else."

"Sure, but can you tell me anything about that guy? You recognized him and called him by name."

"Yeah, we know him. His real name is Reed Miller. But we all know him as Tick Tock. He's a patient at the Allenwood Mental Institution, a couple miles from here. He's broken out a few other times. He had a mental breakdown in the Navy. He used to be stationed at the base on Peterson Drive in Florida. After going AWOL, he's had many violent encounters with people. They keep him fairly medicated because he kept breaking out of the Florida asylum and returning to his home to try to murder his own mother. Blamed her for institutionalizing him."

"Oh, my God! That's horrible! And his poor mother must have been so frightened! He kept asking us if this was Peterson Drive. I thought it was a joke because our last name is Peterson."

"No. Just a bad coincidence."

The doorbell rang, bringing the crime team into the once calm and quiet home.

———

The officer held the door for Missy as she slid into the back seat of the patrol car for the short ride to the hospital. She felt like a criminal sitting on the hard, plastic seat captive between car doors with no interior handles. A metal grate separated her from the driver. She was locked in. It all felt like a bad dream.

The car pulled up to the hospital entrance. The officer jumped out and opened the door so Missy could exit the vehicle. She thanked him, quickly turned and ran into the building. After stopping by the information booth, Missy hurried down a white, sterile brightly lit hallway and located the waiting room. A woman was sitting in a chair in the corner, hunched over with head down and greying hair all askew.

Her pink cotton sweater was pulled tightly around her shoulders.

"Mom?"

Her mother looked up. She was exhausted. Her eyes red rimmed from crying.

"Missy?" Mrs. Peterson jumped up and hugged her daughter. They stood locked in embrace for several minutes. Tears flowed freely down their faces.

"Your dad is in surgery. He's lost a lot of blood. They suspect a major artery was severed. It's going to take a few hours to repair the damage ..." Mom's voice dropped to a whisper. "... assuming it *can* be repaired."

Missy and her mom decided to walk over to the cafeteria while they waited. Arm in arm, they passed through several austere, fluorescent lit corridors. Outside they could see the grey light slowly turn yellow as the sun began to rise to a new day.

While they sipped from cups filled with lukewarm acrid coffee, Missy shared what the cop had told her about Tick Tock, real name of Reed Miller. Her mom listened listlessly, too worried about her husband to really care, and as they talked, quiet stripes of bright light began to stream through the blinds of the windows.

Missy looked up when she noticed a man in uniform walking briskly through the cafeteria headed in their direction. She was astonished when she realized it was the officer that had dropped her off at the hospital a few hours ago. His expression was grim.

"Mom, this is the officer who brought me here."

"I'm glad I was able to find you." He was huffing and puffing and out of breath.

"What's wrong?" Missy's mom sounded frightened, and her blood shot eyes were wide and scared.

"When our patrolman arrived at the police station to transfer Miller into the jail, he was ready for him in the back seat. His legs were pulled up to his chest, and when the door opened, he kicked my partner hard right in the middle of his chest and knocked him to the ground."

"Oh, my god ..." Mom whispered.

"He bolted. Sprinted into the darkness before my partner could even pull his gun. We have an APB out for him. We also planted two officers outside your home just in case he returns. We think that is unlikely ... at least tonight." He grimaced.

Missy's pulse raced. "You mean he's free?"

"Yes, ma'am. Miller was handcuffed, but I can't promise that will slow him down."

"What do we do know?" Missy's mother's voice was high and taut, on the verge of a yell.

"Just wait here, Ma'am, for news about your husband. I have to go join in the pursuit. We'll find him."

The officer left.

Reed Miller was on the loose.

Missy and her mother sat in the cafeteria under the glare of the florescent lights not knowing if they were safe, if they could ever go home again, if their loved one was going to survive. They tightly held each other's trembling hands . Tears ran down her mom's face . The room was cold and still.

The clock on the wall above the table made its little insistent sound … tick tock, tick tock.

AUTHOR'S NOTE

"Tick Tock" is loosely based on a very frightening experience I had in high school. One spring weekend evening, I was waiting for my older sister to return home from a date. I thought I heard her coming up the driveway, so I opened the kitchen door to greet her. Right in front of my face was this young, muscular guy in a buttoned-up woolen peacoat with glazed eyes staring right at me. He appeared to be high as a kite. I jumped a foot and ran inside the house, terrified.

From this encounter, "Tick Tock" emerged.

BN

THE WOOD WITCH

SARAH VAN GOETHEM

IT'S EITHER LOVE *or hate with the Wood house,* Bea thinks.

She retrieves the key from the lockbox and opens the massive front door of the old manor. The rusted hinges creak, announcing her arrival. She's shown the house 17 times now. Seventeen wasted commission-less hours, plus another hour afterward, each time, for the hairs on her scalp to lay flat again.

I hate this house, she thinks.

The counter in the kitchen is littered with realtor cards. Apparently, no one can sell this house. Bea pulls the listing sheet out of her binder and looks again at the details. Six bedrooms, two baths, formal dining room, living room with wood fireplace, office/den, and parlor. Bea knows the appeal: country living, phenomenal character, hardwood floors. She also knows the downfalls: galvanized plumbing, oil heat, leaking roof, enclosed kitchen. But that's all fixable, compared to—

"Miss Brooks?"

Bea jumps, dropping her binder. The listing flutters to the floor.

"You scared me," she says.

It's an accusation; she hates being surprised. She doesn't bother to pick anything up, instead she steps over the mess and extends a hand to the tall blonde man. "You must be Mr. Morris?"

"Booker." His handshake is firm; he hasn't softened it because she's a woman, and she straightens her shoulders in approval. "Call me Booker."

"Beatrice," she says. "Bea, for short." She thinks Mr. Mor— Booker, is exactly what she expected from his deep voice on the phone; all chiseled features and clean shaven with his polo shirt and dark jeans. She forgives him for sneaking up on her and is glad she slicked some argan oil through her curls and applied her favorite Heartbreaker gel lipstick. "I'm so glad you made it," she tells Booker, and she means it.

He's looking around the kitchen, taking in the water stain on the ceiling, the dust bunnies on the floor, the cobwebs in the corners. "You didn't think I'd come?" he asks. He runs a hand over the counter, collecting all the cards in a pile, then smiles at her. "Seems there's been a few before me."

Bea feels the familiar tickle that runs up her neck, the strokes in the roots of her hair. "A few were no-show's," Bea acknowledges. "Some turn around in the driveway after seeing the state of the house. Usually the city folks."

Booker nods. If he's offended at her *city folks* comment, she can't tell. "It *does* give off a certain horror movie impression," he says. "You know, like *The Conjuring.*"

Bea swallows. "Or *The Haunting.*"

"How long has it been vacant?" Booker leans over, picks up the listing sheet.

Bea's chest prickles with heat; she's forgetting she's supposed to be in charge. She scoops up the binder, forces herself to start the tour. "Two years," she says, and adds a shrug. She doesn't say that it's been vacant on and off (more off than on) for the past 90 years. She's researched all the history on the house, though she doesn't know yet if she'll offer any of it up to Booker. "Tough sell so far out here. Needs some money sunk in." She doesn't want to oversell it, instead she plays the part of the truthful realtor—sort of. "It needs new plumbing and windows. A new roof." Bea leads Booker into the dining room. "*Gorgeous* woodwork," she adds.

Booker runs his fingers over the thick trim and nods. "Can't find these quality details in a new house."

"No, you can't," Bea says, giving Booker time to look around. It's a time capsule. You'll never find these features elsewhere." Not the vintage wallpaper, the Victorian architecture, the pocket doors, the window transoms, and definitely not the heady scent of gardenia that always seems to pop up unannounced. No, there's no other house quite like this one. "Everything comes with it," she says, "all the window coverings and furniture you see."

"Everything?" Booker asks.

"*Everything,*" Bea says.

"What about the wall hangings?" Booker asks, looking at the portrait of the 1920s socialite above the fireplace, with pearls and fur and heavily painted lips.

"Everything," Bea says. "That portrait hasn't left the wall since the Jazz Age."

Booker continues to stare at the painting and Bea nudges him. "This way."

She shows him up the wide staircase, where he runs his finger gently over the banister, making a clean line through the dust.

"What about the knick knacks?" he asks, as they pass a glass vase with fake red roses in the hall. They're ridiculously bright against the gloomy interior of the house, and they make Bea cringe.

"Everything," Bea confirms, purposefully steering him into the bedroom with the cold patch. *Maybe I won't have to say anything,* she thinks. *Maybe he'll feel it himself.*

"What about the sheets and the light fixtures and …" Booker stops at the dresser and picks up a matching antique silver-plated hairbrush and mirror. "… personal items?"

Bea stares at the strands of coffee colored-hair in the brush and leans against the old radiator for support. "Everything," she says, and shivers.

I hate this house, she thinks.

"There's a great view from this room," Booker says.

Bea doesn't bother to look; the heavy scent of gardenia is making her feel nauseous.

Eighteen minutes later (Bea checks the time on her phone), they are back outside. The October sun warms Bea through her knit sweater and her goosebumps disappear. She waits while Booker makes a quick inspection of the foundation, basement, and brick siding. The fields around the house are tall with golden corn, and Bea thinks it's the same color as Booker's hair. *I wonder if his hair feels like corn silk, too, all soft and glossy.*

It's been so long since she's had someone. It makes her feel empty—like this house.

Booker walks toward her. "Two hundred thousand," he says. "Write it up."

Bea gapes. Not because it's one hundred thousand below asking and a ridiculous lowball offer, not because every other house in or outside of Shadowmoor sells in a bidding war, and not because Booker Morris is clearly a city-slicker who knows nothing about the Wood House on Mulberry Line, in the township of Addison. But because she hasn't told him the whole truth.

She hates being deceptive as much as she hates this house. But, damn, she so badly wants to sell this house, to not have to show it again.

"Do you want a home inspection?" Bea croaks, scribbling notes. She really should tell him. *What's commission on two hundred thousand, anyway?* she ponders, running the numbers in her head. *Five percent, but I'm not the listing agent, so I can only expect the seller's portion, so two-and-half percent ... so, five thousand dollars, minus what I owe the agency, on a 60/40 cut ... so, 60% of my total commission is ... three thousand dollars.*

Three thousand. Three months of mortgage payments on her cozy little craftsman in town. It's only her to make the payments, after all.

"No," Booker says.

"No?"

"No ... I don't need a home inspection."

"Right." Bea slashes off inspection. *Three thousand. I could upgrade the car, trade in the old Honda Civic for a Ford Escape.* "What about financing?"

"No," Booker says.

Bea raises her eyes warily. She doesn't get too many of those—the ones that don't need financing. Now she's suspicious. Has he inherited money, coddled some old relative just waiting for them to croak? Or is he a criminal, a dishonest business tycoon?

I'm probably not going to tell him, she thinks.

"I lost my wife," Booker says. "We had life insurance." He turns his back to her, maybe so she won't see his eyes glass over, or maybe so he won't see her sympathy.

Bea sighs, wishing the ground would swallow her up. Booker Morris is an honest, heartbroken, incredibly handsome man.

He saunters over to the apple tree, kicks at the rotten ones that have fallen on the ground. "Do you make pie?" he asks her.

"What? No." *No, I don't make pie. I'm too busy showing this sinister house. Had his wife been some 1950s bow-in-her-hair type? Is that what he likes?* She wonders.

Booker smiles. "You didn't even know the tree was here, did you?"

"What? Yes, of course I did." What the hell? Of course, she knew there was an apple tree, she's shown this house *17 bloody times.* She knows every nook and cranny in this ghastly house.

"No, you didn't," Booker says.

"No, I didn't," Bea admits. Trees are not on her radar, only foundations, siding, and the age of furnaces. She wishes Booker would stop looking at her like her like he knows her, with those penetrating brown eyes.

Booker twists two red apples loose, presents one to her. "I think I'll like it here," he says. "Do you live close by?"

"What? Oh yes. In town," Bea stammers, still thinking of the commission. "Sixty-five Primrose, cozy little yellow house …" Her voice trails off, she's said too much.

Three thousand. It isn't worth it. Maybe she doesn't mind him looking at her, after all. She definitely wouldn't mind his dimples around town. But it isn't worth it. He'd dump her when he found out anyway, ditch her for being a liar.

She hates her honesty almost as much as she hates this house.

"It's haunted," Bea blurts out. "The house."

Booker sets the apple atop her clipboard, since she hasn't taken it. He turns, stares up at the Wood House, with its perfect symmetry, its identical proportions on either side. *It's like a face*, Bea thinks. She'd never noticed that before, either. The goosebumps on her arms return.

Booker bites into his apple with a loud crunch. A crow flies up and out of the apple tree, and lands on the roof.

A gust of wind blows the front door shut, and Bea is glad they are outside, glad the key is tucked safely in her pocket. She has the uncanny feeling that the house has just set its jaw, clamped down on Booker's decision.

But Booker only smiles at her. "Haunted," he says. "Well, of course, it is."

—

Booker moves into the Wood Manor on a Friday, 36 days later. Bea banks her $3,000 check, buys two bottles of Merlot, and goes home to contemplate the basket of apples on her counter. Booker had insisted she take them when she dropped off his housewarming gift— a survival kit for when the power goes out. It was the most logical thing she could think of: candles, flashlights, bottled water, battery-operated radio, and lighters.

She wonders what Booker will think the first time he opens it, in the dark, at night, and sees the box of salt.

—

Bea awakens to a pounding on her door. She reaches for her phone, squints into the bright screen, and looks at the time—3:00 AM.

What the hell? Probably teenagers, she thinks, *getting a head start on their mischief for Devil's night.* They'd been known to start a week in advance before, draping houses in toilet paper and smashing eggs on porches.

The banging continues and Bea wrestles with the covers, finally winning her escape. She stumbles to the front door, unafraid, ready for battle. She'll show those kids who is boss.

She throws the door open.

Booker is standing under the porch light, rubbing the short hairs on his chin.

Bea clutches the doorknob, unsure of his presence. She would love to see him, in daylight, when she knows he's coming. She isn't ready for him right now.

"It's haunted," he says. "The house." His eyes are wide, unseeing.

"Yes." Bea steps aside, lets him enter. "Did you not believe me?" she asks, trying to keep her voice even.

"Well, no, not really. I thought you were having fun with me."

I'd like to have fun with you, Bea thinks. She realizes she hasn't covered herself. Her sleepshirt seems inadequate, too transparent, though Booker hasn't looked at all.

"I'm sorry, I don't know anyone else." Booker gazes around the dimly lit living room, but Bea can tell he isn't seeing her cheap sofa or mismatched end tables. He seems lost in his own thoughts of the Wood House.

Damn, I hate that house, Bea thinks.

"I'll be right back," she says. "Go on through to the kitchen." She hurries to her bedroom and slips on a fluffy housecoat. She pinches her cheeks and runs her fingers through her hair. She thinks of Booker, in his rumpled shirt and his clinging jogging pants. *How does he look so damn good in the middle of the night?* She'll light candles, she decides. Candlelight will be more flattering to her pale face, and more romantic.

Booker is sitting in the dark, fingertips tapping on the kitchen counter, when she returns. She flicks the light on, adjusts the dimmer to low. "Tea?" she asks.

"Whiskey?" Booker returns.

"No, sorry." Bea holds up a bottle of already-opened red wine.

"That works."

She pours two glasses and slides one over the counter to Booker, letting her hand graze against his. "So," she says.

Booker takes a sip. "So."

"It's haunted." Bea feels like she does during house showings, leading people, prodding them to get their thoughts. She doesn't say *I told you so.*

Booker takes a large gulp. "It's a woman. The one in the picture."

"You've seen her, then?" Bea sips her own wine and thinks of the lovely girl in the painting. It makes her aware of how ridiculous she must look—like an Easter bunny, all cottony and soft. It's not the effect she would have liked. She was wrong to put on the housecoat.

"Yes. Who is she?" Booker asks.

Bea sighs. "Opal Wood. Hardly anyone actually sees her."

"Opal." Booker drinks the rest of his glass, runs his tongue over his lips. "Opal," he says again. "Opal. Like the stone, with all the iridescent colors."

"Sure." Bea refills both of their glasses, lets him go on.

"She was so …"

Bea waits for the word … *beautiful? Young? Striking? Frightening?*

"… happy."

"Happy?" Bea asks.

"Gloriously cheerful." Booker nods, confirms his own thoughts. "Absolutely delightful."

"That's ridiculous." Bea has felt the energy herself, the ominous cloud of dread that drapes over the house. *Fuck, I hate that house,* she thinks. "What makes you think she was happy?"

"She was dancing," Booker says. "Well, more like floating. And laughing."

Bea crosses her arms. "Well, people who are happy do not throw themselves off roofs," she says.

"Right off?" Booker's jaw hangs open and Bea is overcome with the need to close it for him, to run her finger over his bottom lip.

"Straight off the witch's seat of the chimney," she says, flicking her hand to mimic Opal's fall.

"Say what?"

"The witch's seat." Bea doesn't know if this is true, or simply Shadowmoor folklore. "You know? The little stone blocks that stick out of the chimney? Originally used to protect the roof from seeping water?"

"No." He doesn't know houses like she does. Most people don't.

"Well. Anyway." Bea thinks for a moment, knows where the truth is. "Wait," she says. "I'll show you." She goes to her bookshelf, searches blindly. She won't risk turning on more lights, letting Booker see more of her, undone. Finding what she wants, the thickest leather-bound book on the shelf, she returns to Booker. She studied the book obsessively when she got her realtor license; she wanted to be the realtor who knew all the town history, and now she is. She presents *The History of Shadowmoor* to Booker.

Bea flips to the exact page and shows Booker the same portrait of Opal that hangs in the Wood House—his house.

Booker presses his pointer finger to Opal's neckline and draws circles where the pearls are.

Bea follows Booker's gaze, still on Opal. Bea is aware how lovely the girl is, how young. She shrugs off her housecoat in the hope of drawing Booker's attention to her and away from the dead girl. After all, Bea is here, alive, breathing, and willing. "Her father was going to marry her off," Bea says. "See? This photo was taken in 1928. Before the stock market crashed."

"I see," Booker says.

Bea leans in, lets her side press against his. He smells like whiskey and wood smoke and, now, red wine. "Her father lost all his money and wanted to save the manor. Back then, it was one hundred acres of farmland, before the house was severed off in the eighties."

"So, he wanted to marry her to someone wealthy?"

"You're a quick study," Bea tells him.

"But," Booker frowns, puts the pieces together, "she loved someone else."

"Very quick," Bea says. She almost giggles; she hopes he isn't quick in other ways.

"Someone she couldn't have."

"*Extremely* quick."

"But, who?" Booker's face is flushed and his glass is empty. He looks up at Bea, his body warm against hers.

Bea pours him more wine and wonders if he will make the first move. Instead, Booker turns back to the book and flips the page. "What's this?" he asks.

Bea tries to regain the moment, leaning in closer to see, though she already knows what he's looking at. "Opal wrote a love letter, before she … well, ya know … the roof."

She wants to linger longer, stay nice and close, but Booker is reading the photocopied letter. He doesn't notice as she retreats with a loud sigh.

Bea already knows what the letter says, she's read it before. She hopes it will make Booker feel all passionate and lovey-dovey.

> October 31, 1929
>
> Dearest Love,
>
> It's silly to think I didn't recognize how much I loved you, until I was destined for another. For years, you have cast a spell on me, unknowingly. It is your voice I hear, the whisper in my ear on summer mornings, it is your embrace I feel in the warmth of the fire in the winter. You enchant me, enfolding me into your arms until I become part of you, not knowing where you end and I begin. In the depths of your eyes, I see myself dancing, in your mouth, I am consumed. I love you from the tiny veins in your feet, all the way to the scar on your ear.
>
> I will never leave you,
>
> Opal

Bea rummages in the drawer and finds candles. Booker is still absorbing the letter, and Bea fills the silence by lighting the candles. The mood in the room has changed, she can feel it. It's less awkward now, warmer and more snuggly. Nothing like a bottle of wine and a love letter from a ghost to make sparks fly.

"It's rather an odd letter, don't you think?" Bea asks, breaking the silence.

Booker looks around the candlelit room, seemingly surfacing, and his eyes settle on the foil-covered plate. "Don't tell me that's apple pie." He smiles, finally, and Bea melts.

She tugs at her nightshirt, wondering (hoping?) if he'll see through her, too. "Yes," she admits.

"But you don't make pie." He's teasing her now. But, she doesn't want to talk about pie.

"Yes. Well …" She retrieves a plate from the cupboard and cuts him a slice. She pushes it over, looks at him through her lashes as he thanks her. "It's always love, you know—these things with ghosts. It's always the reason they don't cross over, why they stick around and haunt places."

Booker jabs his fork in and takes a bite. "What will I do?"

Me, Bea thinks. Instead, she leans over, purposefully letting her nightshirt slip dangerously low. "Sell?" she suggests.

"No." Booker's face darkens. "It's *my* house."

Fucking hell, I hate that house, Bea seethes. Booker has barely noticed her; he's too focused on his stupid house and stupid dead Opal.

"I know someone," she says, turning to rinse out the wine bottle for recycling.

"Like a ghost hunter?" Booker points his fork at her. "This pie is good. You lied. You *do* bake."

"I didn't lie. I didn't know I could." She's short with him now. She can't help it; she craves attention, someone to love her. But, Booker is oblivious. "Sometimes we discover things about ourselves, I suppose."

She only wishes Booker would discover her.

Booker flips the page back to the photo of Opal. "Maybe that's true," he says. "Mind if I borrow this book?"

"Suit yourself," Bea says. "I'll call the ghost hunter."

———

Alfred Russell is 58, with thinning hair and a protruding paunch. He's lived in Shadowmoor his whole life, like Bea, and thus, has been to the Wood Manor six times already in search of the ghostly inhabitant. Bea says as much when she introduces him to Booker the next night.

"What makes you think it will work *this* time?" Booker asks, letting them in.

"It *always works*." Alfred hauls in his equipment—an audio recorder, a camera, and an EMF meter—all his ghost-hunting gear. Bea knows what everything is, she's helped Russell before.

"If it works, then why is Opal still here?" Booker is leaning against the doorframe, arms crossed.

Bea flinches when Russell's eyes lock on her, like an accusation. "Alfred investigates paranormal activity," she explains to Booker, "he doesn't perform ... exorcisms." Bea twists her hands together behind her back; being in the house is already making her scalp crawl.

I fucking hate this house so much, she thinks.

"Exorcism sounds harsh," Booker says, steering them into the living room. "She isn't a demon. She's a lovestruck girl. That's all."

"Yes," Bea says. "a spirit."

"A ghost," Booker says.

"A witch," Bea says. "The Wood Witch."

"A ghostly witch?" Booker frowns, jiggles the ice cubes in his glass. Bea knows its whiskey; she smelled it when he opened the door. "What makes you think she was a witch?"

"*Is* a witch," Bea corrects.

Alfred clears his throat. "My grandfather told me. Everyone in Shadowmoor knew. It was obvious. She had a pet crow, some said it could shapeshift, but was mostly a crow. She'd send it out to do her bidding."

"What bidding?" Booker asks.

"Eliminating her betrothed." Alfred taps his EVP recorder wrist band. "He died, mysteriously. Drove his car into the tree at the end of the lane."

"You don't say." Booker's eyes land on Bea.

"You mean the apple tree?" Bea asks Alfred. She's never heard that part before. She hates that she didn't know this tidbit. She tips the tables, adding what she does know. "Opal stopped going to church. She dressed scandalously, a real flapper. Wore red dresses and red lipstick and drank ... red wine." Bea fumbles over her words, thinking of the wine last night, and rushes on. "She stole a horse and was found drunk in the rye field."

"She screamed at people," Alfred adds. "Swore and cursed."

"She had a wart." Bea widens her eyes for effect. "Down there."

"Down there?" Booker asks, eyebrows raised. "How on earth was that determined?"

Bea thinks he's smiling, but she can't be sure. "She was naked in the rye field." Bea berates herself inwardly the moment she says it; she doesn't want Booker thinking of Opal naked, or *anyone* naked, that isn't her. She flops into a stiff wing chair.

"Ahhh." Booker smirks, then turns to Alfred. "I don't think I require your services," he says.

"Excuse me?" Alfred looks to Bea for help, but she only shrugs. She won't be sad if Alfred leaves, if it's just her and Booker.

"If you're only here to determine that my house is haunted, well, I've already done that." Booker goes to the side table and pours himself some more whiskey, straight. "What I need is for Opal to leave. It's my house, now."

Alfred sputters. "Then, you need me. I can find her."

"I already found her." Booker points at the staircase.

Bea follows his gaze up the mahogany steps with the curving ornate banister. She looks around at the old floral wallpaper and the candelabras, but sees nothing. She can tell Alfred sees nothing as well. But just as Bea is about to say so, she feels the blast of cold air, accompanied by a shiver that crawls up her spine and into her hair.

Booker pours two more drinks and hands them around. "So, I'm the only one, huh? The only seer. Interesting."

"What does it mean?" Bea asks Alfred.

"I'm not sure," he says. "But, I don't drink."

"Me either," Bea says, but takes a sip anyway. The old clock on the mantle bongs three times as she continues sipping. "Did we not just get here?" she asks. "At ten?"

Booker pulls out his phone. "It *is* three," he says. "How in the world?"

"We told you," Bea says. "She's a witch. She manipulates time."

"I'm staying," Alfred says.

"I'm having your drink," Bea tells Alfred.

They traipse from the bottom of the house to the top, together. Bea stays nice and close to Booker on all three floors. Alfred lugs his equipment around, snapping excitedly like a live wire. Always, Bea knows when he will pick up electromagnetic activity; she feels it crawl up her neck beforehand. She watches Booker closely, the way he pets the old stone foundation, how he caresses peeling wallpaper, how he massages the wood into the fireplace. If he sees Opal again, he doesn't say.

Still, Bea is on guard. *I hate this house,* she whispers whenever Booker and Alfred are out of earshot.

In the basement they find ceramic bottles with nails and bent pins.

"Spell bottles," Bea explains. "Someone tried to aggravate Opal out."

"Someone like who?" Booker asks.

"Other owners," Bea says. "People like you, people that want it to be *their* house." Bea thinks Booker will commiserate with the other buyers before him, but he doesn't.

"Poor girl," he says, instead.

In the attic, Booker finds old shoes in the rafters.

"To protect the occupants from her," Bea says. She stumbles slightly, feeling tipsy from the whiskey, and Booker catches her. "There are sure to be more, in the walls and in the floorboards." Her breath hitches; she doesn't want him to let go.

"Poor girl," Booker repeats, righting Bea.

Bea scowls.

"You see?" Alfred asks. "It's all been tried. She won't leave."

Bea can tell Booker is deep in thought as they settle themselves, sometime later, by the fire in the living room. Time passes slowly now. Booker makes Bea and himself another drink—more whiskey. Alfred yawns and fiddles with his equipment, downloading footage onto his computer. Bea tucks her feet underneath her on the wing chair and tries not to stare at the portrait of Opal, though that is exactly what Booker is doing.

Bea wishes he would look at her, instead.

Damn this house, Bea thinks.

Booker snaps his fingers. "Of course, she *can't* leave," he says.

"She can't?" Bea asks.

"Not without her love."

"And we're supposed to figure out, decades later, who that was?" Bea hears the sarcasm in her own voice.

The fire crackles and an ember shoots out onto her lap. She jumps up, brushes it off quickly.

Booker stomps on it. "That was close."

"So is this," Alfred says. "Listen." He presses PLAY and they listen to the static, waiting for the sound of something they can interpret.

Bea hears nothing.

Booker sinks into the couch. "My God," he says.

"What is it?" Bea asks. "What is it? I couldn't tell. *What is it?*"

Booker's head is thrown back over the old sofa. "She said ... *I love you.*"

Bea rolls her eyes. "She did no such thing," she says. "You have such an imagination. You're cut off of the booze."

Booker's head snaps up. "Do I sense jealousy?" he asks.

"Of a dead witch?" Bea glares at him. "I'm leaving."

"Oh, don't leave," Booker says, reaching for her.

"Well, *I'm* leaving," Alfred says. "I'm exhausted."

"Goodbye," Booker says.

Bea stays, only because Alfred doesn't, and because she's drunk.

Booker is rereading the love letter and Bea pours herself another drink, red wine this time, and wonders why Booker didn't offer her that in the first place. He should have known she liked it best, after last night.

"It's divine," Booker says. "Such a deep love, so profound, such beautiful words."

"You like words?" Bea asks. "What are you, a writer, or something?"

"Or something," Booker says.

"Oh, I get it." Bea giggles. "Booker isn't your real name. You've changed it to suit yourself. BOOK-*er*. Appropriate."

"No, no," Booker says. "It's pure coincidence, I promise you. Like something dropped in your lap, a fluke, an accident, something you didn't know you needed."

"Like this house?" Bea asks.

"Like this house," Booker says.

I hate this awful house, Bea thinks.

She's feeling bold, now. Now, that Alfred is gone and she has liquid courage. Now, that they are alone. "What else *do you need?*" she asks. She's had enough, enough of the games, enough of the dead girl ghost-witch, enough of this blasted house.

She ambles over slowly, feels the fire lighting her face. She knows her hair is glowing red like a sunset, her lips stained from the wine. She thinks maybe in this moment, she is almost as pretty as Opal. Maybe. And Booker is looking right at her, finally.

Their eyes stayed locked as Bea goes to him and straddles him. Her knees press into the back of the sofa and she runs her fingers through his hair. It's not like corn silk at all, it's coarse and thick—unexpected. His hands move to her hips and she lowers her head to kiss his neck; she doesn't want to kiss his lips just yet, she wants to draw this out, make it last.

Light flickers on and off from the antique chandelier overhead and Bea remembers—they aren't alone. She raises her head.

"She's here," Booker breathes. He looks around, trying to find Opal. He stands, taking Bea with him, and deposits her lightly on the floor.

"*I'm* here," Bea says. But her voice is weak, and she isn't sure she said it at all. The temperature drops by a few degrees and she shivers.

"She can't leave." Booker grabs the book. "*You have cast a spell on me*," he reads.

Bea wishes she could cast spells—love potions, to be exact.

"It could've been anyone." Bea slumps into the same chair as before; it's hers now. The moment has passed. "It might've been the neighbor, or the banker, or a lumberjack." Booker isn't listening, but she goes on. "Or the stable boy, or the chimneysweep, or the lamplighter. *Anyone*," she stresses.

"It wasn't just *anyone*," Booker says, intent on the letter. Bea is sorry she ever showed him the history book. "*It is your voice I hear, the whisper in my ear on summer mornings, it is your embrace I feel in the warmth of the fire in the winter.*" Booker leans toward the fire, appears to listen to something beyond.

"Are you quite alright?" Bea asks, pulling a throw blanket over her and shutting her eyes. She's suddenly so tired. So very, very tired. And cold.

Bloody hell, I hate this house, she thinks.

"I have a scar," Booker says, settling on the sofa again.

"Yes, well I bake pie," Bea murmurs.

"But, *I* have a scar," Booker insists. "I have a scar, I *do*." He says it over and over again as Bea drifts away.

———

The morning comes in a crash of light, a shard that pierces through the slit in the drapes. Bea moves her tongue around her mouth, presses a hand to her throbbing head.

Then, she jolts upright, remembering.

She's in the Wood House. She scans the room. She's alone.

Except she isn't. The chill is creeping up her neck again, niggling into her hair. But it's also inching downward, snaking down her spine and over her arms.

I hate this house, she thinks.

She lets out a breath, stares at the cloud of fog in front of her face.

The fire has died. There's no heat.

"Booker?" she calls.

She goes to the sofa where he was sitting last night, looks down at the history book. A page has been torn out. The cold is in her legs now, working its way to her toes. She cups her hands around her face and breathes warm air.

"Booker?" she calls.

She hears a latch creak, from upstairs, and instinctively knows where it's coming from. "Booker!"

Bea goes to the front door, where the care package she brought Booker is still sitting on the floor, unopened. She roots around, finds the box of salt. She dashes to the stairs, and goes up and up and up. Time folds away, gets lost somewhere, before she reaches the top. She wonders if maybe she's still drunk, but dismisses the thought when she hears the tinkling laughter. The stairs are never ending and she thinks she may die here, surrounded by the laughter. She heard it once before, on another showing, years ago. It's tucked into the corners, reverberating off the floorboards. It's everywhere and nowhere.

Booker thinks of the laughter as happiness, but Bea knows better. It's pure madness.

She comes to the door she wants, the door of the cold room— Opal's. Other owners have tried to change the bedroom, to remove the ancient items: the brush and mirror, the music box, the clothes, the jewelry. No one has ever succeeded.

The door is shut, locked, and cold as ice. Bea bangs on it. "Booker!"

She bangs and bangs and bangs. Her fists are raw and her palms red when she finally stops. She stands with her ear pressed to the door and listens. She hears the footsteps on the roof, just as the door swings open on its own. The room reeks of gardenia.

Bea doesn't want to go in, but she has to. "Booker?"

The lace curtains are flapping frantically, swelled up with a howling wind. It's not day—it's still night. She's been deceived.

"I hate this dreadful house," she says aloud.

She tosses salt everywhere, throws it across the floor and at the walls. Then, she wraps her arms around herself and rushes to the side window, the one that opens onto the roof. She can see straight over to the chimney, to where Booker is crouched in the moonlight.

"Booker!"

He startles, nearly loses his balance, and Bea gawks in horror.

"You scared me," he calls. "A close call. But look, your witch's seat saved me." He's holding onto a protruding stone block in the chimney, the one Bea has imagined Opal resting on when she takes a break from her nocturnal adventures.

Bea is dizzy just watching him and she grips the window ledge. "Come in," she begs.

But Booker is reading the love letter again, clutching the torn piece of paper as it flails in the wind. *"In the depths of your eyes, I see myself dancing, in your mouth, I am consumed. I love you from the tiny veins in your feet, all the way to the scar on your ear."*

A crow lands on the eavestrough, black as the sky, and spreads its tail feathers like a fan.

Caw, caw, it says.

"Booker!" Bea says.

He raises a bare foot, blue with cold. "I have tiny veins," he says. Bea realizes, with dismay, he isn't talking to her. He's talking to the bird.

"No," Bea says.

"I have a scar," he says, excitedly, "on my ear."

"No." Bea feels warmth fill her, a rising red fury. "Booker, you raging lunatic, get back in here."

"*I will never leave you,*" Booker says.

The crow spreads its wings, floats into the air.

Booker spreads his arms, slides off the roof.

The heat leaks out of Bea. She staggers backward, shuts her eyes. She can hear music now, the wedding march. She can barely breathe; the air is so cold her nostrils stick together.

She has to get out.

She heads past the dresser, where a wooden jewelry box is open, a tiny bride twirling to the song. Pearls are draped over the edge. Before she can change her mind, Bea snatches them and runs.

The stairs take too long, but Bea keeps going. Down, down, down. She refuses to let go of the pearls, even when her mouth has gone dry and her lungs burn.

Finally, she's there, clawing her way out the front door and across the lawn. She blinks in the heavy sunlight, turns her face greedily to the warmth. It really is morning, now.

She sees Booker's body, lying limp and broken, a few feet away. "I hate you!" she screams at the Wood House, and sinks to her knees. She knows what she has to do, how to end this madness, how to get rid of the Wood Witch.

Bea is weak, her legs and arms are jelly. She crawls to the dining room window, where she knows she will find the length of twine hanging, strung with hag stones. She knows, because she put it there. After her very first showing of Wood House, she scoured Shadowmoor for stones with holes, and painstakingly slipped them onto the string. Her grandmother had told her, years ago, that hag stones could ward off spirits of the dead. Bea tried to block the Wood Witch. In her own way, she tried. Oh God, how she tried.

She'll try again now.

She pulls herself up against the bricks of the house, reaches for the stones. Overhead, the crow circles.

Caw, caw.

She intends to slip the pearls onto the stones, entwine the two, like a double necklace. But she finds herself frozen in place, unable to move.

Opal is screeching now and it mixes with the caws of the bird.

Bea tries to stretch her fingers, flex her arm, kick her legs. Nothing will budge. She imagines herself stuck here for eternity, growing old and gnarled and rigid. No one will ever know what happened. The ivy will cover her, consume her.

And then, she knows.

"You enchant me, enfolding me into your arms until I become part of you, not knowing where you end and I begin," Bea whispers. It's strangely comforting—a moment of connection.

The crow swoops in and plucks the pearls from her hand. The spell breaks, and Bea sinks to her knees.

She stares at her empty palm. She knows where the pearls will be returned to— the jewelry box, in the room that never changes. She failed. She's no longer frozen, but she can't shake the feeling.

She creeps slowly over to Booker. He's facedown and Bea is glad; she doesn't want to see his eyes that weren't for her.

She reaches for the paper still locked in his hand. She unfolds the love letter gingerly and sits back to read it.

When she's done, she looks up, into the face of the Wood House. Sure enough, Booker's figure is in the right eye, palm pressed to the glass, staring down at her. Another figure is in the left eye, a swirl of crimson with glossy pearls.

"I can see you now," Bea whispers to the Wood Witch.

The mouth of the house gapes open, with the familiar creak, inviting Bea in, once again.

An eternal invitation.

"I love you from the tiny veins in your feet," Bea reads, *"all the way to the scar on your ear."*

Her eyes slip from the hairline cracks in the foundation, where the ivy has wormed its way in, to the blackened bricks of the chimney, on the right side of the witch's seat. She forgot to tell Booker about the long-ago chimney fire—the scar on the ear.

She's startled by a mad laugh, and realizes, this time, it's her own. It's uncanny how much she sounds like the Wood Witch. She pokes Booker in the shoulder, fevered with the revelation. "You were right," she says, "Opal *is* happy."

Bea laughs some more, then sobers suddenly. "But you were so wrong, Booker, my love. She didn't write the letter to *you*." Bea pets his head, moves his hair aside to see the scar on his ear. "Unfortunate," she mutters. "A fluke, pure coincidence, a tragic accident." She lowers her face, whispers in his unfortunate ear. "Do you see, now?" she asks.

"No, of course, you don't," she continues. "You only saw what you wanted to see. We could've been happy, you know. The way Opal is—with this house." Bea snorts at the irony. "Opal is in love with the Wood House and you're in love with Opal … but who is in love with me?"

Bea rises, shoves the letter in her pocket. She should phone someone, she thinks vaguely. Maybe the police. But a jolt of logic grounds her. What will happen to her if she does phone someone?

Beatrice.

Bea whips around.

The two figures are still in the windows, but it isn't either of them that has called for her.

Beatrice. It's her name again, like a shuddered breath in a doorway, like a wisp of a kiss in a billowing curtain.

And then, Bea feels it. The magnetic pull, sucking her in.

It's the house that has always wanted her, but the Wood Witch kept her from seeing it. *Love and hate are so close,* she thinks, with tears in her eyes.

Bea remembers how it felt when she was frozen, when she thought she would become part of the Wood House, covered in ivy, always belonging. The empty space inside her fills with warmth.

It's overwhelming to Bea; she's never known the intensity of being the beloved. She runs back to the house and slips through the cavernous front door.

Bea hears the Wood Witch's jealous shriek as the Wood House enfolds Bea in a loving embrace.

AUTHOR'S NOTE

My mother introduced me and my sister to "haunted houses," when we were very young. We'd spend weekends traipsing around the countryside to find abandoned houses to trespass, and though we never found ghosts, we were usually given a healthy dose of fear, either by Mom (who found second staircases to creep up and surprise us) or the possibility of being caught (owners lurk around every corner and according to Dad we would go to jail, and we'd only get one phone call, and don't make it him).

It didn't surprise me when I became a realtor for a short stint, but it quickly became clear that my favorite parts of the business were either the write-ups/house descriptions or the abandoned/derelict properties. Run-down Victorian house on Elm street? I'm in. Decaying farmhouse in the backcountry? Pick me. It wasn't trespassing anymore, it was legal! But somehow, not as fun.

Old and abandoned houses whisper to me. It always seems as if there is a story left untold, brushed into the corners and forgotten in the walls. Having a house as a character in its own right was highly appealing to me, as I'm always fascinated by the love certain people bestow on places. Thus, the Wood House came into being. But, I wondered, could a house love someone back?

The character Beatrice sprang off the page as the beloved, as someone who seemingly has it altogether, but is missing that vital piece of life—a connection to someone or, in this case, something.

The two were a perfect match.

SVG

MIRROR, MIRROR

ELLIE COOPER

"I REALLY APPRECIATE the ride," he said. "Not many women would these days, but you can trust me."

I glanced at the stranger in my passenger seat. He was 15 years younger, but I'd been giddy as a teenager when I'd led him across the parking lot to my sensible, white Corolla. His shoulder-length blonde hair was different from the close-cropped hair of oppressive bosses, fathers and lovers. A tattoo wrapped his bicep like a pale green vine. His jeans were tucked into black lace-up Doc Martens. His left arm now dangled loose on the back of his seat just inches from me.

"You'll have to tell me if I need to make a turn or anything." I spoke too quickly, nervous now. The mirror's effect was wearing off like a short-acting drug. My hand swept the side of my face below my right cheekbone, an unconscious gesture or bad habit like a girl who bites her nails or picks at ugly scabs. I caught myself. Perhaps he didn't notice, but he was on my vulnerable side, where the scar hung, too dark for the rest of my face, dimpled like spackling the plastic surgeons forgot to smooth. It grew agitated when I had a fever, became embarrassed or stood beneath a bright light. I'd worked hard to be rid of it. I'd been to herbalists and faith healers, read books on Native American remedies and Voodoo spells. Finally, I gave up and covered it with expensive French make-up. I glanced again at this stranger in my car. Another one of my mistakes I now feared.

I tried to remember my way back to the auction house, the red barn perched high on a hill, 30 miles outside of Austin. It had been postcard perfect earlier in the day, white picket fences and cattle grazing in fields of bluebonnets. The smell of fresh cut hay had been in the air when he'd asked for a ride. Now every time I asked, he said his sister's place was a little farther. A little father down this dark, one-lane country road. I'd never find the highway. All I could do was stay between the white lines.

I glanced quickly in his direction. The night bathed him in shadows as it had when he'd stood in the soft glow of the building's lights while I searched for my car keys. I'd gone to the auction for the

"Littles"—the out of print book, chipped plate, milk glass or knick-knack—that would fill the shelves and empty spaces of my lonely existence. I'd found what I needed but had foolishly let it slip away.

His head had bobbled staccato like a little bird as he listened to Seattle Grunge over a pair of headphones.

"You didn't find anything you couldn't live without? he said.

I looked around, but he spoke to me.

He continued: "It was an okay auction. I only got some junk here for my sister who just got married." He pointed to a cardboard box at his feet.

And there I saw *it*—the mirror—propped along the side of his box.

I rushed forward and joined him in the shadows. I bent down and took the mirror without asking; I cradled it like a child with a found toy.

"It was supposed to be in Box Number Six," I said. "I won the winning bid. Somebody must have switched it. It's mine—really."

I was breathless and expected him to protest. I forgot my rule about not looking strange men in the eye. I only had 40 dollars left, but he might take a check. At flea markets and garage sales, I'd learned to haggle, offering half the asking price, hiding my interest in whatever caught my fancy. But it was too late for that. Too late to pretend *it* was unimportant. I rubbed the silver that was almost black with tarnish. I turned the mirror slightly and caught more of the light from the parking lot, and there I was as I'd been when I first found it buried beneath hand-embroidered pillowcases and a pile of yellow curtains. I saw myself as I'd been a long time ago. As I'd been when Mother sat me on her lap and brushed my hair until my scalp tingled. As I'd been when she told me some day, I'd have a man to love me and children of my own. The safe, happy times before the cancer took Mother. Before Father had come into my room and started throwing my things, because I'd been late with dinner. Before her mirror broke and things turned bad. Before I'd run away and had the accident. A time when I was pretty.

"That a magic mirror, or what?" he asked.

His headphone rested around his neck, but his head still bobbled as if he listened to some internal music only he could hear. He wouldn't take my money. He gave me the mirror, because it meant something to me, he'd said. And now it lay face down on the back seat directly behind me. I could keep it near me always, in the car, if I wanted. I could look into it any time I felt bad or ugly. It had almost slipped away like a foolish old woman's lost youth and unfulfilled dreams, but he'd given it back to me. I'd been so grateful. He'd been waiting for a taxi he said, but I'd led him to my car instead.

"Yeah, I knew it was something special when I saw you inside like a little girl with her looking glass. You looked pretty from your good side. You use them fancy moisturizers and make-up they sell on TV? You work out?"

"What? You saw me?" I spoke without taking my eyes from the road, my voice barely a whisper.

"What's your name?"

"Lillian." Eyes still focused on the treacherous road.

"Pretty Lilly. I like that." He reached over and touched my scar, letting me feel the ragged edge of his fingernail. "Bad accident, or your old man slice you?"

No one besides Mother had ever called me Lilly. My face burned like the time I'd applied dilute Clorox on a cotton ball and tried to bleach the scar. I could feel it turn a deeper purple. I brushed his hand away like it was a gnat. Something was wrong. I'd taken a wrong turn from my cautious existence.

He leaned back in his seat. "Yeah, it's my lucky day you came along. I'm real surprised after them two girls that disappeared from these parts recently. You hear about them? Maybe just a little write-up in the paper. The one that worked nights at Walmart and then the other one. Margaret was a real looker, nice tits. Joanne something or other, had them big, chubby, cellulite thighs. You know what I mean? She didn't take care of herself like you. Both disappeared on their way home. A woman's got to be careful. You careful? Yeah, you looked real good from the side, talking to that fat, old counter woman."

He spoke of the auctioneer's wife who ran the snack bar. I'd rushed to her like a foolish child needing the wrong, righted—the hurt kissed away—after I'd won the winning bid and found the mirror missing from my box. "What kind of place is this, anyway? It was here!" I'd held up the cardboard box with the big black "six" written on its side.

The woman had been slow, lethargic and spoke with a sing-song German accent. She wasn't Mother.

"Oh, I'm so sorry, dear," she'd said. "These things happen. Somebody fancies something in this box and something else in that box, but they don't want to pay for two boxes, so they put everything together in one box, and make sure they get the winning bid. It happens. We'll get you next time. You don't have to pay, dear."

I'd shoved the box at her. I'd whirled and run to the parking area where men loaded their Ford F150s and Suburbans with elaborate armoires, massive tables with legs carved like carnival balloons pinched and twisted into intricate shapes. My muscles ached from sitting on a hard church pew in the last row of the bidding area for hours waiting for my box to be auctioned.

I now remembered something else the auctioneer's wife had said as she'd passed out the bidding cards. *We have something for everyone.* Her words now stung. I glanced at the man beside me. He'd been waiting for something more than a taxi.

He still talked about the missing women. I tried to recall the one-inch pictures of the smiling, dark-haired women from the City-State section of the *Statesman*. Had their bodies been found? I breathed deeply to push the panic down, but it clawed against my chest like a wild animal trying to break free. The night was darker than the city nights I was used to. No street lights or familiar landmarks to guide me home. There were no stores or stars. No place to turn around. I looked quickly to my left, and then quickly past him, to the other side. There was only a low sloping drainage ditch, the same as on my side. I knew there were mesquites, live oaks, prickly pears and life beyond, but all I could see was myself lying in a field alone, insects crawling over my cold flesh. Only the headlights ahead to guide me.

"Pretty Lilly, slow down," he said. "You'll get us both killed."

I lifted my foot from the accelerator and watched the speedometer drop. Yes, slow down; you're not dead yet. Had he actually confessed? But the details, how could he know the intimacies of both women? Think, damnit. Think! Should I lie and say I knew Kenpo Karate, that my boyfriend was a detective and would hunt him down, or that I was HIV positive? I was exhausted and wanted it over. It would be, of course. Why else had he bragged, unless he knew I'd never repeat any of what he said. I didn't want to hear him, but he kept babbling. I wanted to give up, stop the car. I knew I couldn't outrun him, and after death, it wouldn't matter. But the torture could go on for hours, days, weeks. I wanted quick. But how? I glanced at him. It wouldn't be a quick death, one shot to the head. Perhaps I could hit a tree, maybe the crash would kill me. I studied him as he talked. Yes, he had the advantage, he was in control. I rubbed my scar. Find his Achilles' heel, everyone had theirs, I hoped. I forced my mouth open and tried to speak.

"Your sister," my voice broke. I tried again: "Your sister. You say she's recently married. Is she younger or older?"

Get him away from the other women and back into my world. It was a slim chance. I wasn't a psychologist, but something I'd read came back to me. *Stand your ground. Don't go with him.* But it was too late for that!

He didn't answer, but he'd stopped his monologue. That's good.

"Any kids," I asked. "Your sister?"

He was quiet now, but I heard the blood pound in my ears. Maybe I'd reached him.

A small hiccup sounded deep within him followed by childish laugher that choked his words. "Yeah, it works every time." His voice deepened. "Hell, after Ma saw me come out, she made sure there wouldn't be any more. She didn't even want me." His hand slapped the back of my seat.

I clung to the steering wheel. There was no sister, and I was in some unfathomable abyss. I'd taken him to a worse place, if that were possible. It was pointless, but I forced myself to continue. "I'm an only child, too. It was hard, very hard at times, but—"

"That so? Well, that makes us kind of related, don't it?"

"There were times—"

"You aren't wearing a ring, but that don't mean nothing now days, does it? You got a boyfriend, or you in between? I'll bet a fine lady like you has been married, what two-three times? He don't mind you out late like this? Hell, you didn't have to give me a ride, you know. I'd already given you your sorry, old mirror." He glanced towards the back seat.

His words were grievous, and he was back in control. I wanted to ignore him, but I wanted him to stop even more. "I liked you," I said. I knew it was a stupid thing to say as soon as the words slipped out. "I mean, I thought we could get to know one another, be friends, maybe."

"Yeah, I know lots of women like the way I look." I could see him flex his muscles and pump his chest; he tossed his lovely hair from his shoulders like Fabio on the cover of a romance novel.

Perhaps I could outlast him, keep him talking, keep driving until morning, wear him down. He'd grow tired eventually, wouldn't he? No one killed in the day light, did they? Didn't all bad things happen in the dead of night—Mother's death, my accident. Perhaps we could find an all-night store and stop for a soda or beer. Maybe the clerk could hit the panic button around his neck or under the counter, before he—he what? Before they found my body days, weeks later after the insects had taken control. Work would call me at home tomorrow when I didn't show up and eventually the police. But by then, it'd be too late. For the first time all night, I thought of Harlan. Harlan who didn't want to marry me. Harlan whose relatives I'd never have to cook chicken cordon bleu or veal parmesan for again on Sundays. Harlan who only had to ask and I'd pack an overnight bag and hurry to his place. Harlan might not miss me for days. I thought of the bottle of Chardonnay on the back shelf of my refrigerator that I'd bought for him. I brushed my scar. *Who could ever love you*, it said.

My anger fueled me. "We could drive into town, any place, it wouldn't take that long, we could—"

"We'll party when we get to Doug's. It's just up ahead."

No, not two of them. "Listen, it's a nice night, we could catch the interstate, drive down to San Antonio, maybe keep going all the way to the coast. That'd be nice, wouldn't it?"

He didn't answer only stared out the window. How much time did I have? Ten minutes, maybe. I eased my foot from the accelerator, so he wouldn't notice. My thoughts raced like a train about to derail. I rubbed my scar again. *The mirror. Maybe, just maybe.*

"You know it's my lucky day, too." I choked on the words but forced myself to continue.

"What?"

It was my turn to lie. "The mirror's turn of the century. There's an engraved mark on the back handle that's almost worn off. Fools at the auction don't know anything. You probably thought it was something sentimental. I wasn't going to say anything, but we're friends now, right?"

"Yeah, I thought it was valuable," he said. He seemed to cheer up and reached behind me for the mirror. He rubbed his big, strong hands over it, making me cringe. "How much you think it's worth?"

Suddenly, without thinking, I snapped on the interior light. "Why don't you take a look."

"Cool," he said. He held the mirror with one hand and fluffed out his beautiful hair with the other. I saw him better in the light. He was perfect. His skin flawless, his features Greek sculpture. His beauty—I bit down hard on my lip to stop the awful truth—he was everything I'd always wanted to be.

When I could, I turned to face him. He still stared at himself. Gently, I put pressure on the brake. He began to change chameleon-like before me; his shoulders sagged; his features softened. I stopped the car but kept it idling. I leaned carefully towards him to see what he saw, as he was a long time ago. The lovely, beautiful child. His hair even lighter like spun gold, his skin mother-of-pearl. But something was wrong. He was crying.

I wanted to ask why, but I had to act fast. The mirror's effect was temporary. "Look it's getting late, we have to hurry, get you home."

"Fuck you."

I recoiled as if his hand had struck me. "You want to get out and walk to your friend's house? Maybe you could spend the night?"

"Hurry up, don't stop, it's just up ahead. Hurry, please."

He hadn't noticed we were already stopped. He began to cradle his left arm to his body. He shook. I could see the bone in his forearm was slightly bent at an angle as if it hadn't been set properly. My hand touched him lightly on the shoulder, but his good arm struck out at the empty air around him. When he'd quieted, I whispered. "What's wrong with your arm?"

"Uncle Doug."

I hit the gas hard and looked into the darkness for some sign of Uncle Doug, but all I saw in the headlights were rural mailboxes and a whiskey barrel with red verbenas. The houses were far between and set back from the road where screams in the night might go unheard.

"He's not really my uncle, but Ma told me to call him that," he said.

"Your Ma, where is she now?"

"The day after Ma died, he went out and got a woman. I could hear them laughing. Laughing at Ma and me. It wasn't even his house. It was mine, all mine."

"Go on," I said.

"He'd bring home women he'd pick up in bars or lonely waitresses at all night truck stops or sometimes runaways like Marie, but I knew what was going on."

"What?" I said. His silence worse than the truth.

"Marie was different. She liked me and was nice, fixed my breakfast sometimes, and I could talk to her. I can talk to you, too, can't I?"

I could feel his eyes on me. "Yes, I love it when you talk to me. You can tell me anything you want."

"Uncle Doug, he was mean and saw that Maria liked me better than him. She tried to warn me. She snuck into my room late one night, one eye all swollen shut. We've got to get out of here, she'd said. There was fear on her, I could smell it, you know what I mean?

His nostrils flared. "Like you," he said. He turned back to the window. "We threw my things into a backpack, but he came in."

"Your uncle?"

"He hurt her bad, taught her—her manners, he said, but he never touched me, at least, not my face. I got scars all over my body, you wanna' see? Afterwards, it got easier, he took care of me. We became a team. Him and Me. My looks lure them, you see. I'm sucker bait, and Uncle Doug reels them in. That's what he says. See women like me. Uncle Doug won't let me cut my hair. But they all asked for it, you know. I didn't force them to come with me like I didn't force you. Margaret was the first one that was strong and fought real hard. You gotta' separate yourself from them, Uncle Doug says. It's like a primitive tribe, they weren't family, not really human, but just ours for the taking—"

"No!" My voice reverberated in the confines of the small car. The mirror's effect was wearing off. "Look again, into the mirror, farther back before the pain. Try. What do you do for fun?" A dangerous question for this man, but the boy couldn't have been more than 12.

He looked at himself again. "Hang out."

He wiped his nose with the back of his hand. "Play video games. At the Pack-N-Sack. Roy has a stack of *Playboys* he lets me look at in the storeroom. It's there, just ahead."

"What?"

"Pull over, now. Stop the car."

I almost missed it. The deserted, boarded up convenience store, totally dark. By the look of the sign, it had changed ownership at least once since the boy had known it. It wasn't what I'd expected, but I hit the brakes hard. My hand was on the door handle, but he opened his side first.

Please just go.

He turned towards me. "You got some quarters I can borrow?"

I emptied my change purse into his outstretched palm and gave him the two twenties I'd tried to give him earlier for the mirror. I watched him get out and adjust his headphones. I should have gone then, but I found myself in the quiet eye of a storm, my fear gone. We were joined, my knowledge, his deeds. He'd tried to run away also but had only gotten this far. His beauty had been corrupted and used against him. I ached for the boy. If my father had been worse, I might—but I stopped my thoughts. He turned back towards me. His handsome lips tightened into an ugly sneer. He was changing back. *No, just go, please.* He took a step toward my car, and instinct took over— his and mine. The automatic door locks clanged like prison gates, but he slapped the roof of my car, and I jumped as if his hand had finally found me. My foot hit the accelerator.

At a crossroad, I stopped. I couldn't get enough air; his stale boy's sweat permeated the car.

Or was it my own smell?

Should I phone the sheriff and tell him I'd spent the evening with some nameless monster?

I didn't know whether to turn left, right or continue on. I was lost in a web of dark county roads, not knowing where I'd been.

I looked for him in the shadows of my rear-view mirror. There was only darkness, but I knew he was out there waiting for me or someone else. Yes, and I knew he'd always be there. Waiting. My hand rubbed my scar again, and I thought of Mother, and then the auctioneer's wife. *We have something for everyone.* I rolled down my window and tossed the mirror far into the night, my tires crushing loose gravel like broken glass.

AUTHOR'S NOTE

My first husband was an avid auction-goer, which is where I devised the setting for my story. I would often accompany him and observe how people waited hours for particular items to be auctioned, and then witness their dismay if they didn't win the lot. It was surprising to me how people would grasp for items they never knew existed, things they didn't need and previously hadn't wanted. I was thinking of the evil queen and her mirror in the fairy tale "Snow White" when I decided to use a mirror as a literary device for my story. The mirror enabled both the protagonist to see herself as she really was—not someone horribly disfigured—as well as to show the antagonist's nature as he had been as an abused child.

EC

THE TWO WITCHES

CARRIE Sz KEANE

THE SMELL FROM the poultry factory was a fog. It rolled across the parking lot, fuming, a gas of chicken carcass, chicken shit, and blood. It choked. The factory, standing alone and surrounded by corn fields, pushed smoke from spires, coiling the malodor up, out and around, pervading. The incinerated feathers and flesh of birds wafted across the town.

I can no longer eat meat.

I pulled into my assigned parking space, the word *clinician* painted with a stencil on the hot asphalt. The Perdue plant, a place I called The Chicken of Oz, was a place where migrant workers landed after suffering the long path, a yellow brick road, from Mexico, El Salvador, Haiti. The wizard awaited them in Emerald City, a promise of freedom and the greenback paper dollar. The men and women literally slaving therein were cowardly lions looking for heart, scarecrows of agriculture, animal husbandry, farmers, tin men, industrial workers. I was Dorothy—naive, young, and simple, representing the American people, *Everyman,* led astray and seeking the way back home.

My patient's name was Soledad Sullivan. She turned out to be a good witch. In Spanish, the name Soledad translates to loneliness and solitude. Sullivan, obviously, is an Irish name. I thought the name to be a curious combination, a lovely alliteration. We had this in common. I also inherited an Irish surname through marriage. I also have an alliterative name. Soledad also worked in the chicken factory, in sterile processing, a fancy name for slaughter. We each received a frozen chicken on pay day, a turkey on Thanksgiving and Christmas.

On Fridays, I managed the in-house women's health clinic. It smelled like bleach and raw meat. Stainless steel tables and crisp white walls made the place sterile, but outside of the door to my little office was a factory where chicken catchers processed as many as 50,000 chickens in an 8- to 12-hour shift, lifting three and four at a time in each hand, cramming the birds into steel cages known as "the hole." Forklifts loaded the dirty white chickens onto conveyor belts that rolled into the plant. Inside, in cold, dark, wet, refrigerated rooms, workers hung the birds on metal hooks, upside down by their feet. Electricity zapped the chickens to stun them, before their necks were sliced open to kill. Their blood dripped into tanks the size of wading pools.

I was not allowed to venture past the locked double doors that led to the processing plant. Instead I was dealing with the blood flow of women, not chickens. My job was as the midwife to the chicken workers.

The chicken factory housed its own women's clinic so that the ladies who worked there wouldn't have to leave work as deboners and live prodders for prenatal and gynecology appointments. The women, mostly Latinas and some Haitians, would come to see me on their breaks, wearing hairnets under hardhats and high gum boots over disposable yellow rubber jumpsuits. Their chief complaints were swollen ankles from standing for 12-hour shifts and carpal tunnel from repetitive cutting motions. My job was to give out ibuprofen to crampy menstruating women, to listen to the fetal heartbeats of the pregnant girls, to provide herbs for the menopausal, to give pap smears and breast exams, to test for STDs, and to hand out contraception for free, like candy from a basket that hung on my arm.

I was Soledad's midwife. My name is Care. From birth, her destiny was to be lonely and mine was to give a shit.

Over the years, as a midwife, I have become obsessed with what people name their babies. Duchess, and King George, Awesome, and Onasty, pronounced Honesty, Pixie Pearl and Konfidence. Yes, Confidence. With a K. Rarely, Matthew or Carol. Every Angelica is born a beauty, an angel. Every Norm, normal. And nearly all Brendas are husky horse-mouthed women who work long hours and have fat calves. Everybody grows into their name. A name, hung around the neck of a newborn like a badge, becomes, in some ways, their definition. Soledad, I would come to understand, had a life defined by sorrowful solitude.

Soledad came to the clinic nearly every Friday, for this or that. I quickly learned that she didn't have anything wrong with her, but was just looking for company, looking for an excuse to leave the production line, to take a break from the cold refrigeration and blood smells of dead chickens. I enjoyed her visits. Her English was excellent. My Spanish was poor. She would translate for me, especially for patients whose Mayan dialect was impossible for me to understand.

"She is not Mary," she said one afternoon, pointing at Mary, who was undressed, with a gravid belly and swollen, veiny breasts, sitting on the examination table.

"She isn't married?" I responded.

"I no Mary," said the young woman, pointing, jabbing a finger, at herself.

Squinting to understand, I questioned, "You know Mary?"
"She isn't Mary," Soledad said again, rolling her eyes.

"Oh … who is she then?"

"Don't you worry," she nudged me, wink wink.

With her accent it sounded like she said, "Don't chew worry." I had a tendency to chew worry, like cud. I bit the insides of my cheeks. I fretted my nails down to the quicks. I worried.

I looked at the chart in my hands. The label read, Mary Santiago Rivera, with a birthdate that read: 12/04/1962. This would have made "Mary" 51 years old. She was 36 weeks pregnant and looked no older than 25. The fact registered that I had already met three other women named Mary Santiago Rivera. All of them 51 years old. Name-sharing and identity fraud were pervasive in chicken factories. All of us turned a blind eye. Even, and especially, the administration, who knew that most of their employees were illegal and using fake or borrowed documents. Who else would they get to do this awful work? At this awful pay rate? This is not my problem, I thought, as I ripped my cuticles and chewed on my worry. I can't take on the whole world.

Two weeks later, "Mary" showed up to the hospital where I also worked, huffing and puffing, squatting in the hallway with an urge to push, yelling, "No puedo!" Mary had presented to the unit with a different name, and no paperwork."Si! Tu su puedes, Carlita!" I said.

She smiled at me when I spoke her real name, as if she knew I was one of the good guys. She wouldn't be turned away by me, no matter who she was, or who she said she was. Good guy, or not, turning away a woman in labor, no matter her legal status, or race, or lack of insurance, was against the law.

Her baby, a girl named Linda, which translates to cute, was born an American citizen. Linda was oh-so cute, with enormous brown eyes, toffee skin, and a dimple in one cheek. "Que gordita!" I said, pinching her fat chin. Carlita was so proud, but Mary Santiago Rivera, age 51, would be back to work the next week as if nothing had happened, plunging chickens into foamy hot water, loosening and removing feathers before the birds faced the cavalry of machines and blades.

One device removed their feet. Another jammed a cylinder into cavities, reaching through 16 birds at a time, emerging with the guts in one grab.

Mary and Soleded had the job of hosing down stainless steel sinks, counter tops, and floors, redirecting fat, feathers, and meat scraps into bloody channels coursing beneath steel grates in the floor.

My job, delivering babies, and doing gynecological procedures, was also bloody and messy. And, some days, the sheer number of women coming in the door, pregnant, panting in labor, shrieking, or with relationship woes, and strange itches, made it feel like I worked in a factory too.

Soledad started showing up with laboring women to the hospital, in the middle of the night and on weekends. She would say that they needed a ride, or that they asked her to come since their own *madre* or *tia* was in Nicaragua or Honduras. Always, she would be right on time for work in the factory the next morning, both as a translator, but more as a patient navigator, to help me steer the immigrant patients who worked in the factory toward community resources. I needed her there. She fit the role perfectly, embracing all us women, equally, with hard won love. These were women who had experienced so much trauma in their lives. They had endured poverty, abandonment, rape, slave labor, homesickness, violent migration from their home countries to end up working at a chicken slaughter house in the middle of the eastern seaboard. My Spanish skills allowed me to ask them their birth dates and to tell them that I liked their skirt or hair, but I had no idea how to breach the sensitive social subjects like leaving behind beloved children. To come to America. To make money. Perhaps to never see their children again. Soledad treated them like her daughters, acted like a sage, and earned the nickname, "Baba Yaga."

The word *witch* once meant wise. Baba Yaga was a witch from an old Slavic tradition that, in many societies, was seen as the keeper of wisdom and tradition for the family or tribe. Baba Yaga was said to be an ugly old crone of a woman who lived in a ramshackle hut in the woods, which was elevated on a pair of giant chicken legs, so that it could move around. Although she is mostly portrayed as a terrifying spinster, Baba Yaga can also play the role of a helper and wise woman, guardian spirit of the fountain of the Waters of Life and of Death. From *The Story of Baba Yaga*, "The Earth Mother, like all forces of nature, though often wild and untamed, can also be kind."

Baba Yaga is the Arch-Crone, the Goddess of Wisdom and

Death, the Bone Mother. Wild and untamable, she is a nature spirit bringing wisdom and death of ego, and through death, rebirth. Anyone who entered her home to search for wisdom was given knowledge and truth, advice and magical gifts, but only if the seeker was pure of heart. She is all-knowing, all-seeing, and all-revealing to those who would dare to ask for help. She is a healer, looking after the birthing and dying. Sometimes she is thought to have the power of life and death itself.

Witches and midwives. Chickens and babies. Lonely and empathetic. Soledad and Care. We became a team.

As an older women, Soledad became a pseudo-mother or "Baba Yaga" to the rest of the chicken community. She began to take great liberties with her translation services. I asked a patient, Clara, how she felt. In Spanish, the pregnant woman answered, "Yo tengo muy cansada." I knew this to mean that she felt tired. Soledad translated, "She say she need new shoos."

Over time, I became interested in Soledad's truth. We worked closely together, and in a sense we became unlikely friends. I was a newly married 20-something, freshly out of an ivy league university, working my first job in an "underserved" factory health clinic. I was a privileged white girl, working for the indigent poor, as a way to pay back my government service scholarship. She was the indigent poor. Besides that, I knew nothing about her. She never shared her personal story with me, never mentioned children at home, or how she came to have an Irish surname. She never had to hurry out the door to make dinner. She didn't speak of vacations or visits home to see her aging parents in Mexico. She spoke her secrets in silence.

She asked me if I wanted children. I told her we had been trying, for three years. I cried a little. She asked me if I tried *ventosas*, Mexican fire cupping. No. I hadn't tried that yet. I had tried everything else. Mustard seed. Eating the core of a pineapple. Sex with my legs above my head. Thai massage. Not thinking about it. Constantly thinking about it. A Lingam stone put under the mattress.

"Que es según Dios," she said, sighing, pointing to the sky.

It is according to God.

When I finally asked Soledad her story, she told me it was between herself and el Jesús Cristo. A year went by. More nights, more laboring mamas, more botched translations, more blood, more clinic days, more and more truckloads of chickens. A freezer full of naked frozen raw breasts and drums. Still, no baby for me. Still no story from Soledad. She and Jesus must have been working it out, together.

On the night of summer solstice, Soledad came to the women's clinic after her shift, holding a live pure white chicken under her arm. She had on a bloody apron. The chicken squawked and screamed. She was ready to make a sacrifice. She was ready to share her story.

In Santeria, The word ebó comes from Yoruba and means both "sacrifice" and "offering" because these two things are interconnected. Sacrifice doesn't always mean cutting an animal's throat and offering blood. Sacrifice means giving up something that means something to you, as a way to show you're devoted to the Orichás, the intermediaries between the Gods and humans. It is proof that you appreciate what they do for you. Divine providence: to live out your life as providence decrees, a timely preparation for future eventualities. Soledad's sacrifice right now was an offering of her story, her self.

That evening, under the waning solstice moon, sitting Indian-style on the beach, we honored our heartache with very simple gifts, a glass bowl of fresh water, a few pieces of fruit, a candle, some flowers, a cigar, a small dish of honey and molasses, a small glass of rum.

We built a fire of driftwood.

We cut the throat of the white chicken.

We dripped its blood into the fire.

We cried.

Tears and blood mixed with the curling smoke.

Santeria.

Mi amiga sorrowfully told her story.

Soledad had met her first husband, Mike, in Texas when she was 15 and working as a dishwasher at a mess hall in Fort Bliss. If only she would have realized the irony in the name Fort Bliss. Mike was a soldier in training and Soledad had crossed the border from Mexico to get work. It was 1960. They fell in love. She was pregnant within the first three months. They married in a Baptist church in El Paso. She didn't understand one thing the pastor said. Mike was immediately sent to Vietnam. Soledad, now 22 weeks pregnant with twins, and barely able to speak English, was sent to live with her new in-laws, Elnor and Francis Sullivan, in Seaford, a flat farm town in Godforsaken Delaware.

Elnor treated Soledad like a slave, constantly yelling at her, forcing her to do all the heavy lifting at their poultry farm now that Mikey was away at war. Soledad taught herself to speak English by reading Betty Crocker cookbooks. The twins, boys, were born 6 weeks early, by cesarean, in a hospital in the middle of nowhere, and upon discharge were handed over to Elnor, the mom-mom, like they were her live prizes for enduring this "wetback" in her home.

When the boys were three, Mike came home from Vietnam, but he was a changed man. He berated Soledad and the twins. He was violent and withdrawn. He had a limp and chain smoked. They had two children together, had been married for nearly four years, but had only known each other for about 4 months. She was immediately pregnant again. When Soledad was three-and-a-half months pregnant, Mike kicked her in the stomach because one of the boys spilled his coffee. She lost the baby, hemorrhaged in the hospital, had to have a D+C, and got an infection. She spent a week in the community hospital. Neither Elnor nor Mikey came to visit.

A nightshift nurse attempted to speak minimal Spanish to Soledad, by asking her if she had any "dolor" and offering her ice by saying "yellow" instead of "hielo." By now, Soledad was fluent in English, but no one had ever attempted to speak Spanish to her in Delaware, so Soledad asked the nurse for help. The nurse gave her 30 dollars. When Soledad finally got home, she waited until the middle of the night, carried both boys down the steps in their pajamas, put them in her father-in-law's brown Chevy Vega, and drove away. She put the car in gear, and started south, toward Mexico.

In North Carolina, she was arrested and ultimately charged with two felony counts of child abduction and one count of auto theft, and sentenced to 14 years in prison. The twins went back to the poultry farm to live with Elnor, Francis, and Mike in Seaford. Soledad didn't see her kids again until they were 22 years old. They wanted nothing to do with her. They still don't. Now, Soledad is 65. Her boys are grown. They have children of their own. Her sons, with American names, David and Dennis Sullivan, think she abandoned them when they were babies. The only part of their Hispanic culture that they don't renounce is their deep tan skin.

"I am a crone. I am Baba Yaga, forest dweller, sage. I am wise and alone," Soledad chants as she dips her thumb in honey and traces the sign of the cross on my forehead. The heat from the fire, in the dark, in the sand, with the roars of the ocean, intensify the prayer. "You are Yemaya," she tells me. You rule over the seas." Yemaya, explains Soledad, is the patron goddess of pregnant women. She is associated with saltwater, rain, healing, ducks, peacocks, fertility, the full moon, the stars, the subconscious, creativity and female mysteries such as menstruation, conception, pregnancy, childbirth and menopause. She acts as a spiritual mother to all who feel lost and lonely.

All life starts in a sea, the saline amniotic fluid inside the mother's womb is itself an ocean, where the embryo must transform through the form of a fish before becoming a human baby.

"Always listen and offer maternal love to anyone who needs a mother. You are *la madre de todos*, the mother of all. You may not have children of your own, but all of the world's children will be yours." She draws a fish in the sand and fills in the shape with pieces of seashells. She tells me that my children are uncountable, like fish: glittering, fast, fleeting, vast schools of fish. We spend the whole of the night, Soledad and I, practicing witchcraft together, ensuring that I will always be there to witness all the children being born, to be *la madre de todos* and *la amiga* of Baba Yaga.

AUTHOR'S NOTE

Everyone has a story, it's said.

Day after day, we pass each other in the streets, work side by side, exchange money, sit next to someone on the bus, ride the elevator up together.

Sometimes we even ask, "How are you?" not expecting an actual answer. We are all strangers, sometimes even to our own selves.

Soledad Sullivan was my patient. She sat on an examination table in a women's clinic, basically naked in the thin paper gown, with her feet in stirrups, when she told me that she had two children but that she hadn't seen them in over 20 years. I was her midwife. I was sitting on a metal stool between her legs, getting ready to perform a pap smear. From that very vantage point, I have heard countless women tell me their stories of loss, abuse, love, infidelity, eroticism, anger.

Her story piqued my interest because she was very cheerful despite her multiple tragedies. I wrote this story, which is as much about the immigrant experience as it is about the global story of motherhood and womanhood. And about finding friendship in the most unlikely of settings: a chicken factory.

CSK

RED

JUDITH SPEIZER CRANDELL

MY ANKLES AND WRISTS are untied. My captor, Sargent, must have released them when I was unconscious. Grateful, I semi-recline against the fresh ivory-colored pillows. But when I finger the spiked dog collar he clasped around my neck earlier, I become angry. Goddamn it, there is nothing to be grateful for.

Now entering the bedroom, my captor's dressed in a belted maroon robe and carries a wooden bed tray. He sets the tray down on the floor, and pushes and prods me into a short baby pink velour bathrobe, then eases me against the pillows on his bed. I try sitting up, but it hurts even with the soft pillows, so I slip back down.

Before he places the tray across my lap, he takes a thin ice pack from his pocket and shoves it under my tail end. "For a first-time rear entry, there is a bit of pain, but worth it, right, Red?" He laughs as he settles the tray.

"My name is Rochelle. I told you that."

He lightly touches my red hair. "But to me you are Red, just like the others."

What others?

I try to appease him with a half-smile as he lifts the silver lid, revealing a blue Wedgewood plate of eggs. Beside it blooms a single red rose in a Limoges vase.

"This is like a honeymoon, Red, isn't it? I told you my fantasies all feature redheads, like my mother and sister." He giggles. "I hope you like veggie omelets with feta cheese—my *specialité*." He sits at the edge of the bed, legs crossed, gazing at me expectantly. Is my rapist awaiting accolades for the perfect omelet?

Instead, I reach with both hands for the heavy blue-glazed coffee cup. "I'm not used to this kind of attention. I survive on a mug of coffee, while I toast half a bagel and bag a piece of fruit to eat at my desk." I think longingly of my work cubicle. Again I tug at the tight spiked collar. He ignores my feeble attempts to unfasten it.

He rubs my left leg through the extra-soft down comforter encased in a white-on-white Grecian Urn patterned duvet. "Well, Sargent is here to change all that, Red. You deserve to be kept in luxury. Of course, on my workdays, the routine will be different."

"Routine will be different" hangs over my head, a guillotine. Every word drips evil.

Who the hell is this man? What does he do—besides tie redheads up and fuck them? I shudder. I don't want to think about that. I need to plan my escape. Somehow I will trick him and run away. Who cares if I still sport a skimpy robe, a spiked metal chained choke-me collar? Who cares if people think it's Goth jewelry or I'm into S&M? What the hell do I care about judgements? My damn life's on the line.

"First-rate eggs," I utter in a false friendly voice, as I continue stuffing rubbery pieces into my mouth with a plastic spoon. I realize he doesn't trust me with real implements. Maybe he doesn't think about me smashing a delicate china plate or heavy crystal glass and attacking him with a shard. Could I do that? Serve him for breakfast in lots of pieces? As if reading my mind, he quickly removes the tray with all its potential weapons.

I pull the covers up to my neck. Then I stare at him suspiciously. "Aren't you eating?" *Is the food I ate full of date rape drugs or horse tranquilizers?*

Just then, a white bird flies into the room through the open door. "Meet Golden Boy, my loyal Velcro bird—a white cockatoo who talks and cuddles—my darling companion," Sargent says. The bird circles me with a purple ribbon dangling a golden key. Is this the bedroom key my captor uses to lock me in his torture chamber? I try not to stare at it. Too late. Sargent notices.

"Good boy," he says, tearing off a piece of toast to coax the bird. "Bring that to Daddy." As the bird drops the key, Sargent grabs it, grinning.

"Welcome, Red," the bird says. *Has Sargent taught him to say that to all the redheads coaxed into his house?* At the thought, I gag on my coffee.

Sargent pats me on the back. "My sweetness, take your time. We have all day . . . and beyond." His voice lilts. His bird soars.

On high alert, I carefully move the bedtable, sling my cramped legs out from the covers onto the floor and tighten the belt on the robe. "Time for this redheaded girl to get herself showered and dressed." I try to talk with enthusiasm, to mask my creeping dread and excruciating pain. I stand, shaky and confused.

"I am prepared to join you," he declares as the corners of his mouth curl up slightly.

"Um, I need privacy. A girl thing. To get all fresh smelling." I cringe with the false words. Scrutinizing the green velvet curtained windows, I wonder if I could escape that way or if they are barred or covered with wood, metal . . . my imagination races.

Once more, I tug at the spiked collar. "Can you remove this?" Frustrated, I tug harder. "I'd hate to get it wet in the shower."

His shoulders droop. His head touches his chest. He resembles a little boy told he can't have his way. Would it help if I sat next to him and put my arm around him? But it hurts too much to sit. He had rammed himself back there so hard, so suddenly, against my will, my rights, then my body shattered.

My hatred for him fills me. Pure hatred. *I hate him. Hate him.* My breathing is shallow, as I inhale and exhale hate. Finally, I say through gritted teeth, "I'm not a very experienced woman, like maybe what you're used to."

He stands abruptly and knocks me away from him. I grab the black teak dresser to steady myself. "Do not mention those other bitches!" He is yelling now, pounding the air with clenched fists. "Not unless you want to end up the same way."

Oh my God, what does he mean . . . Meekly, I reply, "I'm sorry. No, I won't. Never again." I trip over my words. Terrified, I regress and chew a fingernail.

He shoves my hand out of my mouth and slaps it. "Do not do that again, Red. Do not bite your nails. That's not lady-like. That's not *romantic.*"

OK, what's that about? This guy is a lunatic going from one mood to another. I need to outsmart him. I need a story. "Sorry, Sargent. When I'm confused, I do this. Chew my nails. My mother tried iodine. I really didn't mean to offend you."

Shit, shit. I hate him. He is crazy.

"Let me get washed and dressed. I promise I will —" *What was I promising?*

Sargent supplied the word. "*Behave.* You promise to behave. Right, Red? And that collar, that's a gift. A *memento mori* of sorts."

Fuck! Doesn't that mean, "Remember, you must die?"

Hands sweating, heart racing, I long to be home, at work, with people I know and trust. Sane people. Are my officemates wondering about my absence from our cubicle jungle? I hope so. My mother and I rarely speak, so she won't notice I'm gone for weeks, months maybe– *I want to be anywhere except here in this dark room, this dark house with this dark stranger, but who will find me, who will save me?*

"Go, Red, go use the bathroom. I'll be here upon your return."

Shit. That's what I'm afraid of.

Quietly, I obey. I look around—damn, no window for escape. I turn the lock on the gray bathroom door.

Cheerfully, from outside, he calls, "Oh, that lock? It doesn't hold but if you feel safer …"

Then I friggin' hear him snort! "Have everything you need, Red? Since I'm a good guy, don't worry. I'll give you some '*pri*-vacy,' sweetheart."

Frantically, I peer around. *Is there a camera in the bathroom, the bedroom … everywhere?*

I yank the shower knob. *I am so dumb! People warn the Internet is dangerous! I mean, stupid Rochelle, a dating site hookup and you walk straight into a maniac's house.*

"Meet at a public place," I read in *Cosmo.* I had never even slept with a guy. I had to be goddamned careful. But I got tired of being alone. Well, I'm not alone now, am I?

I hug my naked body, finger the "you better behave" collar, as the scorching water rushes down. Blood mixed with the water pools at my feet. I feel nauseous and faint. How badly had he hurt me? There's so much pain where he forced himself into me.

"Calm down, Rochelle," I say aloud—now I'm talking to myself. That's what fear does to you. I'm a nut job just like him. I choke on my sobs. I don't want him to hear me.

Did he lie about "privacy?" Is he still standing guard outside the door?

"Hey, Sargent," I call out. No answer.

But a minute or two later, I hear, "Do you need me, Red?"

Loudly, I idiotically ask, "Does it matter what towel I use?"

Lame, lame, stupid me. And why the delay in his answer? A camera *and* a microphone. He heard me right away, but tortured me by withholding a response? No, no, I am being paranoid. I just need to put the robe back on, waltz out and ask for my clothes, which is exactly what I do.

"*Viola!*" he says, pointing to a carefully arranged outfit, resembling a body laid out on the white duvet. The ensemble includes black lace panties and matching bra, a chic pale lavender off-the-shoulder raw silk blouse and pegged blue jeans. The clothing appears to be a 16, my size exactly. *Whose clothes are they? Oh my God, could they be an earlier victim's?*

"*Perfecto, n'est-ce pas?*" he purrs, strokes my cheek and hands me one item by one item, each gently swinging from his fingers, which I just noticed are manicured and small, matching his feminine hand movements.

I rush back to the bathroom and shut the door, even if I can't lock it. *Surely, I am the most asinine no-longer-a-virgin who ever lived! Now would I be the most foolish non-virgin who ever died?*

A dog collar, a fiendish white bird who appears to nibble human flesh. This sick, sexual predator and his sidekick. Now what?

I am unmoored. I have to get out of here. Shit, I don't know where I am! The address I gave the Lyft driver is where? In my purse. Where's my purse, my clothes? I grip my right arm and dig my nails in. Now my arm *and* my rear end hurt. I leave blood on his pure white towels. Who the fuck cares.

Think, Rochelle, think!

OK. OK. I will sweetly ask for my clothes, my purse, throw in a "Dear Sargent, when can we meet again?" Then I'll call Lyft and be on my merry *very* alive way.

As I calm myself, formulate my plan, he bursts into the small bathroom, bird hooked onto his shoulder, nuzzling his ear. Sargent smiles, an evil, contorted grimace as he removes the dog collar. That feels better. But then I see he is holding something in front of my face. It's a fucking ragged rope ending in a noose. Patiently, he awaits my reaction.

"No, no. Don't," I yell. I struggle in vain to push past him, to leave the locked room, but his arms are bars. I try to bite the hand holding the noose. But the damn bird jumps on my neck and bites it. I crumble in terror, muscles going soft, the eggs! I hit the freezing tile floor.

"Good-bye, Red. Good-bye, Red," Golden Boy squawks.

Shit, are the last words I ever hear going to come from a goddamned bird? I look up, to the ceiling, to heaven?

Sargent stands there, bird on shoulder, smiling with the grimy tattered rope swaying above me dangling from his dainty, flawless hands.

AUTHOR'S NOTE

The concept for "Red" came to me in a dream. A nightmare. I recall this fuzzy-red-headed naive and likeable 20-something virgin wandering into a stranger's vivid split-level suburban house. I recall a white bird perched on a 40- or 50-something professional guy's shoulder, nuzzling him. Something seemed menacing and evil about the man, the bird, and the house. I felt there were secrets literally buried in the backyard and that this red-headed girl was not going to escape unscathed—if at all.

This weird tableau burned itself into my dream brain. When I awoke, the vision awoke with me. I knew I had to use these elements in a story. At first, I thought I'd write a novel or novella. But truthfully, I did not want to live that long in the darkness of what promised to be a pulsating noir tale. Ironically, a writing friend had her own dream about it and suggested crafting a short story out of these weird elements.

So "Red" was born—or rather ripped—from the womb of my imagination. I had read *The Collector*, *Girl on the Train,* and other dark tales, including several noir anthologies. I had previously written a very dark novella, *The Whore of Desert Sorrows*. But after that, I didn't think I'd return to such a bleak, horrific landscape. Yet I did. And now, if you've read the story, you are part of my dream.

JSC

THE HOLES

CAROLYN GEDULD

The process of delving into the black abyss is to me
the keenest form of fascination.

Howard Phillips Lovecraft

I AGONIZE ABOUT attending his funeral for days, but ultimately decide against it. Then, without further thought, I take my purse and fish around for the car keys. I'm wearing yesterday's white T-shirt, now grubby and odorous from sweat, and black yoga pants. My hair is curling into dark snarls, and I haven't brushed my teeth in two days. My mouth tastes of mourning and loss. I slip on white flip flops. The red polish on my toenails is weathered and half-flaked off. But I'm out of time. I have to leave immediately.

The old Impala rattles to the cemetery. I drive around, finally arriving at the hearse and a cluster of parked vehicles. The service has already started. I walk over and stand at the rear of the crowd, where I'm met by the curious glances of strangers wondering who I am. An elderly couple stand near the casket. His parents; both hunched with age.

Craning my neck, I spot *her*. His wife ... the widow. Older than me, but with a similar plumpness. She wears a severe black suit and an ebony pill-box hat. Like his parents, she stares straight at the casket. She won't notice me, even in my unkempt condition. The children stand next to her, Kelley and Julian, both in their twenties, and Ryan, a sophomore in college. One of the girls holds a baby. The infant leans leftward, reaching pudgy arms toward his grandmother while emitting whiney noises through a pacifier. She pays no attention to the child.

The minister recites Psalm 23.

Though I walk through the valley of the shadow of death ...

Glancing around, I notice that the cemetery is in a slump between two rises. It resides in a valley of sorts—a valley of death. Nonetheless, an attractive place to spend eternity. Because the only markers permitted are flat granite slabs, nearly invisible outside of close range, it has the appearance of a park. I'm comforted in knowing that an aged oak tree shades his gravesite. But this pleasant thought is interrupted by the realization that the family has likely purchased a double plot. His and hers.

She will spend eternity under the oak tree in the valley of death next to him. The thought is intolerable. *I'm* the one he loved. Even when he denied it.

More than once he tried to end it.

"This has to stop. It's over. I don't want to see you anymore. Don't try to contact me."

In my heart, I always knew he didn't mean it when he spoke like that. Even if I threw my arms tightly around him, causing him to twist away forcefully, unwrapping my grip and leaving purplish bruises, I knew it was just a mood. I simply had to show up at the right place— his office, his gym, the sports bar where he ate lunch—and we were soon entwined once more. It was only a matter of time before he would admit that he loved me more than *her,* if he could be said to love her at all.

The minister finishes the sermon. Two cemetery facilitators approach and begin the slow process of lowering the casket down into the open grave. Once in place, they remove the straps that hold the coffin and carry them to the pile of fresh dirt several feet away. They each pick up a shovel and wait. Flowers are tossed down atop the casket as, one by one, the crowd disperses. I hurry to my car before anyone can approach me.

I wait while *she* walks to her car. Doors close and engines fire. When the car passes me, she doesn't look my way. Nor do her children. Yet the baby gazes at me from his car seat with widened eyes. His pacifier momentarily stops bobbing in his mouth.

I remain in my car and watch while the two laborers shovel earth into the grave. The pile they shovel shrinks until the hole is filled. The men tamp the soil down using the backs of the shovels. They load the shovels, the straps, and the lowering device into a golf cart parked discreetly nearby and drive away.

Alone, I walk back to the grave site. I scrape up a handful of the tamped soil and place it in the pocket of my yoga pants. I smooth the ground with my foot.

For several minutes, I stand there and speak to you of our love. I promised I will remain forever faithful to you, as you are now to me. It comforts me to know that nothing more can keep us apart.

After expressing my endearments to you, I walk around the cemetery, reading the gravestones, knowing I will be spending many hours here. Not far from the oak tree, I find a concrete bench. This is where I will sit in the future while we speak of our love. Meanwhile, I continue to walk around the area of your grave, hoping to know the land you are buried in as well as I know every inch of your body, everything about you that a Google search could reveal, and everything I learned by using various pretexts to question your colleagues and friends.

Opposite the oak tree, I find a freshly dug grave. As with yours, a pile of fresh earth lies nearby, pyramid shaped, with two shovels sticking upright. I walk to the edge of the hole and peer down. It is easily six feet deep.

I am struck by a sudden impulse to jump in. I glance around to ensure I'm alone. The cemetery office is far away, on the other side of the rise. I sit on the edge, then drop, landing hard and uneven, hands pressed into the cold earth. A sharp pain envelops my left ankle. No matter, I'm not planning to walk for a while.

I estimate the hole to be four feet by eight feet. I'm unable to see over the top, even on tiptoes. I make an attempt, but my ankle cries out in protest. The top is nearly a foot over my head. A rectangle of sky is above me. The walls of the hole are smooth, compacted clay. There is no way out. Gingerly, so as to avoid further injury to my ankle, I sit on the ground.

I calculate that nearly twenty feet separates your hole from mine. The roots of the oak tree, extending to both resting places, connect us. As long as I remain here, we maintain our attachment. I place my hand on the wall nearest to you and smile.

It occurs to me that I should lay flat on my back, just like you. In this way, I can watch the clouds and later, when night falls, gaze at the stars. There is no doubt in my mind that I will remain here throughout the night. Even if I want to leave, there is no one to aid me. I am content to stay.

As afternoon fades to evening, I imagine a casket being lowered into the hole atop me. It will stop, leaving just enough space to avoid crushing me. Distantly, I imagine the words of a service being spoken above, including the Psalm 23 again. I will free my hand enough to stroke the smooth wood on the bottom of the casket. In my imagination, it is you, my love, in the coffin atop me. I imagine a thud, as the first shovelful of earth hits the curved wooden top. After a few

more thuds, the soil seeps around the sides of the casket, filling in everything except a thin pocket of air between us. As the soil is tamped
down and the crowd departs, I imagine using the last of the air to pro-
claim my love for you one last time.

By mid-evening I feel ravenous. I have not eaten in two or
three days, since learning of your death. The hole in my heart is
eclipsed partially by the hole in my stomach. I begin taking bits of earth
from my yoga pocket and consuming it. *Your* earth from *your* gravesite
enters into *me*. Swallowing what was above and around you is yet another way of having you with me, *within* me. I savor each mouthful of
you, satisfying my craving to be blended with you, to have another way
of not being separate from you.

In this almost delirious state, I refuse to doze off, even though
the rectangle above me darkens. I now have what *she* will never have,
even if for only one night. Somewhat to my surprise, my hatred of her
seems to lessen. I understand that even if she were buried next to you,
she would never possess you the way I do.

I awake, clothing damp with from groundwater that has seeped
through the clay. I try, unsuccessfully, to escape this earthly hole. I call
out for help. To my good fortune, a trio of passing mourners hears my
call. I explain that I'd taken a stumble. They don't question this explanation.

Driving home, I am struck by the realization that I can still be
with you. The grave has already been dug. I consider the notion that
the presence of this open hole is, perhaps, merely coincidence, but re-
mind myself there is no such thing as coincidence. It is there, for me,
for us.

That evening I shower and dress for the event to come. A second realization strikes me. The baby at the funeral. The baby had
looked at me. He knew. He obviously knew that he was really *our* baby;
yours and mine. Not yours, not *hers*. He belongs with *us*.

The abduction will be easy. Surprisingly so. I will bring him to
the cemetery that evening, while across town family and authorities
conduct frantic door-to-door searches. We will stand at the open, gaping hole, and I will stare down into its darkness, a black, endless abyss.
Overhead the thunder of an approaching storm will break the silence
of the night. I will drop into the chasm, baby tight in my arms.

The three of us—you, me, and baby makes three—together in
the valley of the shadow of death, fearing no evil, no restraining order,
no blocked calls, no unfriending, no caving in to *her* demands or to the

needs of your other children. These temporary impediments are less than the annoying drone of a mosquito.

The infant will be crying. I will retrieve the handgun and the skies shall bleed rain. Two bullets in the chamber. One for each of us. The first shot will be lost beneath a thunder clap and the crying will abruptly end. I will place barrel of the pistol to my head, slowly squeeze the trigger, and the three of us shall be joined together for eternity.

AUTHOR'S NOTE

Truthfully, I never know where the stories I write come from. When I'm writing a story, it always feels like it's coming through me rather than from me. I also never know how my stories will end. I just keep writing, channeling the words like a medium with a keyboard in lieu of a crystal ball.

CG

BRB

DAVID YURKOVICH

HELLO THERE.

You may be wondering, "Why?" As in, "Why is Nick, your friendly neighborhood, average-looking middle-aged white dude, beloved across social media, dressed in his middle-management off-brand Oxford and elastic waistband Sears trousers and weathered leather loafers, livestreaming to his network of 227 friends while standing in his garage, perched upon a wooden kitchen chair with a well-crafted noose affixed firmly around his neck while Armageddon sweeps across the planet?"

I will tell you why.

Most of the responsibility rests with the parents. Not my parents, both of whom are long dead and, hopefully, not partaking in the carnage occurring outside my single-car garage. No. I am referring to those parents who, in lemming fashion, followed the crowd nine months ago and ultimately ruined Halloween for the dead and, in so doing, brought about the terror that is presently ravaging the Earth. Perhaps if I had kids of my own I'd understand it better, though I kind of doubt it. Collectively, a minority of individuals took action and changed what should not under any circumstances have been changed. They lost sight of an important reality: Halloween, the Halloween that once was.

Permit me to take a few steps back, figuratively speaking, to explain, and forgive me if the following reeks of information dump, but as I'm sure you know, time is no longer a luxury for any of us, and I'm certain that it's just a matter of time before the entire web or internet or blogosphere is taken permanently offline.

The event once known as Hallowe'en was never solely about candy and dress up. From its early origins in Celtic-speaking lands, throughout Europe and the holy days of obligation in which church bells were rung for those souls in purgatory, to candles burned in Ireland for countless ages to alight wandering souls back to their homes, Halloween had always been a means to honor the dead, to aid the lost souls roaming the earth. Halloween was synonymous with October 31st as sure as Christmas was with the 25th of December.

Everything, of course, changed during the 20th century due to the monetization (a word I became intimate with during my many months of management training) of Halloween. Did you know that last year's Halloween spending exceeded $9 billion dollars? Now you know. Much of this was fueled by pop culture. Super-heroes, zombie movies, Disney. That's a lot of plastic Mouse ears and Spider-Man masks, a lot of which eventually found its way to landfills. And with each successive year, the true spirit of Halloween gave way to consumerism.

Not that it mattered much to the dead. Each October 31, Halloween night, the rituals still occurred in one form or another. Jack-o-lanterns aglow with candles, offerings of food to strangers donning costumes. To say nothing of the cults and cultists offering up sacrifices in the form of rats, snakes, or chickens. All Hallows' Eve may have devolved from its origins, but the souls of the dead remained satisfied with the end product.

Which brings us to Bonnie Britton—Christian, mother of three, and an overzealous zealot with a flair for fanaticism and 5,000 friends on Facebook. You probably heard of the Trick-or-Treat Petition. Maybe you were one of the 450,000 or so who signed it. What you probably don't know is that the petition was created by Britton. Her chief complaint and reason for the petition was that each year Halloween occurred on a different day of the week. Britton, and the parents who supported her, decided the world would be a better place if Halloween were held on the last Saturday of each October, thus avoiding the need to send their kids out for tricks and treats on a potential school night. Parents took the idea like bats to a mosquito. Despite outcry from dozens of groups, including several Christian denominations, the petition was adopted just nine short months ago and Halloween as we know it, well, you know the rest.

What none of us knew, even though we should have, was that the dead didn't exactly welcome this new concept with open arms. Turns out that without All Hallows' Eve, their souls were doomed to roam the earth, to *unlive* in eternal unrest.

This they did not like.

Which is why, if you have been paying attention to the news or glanced at your phone or, God forbid, looked out the window on this first day of November, the day after what should have been a night to honor the souls of the dead, you no doubt have seen the carnage that is wreaking havoc across the planet. The apparitions, which, in years past, were largely invisible out of respect to the living, appear now both uninhibited and unrestrained. They are, in the words of the late Paddy Chayefsky, mad as hell, and not going to take this anymore. Thus the devouring of humanity that is currently in progress.

I know what you're thinking. You're thinking, "Well that sucks, Nick, but at least those of us who are devoured can then get to join in the fun." Not true, as it turns out. Apparently, as the dead eviscerate the living, they also eradicate their souls. This much I've learned from watching the CNN special report "The End of the World" broadcast this earlier this morning. Scientists claim that by all estimates, humanity as we know it has maybe another week, though probably far less.

Which brings us back to my present location, atop a chair in my garage. I'm no scientist, and am certainly no theologian, but those of you who have subscribed to my YouTube channel—Nick Fixes Everything—are likely familiar with my doctrine, *every problem has a solution.* The solution to this particular problem, however, cannot be recorded and edited for broadcast at a later date. The reason for this will soon become apparent. Here, then, is the Nick fix.

As I've stated and as you doubtless know by now, the undead are coming to rip you and me apart. However, by my recollection, the undead cannot have at me if I'm already dead. If I'm deceased, you see, then I'm on the winning team. Having never died, I am not certain what this means. But if I'm correct, my spirit will join with the spirits of the dead who are wiping out humanity by the second. Perhaps I'll enter a state of soul sleep. Again, I'm not a priest and I don't claim to have all the answers. But I firmly believe this solution to be preferable to the alternative, so I invite you to try it as well. The beauty of this plan is its simplicity. One swift kick of the chair, and then swing, baby, swing.

Quick and easy.

If you're ready to join me, it's essential that you know how to tie a proper hangman's noose. If you do *not* know how to do this, be sure to visit my YouTube channel and scroll until you find Episode 137: *Five Minutes to the Perfect Hangman's Noose.* Don't forgot to comment if you like the video.

I, of course, have no doubt that what I'm about to attempt is going to hurt. Most likely, "hurt" is an understatement. Nevertheless, it'll be quick, less than ten seconds to unconsciousness and only four minutes to my demise, and I much prefer this to the looming alternative. Well, I hope you found this tutorial helpful, and perhaps I'll see you on the other side.

And so, without further ado…

AUTHOR'S NOTE

When I recently learned that the Halloween & Costume Association had launched a petition to implement a National Trick or Treat Day, I vomited blood for several hours. Posttransfusion, I realized that I had no choice but to write the "BRB." The Association busybodies claim that Halloween results in 3,800 injuries per year. A drop in the bucket compared to the planetary annihilation that will certainly follow if Halloween is tampered with. The blows of Great Cthulhu will seem like candy kisses compared to the pain you will suffer should All Hallows' Eve be altered.

Consider yourself warned.

DY

ABSOLUTE MONSTERS
AUTHOR BIOS

AMIRAH AL WASSIF

A prolific author residing in Egypt, Amirah Al Wassif is a freelance writer, poet, and novelist. Five of her books were written in Arabic, and many of her English works have been published in various international literary and cultural magazines around the globe such as *Praxis Magazine, The Gathering of Tribes, Credo Espoir, Reach Poetry, Otherwise Engaged Literature and Arts Journal, Cannon's Mouth, Mediterranean Poetry, The BeZine, Spill Words, Merak Magazine, Writers Resist, Bosphorus Review of Books, Writer NewSletter, Call and Response Journal, Echoes Literary Magazine, Better Than Starbucks, Envision Arts, Women of Strength Strong Courage Magazine, Chorion Review,* and *The Conclusion Magazine.* Al Wassif is the author of the poetry collection *For Those Who Don't Know Chocolate* and the children's book, *The Cocoa Boy and Other Stories,* both of which are published in English. Her works have been translated into Spanish, Arabic, Hindi, and Kurdish.

DAN ALLEN

Dan Allen is Canadian and enjoys spending time off the grid in Northern Ontario. His story "Above the Ceiling" (originally published in 2018 in *Home Sweet Home* [Millhaven Press]) is featured in Bards and Sages 2019 anthology of *The Year's Best Speculative Fiction.*

Allen's most popular publication to date, "Sympathy for the Zingara," can be found in the March 2019 edition of *ParABnormal Magazine.* Other recent and upcoming works include "The Basement" (*Horror Zine's Book of Ghost Stories*), "Where Only the Mosquitoes Sing" (*Monsters We Forgot*), "Footprints" (*Through Death's Door*), "Become the Beast" (*Erie Tales*), and "Corn Stalker" (*Fears of a Clown*).

Allen is currently completing his first novel, an epic tale spanning the decade before and after a devastating disaster that alters the lives of the people in Joshua Ridge. It's a nostalgic tale of young love and heartbreak, loaded with both real and supernatural horrors.

More at danallenhorror.com.

BERNIE BROWN

Brown is an Iowa farm girl transplanted to Raleigh, North Carolina. She has published nearly 40 short stories and essays, sews well, and plays the harmonica badly. She holds both a bachelor's and a master's degree in English from the University of Nebraska at Omaha, and is a Writer-In-Residence at the Weymouth Center for the Arts, and a Pushcart Prize nominee. In 2019, her short story, "The Best Shot," set in Iowa, was published as one of the contest winners of the Grateful Steps Pub-lishing contest. Brown's debut novel, *I Never Told You,* was released in October 2019 by Moonshine Cove Publishing. Her Iowa childhood, travels in the States and Europe, and her contemporary life in Raleigh influence Brown's writing. More at berniebrownwriter.com.

RACHEL M. BROWN

A native of the UK, Rachel Brown now lives in Somerville, Massachu-setts, with her husband, Ethan. She works as an attorney for the City of Lowell, an old mill town north of Boston, and switched to law after a former career as a college professor in philosophy. Her short stories can be found in the anthology *Seascape: Best New England Crime Stories 2019* (Level Best Books). Brown has been working on creative writing for several years, and has a complete novel draft (psychological sus-pense), as well as other short stories. She has also won two flash fiction contests at the New England Crime Bake annual mystery conference.

CATHARINE CLARK-SAYLES

Catharine Clark-Sayles is a recently retired doctor who has been prac-ticing internal medicine and geriatrics in Northern California. She com-pleted an MFA in poetry and narrative medicine at Dominican Univer-sity of California in 2019. The child of a career Air Force officer, Clark-Sayles also served in the Army which sent her to medical school and then to San Francisco for her internship and residency. Her plan to get out before an earthquake knocked the whole state into the Pa-cific was upended by falling in love with California and by the novel experience of living in one spot for more than three years. After 40 years she is still living in California. She has published poems in many journals and anthologies. Tebot Bach Press has published two full col-lections of her poetry: *One Breath* and *Lifeboat*. A chapbook of narrative poems from her military childhood, *Brats*, was published by Finishing Line Press in September 2018.

TERRI CLIFTON

Terri Clifton is a writer, photographer, and Delaware coast native who was awarded a fellowship in 2013 for Emerging Artist in Literature by the Delaware Division of Arts. Her short stories and poetry have been published in several anthologies and journals and she has recently completed two novels. Clifton's nonfiction book, *A Random Soldier*, was published in 2007. Passionate about nature, art, and dance, Clifton resides with her husband, a wildlife artist, on a historic farm along the Delaware Bay.

ELLIE COOPER

Cooper's passion has always been the written word—as a teenager, folk songs and the poetry of Leonard Cohen, and, later, the southern gothic writers such as Flannery O'Connor and Carson McCullers. She has written secretly throughout her life—mostly in the early morning hours or late at night—in between the demands of work and family. After being laid-off as an executive assistant a few years ago, Cooper retired, dusted off old pages and tried to hone new skills. She took creative writing classes at a local college and has since been published in the *Rio Review, Mused Literary Review,* and *2 Elizabeths*. Most of Cooper's work centers around women and their relationships which are often flawed, sometimes dysfunctional and occasionally dangerous. A native Texan. Cooper and her husband reside in Austin. Besides writing, Cooper enjoys gardening with xeric plants, hiking the greenbelt, ballroom dancing, and exploring state and national parks in a small Casita RV.

SHUTTA CRUM

Shutta Crum's poems have appeared in numerous publications since the 1970s. Her first chapbook, *When You Get Here*, will be published in 2020 with Kelsay Press. She also has published several children's books written in verse including *Thunder-Boomer!*, a *Smithsonian Magazine Notable Book,* and an *American Library Association Notable Book*. More at shutta.com.

JOHN DAVIS

John Davis is the author of *Gigs* (Sol Books) and a chapbook, *The Reservist*. His work has appeared recently in *DMQ Review, Harpur Palate, Iron Horse Literary Review, One* and *Terrain.org*. He moonlights in a local blues band.

DAVID W. DUTTON

David W. Dutton is a semi-retired residential designer who was born and raised in Milton, Delaware. He has written two novels, several short stories, and 11 plays. His musical comedy, *oh! Maggie*, created in collaboration with Martin Dusbiber, was produced by the Possum Point Players and the Lake Forest Drama Club. He wrote two musical reviews for the Possum Point Players: *An Evening With Cole Porter* (in collaboration with Marcia Faulkner) and *With a Song in My Heart*. He also wrote the one-act play, *Why the Chicken Crossed the Road*, commissioned and produced by the Delmarva Chicken Festival. In 1997, Dutton was awarded a fellowship as an established writer by the Delaware Arts Council. In 1998, he received a first-place award for his creative nonfiction by the Delaware Literary Connection. His piece, "Who is Nahnu Dugeye?" was subsequently published in the literary anthology, *Terrains*. More recently, Dutton's work has appeared in the anthologies, *Halloween Party 2017*, *Solstice*, *Equinox*, and *Aurora*. In fall 2018, Dutton's third novel, *One of the Madding Crowd*, was published by Devil's Party Press. In 2019, it was awarded best original novel by the Delaware Press Association. Dutton, his wife, Marilyn, and their Rottweiler, Molly, currently reside in Milton.

LISA FOX

Lisa Fox is a pharmaceutical market research consultant by day and fiction writer by night. Her short story, "The Fruit Stand," appears in the Devil's Party Press anthology *Suspicious Activity*. Other works have appeared in *Theme of Absence*, *Unlikely Stories Mark V*, *Credo Espoir*, *Ellipsis Zine*, *Foliate Oak Literary Magazine*, and at ubiquitousbooks.com. Fox placed third in the NYC Midnight 2018 Flash Fiction Challenge, from a field of over 3,000 writers worldwide. She resides in northern New Jersey with her husband, two sons, and their oversized dog, and relishes the chaos of everyday suburban life.

R. DAVID FULCHER

R. David Fulcher is an author of horror, science fiction, fantasy, and poetry. His major literary influences include H.P. Lovecraft, Dean Koontz, Edgar Allen Poe, Fritz Lieber, and Stephen King. Fulcher's first novel, a historical drama set in World War II, *Trains to Nowhere*, and his second novel, a collection of fantasy and science fiction short stories, *Blood Spiders and Dark Moon*, are both available from authorhouse.com and amazon.com. Fulcher's work has appeared in numerous small press publications including *Lovecraft's Mystery Magazine, Black Satellite, The Martian Wave, Burning Sky, Shadowlands, Twilight Showcase, Heliocentric Net, Gateways, Weird Times, Freaky Frights* and the anthologies *Dimensions* and *Silken Ropes*. A passion for the written word has also inspired Fulcher to edit and publish the literary magazine, *Samsara* (samsaramagazine.net), which has showcased writers and poets for over a decade. Fulcher resides in Ashburn, Virginia, with his wife Lisa, and their rambunctious cats.

ANDREA GOYAN

Andrea Goyan is a writer, actress, and master Pilates instructor. Her short story, "My Neighbor's a Fucking Monster," appears in the Devil's Party Press anthology, *What Sort of Fuckery Is This*? Other recent work by Goyan can be found in *On Loss: An Anthology, Dirty Girls Magazine* (May 2019), and *Newfound Journal* (October 2018). Goyan was shortlisted for the 2019 Anton Chekhov Award for Very Short Fiction. An accomplished playwright, she lives in Los Angeles with her husband, a dog, and two cats.
More at andreagoyan.com.

CAROLYN GEDULD

Carolyn Geduld is an author and mental health professional residing in Bloomington, Indiana. Her fiction has appeared in numerous publications including *The Writing Disorder, Pennsylvania Literary Review, Persimmon Tree, Not Your Mother's Breast Milk, Dime Store Review, Duel Coasts*, and *Otherwise Engaged*.

JAMES GOODRIDGE

Born and raised in the Bronx and now located in the Yorkville section of Manhattan, Goodridge has been writing speculative fiction since 2004. After ten years as an artist representative and paralegal, he decided in 2013 to make a better commitment to writing. Goodridge is currently at work on *The Passage of Time Saga*, a series of short stories in the occult detective genre featuring Madison Cavendish and Seneca Sue, living vampire and werewolf occult detectives. He has written a series of Twilight Zone-style short stories entitled *The Artwork (I to V)*, and runs the Facebook writers' page: Who gives you the Write. Goodridge also pens an annual series of blogs for Black Horror History Month at horroraddicts.net He is a member of the Black Science Fiction Society.

ROBERT LEWIS HERON

Scottish-American author and poet, Robert Lewis Heron, is an architect and accomplished artist (traditional and digital) living in Maryland. His unique voice for storytelling captivates his readers by twisting and tormenting their imagination. By sprinkling a dry sense of humor throughout his writing, he makes any harshness a wee bit more palatable. Expect the unexpected on entering his world of woe and wonderment. His writing has been compared to Tartan Noir author, Christopher Brookmyre.

ROBIN HILL-PAGE GLANDEN

For 20 years, Glanden worked as a professional actor, musician, and writer/editor in Philadelphia, New York City, and Los Angeles. Glanden edited books for Los Angeles public relations guru, Michael Levine, and several of her non-fiction articles were featured in two Los Angeles magazines. Family matters brought Glanden back to her home state of Delaware, and she's now working as a freelance writer, editor, and performance artist. Her short stories have been published in several *Rehoboth Beach Reads* anthologies, and she has won awards for her fiction from the Delaware Press Association. Her poem, "Change Your Feng Shui, Change Your Life," was published this year in the *Dreamstreets* literary magazine. Another poem, "Worry and Wisdom," was published recently in the anthology, *Delaware Bards Poetry Review*. Glanden is a regular contributor to two of the *Guideposts* magazines, *Mysterious Ways* and *Angels on Earth*, where she writes true accounts of curious "coincidences" that have occurred in her life. Glanden conducts workshops for writers, and performs her poetry and original music with her husband, Kenny. Glanden also produces cabaret shows and performs in various local venues.

CARRIE Sz KEANE

Carrie Sz Keane studied journalism and English at the University of Maryland. She apprenticed as a midwife in rural Appalachia in Kentucky before studying nurse-midwifery at Yale University where she was awarded a humanities honor in creative writing for a piece entitled "Modern Nurse Nancy," a story about working night shifts as a new nurse on a postpartum unit. It was later published in a Canadian nursing textbook. Upon graduating in 2004, Keane began journaling and writing stories of her work as a midwife. She is actively writing a journalistic memoir of her career. Keane works at an active obstetrics and gynecology practice in Delaware as a sexual health clinician, providing prenatal care, contraception, annual examinations, STD screenings, and birth support for females. Her stories and essays, which have been published in multiple anthologies, focus on maternal health in America and her role as a witness on the frontlines of female healthcare.

DOYLE WELDON KNIGHT

Doyle Weldon Knight is a novelist, short story author, occasional poet, and subsea engineering consultant who lives in central Louisiana. A life-long reader, with a preference for the macabre and supernatural, in 2016, he discovered a passion for writing. After 36-years of life with a beautiful southern belle, a 40-year career in the oilfield industry, residences in Scotland and Brazil, two daughters, one son, and three Yorkies, he finally found his calling in life. He is Pap-Pap to two year-old grandsons.

HEIDI LOBECKER

Heidi Lobecker writes short fiction about weird and wonderful characters in uncommon and unusual situations. She majored in English and takes some of her inspiration from her love of Shakespeare. Living in rural New Jersey, she spends her free time outdoors, hiking, biking, camping, and sailing with her husband and two sons. She works as an IT Product Manager. Her go-to question is, "Did you test it?"

PAUL MILENSKI

Paul Milenski works on assignment as a Care and Protection Investigator for the Massachusetts Trial Court and writes fiction and poetry full time. In addition to the United States, Milenski's work has been published in the Commonwealth Countries, China, Singapore, Chile, Germany, Denmark, Russia, Turkey, Iran, South Africa, and Poland. Milenski resides with his wife, B-Mile (a local television celebrity), in Dalton, Berkshire County, Massachusetts.

ALICE MORRIS

Alice Morris holds a MS in Counseling from Johns Hopkins. She comes to writing with a background in art, and writing for art published in *The New York Art Review* and a West Virginia textbook. Her poetry appears in such places as *The White Space-Selected Poems, Delaware Beach Life, The Broadkill Review, Rat's Ass Review, Backbone Mountain Re-*

view, *Paterson Literary Review*, *Gargoyle*, and in several anthologies including *What Sort of F*ckery Is This*, and *Halloween Party 2019*. In 2018 Morris won 5th of 6th place in a Clutch-themed fiction contest, and she received the Florence C. Coltman Award for Creative Writing. In 2019 she won second and third places respectively for a single poem and a single short story in the Delaware Press Association Communications Contest. Her poem *Watercress* was a finalist in the 2019 Art of Stewardship contest. In 2019 she was nominated twice for the Pushcart Prize, then became a Pushcart Prize finalist. Her work is forthcoming in two anthologies and in Gargoyle #73. Morris is a member of the Rehoboth Beach Writer's Guild, and Coastal Writers. Presently she is working on her first full-length poetry collection.

BAYNE NORTHERN
After publishing the Executive Summary to "The Future of Independent Life Insurance Distribution," Bayne Northern transitioned from writing nonfiction to fiction. Her work has appeared in several anthologies including *Equinox*, *Solstice,* and *Suspicious Activity*. She is currently completing her first novel, *The Bitch Seat*, situated in the financial services industry. An avid short story author, Northern is also an active volunteer with the Village Improvement Association and a resident of Rehoboth Beach, Delaware.

DIANNE PEARCE
Dianne Pearce founded The Milton Workshop in 2015, and Devil's Party Press in 2017. She is a graduate of both the West Chester University and Vermont College writing programs, earning an MA and an MFA. Pearce has taught writing in Delaware, California, Pennsylvania, and Maryland. She sometimes takes on editing projects for other writers, and has done both writing and advocacy for causes close to her heart, among them adoption, developmental disabilities, and animals. Pearce is an adoptive parent of a wonderful daughter, Sophie, and is married to her best friend, David Yurkovich.
More at dpearcewrites.com.

MARK ALAN POLO
Mark Alan Polo has been an interior designer for over 30 years and is President and Owner of The Urban Dweller/Polo M.A. Inc., with offices in Northern New Jersey and a satellite office in Delaware, where he currently resides. A part-time writer for the past 15 years, Polo's short story, "Fifty-Five," appeared in the 2016 award-winning *Beach*

Nights anthology (Cat & Mouse Press). His debut novel, *Mosquitoes and Men*, was published in 2019. He is at work on a second novel.

PRATT-HERZOG

Patsy Pratt-Herzog is an emerging freelance writer from Southwestern Ohio. Her favorite genres to write are sci-fi and fantasy. When she's not writing, she enjoys painting and riding roller coasters. She shares her house in the burbs with her husband, Tim, and three chunky cats. More at patsyprattherzog.wordpress.com.

JOSEPHINE QUEEN

Josephine Queen grew up in England and moved to the US in her early twenties. She now resides in the northeast with her husband and daughter, writing flash fiction and short stories in a variety of genres, though a disturbing number end up as scary stories. Queen is currently working on a middle-grade fantasy novel and a collection of ghost/horror tales. Queen's writing has been published online at 101 Words, Nutshell Narratives, and Christopher Fielden's 81 Word Challenges. More at josephinewrites.home.blog.

J. C. RAYE

J. C. Raye's stories are found in anthologies with Scary Dairy Press, Books & Boos, Franklin/Kerr, C.M. Muller, HellBound Books, and Death's Head Press. Other publications are on the way in 2019 with Belanger Books, Rooster Republic, and Jolly Horror. For 18 years, she's been a professor at a small community college, teaching the most feared course on the planet: public speaking. Witnessing grown people weep, beg, scream, freak out, and collapse is just another delightful day on the job for her, and seats in her classes sell quicker than tickets to a Rolling Stones concert. She also loves goats of any kind, even the ones that faint.

RUSSELL REECE

Russell Reece's poems, stories and essays have appeared in a variety of journals and anthologies including *Blueline*, *The 3288 Review*, *Memoir Journal*, *Crimespree Magazine*, *Edify Fiction*, *Under the Gum Tree*, *The Broadkill Review* and others. Reece has received fellowships in literature from The Delaware Division of the Arts and the Virginia Center for the Creative Arts. His stories and poetry have received Best of the Net nominations, and awards from the Delaware Press Association and the Faulkner-Wisdom competition. He recently he won the Pat Herold

Nielsen Poetry Prize in Chester River Art's 2019 Art of Stewardship contest. Reece lives in rural Sussex County near Bethel, Delaware, on the beautiful Broad Creek.

More at russellreece.com.

LINDA RUMNEY

Linda Rumney started writing after a painful break-up, a near-miss nervous breakdown, and a discovery that she'd spent a lot of time making others happy while being miserable herself. She has written nine feature film scripts, seven short film scripts (two that she directed and produced were inducted into the National Screen Institute of Canada), two novels (one that took her to the Squaw Valley Writer's Community in 2018), and a collection of short stories since 2011. She has found her joy! Rumney currently works as a palliative nurse clinician, guiding and supporting patients and their families toward a "good death."

JAMES MICHAEL SHOBERG

James Michael Shoberg is a director, designer, and award-winning actor and playwright. His writing credits include numerous fringe plays and collections of both monologues and poems. Shoberg is also the Co-Executive Producer, Artistic Director, and Resident Playwright of The Rage of the Stage Players, a fringe theatre company in Pittsburgh, Pennsylvania. In 2011, he received the permission of The Butcher Brothers and Lionsgate Films to write, produce, and direct a world premiere stage adaptation of their award-winning independent horror film, *The Hamiltons*, for The Rage of the Stage Players. Shoberg's unique brand of twisted theatre has attracted both national and international attention. In 2016, iconic horror writer and director, Tom Holland (*Child's Play*, Stephen King's *Thinner*), tapped him to write, produce, design, and direct an official stage adaptation of the 1985 vampire film *Fright Night*, which celebrated its world premiere on October 5, 2018. Shoberg's most recent endeavor is a book of horror poetry.

DANTE J. SILICATO

Dante J Silicato lives in Milton, Delaware, with his beautiful wife, Gwendolyn, and mischievous dog, Frank. He holds a bachelor's degree in political science and history from the University of Delaware, and a master's degree in early American history from West Chester University of Pennsylvania. An avid traveler, poet, and observer, Silicato currently spends much of his time as a ranch hand on a small sustainability farm and as a craft beer tender at a local brewery.

JUDITH SPEIZER CRANDELL

Having resided on both coasts and in between, Judith Speizer Crandell has happily landed in Milton, Delaware. Solitary walks along the Atlantic beaches soothe her soul. Shared beach walks with her husband, Bill, a fellow writer, and their rescue dog, Windsor, enliven her soul. Proximity to the ocean fuels her creativity. An award-winning writer and teacher of fiction and nonfiction, she's received residencies at Yaddo, A Room of One's Own (AROHO), as well as selection as a semi-finalist in the Tucson Festival of Books Literary Awards Competition. She attended writers' conferences at San Miguel Allende, the Joiner Center/University of Massachusetts, Mendocino and Byrdcliffe. The Maryland State Arts Council granted her their Individual Artist Fellowship for her novel, *The Resurrection of Hundreds Feldman*. Most recently, her new home state chose her to attend the Delaware Division of the Arts and the Delaware Arts Council 2018 Seashore Writers Retreat. Her fiction has appeared in publications including *Cleveland* magazine, the *Hudson Review*, the *Sun* and *Gamut* and most recently in the anthologies *Halloween Party 2017*, *Solstice*, *Equinox*, and *Suspicious Activities*. Her general background includes print journalism and speechwriting. *The Woman Puzzle*, one of her novels, is scheduled for 2019 publication. judithsca.wordpress.com

SARAH VAN GOETHEM

Sarah Van Goethem is a Canadian author who spent a short time as a realtor, until she realized she more thoroughly enjoyed trespassing at abandoned (and haunted?) houses. Van Goethem has won awards for her short stories and has several floating around in other anthologies. Her novels have been in Pitch Wars and longlisted for the Bath Children's Novel Award. Van Goethem is a self-described nature lover, a wanderer of dark forests, and a gatherer of things vintage.

ELIZABETH VEGVERY

Elizabeth Vegvary studied creative writing at California State University, Sacramento before dropping out to manage the import section of a famous record store and misspend her youth. Years passed and now she lives in a small enclave in the foothills of the Cascade Mountains. When she's not taking long walks in the dark woods with her husband and her dogs, she's far too often wandering alone with her thoughts. She's been writing for most of her life, absent a two-decade sojourn to raise her babies, become a certified lactation educator and hang a professional photographer shingle. Currently life is smaller, but the words are bigger. She manages her husband's business and edits a monthly parenting magazine. Her work has been published by Zoetic Press, Rozlyn Press, and *Oberon Poetry Magazine*.

DAVID YURKOVICH

David Yurkovich is an award-winning writer, illustrator, and graphic designer. Published works include *Banana Seat Summer*, *Glass Onion*, *Altercations*, *Less Than Heroes*, and *Death by Chocolate: Redux*.
More at yurkoverse.com.

A DEATH IN THE FAMILY

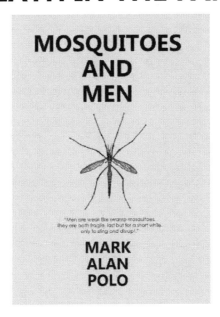

After a twenty-five-year absence, Faustus Madigan returns home to Grey-haven, a formerly illustrious 18th-century plantation in Peaceable, South Carolina, for a most unanticipated family reunion.

Titus, father to The Madigans, is dead.

Faustus steps through the doors of the home he'd fled quarter of a century ago. Yet, nothing can prepare Faustus for the changes that have occurred in his family members following his departure from Peaceable, so many years earlier. Nor can he foresee the monumental shift in the family dynamic that has occurred because of Titus' death.

Faustus' siblings, the heirs to Greyhaven, yearn to take hold of the reigns bequeathed them. They have plans of their own for Greyhaven's future and are determined that no one—family or otherwise—will stand in their way.

There is always a price to pay for survival.

MOSQUITOES AND MEN

A Southern Gothic novel by **MARK ALAN POLO**
Available now at AMAZON and at finer bookstores worldwide.

BROKEN ... BUT NOT DEFEATED

"Daddy. Wake up, Daddy!"

On the night before her eighth birthday, Anne Bergman calls out these words to her beloved father.

He never answers.

He never wakes up.

For the rest of her life, Anne is haunted by that moment in time and the nightmare that follows.

When her unstable, narcissistic mother, Irene, remarries, Anne is plunged further into darkness. Bernie is young, powerful, and lecherous, and he desires his new teenage step-daughter.

Powerless against Bernie's sexual assaults, Anne furtively seeks solace in the shadows, existing in constant fear. With no help forthcoming, Anne's life is an open wound.

At 15, Anne is the adult in a house occupied by her mentally ill mother and her frightened, disturbed younger brother. Lost and defeated, Anne is a broken adolescent, attending to everyone's needs except her own. Repeatedly tested by the people in her life, Anne compartmentalizes her brokenness as she struggles to retain her sanity. Anne is always a puzzle piece away from falling apart.

Pregnant at 19, Anne flees into, and then out of, a doomed marriage. To save herself, she makes the difficult decision to leave her two children, as well as her husband. She journeys across the country, from the East Coast to the West Coast, seeking recovery and peace. Along the way, Anne enters into a significant relationship with a Vietnam vet whose struggle with Post-Traumatic Stress Disorder mirrors her own. Deep inside, she knows somewhere, somehow, she must move from victim to victor.

Can a broken woman accept her brokenness and move on?

THE WOMAN PUZZLE

An original novel by JUDITH SPEIZER CRANDELL
COMING SOON FROM DEVIL'S PARTY PRESS.

SUBSCRIBE AND SAVE!

Whether it's our award-winning
short story collections
or full-length novels,
DPP has the talent to take your
imagination to new and exciting places.

Our authors have lived a lot,
seen a lot, and done a lot.
Like a good cut of beef
(or tofu if you prefer)
they're well-seasoned.

2020 will see a series of all-new DPP releases.
Subscribe and save today so you'll never miss a title.

Complete details at **devilspartypress.com**

Made in the
USA
Columbia, SC